GALLIMORE

an historical family saga spanning London to the early Australian settlement of New South Wales and the Victorian gold rush

DOROTHEA COBB

First published 2020

I acknowledge Aboriginal and Torres Strait Islander people as the First Peoples of the land on which this story takes place, and I pay my respects to elders past, present and emerging.

Gallimore

Cobb, Dorothea

A catalogue record of this work is available from the National Library of Australia.

Original Australian landscape painting by Dorothea Cobb.

ISBN 978-0-6489592-0-5 (paperback)

ISBN 978-0-6489592-1-2 (ebook)

Published by Deborah Parker

gallimore2411@gmail.com

Mum

I'm sorry you didn't live to see the publication of your novel come to fruition, but I hope I have honoured my promise to you and done you proud.

Your loving daughter
Deb

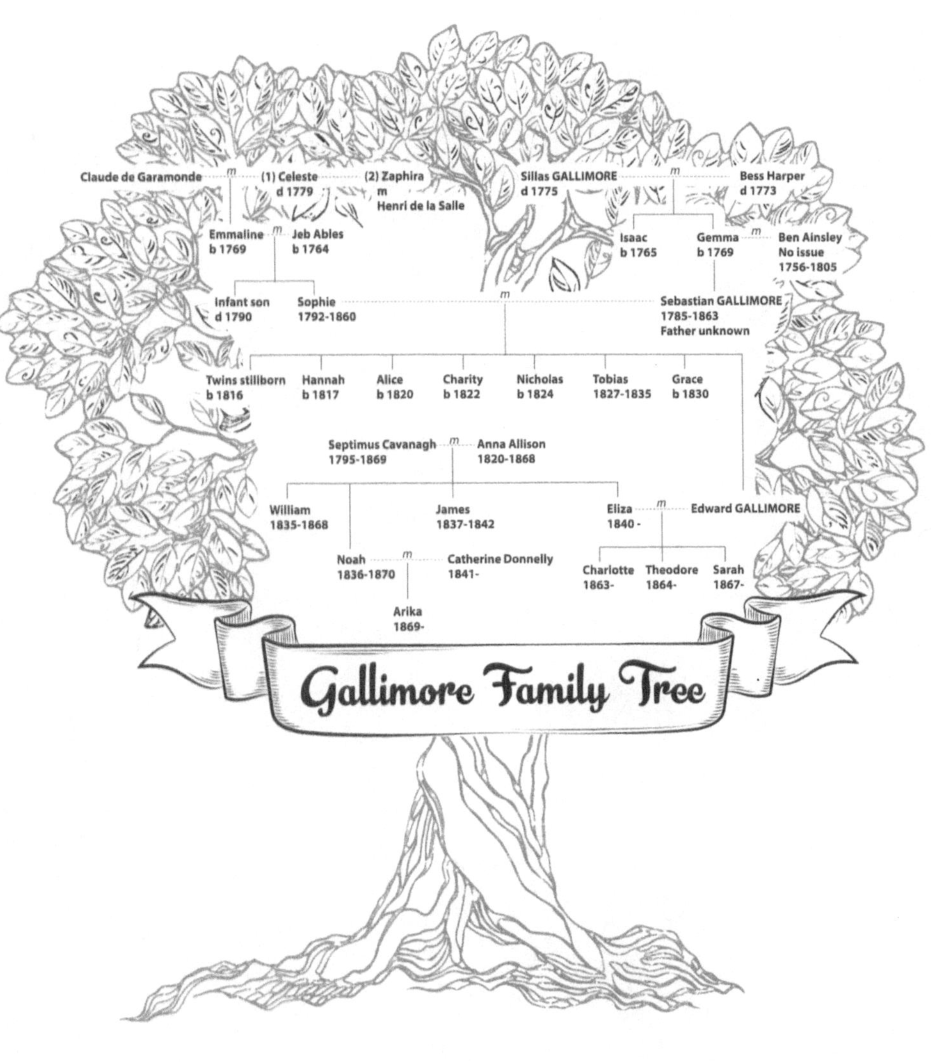

Claude de Garamonde
(1) Celeste
d 1779
(2) Zaphira
m
Henri de la Salle
Sillas GALLIMORE
d 1775
Bess Harper
d 1773

Emmaline
b 1769
Jeb Ables
b 1764
Isaac
b 1765
Gemma
b 1769
Ben Ainsley
No issue
1756-1805

Infant son
d 1790
Sophie
1792-1860
Sebastian GALLIMORE
1785-1863
Father unknown

Twins stillborn
b 1816
Hannah
b 1817
Alice
b 1820
Charity
b 1822
Nicholas
b 1824
Tobias
1827-1835
Grace
b 1830

Septimus Cavanagh
1795-1869
Anna Allison
1820-1868

William
1835-1868
James
1837-1842
Eliza
1840 -
Edward GALLIMORE

Noah
1836-1870
Catherine Donnelly
1841-
Charlotte
1863-
Theodore
1864-
Sarah
1867-

Arika
1869-

Gallimore Family Tree

INTRODUCTION

Gallimore
June 27th, 1891

My darling daughter Arika,

It was a long time before I could go through your father's
papers, and when I found his journals, I put them aside to read
at a later date. The first nine journals, all in his beautiful
handwriting, deal with his day-to-day life from when he left
home to go with his father (Grandfather Septimus, who, of
course, you and I never met), through to his life in the
goldfields. They make marvellous reading, and I hope that, one
day, you will enjoy them as much as I do. I still regularly dip
into them. As we have discussed, these journals are yours to
have at any time you wish.

There is, however, a tenth journal. It begins on the day he eventually came back to Sydney to meet up again with his family. As
I read it, I got the shock of my life! Is not life bizarre? How it
twists and turns! This tenth journal, and my own, will only be
available to you after my demise. I have left instructions in my
will as to their whereabouts.

Dearest Arika, I hope that in your travels you will find what you seek. I miss you dreadfully and long for the day of your return. Until then, I am, as always, your loving mother,

Catherine Cavanagh

PART 1

1765

Silas Gallimore looked with more than a little alarm at the rising waters lapping at the ancient wooden wall of his makeshift shop under the steps of the bridge at Blackfriars. Even though it had escaped the Great Fire, time and rats had done a great deal to undermine the construction, and now it looked like Old Father Thames was going to finish it off.

Up till now, life had been fairly good to Silas. As a cobbler, he earned enough to pay the rent on his tiny, dilapidated shop and the two rooms in the very modest house in which he and Bess lived, not a mile away. He worked hard and kept long hours, but he was happy, especially now that Bess was expecting. Silas always thought that Bess could have done a lot better for herself than to marry him. For one thing, she could read and write, which was a lot more than he could do. To his everlasting delight, however, she had chosen him.

Bess's meagre possessions included a large, dog-eared book of stories, myths and legends which she treasured and from which every evening after supper she read aloud. He listened, enthralled, enchanted by her. It seemed to him, as he watched her reading, that he loved her more and more every day. A single tallow candle would be flickering beside her as she read, and soft shadows would dance in the corners of the room. Every now and again, Bess would give a little cough, which only happened when the candle was lit in the evenings. He resolved that, one day, he would be prosperous enough to buy wax candles. Bess could have as many as she wanted, and then maybe she wouldn't cough.

On some nights after their meal of sheep's heads or, if he'd had an especially good day and someone had paid him well, perhaps rabbit pie, they would sit down together and play a game of whist. Life was good.

Today, however, Silas was concerned for two reasons.

First, Bess was close to her time—it could be any day—and she was very tired when he came home each evening. She often appeared to have a fever but always brushed his concerns aside, saying that it was a normal part of her advancing pregnancy.

And second, the rising water. He knew that, every spring, Mother Nature would see to it that Old Man Thames would flood and recede, but this time the flood-tide seemed higher than usual—or maybe he was just more fearful and jittery at this time.He was just setting up shop for the day when his musings were cut short by the sudden arrival of a puffing, panting Mrs Bunting, who almost collapsed after breathlessly telling him to go home quickly, because Bess was in heavy labour and calling for him.

The eight hundred yards he had to travel seemed to him like a thousand miles. His feet hardly touched the ground; he'd never run so fast in his life. All thoughts of the rising Thames had gone from his mind, and all he could think of was his Bess, his beautiful Bess, who needed him now.

Through the lanes he raced in the early-morning misty light, past the costermongers, readying their barrows, and a chimney sweep and his boy, off to clean a cooled chimney before the fire was lit for the day. The great bell of St Mary le Bow, replaced after the Great Fire, struck the hour of seven in the distance, but he didn't hear it, nor did he hear the soft snuffling of a newborn as he ran through the door. He just knew that he had to reach Bess's bedside, and, as he reached it, his heart almost stopped.

She was lying there, eyes closed, white faced, with beads of perspiration still on her forehead. For a dreadful moment he thought she was dead.

Then he became aware of a muffled wail behind him and turned to see Mrs Bunting's sister in the corner of the room, nursing a tiny bundle. She came toward him and, with one hand, parted the folds of a crocheted shawl enclosing a soft cotton sheet.

With absolute wonderment and a bursting heart, he beheld for the first time the face of his tiny newborn babe, and then the face of the woman holding him.

"It's a boy!" she said. She was about to hand the precious bundle to Silas when a soft sigh from the bed made him turn around to see Bess, eyes closed, smiling weakly and holding a hand up towards him.

"Bess. Oh, Bess—I didn't know—I'm sorry I wasn't here—why didn't you tell me? It's a boy! Oh, Bess, I'm sorry, I'm sorry!" Words tumbled and tears flowed as he grasped her hand tenderly and pressed it to his cheek.

Bess raised her eyes to him, gave him a watery smile, closed them again. Her breast rose and fell in an exhausted slumber, only interrupted from time to time by a little cough.

For three days, Silas stayed beside Bess while Mrs Bunting, their kindly neighbour, looked after baby Isaac. Succumbing to a lot of tongue-clicking and tut-tutting from Mrs Bunting and emphatic assertions from Bess that she was well on the way to recovery and that she and the baby would survive without him, Silas went back to his cobbler's shop. To his delight, the floodwaters had receded, and everything was as it should be.

With a smile, he thought, *Life is good. I have my Bess and a son, and I can earn enough to feed us all.* Apart from her cough, Bess grew stronger as the days passed, and she and Silas shared the joys of watching Isaac grow into a happy, healthy little boy. Bess read to them every evening from her treasured book. They never tired of hearing her voice, and soon Isaac began to talk.

One night, Bess cuddled him on her knee between her arms as she read. Isaac's finger seemed to trace along the lines, and he pointed to pictures relevant to the story.

"Look Bess, he's trying to read!" laughed Silas. "Perhaps you should start to teach him—and why not teach me, as well?" And so Bess became the reading teacher to her husband and her son, and at the same time, because it was easier, taught them to write. They were happy days, and there was a great deal of laughter.

These new skills awakened in Silas a hitherto unsuspected talent. He became a skilled and amusing storyteller. Sometimes, the three of them would take it in turns to read from Bess's book, and, at others, Bess and Isaac would beg Silas to tell them one of his tales, which always made them laugh, always had a happy ending and always had a moral. By this means, Silas and Bess instilled in Isaac a sense of what was right and good.

Isaac was four when Bess announced that a new brother or sister was on the way. In due course, little Gemma arrived, like her brother Isaac, on a wonderful warm spring day. Bess had kept well during the pregnancy, and the confinement had been uneventful.

But this time, she took much longer to recover, her persistent cough was becoming more pronounced, and she began losing weight. Silas worked harder and longer, well aware that three mouths now depended upon him. He did so without complaint, happy that he had his Bess, a son and now a daughter to bring sunshine to his life. What more could a man want?

In a few months, however, they would be coldly and crudely thrust into a new life that would change him forever, and it was as well that he could not know it.

TWO SPRINGS after Gemma's birth, Old Father Thames, in obedience to Mother Nature's bidding, rose and rose and kept rising. He crept inexorably towards the cobbler's shop, and Silas was powerless to do anything but watch as the water lapped at the ancient foundations of the building and, bit by bit, devoured them.

"No! No!" he screamed, as he saw the last rotten timbers fall slowly, dreamlike, into the murky, churning, swirling water and drift slowly away upriver, taking with them the contents of his shop. At that moment, elsewhere in the country, James Watt was cementing his name in history by improving the Newcomen steam engine and ultimately having a unit of power named after him.

James Hargreaves was upsetting the Spinners, who thought they were losing their jobs because of his invention, the Spinning Jenny.

Richard Arkwright was adding his bit to the coming Industrial Revolution by inventing the water frame and other mechanical spring devices.

William Pitt the Elder was just coming to the end of his Parliamentary days, and his son, William Pitt the Younger, was just about to begin his.

Arthur Wellesley, 1st Duke of Wellington, was three years old; Horatio, 1st Viscount Nelson, was fourteen.

Captain James Cook was making the second of his voyages of discovery in the southern hemisphere.

Samuel Johnson was busy writing essays, compiling a dictionary and chatting with his friend, James Boswell, who was busy being a lawyer and author and chatting with his friend, Samuel Johnson.

Josiah Wedgwood was perfecting soft porcelain and creating pottery which would bear his name well into the twenty-first century.

And Silas Gallimore could only stand and watch while the rising spring waters of the Thames robbed him of his livelihood and—though he wasn't to know it at the time—his Bess, his two children and ultimately his sanity.

Silas was shattered, but hopeful that this was a temporary setback. Since he had lost all his tools in the flooding waters, he walked many miles each day looking for work. Despite desperate pleadings to every cobbler and shoemaker he came across, it was to no avail. Eventually, an unsympathetic landlord, after first having confiscated every piece of their meagre belongings he could lay his hands on, turned them out into the street.

By now, Bess's cough was more pronounced than ever, and she was very thin. She made light of it by saying that Silas should be happy he didn't have a huge wife who needed cartloads of food to satisfy a voracious appetite. But that did not stop Silas worrying.

In desperation, Silas approached the Parish Beadle. That whiskered functionary, all too aware of the power that his office allowed him, listened half-heartedly as he yawned, adjusted the top button of his canary-yellow waistcoat, tapped his silver-topped staff on the floor and absent-mindedly picked his yellowing teeth with a wooden pick delicately extracted from his inside top pocket.

Once Silas had finished, the man removed his cocked hat, brushed it importantly with his hand and advised Silas that there was "nuffin' to do but have you admitted to the Parish of Ludgate Workhouse."

Silas almost fainted to hear those words. The workhouse was for vagrants, vagabonds and idlers, which he and his family were not; the lonely sick, which he hoped they never were; and the desperately poor, which—he reluctantly admitted to himself—they now were.

Seeing Silas's distress and anxious to be rid of him quickly, the Beadle continued. "Hit's not so bad! Your family will be fed, you'll 'ave a shelter over your 'ead. You'll be able to work as a cobbler to earn yer keep, and hif all goes well, the young 'uns'll be taught a trade."

Silas had no other option, and he was persuaded that the tales of the workhouse as the last refuge of the poor, the sick, the insane and the diseased were maybe, hopefully, a little overstated.

The Beadle said that he would arrange their admission that day and that they were to proceed to the workhouse gate immediately. It was not his custom to be in the company of the likes of Silas and his family for longer than was absolutely necessary.

Having discharged his obligations, he brushed his hands together to be rid of the taint, twirled his whiskers and, brandishing his staff, strutted off with an air of self-importance befitting "a man of 'is 'igh Hoffice." He thought he might now fortify himself with a plate of cold beef and a jug of porter at the Boar's Head.

THE BUILDING CALLED the workhouse had once been a convent, but it was so decrepit that it had been vacated and stood empty for many years. Now, it housed a dreadful collection of the most dejected human beings, all herded together in squalid misery.

Conditions were deplorable. No running water, uneven and broken flagstone floors so cold in winter that those who had to stand for hours on them suffered greatly, broken windows through which the wind whistled and tore at the paper used to mend them, rusted iron bars at the windows, and worst of all, as far as Silas was concerned, separate quarters for men and women.

Surrounded as he was by such a host of abject beings, Silas had never felt so alone.

Silas and Bess had all their belongings taken from them. These would be sold to defray the cost of the keep to the Parish.

"You won't be needing the likes 'o that in 'ere, dearie," Bess was told, as her precious book was wrested from her.

Gone also was their clothing. In return, they were given their uniforms—a gown of very coarse material for Bess, a thin cotton shirt and trousers for Silas. The children were given clothing from a stock-pile of items taken from incoming people and too tattered to be sold. All these items had a large L marked on the back, to denote Ludgate, easily recognizable if they ever had thoughts of escaping. They could then be charged with stealing.

"Men this way, women and children this way!"

That was the last Silas saw of his family for some days.

The Beadle had advised the workhouse master of Silas's late occupation, and Silas very soon found himself in a hot, filthy workroom where the stink of leather, still wet and only just out of the tanning vats, mingled with the odour of unwashed and sweat-soaked bodies, made him heave. The very walls seemed to be saturated with the stench of the sick and the dying.

Bess was employed in the workhouse laundry, where the heavy work of scrubbing and lifting wet washing hour after hour took its toll on her thin frame and left her coughing and ill. Gemma, three years of age, stayed beside her mother, and Isaac, seven, would be shortly apprenticed to the trade of brick-making. After the Great Fire a hundred years earlier, London was still being rebuilt, and many of the formerly wooden houses, especially those of the rich, were being reconstructed in brick.

At the end of a long day, Silas, Bess and the children would some-times see each other as they joined separate lines of people with gruel bowls in their hands. Speaking with members of the opposite sex was not allowed, but no-one could not stop them looking.

Silas was shocked at how thin and pale Bess had become. He tortured himself with the thought that it was all his fault.

One day a week, a boiled onion would be added to their bowl of thin gruel; on another, a small boiled potato; and on Sundays, a slice of dry unleavened bread.

Before long, the constant acrid steam of the laundry and the lack of proper food had a severe effect on Bess. Her cough became worse and worse until, one day, flecks of blood appeared around her mouth and she collapsed. She and Gemma were removed from the laundry area and work went on as usual.

Silas knew nothing of this until Bess's non-appearance at the food line later that day. No Bess and no Gemma. Frantic, he asked their whereabouts and was told that she was ill, was in the infirmary, and was being cared for. Visitors were only allowed on Sundays, for half an hour.

He was horrified when he saw a pale, listless, gasping Bess, lying comatose on a pallet. It was as if she had waited for him. As he held her hand, she gave a deep sigh, and a tiny smile appeared on her lips.

Then the thin face that he knew and loved so well relaxed into a still, serene expression.

For a fleeting moment, he thought she had gone to sleep and was grateful. But when her grasp suddenly relaxed, he knew, with terrible clarity, that she was gone. He knelt, unbelieving and staring at his Bess, and his heart broke. Consumption, they said.

From that moment on, Silas became a living shadow. He lost interest in Isaac, Gemma, and life itself. He sat staring, thinking and remembering, day after day. Totally incapable of work, he, and the children with him, were declared paupers, marked with a large P added to the L on their uniforms.

The workhouse master was given funds from the parish for food and medical care for the inmates. The inmates subsidised their keep by making goods from the leather, wool and metals provided. These goods were then sold for the profit of the Parochial Assembly first, and then the master.

It was, therefore, in the master's interest to minimise the number of paupers to share the food, and to feed them as little as possible. When a non-productive prisoner—that is, a pauper—died, it was one less mouth to feed and a little more for the master himself. To paupers like Silas's family, little food and almost no medical attention was proffered, and death was never distant. Little wonder that the workhouse was the dread and last resort of any family.

How long he remained like this, Silas cared not. The light had gone from his eyes, his heart, his life.

Isaac was, by this time, almost nine and Gemma five years old. Silas stumbled through his days, automatically doing what he had to, and nothing more. In his mind, the Thames had been responsible for Bess's death, and for all he cared, it could have him as well. That way, he and she would be together again.

Isaac took on the role of both mother and father to Gemma and comforted her as he could. He resolved that, at the first chance, he would get them all out of the workhouse. He had no idea how, but he was sure an opportunity would present itself.

It was now winter, and this one promised to be harder, longer and crueller than usual. Isaac knew that Silas was ailing, sinking fast, and was fearful for him. He had to get them all out, and it had to be soon!

He made a plan. One morning, he witnessed five hapless souls newly admitted to the workhouse being divested of their clothing. Their belongings, which he knew they would never see again, were tossed into a heap in a corner, ready for sorting and sending out for sale to an old second-hand shop outside.

Now was his one and only chance, and he would seize it. During their evening meal of thin gruel and bread, he contrived to keep Silas and Gemma close by. Then, grasping his father's arm and Gemma's hand, he hurried them out and down an ill-lit passageway to where he had seen the family being admitted earlier. Breathing fast and terrified of being caught, he quickly caught up an armful of the discarded clothing and pulled his family along.

Into the yard Isaac bustled them, almost dragging Silas. Wide-eyed Gemma, uncomprehending, put her total trust in her big brother.

"Ssh! Ssh! Quickly, quickly!" encouraged Isaac in a frantic half whisper. Up with the heavy iron latch on the high wooden gate, and out they went, into the road and into liberty!

Isaac did not know that their escape had been observed and reported.

"Yes, yes, yes," said the master irritably upon receiving the news. "I care not. If the cold don't get 'em, the runners will! Then 'Is Majesty'll 'ave to look after 'em 'stead of me!"

He was quite happy to have three less to feed, especially after that morning's intake, and decided against recording their disappearance in his log.

"What the Parish don't know won't 'urt 'em." he repeated to himself for the thousandth time in his career, his thin lips pressed together. Winter would not give way to spring without one last flurry, and out of the shelter of the workhouse and its yard, the three escapees were suddenly and brutally assaulted by the freezing blast of the wind. Their thin clothing was no match for it.

Stopping for a few seconds, Isaac said, "Here! Quickly! Put these on."

Teeth chattering, he helped them don the stolen clothing. He had taken them only to conceal the workhouse letters stamped on the backs of their uniforms but was now very glad of the extra warmth they provided.

Since his plan had not extended beyond their initial escape, Isaac was now faced with the realisation that he had no idea where they would go or what they would do when they got there. He only knew that they were never, ever, ever going back.

THEY WERE NOW in another world, the third in Isaac's and Gemma's young lives. It had been three long years since the flood and many lonely months since Bess had passed. With an understanding beyond his years, Isaac knew that any decision about their future would rest with him unless, somehow or other, he could wrest his father from the void he sunk deeper and deeper into every day. First, he must distance the three of them from the workhouse. Perhaps symbolically, he was drawn to the light on the hill to their left.

St Paul's! The great new St Paul's, built by the genius astronomer and architect Sir Christopher Wren, to replace the original destroyed in the Great Fire. For some fifty years, it had stood as a beacon of hope for the people of London. So it did for young Isaac now.

Despite the extra layer, fingers of icy air tore at their thin and patched clothing as they made their way up the hill. The wind whistled up the side lanes, rattling old windows as it went, and gathered itself into a force that tore up Ludgate Hill, taking Silas, Isaac and Gemma with it.

Near freezing, teeth clenched and bare fingers clutching and drawing their clothes about them, they reached St Paul's and looked for shelter from the biting wind. Around the side of the giant structure, into the darkness they went—and at last stumbled into a deep doorway cut into the masonry wall.

Blessed calm! They huddled together, pressed against the thick oaken door. The recess was deep and proved a miraculous shelter from the wind. Isaac had the fleeting thought that it seemed so solid, so strong, that it somehow embodied safety.

Not a single word had been spoken by any of them since they donned the extra clothing, and now none seemed necessary. As one, they sunk to the stone floor in the doorway, utterly exhausted by the malnutrition, the escape, the cold and the hopelessness. They were dimly aware of the great bell striking nine, the sound rolling and rumbling away into the distance as they drifted into a dreamless nothingness.

BY MORNING, the wind had blown itself out and at last made way for spring. Though still chilly, a watery but persistent sun had broken through and promised to warm the east side of St Paul's.

Mr William Brindle, a round, jolly man of about fifty years, was ambling along the side path of the cathedral, humming softly to himself and thinking how glad he was to be alive.

"A lovely day, m'dear," he had said to Mrs Brindle earlier, as she handed him his lunch wrapped in a chequered cloth. "I always like this time of year, so nice and fresh—just like you!" He paused to give her a playful pat on the behind. "If yesterday's wind has blown all the buds off the trees, I shall have a busy day!"

"Go on with you," she said, pushing him gently through the door. "You and your nonsense! Maybe I'll live long enough to see you be serious for once, Bill Brindle."

He put his hat on his head, and, tipping the front brim back with his forefinger, leaned forward to give her a quick kiss.

"Get off with you!" she said again, blushing slightly. For the ten thousandth time, she reflected that it was such a shame that they were never able to have children. Bill would make such a wonderful father.

"Lawks!" said Bill Brindle irreverently, and then, remembering where he was, "Good gracious—Good Lord! What have we here?"

Extracting his spectacles from his inside pocket in such a hurry he forgot to clean them, he twisted their side pieces around his ears and adjusted them on his rosy, chubby nose. He needed to see what was blocking the large, iron-studded door at the end of the eastern side of the cathedral.

Bending down and peering closely at the heap of human misery crouched in the corner, he shouted again.

"Great Heavens! Good Lord!" He reached over and unlocked the great door, then put a gentle hand on Isaac's shoulder. "Come in! Come in, do!"

Stiff from his night huddled down and blinking groggily, Isaac rose and helped Gemma and Silas unsteadily to their feet. Without question, he accepted the invitation, ushering his family into the light and relative warmth of a small room.

"Sit down, sit down!" said Bill, motioning toward a bench along one wall. "I'm Mr Brindle. Now, tell me how you came to be sitting on my doorstep all night!"

"Are you the bishop?" Gemma asked, not knowing how to respond to the first kindly face she had seen in a long time.

"Oh! My goodness gracious me, no!" laughed Mr. Brindle. "No, no, I'm the sexton of this here great cathedral." Then, interpreting their blank reaction, he added, "I'm the caretaker. I've even been called upon in the past to help ring the Great Bell and also to dig a grave or two!"

Looking into their starved faces, he instantly regretted offering this last piece of information. "But that was a long time ago—there's not much call for that sort of thing these days! Are you hungry?"

Without waiting for a reply, he unwrapped his lunch cloth and spread before them a repast such as they hadn't seen for a very long time.

"Please eat!" invited Mr Brindle.

While Isaac and Gemma were ravenously demolishing his meal of thick bread and cheese, along with a goodly supply of pickled onions, he said, "And then you can tell me all about what has happened to you."

Sensing that he was about to hear something that was going to make him very sad, he busied himself fussing over them, making sure that the children had enough to eat and casting a sidelong glance at Silas, wondering what had made the man so detached and disinterested.

Silas sat like a man in a trance, not eating.

"Is this your father? Where is your mother? And where have you come from?" A thousand questions needed to be asked, and soon enough were answered for Bill to know that this was yet another family of poor, wretched souls.

It isn't the first and I don't suppose it'll be the last. He sighed to himself.

"Our mother is dead, and we've run away from the workhouse," confided Isaac. He poured out, in a tumble of words, their story, astonished yet grateful that someone cared.

As Isaac's account unfolded, Mr Brindle became more and more downhearted. He cleared his throat several times and wiped his misted spectacles on his shirt tail.

"Dear me! Dear me!" he said. "Please wait here a while. I will be back in a few minutes!" He left by an inner door, which he closed gently behind him.

"Do you think he's gone to tell the runners?" asked Gemma, eyes wide in alarm. "Please, please, Isaac, I don't ever want to go back to the workhouse! Let's run away now!"

Before she could become too agitated, Isaac enfolded her in his thin arms. "Of course we'll never go back there. I don't know where he's gone, but I'll wager it's not for the runners!"

Through all of this, Silas sat hollow-eyed and silent—blank.

MR BRINDLE RETURNED SHORTLY and at once kneeled close to Isaac.

"Along by the river is a lane," he said softly. "Pump Lane. It's a lane of old wooden houses, now unoccupied. They're going to be pulled down and rebuilt. Go down there and find one to live in until you can get yourselves sorted. Here is two shillings and six pence to start you off. It will buy a little heat and some food."

Isaac was overwhelmed by his kindness. "Oh! Sir, we would be very glad of some shelter, but we cannot accept your money."

"Please!" said Mr Brindle "It is not mine to keep. It's from the church alms box. This is what it's intended for, to help people such as yourselves. Now go! And look after your father. He looks ill, and it will do him good to have some food and a roof—" *Such as it might be*, he thought—"over his head."

Isaac stood and looked at the money in his hand, tears streaming down his cheeks. His heart was so full of gratitude that he was lost for words.

"Go!" smiled Mr Brindle. "Before I get into trouble for neglecting my work!" He would, as usual, have dearly loved to do more, but these were only the latest of a constant stream of souls in need of assistance. He heaved a great, heavy sigh and turned sadly to his labours for the day.

❄

FOLLOWING MR BRINDLE'S INSTRUCTIONS, Isaac, Silas and Gemma made their way to Pump Lane and found themselves standing in front of a long row of decrepit wooden houses with upper floors tottering over the road.

With a newfound lightness of heart, Isaac and Gemma amused themselves for a while, pretending to be gentry looking for a new mansion. They rejected this one and that one—not enough coloured glass in the windows, not enough flowers in the garden, not enough coal in the cellar, and not enough rooms for the servants' quarters!

They never minded that there was no glass in any of the windows, no gardens, no flowers, no cellars, no coal and only two barely habitable rooms, cracks meandering up the walls and across the ceilings. At night, the street would be a dark lane, where the ghosts of lives and times past lurked in the shadows. But Isaac and Gemma were excited and happy.

Silas was remote and silent.

After inspecting their new home, the two children told their father that they were going off to buy some food and maybe a candle and would be back in time for them all to enjoy a wonderful banquet.

They turned out of Pump Lane into Ludgate Hill and then towards Fleet Street. The sounds and the smells of the London morning were becoming more pronounced as they made their way along. Costermongers had set up their barrows of fruit and vegetables. There was a roast chestnut barrow, a pie stall next to a barrow selling a drink of hot spiced ginger, and a muffin man.

"Muffins, hot muffins! One ha'penny each, or three for a penny!" he called, ringing his bell.

Gemma clutched her brother's hand tightly as they made their way along the ancient cobbled road, made more uneven by the intense heat of the Great Fire. There were donkeys pulling carts laden with produce on their way to the market at Covent Garden, a fishwife selling oysters for a penny a lot, a candle seller, a girl selling oranges from a basket, a boy selling boxes of coal for a shilling, and an old woman selling second-hand clothing from a sack.

And beggars! Beggars everywhere!

Soon they managed to purchase a half-quarter of bran bread, a small piece of Cheshire cheese, two dozen oysters, a tallow candle and —for a special treat because they had not seen them for many a long month—three oranges. All for the princely sum of seven pence and three farthings.

As soon as the children were out of sight, Silas grasped the opportunity he had been waiting for. He left the house and walked furtively but purposefully down to the river, making sure he was not observed. He made towards the edge and, waiting for a coal barge to pass, waded into the water until he was waist deep, eventually falling to his knees.

The River Thames closed over his head, and he took a great gulp of water, filling his lungs with it. He half smiled and took another deep gulp.

His head was spinning, his lungs felt as if they were bursting and his world was foggy, but he banished all these sensations. Faintly he heard soft, muffled sounds in the distance.

Though his eyes were closed, he could quite clearly see Bess, in a long, flowing, wraithlike gown that swirled around her, her white arms outstretched toward him, smiling, waiting to enfold him. He moved slowly, dreamlike, toward her and felt himself being swept up and lulled like seagrass—waving, curling, eddying in the ocean current.

A wonderful silver beam of light seemed to dance and twirl and shimmer through the water, down, down, down to touch him.

Then he was drifting, drifting, drifting into a dreamlike place of the most unutterable calm and peace and light.

His life without her had seemed like a never-ending nightmare, but at last—at long, long last—he would be re-united with his Bess in eternity. He was happy.

$$\maltese \quad 3 \quad \maltese$$

In eighteenth-century London, it was not at all unusual for children to sleep anywhere they could find a roof at night and beg or thieve in the streets by day. The alternative was the workhouse, or worse.

Isaac and Gemma had joined these children, somehow existing in the very worst of circumstances. In their sorrow, they kept to themselves, looking after each other as best they could.

Eight years before, on the evening of the day they had moved into Pump Lane, they had followed a small, straggly group of people talking animatedly about a body found in the Thames. Silas was nowhere to be found when they had returned from their shopping foray, and they knew with a dreadful certainty the identity of the dead man.

A grappling iron had been used to drag the corpse to the shore and, before Isaac's and Gemma's horrified eyes, their father's body was drawn unceremoniously through the black mud onto firmer ground.

But when the face had been roughly wiped clear, the spectators, as one, emitted a loud gasp, for it wore an expression of almost sublime peace, almost smiling.

The over-garment was awry, and visible were the dreaded work-house letters, L and P.

"No wonder 'e looks like 'e's 'appy," a toothless old woman said. "'e'll be right glad to get rid of the work'us!"

"Aye," agreed her large, round companion, a man in soiled trousers and tattered shirt. "Poor devil!"

A pause, and then, "But 'es orite now!"

White as a ghost, Gemma had held Isaac's hand so tightly that he had to gently prise her fingers apart, and, grasping her arm, he wheeled them about and started back toward Pump Lane.

"Gemma," he said. "We have to leave him. Before the runners come. As soon as they see the workhouse letters, they'll know who we are, and we'll find ourselves back there, or maybe even in prison because we've run away!"

They had been devastated, frightened, anxious, but some hidden strength had surfaced. And they had survived. They had stretched the alms money for as long as possible, then resorted to scavenging for food and joining the ranks of the beggars.

Sickened by this lifestyle after a very short time, Isaac looked for work. He was able to convince a brickmaker that he had learnt some of the trade.

"We'll see if you are as good as you say you are!" the craftsman said.

He set Isaac to work digging heavy clay from the vast layers of it in and around and under the city, laid down aeons ago when seas had come and gone.

After two back-breaking years of digging and lifting, he was transferred to the brickworks. There he remained, earning enough to keep them fed and clothed, albeit modestly, until a day when a pile of poorly stacked bricks, newly fired and cooled, collapsed on him.

His hard, calloused hands removed, one by one, the bricks crushing his cut and bleeding legs. Though no permanent damage had been done, he had been unable to continue his trade. Their source of money gone, he and Gemma were again plunged into despair.

LONDON WAS, at that time, the largest city in the world, sprawling along both sides of the River Thames. Its citizens were of every description: the richest, the poorest, the lewd, the sinister, the shady, the sick, the young and the old, the dignified, the rabblerousers and the adulterers, the learned and the ignorant and all those in between. There were the great houses of the rich; the rickety, rotten, tumble-down wooden dwellings of the poor; jails; workhouses; churches; taverns; brothels; theatres and markets. There were cobblestoned laneways, muddy lanes, wagon-wheel-rutted roads, paved streets, high-ways, turnpike roads, sinister side-alleys, tow-paths and a small sprin-kling of gas-lit main roads where the rich and well-heeled seemed to attract each other. King George III had occupied the throne for some twenty-three years and was already showing signs of the madness which was to overtake him.

It was through this hotchpotch that Isaac and Gemma wandered one fine night, begging, and found themselves in Fleet Street.

A well-to-do gentleman was just alighting from his hackney carriage, which had stopped under a gas lamp, the better for him to see whether it was only a shilling he was extracting from his purse and not (heaven forbid!) a sovereign, with which to pay his fare.

As he removed his leather purse from the pocket of his maroon corduroy frock coat, the corner of a white silk handkerchief dangled out.

At that precise moment, Isaac and Gemma passed. Gemma deftly removed the item from the gent's pocket, scrunching it up in her hand, and continued to walk on without the slightest hesitation in her step.

She was watched by the coachman, who was very used to witnessing such goings on. He grinned at her, winked, and at the same time touched the brim of his hat with his forefinger with a "Thank you, guv'ner!" to his customer, who was quite oblivious to his loss.

That handkerchief was sold for two pence the following morning. It provided Isaac and Gemma with their first real food in days, setting them on a course which provided a fairly regular income from then on. They sometimes worked together, sometimes separately. Isaac was twenty, Gemma sixteen, and the year was 1785.

Despite her lifestyle, Gemma grew into a graceful young woman and caught the eye of many a male. She bore her mother's softly waving chestnut hair, which she wore in two long plaits, along with her blue eyes, creamy skin and long, sensitive hands. She had her father's almost regal carriage.

Men young, old and in between dreamed of possessing her. Some wondered how she could have come to such circumstances, some dreamed of taking her away from it all, and some simply lusted after her. She was quite unaware of the effect she had as she walked paths both familiar and unfamiliar on her daily expeditions.

"Good evening, miss!" a voice spoke to her from the depths of a dark doorway in an unlit, deserted laneway one night. "How's about a little kiss?"

She stiffened, hesitated, and continued to walk. Soft footsteps approached urgently behind her.

Before she could flee, she was grabbed roughly, twirled around. A rough whiskered face was thrust into hers, strong arms crushed her, and she was forced to the ground.

She bit and scratched, struggled, cried and screamed. But such sounds were commonplace, and no-one came to her aid.

She was aware of a voice swearing coarse oath and of being hit very hard on the face before she blacked out.

Later, through bleeding and swollen lips, she related to Isaac what had happened.

With horror, he surveyed her bruises and her torn fingernails and clothing and swore vengeance there and then.

It was some days later that Isaac returned, shaking, bloodied and ashen.

"He'll never do that again—to anyone," he stammered through lips white with shock. "I think I've killed him."

A few weeks later, Gemma discovered she was pregnant.

$$\text{❈} \quad 4 \quad \text{❈}$$

Daily, Isaac was torn with worry. Had he killed Gemma's attacker? As long as he lived, he would never forget the man's face. One part of him said that the man had deserved all he'd got. But the other side knew that what he had possibly done was murder—and knew the consequences if he was caught.

He told Gemma that he would disappear for a while, until the possibility of an investigation died down. During that time, he met an aged travelling chair bodger, who had to give up his travels because he was "tortured by the screws!" One look at the old fellow's gnarled and twisted hands confirmed this.

Bert Pride—for that was the man's name—related to Isaac how he "was sick of sharing his fingers with the nails! Every time I hits the nail with the 'ammer, me fingers gets in the way, and they are complaining summink cruel!"

Isaac, quickly seeing this as a possible answer to both their problems, asked if he could learn the trade and eventually take over the old man's customers.

"Would it be hard to teach me?" Isaac asked.

"Well, now," said Bert, perceiving this as a golden opportunity but not wishing to make his work look easy. "'Tis a very 'ard business.

There's a 'uge lot of walking to do, and you're away for a long time from the missus." Then, realising that he may have just lost a once-in-a-lifetime chance, he added, "Not that she complains, like, she's quite 'appy when I comes 'ome with the money! And as it 'appens, I was thinking of taking on a happrentice!"

It was clear that Bert had never felt so important in his life.

"I'd be very 'appy to hoffer you the hopportunity, if you was willin'!"

This was exactly the opening for which Isaac had been searching.

Gemma urged him to go. "I'll be perfectly all right! You must give yourself the chance of learning another trade. Give it a trial, at least."

And so Isaac joined Mr Bert Pride—"the bodger codger," as he liked to call himself—and began to learn the ways of the chair-mending business.

His entire collection of tools was housed in a well-worn leather bag, which Bert was now very pleased to be able to hang on young Isaac's back. The bag held a small hammer, some brass nails, a ball of strong twine, a pot of glue made from the hoofs and horns of slaughtered animals and three tins of assorted varnishes, all intermixable.

"Me'oggany colour for them as got such chairs, hoak and helm for the rest!"

Bert really was feeling very important. He had never had an apprentice before, and he had never been one himself! Completely self-taught, he had built for himself a reputation as an honest, hard-working craftsman, and people waited eagerly for his visits. He was proud of his name and happy to introduce 'my new happrentice', Isaac, who will be mending your chairs from now on under my hexpert eye, as I've taught 'im!"

Isaac and Bert took the north turnpike road out of London and started on the first of many miles of travel. A few carriages rattled by, perhaps taking the gentry to their country estates. Sometimes, a mail coach would whirl past or a country cart toiled along. All left behind a cloud of dust which enveloped the two chair bodgers.

Most times, they walked along in a companionable silence. Isaac amused himself with wondering who may have been inside the carriages. He never volunteered any information about himself, and Bert never asked.

In the evenings, when they came to a village, they would put up for the night at a coaching inn. They would take a meal of, perhaps, cold beef with some bread and cheese, and Bert would treat himself to a gin and hot water—and, more often than not, a second one.

"Very good for the screws!" he would say, easing himself gently onto a bench, rubbing his back and massaging his hands. "It surely is doing me good, lad. I 'ope you never gets the screws. Very painful they are, to be sure!"

And next morning, off they would go again, walking through the village, calling, "Chairs to mend! Chairs to mend! Bring out your chairs! You break 'em, we mend 'em! Bring out your chairs!"

Then they would sit down by the side of the road and start their repairs.

Occasionally there would be no business, and Bert would say, "Well, lad, it looks like we won't be eating tonight!" But he was not an unkind man, and he saw to it that Isaac always had something to eat and a bed for the night, though it might be in the stable.

They were gone for many weeks, and Isaac lost count of the times that Bert told his customers that he was now so busy that he had had to take on an apprentice.

At the end of this first trip, Bert announced that Isaac had completed his apprenticeship.

"I've taught you all I know, and you are now a fully qualified chair bodger. You are now on your own. I've put a penny or two aside, and me and the good wife will now look forward to a long old age together. We 'ope you will take an early hopportunity to come and tell us about your travels. Me bag o' tools and me glue is yours now! But if the good Mrs Pride should feel it necessary to break one of our chairs over me 'ead for any reason, I shall expect you to come and mend it free of charge! I can see me business is in good 'ands, and I wish you the very best of 'ealth. I've never 'ad a son' but if I 'ad, you'd be 'im! Look after yourself, lad. I own I shan't be sorry to stop walking all them miles, but I will miss the people."

He clasped Isaac's hand warmly and again wished him the very best. In the short time he had been with Bert, Isaac had become quite fond of him.

"Of course I shall come and visit you," he replied. "And I thank you for the opportunity you have given me. Goodbye, Mr Pride, sir!"

ISAAC SOON PREPARED to make his first solo trip. He expressed his concern about Gemma's advancing pregnancy, but she convinced him that she was very well and perfectly capable of looking after herself, since she had become expert at her chosen vocation.

"Now!" she said. "Get off with you, before you've forgotten everything Mr Pride taught you!"

They were both aware that many weeks would elapse before they met again. Isaac polished Mr Pride's ancient leather bag and looked forward to his journey. He was still dogged by images of Gemma's attacker, and the spectre of Newgate Prison and the gallows was forever with him. He was glad to put a few miles between him and those places.

The week before Isaac was due to return, Gemma went into labour. Without the benefit of family, friend or midwife, she delivered herself a healthy baby boy, who yelled lustily at the injustice of being so violently and suddenly propelled into this world.

It had never occurred to Gemma that there was any alternative to her having the baby, and, now he was here, her maternal instincts took over. She hugged and cuddled him to her breast, cooed and sang softly to him. She loved him fiercely. It was as if he filled some sort of vacuum inside her, and the need to keep him close was overwhelming.

Whenever she wondered how anyone could abandon a newborn, her thoughts went back to her father. It was never a secret that Silas had been left on the doorstep of the Foundling Hospital as a baby. Gemma shed tears of sorrow for him, her mother, herself and Isaac, mingled with tears of joy for her new little one. She hugged him more tightly and decided to call him Sebastian, because she liked the name, and Silas, after her father.

Sebastian Silas Gallimore—it had a good ring to it!

Isaac's visits back home grew rare. Satisfied that Gemma was able to look after herself and Sebastian, he travelled further and further afield. He had probably become better known than old Bert Pride, and, youth being on his side, was able to travel more miles in a day and therefore repair more chairs. He was doing very well. He always visited his old master when he returned and kept both him and Mrs Pride entertained with his tales of Bert's old customers.

Gemma's activities were also flourishing. For a long time, she had harboured hopes of a better life for them all but, seeing no way out, abandoned them. As soon as Sebastian was old enough, he was schooled in the intricacies of the ancient art of the pickpocket. Because of his young age, he made a very proficient decoy.

Some of their most profitable evenings were theatre nights. The old theatre in Covent Garden Square, designed by Inigo Jones over a century before, was one location they chose regularly, though not so often that they became well known.

As the ladies and gentlemen alighted from their sedan chairs and carriages, dressed in their finest evening wear and ready to enjoy that night's entertainment, the young Sebastian would dart into the lamp-light from his hiding place close by, clutching their clothes and squealing that his ma was about to murder him.

Gemma would be hot on his heels, grabbing the boy, disentangling him from coat tails, furs and skirts, and apologising to milords and ladies.

In the ensuing ruckus, purse and watch were transferred from the gentleman and, if it was a particularly successful night, milady's jewellery would be theirs as well. By the time their victims had collected themselves and discovered their losses, the thieves would be well away into the dark. The pickings were pawned the next day, spent or sold on to a fence. Gemma and Sebastian were now making more than an adequate income.

But their way of earning their livelihood came to a sudden end when one evening's victim turned out to be a choleric Jonas Fimbler. He was a man who always had an eye on the main chance, constantly looking for ways to impress the social circles which he yearned to join —and thus found himself at the Theatre Royal on Drury Lane.

Resplendent in his much-worn but well brushed and pressed evening clothes, he progressed slowly on foot to the main entrance.

Hooking his silver-banded cane over his arm, he looked to all the world as if he had arrived in a carriage which, to avoid the crush of people, had stopped only a little way off.

Suddenly, the opportunity to impress more than a few people landed right in his lap. At that very moment, a yelling urchin came rushing up to him, clutching his clothes and screaming that his ma was about to murder him, imploring the guv'ner to take pity on him.

Hot-footing close behind was Gemma, frantically pulling her young son away and jostling against a quick-thinking Jonas.

He had had enough experience in what he viewed as his most important role in life, that of a Justice of the Peace in His Majesty's Bow Street Court, to know what was truly happening. Jonas was proud of the fact that he had personally transported more than a few pick-pockets to the other side of the world, and here was his chance to rid the streets of more of the scum!

He also knew not to grab the child, but a parent, the male if possible. That is, if they *were*, in fact, the parents. After all, how many runners had caught these young ruffians in the hope of finding a parent, only to discover that they were homeless urchins? Those "parents" saw such an event as reducing the number of mouths dependent on them. Out on the streets, there were plenty more young 'uns they could enrol. If the young brats were going to get caught, they were of no use anyway.

A few months earlier, the worthy Justice had been so anxious to impress at an evening's theatre that he had allowed his guard to drop long enough for some scruffy ruffian to lift his purse. He had since kept more than a wary eye out.

This time, he knew what to do.

So it was that Gemma Gallimore found herself wriggling and squirming against the strong arms of Jonas Fimbler, Esquire, Justice of the Peace, and Sebastian began hitting and scratching and imploring Jonas to let his mama be.

Mr Fimbler was exceedingly pleased with himself. He had a large audience of what he hoped were influential people to witness his self-less, and yes, *brave* act of community service.

Immediately he summoned a nearby Runner and handed over his

prisoners. Then he retrieved his cane, wrapped his handkerchief around his bitten hand, and straighten his clothing. He would have been mortified had he been actually injured in such an unseemly scuffle or—worse still—had his clothing been torn. He could ill afford replacement, having to look after his old ma as he did.

Jonas collected himself and puffed up with pride. The ensuing congratulations, pats on the back and expressions of "Well done, sir!" would surely cement his place in the circles to which he aspired.

GEMMA AND SEBASTIAN spent the next few days in very uncomfortable and decidedly unfriendly surroundings as guests of His Majesty George III. In due course, they found themselves in a place of summary justice, that is, the magistrates' court.

They were led to a raised wooden structure with rails all around, like an animal pen. A gentleman in a long, black frock coat and white *jabot* at his throat came into the court and sat down.

"A case of attempted pick-pocketing, Your Worship!" a clerk called out, and Gemma and Sebastian were once more in the presence of Jonas Fimbler, Justice of the Peace.

A knowing smile oozed its way from the thin lips of that gentleman. He was going to enjoy himself more than usual.

"And what do you have to say to that?" he asked the terrified pair in the dock.

Too frightened to respond, Gemma and Sebastian stood, shaking.

Then Mr Jonas Fimbler, Justice of the Peace, with the greatest of pleasure, banged hard his gavel on the bench and sentenced them to "seven years' penal servitude in His Majesty's new colony of Australia!"

Without any further ceremony, Gemma and her son were removed from the court and taken to a "holding house" to await transportation.

The meaning of "seven years of penal servitude in Australia" was not immediately clear to Gemma but was soon spelled out to her in very clear detail. They would be sent a long way away, and since nobody had yet come back from wherever it was, she wasn't sure whether she should be alarmed or not.

They had no way of letting Isaac know what had happened or where they were, but, had he been able to inspect them, the court records would have shown:

1792 Gemma Gallimore, aged 25 years—7 years transportation.
1792 Sebastian Gallimore, aged 7 years—7 years transportation.

❧   5   ❧

And that was how Gemma Gallimore and her young Sebastian found themselves aboard the sailing ship *Hillsborough*, chartered by His Majesty's Admiralty for the express purpose of transporting convicts to His new colony of Australia.

The passenger list was a motley collection of humanity. Above deck were a handful of passengers paying their way to the new world, and their conditions were as favourable as could be afforded. The ladies and gentlemen dined with the captain, and the niceties were observed as far as was possible. Below deck was a rough, primitive, sometimes cruel world of rogues, villains and evildoers. Prostitutes granted favours to sailors in return for extra rations. Tempers became inflamed and fighting was common. Men were separated from the women and children, and there was very little privacy.

Once every few days, small batches of prisoners would be escorted up on deck, well away from the eyes of the ladies and gentlemen of course, to inhale the fresh salty air and see sky and sometimes billowing sails. In these moments, they comforted each other and looked forward to a better future, when they could be together always.

The eight-month journey locked up below deck in the unbearable heat gave Gemma plenty of time to ponder their future. She knew nothing of what to expect on the other side of the world. In some odd way, the whole experience had drawn her and Sebastian closer together. She resolved that, when they were free and perhaps respectable, she would make it all up to him somehow.

They had escaped the typhoid fever that had broken out on board, which she took as an omen of good luck. She solemnly swore to mend her ways and took every opportunity to instil this determination into her young son.

Upon their arrival at Sydney, all the travellers were placed in barracks and organised under the so-called Assignment System. They were then farmed out to private colonists, and, in an uncharacteristic piece of sympathy on the part of the government, families were kept together when possible. Each employer was responsible for feeding, clothing and housing his convict labourers. Some assignees were sent into government service.

Gemma soon learned that the Assignment System had many rules. Her master could take any of his convicts before the courts for breaching them, such as by being drunk and disorderly or being absent without leave. If found guilty, she could be sent to jail for a short spell, flogged or, if the crime was serious enough, put in a chained gang.

But if she behaved herself well, she could earn a Ticket of Leave, which would allow her to work for herself, provided she regularly reported to the police and did not break any rules. Eventually, she could be granted a conditional or free pardon. Under a conditional pardon, she could never return to England. But under a free pardon, she would become an emancipist, as free as anyone else.

It was for a free pardon that Gemma Gallimore would strive.

GEMMA AND SEBASTIAN found themselves assigned to a Mr Benjamin Ainsley. In addition to his business, their new master had built an immense mansion on a hill overlooking a great river which flowed into the harbour some way downstream. He named the house Hillingdon, and it was to have been the dream home of him and his wife, Anna, although they had conflicting ideas on its construction and furnishing.

At one time, Ben Ainsley thought he had everything a man could want. He was tall, lean and handsome. He had more than doubled the great wealth he inherited from his father. And he had a beautiful wife. Anna had been the envy of the elite English social circles in which she had been raised. When she captured and wed Ben Ainsley, she left behind a string of suitors. She saw before her a life of infinite luxury, and when she accepted his proposal, Ben thought life could not possibly be better.

But, as time passed, he saw that something was missing from his marriage. It wasn't that it was childless. That, he left to fate. And it was not that Anna was not an attentive wife. She submitted to him whenever he asked—she saw it as her duty and a small price to pay for the life he had given her. But she never initiated intercourse between them, and he came to accept that, though there was a certain kind of love, there was no passion in their marriage. They had settled into a routine of his work, her socialising, and their regular but monotonous love-making.

The Ainsley family had made a large fortune from tea. But some twenty years earlier, when the British government levied an import tax on the citizens of its own colony of America, its people had revolted, and a great quantity of Ainsley tea had ended at the bottom of the harbour at Boston. Those events were leading to an inevitable war. Old man Ainsley both surprised and upset the tea world when he decided there and then to abandon that business and direct his ships to an industry less politically affected.

When Ben inherited the business, his adventurous spirit got the better of him, and his thoughts turned to the new colony of Australia. An astute businessman, he reasoned that there would be a great need for buildings of all descriptions. He set sail for the Antipodes, taking his reluctant wife with him.

Over the next few years, he brought from England the various pieces of fine furniture, furnishings, coloured window glass and building materials that made up the lavish furnishing of his new house. Not far away, he had established a brick and stone works and required an ever-increasing band of workers both there and at Hillingdon.

Anna never came to terms with the lack of a social life in this new land, said her life there was primitive and departed for England with the stated intention of never returning until he came to his senses. But any possibility of their reconciliation had been dashed forever, as the ship on which she was travelling had foundered in mountainous seas as it ploughed its way around the Cape. All on board were lost.

Benjamin Ainsley had wept. He wept for her lost life, and though he didn't understand why, he wept for himself. He immersed himself in his business and mentally shut himself away from intimacy with anyone, male or female. He was respected by his employees as a man who was stern but not unfair. Most recently, he had requested a further twenty convicts from the next transportation.

Upon their arrival, Gemma was put to work at Hillingdon as a maidservant, and Sebastian, too young to work at the quarries, was assigned to the gardener's care at the house. The other eighteen convicts, all men, had been housed at the brickworks.

Over the following months, Gemma was under the tutelage of Ben's housekeeper, Mrs Dainty, the wife of the head gardener. Mrs Dainty was an exacting but just woman. Both she and Mr Dainty had been where Gemma and her son now were, and she was sympathetic, though it would never have done to show it. The Dainty couple looked after Ben and oversaw the large staff that looked after his home, both inside and out.

Their master was a Christian man, and every Sunday afternoon, he granted his household staff leave to occupy themselves as they wished. This was a precious time for Gemma and Sebastian. Unable, because of their status, to leave the grounds through the high, wrought-iron gates, they enjoyed each other's company as they walked through the gardens hand in hand, sat under an imported English tree, dallied by a fountain tinkling in the afternoon sun, strolled down to the river's edge at the bottom of the grounds and told each other about their days.

Sebastian showed his mother the special garden beds on which he had worked and was excited at being able tell her the names of various plants. At each meeting, she reminded him to be respectful and obedient and to remember their goal: freedom. She implored him to never do anything to put that goal in jeopardy.

Sebastian was kept busy in and around the grounds. Because of his years, he was given fairly light duties, but they were many, and he collapsed, exhausted but not unhappy, at the end of each day. He looked forward to Sundays, when he could have his mother to himself for a few hours.

Gemma, for her part, was happy to be where she was and drank in every detail of the Ainsley mansion. She loved to polish the wonderful English mahogany sideboard, laden with suites of Wedgwood china. She dusted the portraits of unknown Ainsley family members, past and present. She marvelled at the heavy imported furnishings. And she dreamed.

She dreamed of her eventual pardon, her mother, her father, her future and Isaac. Poor Isaac! What had become of him? Where was he? What was he doing? Was he well? And—with a sudden jolt—was he alive? So many questions she asked, nursing a forlorn hope that she might someday have answers.

On her daily rounds through the house, she occasionally came across Ben himself. She always dropped a small curtsey, which he acknowledged with a sombre nod.

So it was with a great deal of surprise that, one day, as she stood in the library marvelling at the countless books, leather-bound and gold-lettered, and running her fingers across their spines as if to caress them, she turned at a small sound and saw Ben in the doorway.

He leaned, relaxed, against the jamb, since he had been there for some time, and regarded her with a quizzical half-smile.

But when she whirled around, culpability written all over her face, he returned to his usual austere expression and asked, not unkindly, "Do you like books, Gemma?"

Too stunned to reply, she nodded, lips pressed tightly together.

"Can you read?"

"Oh, yes, sir!" she replied, hesitating as if she had committed a further crime.

He nodded, turned, and was gone, leaving Gemma in a lather of guilt. Three years into her seven-year sentence, she hadn't put a foot wrong. Did he think she was stealing his books? Would this jeopardise her chances of a free pardon?

She could hardly focus on her work for the rest of the day, torn between confronting him and pleading and waiting to hear the worst from him. She even contemplated running away, though she quickly dismissed the idea. She resolved to simply keep out of his way.

ONE DAY, there was to be a grand ball at Hillingdon. The ballroom was one of Gemma's favourite places. It fitted her notion of all that was graceful, grand and beautiful, part of a world about which she could only dream. The room was a very long one, and in the middle were two large marble fireplaces, back to back. In the space between the sides of the hearths and overmantels, and the walls on either side of the room, were floor-to-ceiling folding doors. They were normally closed, making two smaller rooms, each with its own fireplace. Gemma had seen them opened only once, during the redecoration.

The former Mrs Ainsley had had the house decorated in a rich and overly ornate style. It had not suited Ben, but he had been busy over-seeing the establishment of his business and saw it as a means of keeping his wife occupied and happy. Knowing that money was no bar, she used it with abandon, and he never interfered. Once or twice, he intimated that it was a trifle overdone and perhaps not in the best of taste, but he had been brushed aside. Hillingdon was to be the greatest house anyone had ever seen, and she was out to impress. After her death, it was gradually redecorated in a more subdued, though still opulent, style.

Gemma stood in the doorway of the great room, now opened fully. Her eyes swept around and down, up and across. She was awed by it and loved every corner. The carpets had been removed and the floors polished in readiness for dancing. Fires had been laid in both fire-places, in case it should turn chilly. All was almost ready, and the setting sun caught the crystals in the giant chandeliers and danced and twinkled amongst them, sending a kaleidoscope of colour darting around the room. Sheer floor-to-ceiling curtains billowed and fluttered in a zephyr breeze, and, on either side, heavy brocade curtains were tied back with tasselled sashes, ready to be released should it turn too cool.

The room was decorated in two soft shades of green, with touches of the palest lavender here and there, heightened by trims of white. Gold leaf embellished the elaborate cornices and ceiling roses. At the far end of the room, a long banqueting table had been laid with sparkling white damask supper cloths, gleaming silver, beautiful English china and an immense floral arrangement at the centre, all awaiting the arrival of delicious foods from the kitchens.

Gemma took a step or two inside, closed her eyes, and sighed deeply. She imagined long skirts whirling and coat tails flying in lively dance, then, more sedately, soft skirts swaying and elegantly shod feet peeping out now and then from beneath the hems. She imagined the music of the orchestra, hidden behind a large arrangement of potted palms.

"Isaac, oh, Isaac," she said, with an ache in her heart. "If only you could see this, be in it, a part of it, as I am this minute!" And she felt her eyes become misty. She clasped her arms around herself and swayed ever so softly to the imagined music.

"Do you approve, Gemma?" a soft male voice asked, from close behind her.

Her daydream interrupted, she turned to see Benjamin Ainsley, his kind brown eyes regarding her. Still partly in a reverie, she could barely separate herself from the magic that engulfed her.

With eyes still half closed, she breathed, "Oh, yes! So beautiful! It's just right, just perfect!" Then suddenly, reality overtook her, and she stammered "Oh! Oh! I'm so sorry, sir."

Eyes cast down to the floor, she said again "Sorry, Mr Ainsley, sir!" and fled. Her heart racing, her cheeks flaming, she felt as though she had been caught stealing. Stealing? That was how she had once existed, long before, and it was a time to which she never wanted to return. A long time afterwards, in another life, she would smile at these thoughts.

Benjamin Ainsley's heart lurched. With a startling suddenness, he realised he desired her as he had never desired before. A bolt of ecstasy speared through his body and down to his very core. He resolved that he would make her his. He stood unmoving for a long time, electrified by a forgotten awareness, a fathomless longing, an unrequited yearning...

What a truly exquisite, beautiful woman! he thought. *But she is like a frightened animal! Why?*

He would have to tread gently and carefully to gain her trust. Then there was the difference in their social position. Her seven years' servitude was almost finished. He was a patient man, and he would wait. He was determined to have her.

He imagined the mane of chestnut hair, freed from its daily restraints, loose and soft against his bare chest. He imagined caressing that wondrous body, whispering words of love and wanting. He would possess her, and nothing and no man would stop him.

He wanted to know all about her. How had she come to be there with him? He was unreasonably jealous of whoever had fathered her child. Where was he? Ben only knew what her papers had stated:

Gemma Gallimore, transportation 7 years, pickpocketing.

His head spun with countless questions—and the one burning desire. She had awakened in him a passion he had long ago subdued, and he would go mad if he could not have her.

❧ 6 ❧

Only nine ex-convicts attended the modest ceremony which marked the end of their penal servitude and the granting of their free pardons.

Of the original twenty assigned to Benjamin Ainsley from the *Hillsborough* transport, one had died of natural causes, one had been killed as the result of a violent fight, three had been transferred to a chain-gang, and six had been granted conditional pardons only. For his assignees, Ben liked to make the occasion special, and he conducted these gatherings personally. He commissioned scrolls from a calligrapher and presented them to the ex-convicts, preceded by a short address to express his sentiments.

"In the name of His Majesty King George III, it is with pleasure that I present these scrolls, to officially proclaim that you are now free persons, 'free' in the sense that you are able to leave the bonds of my employ and work for yourselves. As a gesture of my faith in your achievements, I offer each and every one of you the chance to remain with me as a free person. That means that you will henceforth be paid a fair and proper wage for your work. The choice is yours. I wish you the very best of health and prosperity, wherever your decisions may lead you." With a slight hesitation, and a deep intake of breath, he added. "And may God bless us all!"

So saying, he presented the scrolls, shaking the hand of each recipient. As an acknowledgement of Sebastian's age, he patted his shoulder and, coming to Gemma, savoured her hand in his and swore to himself that he experienced a mild electric shock.

"I will leave you now to speak amongst yourselves and think about your futures." He left the gathering and, unbeknown to them, moved to an upper window from which he observed the gathering of seven men, one youth, and one woman—one exquisite woman.

There was much excitement among the nine ex-convicts and much to talk about. Gemma and Sebastian had not set eyes upon any of the seven men present since alighting the *Hillsborough* eight years earlier. All were very much interested in each other and shared their stories: why they had been transported, their fortunes since their assignment, and their unanimous judgment of their master—a stern disciplinarian, but a just one.

A tall, fair-headed man occupied a deal of Gemma's attention, and Ben, watching from his viewpoint, felt a pang of envy. Gemma asked her companion why he had been convicted. He had once, he said, been a bavin-maker, until one long and hot summer, when his hand-hewn faggots had not been required a great deal. He had been very thirsty and hungry after a long day calling his wares to no avail and, in desperation, grabbed a half-quartern loaf of bread from a baker's stall on his way home. The baker, who apparently had no sense of humour, hailed a Bow Street Runner to apprehend him. All this he told to Gemma with such an amusing slant that she had laughed outright. Everyone was so caught up in the merriment of the day that it seemed a great cloud had been swept away, leaving only sunshine.

Ben, still watching, saw Gemma throw her head back, grasp the arm of her companion as if to steady herself, look into his eyes and smile joyously. Her eyes sparkled, and her face had come alive.

He was seized by a passion of jealousy and longing. He was surprised at the depth of his feeling. It was new to him, and he must be wary. Such intensity could be dangerous. It could blind a man and make him do things against his better judgment.

He wasn't to know it, but Gemma was also surprised by her own reaction. She had worked so hard and waited so long for this moment that she had momentarily forgotten her terror of men. Her one close encounter with the opposite sex, apart from her father and brother Isaac, had engendered in her a deep-rooted suspicion of all males. She had always shrunk from physical contact of any kind, and now she found herself grasping a man's arm!

A small part of a great weight seemed suddenly to have been lifted from her, and she was left wondering.

Gemma's partner looked down at her. "I hope I will see you again! Now that I'm free, I intend to stay with the master long enough to get some money, then start out on my own."

Gemma, slipping back into her cautious ways, replied, "Maybe we shall meet—who knows?"

"Where will you be?" he asked. "What will you do?"

"I really don't know," she said, lost in thought for a few seconds. "I have a brother I love dearly back home. I would very much like to see him again. Maybe I will try and... find him, somehow..." Her voice trailed away.

"Well, I hope we'll meet again somehow, sometime!" he reiterated at the end of the afternoon, running appreciative eyes up and down her body as he smiled and left.

Gemma returned to her quarters. Now that she had her freedom, so precious and hard-won, she didn't quite know what to do with it. She had dreamed about it, waited for it, worked for it, but now it was somehow surreal.

Her thoughts were interrupted by a smiling Mrs Dainty, who, upon entering, clasped Gemma warmly to herself and kissed her.

"Gemma, Mr Dainty and I are so proud of you and Sebastian. You have done very well, and you deserve every happiness!"

Gemma was overwhelmed by the soft embrace. She remembered a long, long ago time when her mother had put her arms around her, held her warm and safe. Gemma wanted to stay there forever, and tears sprang to her eyes and spilt over.

"My dear!" said Mrs Dainty, holding the weeping Gemma even closer.

Further words seemed unnecessary. Mrs Dainty thought she knew exactly how Gemma felt; she could clearly remember the day when she herself had been granted her pardon.

An unexpected tap at the door prompted Gemma to disentangle herself from Mrs Dainty's embrace, dash her hands across her eyes, and blow her nose hard before the door was opened.

Ben stood there—and was momentarily lost for words. Questions flew through his head at lightning speed. When he had last seen her, she had been so happy, and now... He wanted to enquire but thought better of it. If he asked her, it might start her tears again, and he couldn't bear to see her so distressed. So he simply swallowed and said:

"Gemma, when you have a minute or two, will you please come and see me in my study? I should like a word with you."

He didn't want to see her so upset any longer and, without waiting for a reply, turned and left.

"Now," said Mrs Dainty, "dry your eyes, my dear, and go and see the master. I wonder what he can want of you?"

Gemma did not see her turn, wink and smile at her husband over Gemma's head.

ONCE SHE RECOVERED HERSELF, Gemma straightened her hair, smoothed down her clothes, and walked the several long passageways to Ben's study.

The door was open, and before she could knock, he called, "Come in, Gemma, and sit down, please." He indicated a deep, upholstered leather chair.

Gemma crossed the room and sat timidly on the edge of the chair. She had never been invited to sit down in her master's presence before, would never have presumed to do so. She folded her hands in her lap and looked down at her feet, totally subservient.

Ben had to fight an impulse to grasp her hands, lift her up and crush her against him. He could feel his face in her hair, his arms pinning hers.

He steadied his voice with an effort. "Gemma, Mr and Mrs Dainty have decided to return to England and..."

Gemma's head snapped back in disbelief, and her lips parted as if to ask him to repeat what he had just said.

Ben wanted to force his mouth down on hers, and kiss her forever, but instead, he continued.

"... And they wish to join the next ship for the home country."

Gemma still stared at him; she could not believe her ears.

"I have spoken to Mrs Dainty and she tells me you are more than capable of filling her shoes. I don't know what you have thought to do, but you would be doing me a great favour if you stayed on at Hillingdon. You will be paid, of course, and moved into Mrs Dainty's rooms. You may keep Sebastian with you, and he may do as he wishes. But I would very much like him to remain where he is; Mr Dainty tells me that he is keen and able!"

Ben looked at her, and his heart melted. She looked so forlorn, the last remnants of her tears still evident. He wanted to protect her, stop the world ever hurting her again.

The day had all been too much for Gemma, and her eyes welled up again. She sat there, head downcast, as channels of tears coursed silently down her cheeks, dropped off her chin and splashed onto her folded hands. She made no sound at all.

Ben turned away. He didn't want to cause her any more pain by looking at her, and he could not trust himself not to gather her to him and kiss her tears away. He took a silk handkerchief from his top pocket and gently placed it on her hands.

He wanted to get down on his knees and beg, to implore her to stay, and he felt quite brutal when he left the room, saying, "Let me know when you have decided what you would like to do, please, Gemma."

AT THE END of the day, it seemed to Gemma that she had shed more tears than she knew she could. She felt drained, dry and ragged. She fell into her bed—and soon into an exhausted, dreamless sleep.

Next morning, she woke and the world had felt totally different. Yesterday had happened, could not be undone, and tomorrow was yet to come. There was now a purpose to her life, a new fresh purpose that stretched before her into infinity.

It wasn't the same as working for her pardon. That had an end to it, a conclusion. But this, this was different—the world was hers. Inexplicably, she felt clean and pure.

She bathed and dressed, and with a new, clear vision, approached Ben's study door.

"Good morning, Mr Ainsley, sir! Thank you for your offer. I am sorry that you will be losing the Daintys, but Sebastian and I would be happy to stay here."

Ben was astonished at the change in her demeanour. She was again efficient, collected and respectful—and distant!

His emotions were in turmoil. Yesterday, when she was so tearful, he had desired her and felt gentle and protective. Now she was cool and aloof, he was overtaken by an almost violent lust. What was it with this woman? A vision of her insinuated itself into his every waking hour. He would have to be careful, he told himself, or she would end up destroying him.

Gemma could not know what control Ben had to exert over himself, and he gave no indication.

Businesslike, he said, "Thank you, Gemma. I'm relieved! Mr and Mrs Dainty will be leaving within the next three weeks. I will put in hand the necessary arrangements to transfer you and Sebastian to your new quarters."

❦   7   ❦

Claude de Garamonde was on his way to the bank from his elegant home at Number 2, Grosvenor Street, in the area named Mayfair, so called after the fair held there on the First day of May in medieval times. The hood of his carriage was raised. He was in a thunderous, black mood and didn't want to have to acknowledge anyone along the way.

Claude was the last of his line. If he died without an heir, the old name of de Garamonde would cease to exist. He had managed, through rigorous efforts of skulduggery, business acumen and plain good luck, to gather and grow the remnants of the family fortune. To his everlasting chagrin, the old title of Count was sent into oblivion at the death of a childless cousin, but he nevertheless managed to perpetuate the bearing and lifestyle of his aristocratic forebears.

When he met Celeste Duvalle, he saw in her two reasons to propose, one as important as the other. She would bring to the de Garamonde name great riches and a son. Her beauty was a bonus, but secondary. He was happy to shower her with jewels and fine silks and show her off. At the beginning of their marriage, she had shown little interest in his ardent overtures, but he left her in no doubt that the sole reason for her being where she was, was the continuation of the de Garamonde name.

With only the faintest hint of disappointment in his voice, Claude announced to his fellow directors that his wife, Celeste, had delivered a daughter that very morning. He had stayed home long enough to establish the sex of the baby, then summoned his footman to order the groomsman to make ready the landau and two blacks, forthwith—and to have both hoods raised—ready to transport him to his place of business, the Bank of England. He had wasted enough time!

It was just like Celeste to do this to him! She had not wanted a child anyway, but to give him a daughter was just too terrible. It was pique, that's what it was, he told himself. He had given her everything she had ever wanted, and much more besides, and how had she repaid him? With a *daughter*!

Well, he'd fix that soon enough. He'd get her pregnant again, straight away, and her usual protests would fall on deaf ears. If it came to a point, he'd force himself on her, that's what he'd do! The more he thought of the injustice of it all, the blacker his mood became.

Celeste, for her part, was delighted. Having reconciled herself in her pregnancy to its inevitable conclusion, she had reluctantly accepted her removal from society for a few months. Now, she was glad it was all over!

And, she thought, a daughter was infinitely preferable to a son. There would be pretty dresses, dainty handmade shoes, gorgeous hats, parties, dances, a "coming out" and so many grand balls! She could see her daughter now, coming down the grand marble staircase, slowly, elegantly, to the envious, hushed stares of her friends, her husband's peers and their ladies. Oh, it would be an endless delight!

She called her daughter Emmaline. Emmaline de Garamonde would set society on its heels one day, Celeste would make sure of that!

Her gaze dropped down to the sleeping babe beside her, and of a sudden, she decided she was exhausted. She had done her duty! She had no intention of suckling the baby herself; there were wet nurses for that sort of thing. The idea was quite abhorrent to her—disgusting, really!

Celeste was carried from the birthing room and never wanted to see inside of it again. She would issue a directive for it to be sealed immediately. She was dressed in a fresh silk nightgown and peignoir and laid herself back on hand-embroidered pillows in her own boudoir. She drew a deep breath, smiled a tiny smile, sighed contentedly, and closed her eyes.

When she awoke, she must remember to give instructions for the door adjoining hers and Claude's rooms to be permanently locked.

BY THE TIME she was five, the dimpled, curly-headed Emmaline was the darling of the de Garamonde household, albeit in different ways to each person. The servants adored her, and she would oft times creep downstairs to find cook, who would provide her favourite tidbits. Her governesses saw to it that she was educated to perfection and turned a blind eye to her sorties downstairs. Her mama spoilt her dreadfully, and her papa, despite his earlier misgivings, had warmed to her. If he was in the right frame of mind, he even endured her sitting on his lap for a short while, and once, she even made him smile, against his better judgment, when she tickled him beneath his well curled side-whiskers.

Emmaline was vaguely aware that her mother and father maintained an ever-increasing frigidity between them, but she had no way of knowing that this was not normal between mamas and papas. She was always very careful not to hug her mama too tightly for fear of crushing her gowns, and she was ever grateful for the small crumbs of affection that were sent her way. She looked forward to the daily half-hour in the presence of her mother. During her waking hours, her papa was not often there, but if he was, she patiently waited for an invitation to speak with him or even put her hand in his.

One day, sitting in an upstairs window with her chin in her hands, Emmaline became interested in a mountain of trunks being packed into several carriages in the roadway. She was repeatedly drawn from the windows by a knowing governess but managed to escape every few minutes to see the comings and goings below.

She was bewildered when she saw the figure of her mama emerge from the house, dressed in her best travelling wear and hurriedly entering her personal carriage.

Escaping her governess, Emmaline raced down two flights of stairs and out the front door, just in time to see the back of her mother's cabriolet rattling off quickly down the road, followed by another, smaller vehicle travelling with equal haste.

Emmaline did not understand. Mama always told her when she was leaving to stay at one of their country houses. And she always said goodbye. What was happening?

Emmaline could not know what the rest of the household, except her papa, had known for some time. Celeste had fallen head over heels in love with an impecunious poet much younger than she. He made her feel young and alive and she granted him regular access to that which she had denied her husband for five years.

Claude had long ago ceased to beg his wife for the occasional favour and satisfied his carnal desires at several destinations within a fairly close radius of his house in Mayfair.

That day, he clumsily took a tearful Emmaline on his knee and, feeling sorrier for himself than for her, told her that her mama had run away and was not coming back because she had ceased to love them.

Emmaline listened to this news in dumbfounded silence. She would not accept that her mama did not love her anymore.

Had she been asked, she would have said that, of course, she loved her papa. But in truth, his rigid thinking and unbending formality frightened her. She understood that he was the head of the household and that his word was law, and she had learned to keep out of his way when his black moods descended upon him. One night, recently, she had heard loud voices, and even a door being violently pounded, followed by the sound of her father's footsteps hurrying down and into his carriage waiting at the door. She wondered if that had had anything to do with her mama leaving them.

THE OLD, French aristocratic de Garamonde family, small to begin with, had been reduced to three members by a succession of various events. Some had fallen on hard times, been ostracised and allowed to die out, and some had been separated from their heads by the axe in the years leading up to the French Revolution.

At ten years of age, Emmaline was about to meet the rest of her relations. She was told by her papa that it was time for her education to be rounded off. He had left her upbringing in the hands of a string of governesses until that point and now had willingly succumbed to the suggestion of his two older sisters to allow them to complete her education in Paris. He knew that she would be schooled in the proprieties, strictly in accordance with the highest principles.

So, Emmaline sailed to France, accompanied by her father, and was handed into the care of his two siblings, both excited to meet her: the widowed, childless Mignonette and the spinster, Charlotte.

By this time, Emmaline had accepted the fact that her mother would never return, and her aunts had made a point of never mentioning Celeste's name.

Claude dutifully visited Emmaline two or three times a year and was not displeased to see that she was being introduced to the very best of Parisian society. Her manners were exquisite, and she was turning into a beautiful, polished young woman. She had inherited her mother's dark curly hair and long lashes, along with flawless skin which had attracted Claude to Celeste many years before.

During his visits, in the evenings, Claude made time to visit certain establishments where he could be amused by a succession of young ladies, some not much older than his daughter. On one such visit, Monsieur de Garamonde allowed himself to become besotted with a very young, exotic Tunisian goddess, who recognised a wealthy man when she saw one and used all her charms to beguile him. She wrapped her sinuous body around his in the darkest hours of the night, allowing him to taste delights he had never dreamed of, always with the unspoken promise that there were plenty more where they came from!

He had been so blinded by Zaphira that he at once took her to London, installed her in Number 2, Grosvenor Street, Mayfair, and hastily arranged a divorce from Celeste. He had settled the country estate in Lincolnshire on his ex-wife, plus a generous yearly allowance, and married his Zaphira with quite indecent haste, lest she should escape.

And so it was that Emmaline was introduced to her new step-mother who, at seventeen years of age, was just one year older than she was.

❧ 8 ❧

Zaphira had been delighted, almost overwhelmed, by the riches heaped upon her by her new husband, who, at fifty-two, was almost three times older than she was. Her gowns were designed in Paris and brought for his approval to Mayfair, where she was happy to parade in each new creation before his lascivious eyes. The fingers of the silk weavers of Spitalfields were kept busy manufacturing bolts of fabric from which "my lady's undergarments" were fashioned, and Messrs Fortnum and Mason regularly delivered expensive morsels for her to savour.

She roamed throughout the great house, watched by the servants and staff, who talked among themselves of their dislike for their new mistress. She swept from one room to another, regarding her reflection in great mirrors, and stood, nose wrinkled, before large portraits of unknown de Garamonde ancestors, fingering sumptuous hangings, and pirouetting in front of floor-to-ceiling French windows. She sat at the grand piano in the main withdrawing room, ran her fingers over its polished, cream ivory keys, and congratulated herself.

Her new husband was an enigma to her. In the daylight hours, dressed for business or the evening's theatre or opera, he was stiff and proper. But in the deep dark hours of the night, his reserves were totally abandoned. It was then that he was like putty in her hands. She could do as she wished with him, and he never seemed to tire of her.

But as the weeks and months passed, Claude's enchantment did wane. Despite his determined and regular efforts to impregnate her, their marriage was still barren. He secretly suspected her of somehow preventing a conception, convincing himself that you never knew with these foreign people—they were always up to all sorts of trickery!

He was also embarrassed when they appeared in public, as her lack of breeding became more and more evident. He enlisted the help of a sympathetic lady friend to coach Zaphira in the rules of dress and genteel etiquette and employed a language tutor. Claude had personally not minded her thick accent too much, but socially, it was a distinct disadvantage. Zaphira had, for her own benefit and satisfaction, taken on board all the advice her tutoress had to offer, and for her further satisfaction, had cuckolded her husband with her male English tutor.

Still, Claude was determined that he would have her educated to his standards, and, until then, have his daughter on his arm in public. For that purpose, he had Emmaline unwillingly brought back from her aunts in Paris.

The relationship between Emmaline and Zaphira was distant. Emmaline did not admire her father's choice of a new wife but respected his right to choose whomever he wished. Zaphira envied Emmaline's obvious superiority in terms of refinement and so delighted in making it clear that she had the greater claim on Claude's attention—and therefore his status and wealth. These were of little interest to Emmaline, who, apart from her obligatory presence at dinner in the evenings, kept herself at a polite distance.

CLAUDE'S MOODS became blacker and blacker at Zaphira's failure to bear a child. His outbursts at the bank became more frequent and more violent, and his fellow directors, who could not know the reasons, became concerned for his sanity.

After one particularly explosive outpouring, he collapsed, white-lipped, beads of perspiration collecting on his forehead, and clutched his chest. His colleagues, not wishing to have a deceased director on the premises, had him carried to his carriage with a message to have his physician summoned immediately.

Mrs de Garamonde was not to be found at the moment of his arrival. She was in a state of undress, sprawled on a bench in the gazebo in a rarely visited part of the garden, vigorously pursuing a dalliance with a young gardener.

Emmaline was called, and the doctor informed her that her father had suffered a heart attack. He administered some laudanum to his patient, issued instructions that he was to be kept very quiet and promised to visit again on the morrow.

Emmaline was worried and attentive, and, thinking that Zaphira should be informed as soon as possible, went in search of her. She found her stepmother in the garden, walking towards the house, smoothing down her skirts and patting her hair, a satisfied smile on her lips.

Zaphira was unmoved by her husband's affliction. In fact, she welcomed it as a release from the nocturnal duties which she now found repugnant, especially since her voracious appetite was now being regularly satisfied by much younger men. She kept away from him as much as possible.

As he slowly recovered, Claude had time to reflect. He concluded that he had made somewhat of a fool of himself and began to concoct ways of ridding himself of Zaphira before she destroyed him totally.

From time to time, important bank documents required his attention, and these had been despatched to him in the hands of the bank's most reliable clerk. Jeb Abeles was up and coming, and his superiors were hopeful of him reaching great heights. He was a trifle overwhelmed by his task; to visit the private residence of the most senior man in the bank was a daunting prospect. But he told himself he had to subdue his usual reticence if he wanted to move up the ladder. He had to be more assertive, more confident, or at least appear to be so.

A maid admitted him to the hall of the Grosvenor Street house and asked him to please wait while the master was being informed of his arrival.

Jeb looked around the immense hall. The two rooms he occupied would both fit into this one, and then some.

Then a door on the side wall opened, and a smiling Emmaline approached.

"Good morning!" she said. "I'm Emmaline de Garamonde. My father is expecting you and will be with you shortly."

"Jeb Abeles, ma'am, at your service!" Jeb replied, executing a small bow from the waist, and nervously transferring a large envelope from one hand to another.

As he did so, the package slipped from his grasp, hit the marble floor, split open and documents scattered around their feet, some even skittering a small distance away on the highly polished stone.

Jeb was momentarily struck dumb with horror, his mouth open as he surveyed the strewn papers.

"Oh, dear!" Emmaline said, and quickly bent down to retrieve the pages.

"S-so sorry!" stammered Jeb. "A clumsy accident! Allow me please!" He stooped to help her.

Emmaline smiled and handed him her bunch of papers and, in a rush of sympathy, asked, "Would you like to come into the picture gallery? We will at least have something to look at while we wait for my father."

Jeb wished himself a thousand miles away but said, "Thank you!" Then, remembering his resolve, he added, "That would be most enjoyable."

He was a little taken aback by her informality and wished that his replies had not been so stilted, so nervous.

She looked straight up into his eyes, then indicated the gallery door. He entered the long gallery after her. She watched him survey the long side wall of the gallery, clutching his papers tightly, lest he should lose them again.

Again trying to ease his embarrassment, she said, "Didn't people wear amusing clothes in the old days?"

Taking this as a comment, rather than a question, Jeb's eyes took in portraits of young, not so young, old and very old de Garamonde ancestors, many with decorations and one or two with small coronets.

At the very end of the gallery was a large portrait of Emmaline, painted the year before by Sir Joshua Reynolds.

In commissioning the portrait, Claude had at first approached Sir Thomas Gainsborough, noted for his paintings of patrician breeding. Sir Thomas had politely declined the commission, saying that as he had so many to complete and could not undertake another for a while, but that he would be pleased to put Claude's request at the top of his list when he could start again. His would-be client had been enraged by this, and in a fit of pique, gave his commission to Reynolds. That artist, known for his rich colours, had portrayed her in a garden by a fountain, one hand on the stonework, and the other, relaxed and elegant, down the side of a rich sapphire blue silk gown which matched the colour of her eyes exactly. It was an amazing likeness, and Claude was somewhat mollified.

As soon as Jeb saw it, he studied it for a second, then looked at Emmaline as if to compare, and looked back again at the portrait. She was amused by his reaction, and he turned again to find her smiling at him for the third time that day.

He was saved from comment by the arrival of a maid, who announced that Mr de Garamonde was ready to receive him.

Emmaline thanked her, and she and Jeb walked side by side from the gallery, into the study where Claude awaited his visitor.

CLAUDE SAT in his favourite wing-chair, the plaid rug which normally covered his legs folded neatly on a carved chest by his side. It wouldn't do to let a subordinate see him as less than his usual, efficient self. His mind was as lively as ever, but his body was still recovering.

"What have you brought me?" His hand shook ever so slightly as he extended it towards Jeb.

Jeb approached and placed the documents, now neatly back in their covering and in precise order, in his hand.

"Good morning sir! I trust you are well?"

Ignoring this, and opening his package, Claude waved his hand in dismissal, saying he would ring when he was ready. He had no intention of allowing a young clerk, however bright he might be, see that he was unable to stand and could barely see what he was reading because it was so difficult to hold his eyeglass steady. Sometimes, when he raised it to his eyes, he shook so badly that he let it fall, then started all over again.

CLAUDE'S RECOVERY took a great deal longer than he had hoped. He would never relinquish control of the bank as long as he lived. As a result, Jeb's visits were becoming a regular occurrence.

Emmaline always made sure that she was available to keep Jeb company, and Jeb looked forward more and more to his visits. Sometimes they would sit in the library and talk, and sometimes they would walk in the gardens. Oft times they would visit the picture gallery and make up stories about the old people portrayed there. Jeb's sense of the ridiculous would make Emmaline laugh outright, and he loved to see her so enjoying herself. Claude would have had a conniption if he overheard some of their nonsensical tales about his forbears.

Emmaline's natural charm rubbed off on Jeb, and together they made a great deal of fun between them. His humorous side and her quick uptake emerged as they got to know each other better. Sometimes he would describe an event at the Bank and put such a slant on it that they would end up with tears rolling down their cheeks, they laughed so hard.

It was inevitable that they should fall in love—and they did. The day the realisation struck them, they kissed and clung to each other in their special place in the garden, wondering how they were ever going to tell Emmaline's father, and what he would say...

Each had a fair idea, of course, but didn't wish to upset the other by voicing it. Jeb wanted to do the accepted thing and ask Claude for his daughter's hand, but Emmaline prevailed upon him to wait until she had had a chance to speak to her father and prepare him for what was to come. Jeb reluctantly agreed.

WHEN CLAUDE'S recovery was almost complete, he resumed his days at the bank, starting with shorter hours. He made up his mind to give Zaphira a last chance and request that she restore his conjugal rights forthwith.

Zaphira had not yet totally lost her ability to wrap him around her little finger. She managed to convince him that such exertion would not be good for him, might even bring on another attack! She stroked his arm, pouted prettily, and said, quite truthfully, that she didn't want to lose him.

He mistook this last sentiment, and capitulated. An hour later, when his ardour subsided and his obsession with fathering an heir resurfaced, he determined to wait only a little while longer, then he would insist. No excuse would deter him.

Zaphira, meanwhile, enjoyed herself immensely. She had a rich husband to provide everything she wanted, and, because he was ill, freedom to go about town and broadcast her gifts wherever and whenever they were desired. Her body was anybody's to enjoy, and her continual need for gratification was satisfied.

One evening, Claude was standing at the fireplace, a balloon of brandy in one hand, the other arm running along the wide mahogany mantle, and one expensively shod foot resting on the elaborate brass fender. He had had a good day, successfully concluding a major piece of business, yet his mood was pensive. Zaphira had once again displayed bad manners by keeping dinner waiting for her appearance, and a very good pheasant soup had been ruined.

The three of them had dined in a frosty silence, the two women of his household well aware of his brooding resentment. Zaphira had repaired to her boudoir, pleading a headache, immediately the dinner had finished, and Emmaline had gone to her room to prepare for her approach to her papa about her betrothal. She would wait until he had gone to his study and had a brandy or two, and maybe his mood would be more benign.

For his own part, Claude determined that tonight was the night, headache or not, that he would assert his rights, and that was all there was to it. He had waited long enough! He would have his heir at any cost. In fact, he told himself, he was looking forward to it all, including the act itself but even the eventual delivery of his son.

When she did produce his heir, he would instruct his advocate to draw up a fresh will, leaving nearly all to his son and heir first, then Zaphira. All he had done so far since his marriage to her was revoke his will leaving all to Celeste, so at least she was out of it all. That only left Emmaline and his two sisters, Mignonette and Charlotte, and they would be well provided for whatever happened. In the meantime, he would leave things as they were.

AND THAT'S how Emmaline found him: smiling to himself and apparently at peace. His dark mood over dinner had subsided, making her feel more at ease.

"Papa, may I speak with you for a moment, please?" she asked, entering the room.

He shook himself out of his reverie. "Yes, my dear, what is it?"

Emmaline took a deep breath. *How and where in heaven's name do I start?* All her prepared speech had deserted her. She swallowed and hesitated.

Claude, always impatient with indecision, said, "Come, Emmaline, what is it?"

It was now or never, and it had to be now. She was determined.

"Papa, you know the young man from the bank who brought you your papers while you were ill?"

He frowned, trying to focus, and his tone was vacant and dismissive. "Oh, erm... Yes—what's-his-name—er..."

"Jeb Abeles," Emmaline supplied.

"Yes! What of him?"

"Papa..." Emmaline hesitated for so long that Claude, thinking of Zaphira and his need to have her tonight, almost shouted.

"Come, Emmaline, what's the matter with your tongue? What of him?"

Emmaline could see his mounting temper and decided that it was too late to give up.

"Papa, Jeb and I want to be married!"

If the ceiling had fallen in on them at that moment, Claude could not have been more flabbergasted.

"What?" he roared, expelling the word like a bullet. "What did you say?" Perhaps he hadn't heard aright. The hand holding his glass shook, the brandy slopped over, his foot came off the fender, and he glared at his daughter in absolute disbelief.

Emmaline, having gone thus far, suddenly felt very brave. Wishing to spare Jeb such a confrontation, said quietly and with such determination, "Papa, we have made up our minds. We are going to be married, with or without your consent!"

Claude de Garamonde couldn't believe his ears. His world was disintegrating, and it was all to do with women. Confounded females! That's what he got for leaving his daughter in the care of his sisters. They had a deal to answer for! Where was it all going to end? First Celeste, who had left him—*him*—for another man, then Zaphira who would not do his bidding, and now his own daughter who was standing up to him in a way he never imagined possible. What the devil was going on?

Well, it was about time he turned things around and let 'em know what was what around here! Celeste, he could do nothing about. His two sisters were in France and well away from his day-to-day life. Zaphira would get her come-uppance that very night; he would particularly enjoy that.

But now... Emmaline!

He would let her know what he thought about her idiotic ideas, and he would forbid her, absolutely and irrevocably, to carry on with this silly notion. Fancy even thinking of marrying a... a... he couldn't even find the words.

His heart beat abnormally fast, and he collected himself quickly, frightened by it.

"Emmaline, sit down, please. And heed what I have to say." He drew a deep breath. "You are a child, Emmaline. A child, do you hear? You are only seventeen and cannot possibly know what you are contemplating."

Had Emmaline had the temerity to remind him that his own wife was only seventeen when he had married her, she knew he would have blustered, shouted and sworn that that was a different matter altogether.

"This... this... what's-his-name..." he sputtered, "*Abeles* fellow is a junior clerk, for God's sake! He has no prospects! He is not even... Where does he come from? Where's his family from?" He thought his head was going to explode.

He was working himself into such a passion that Emmaline became alarmed. Strung across his embroidered silk waistcoat was a gold chain, with watch and seals suspended. He grasped at those appendages, twisted and turned them furiously in his fingers.

"Papa, please—I care nothing for all that! Anyway, he has no family, and—"

"*Everybody* has a family, Emmaline!"

"As for his prospects," she continued, "we shall get by. We love each other!"

This last statement was delivered with such finality that Claude felt helpless for the first time in his life. But he wasn't going to accept this preposterous proposal without a fight. The emotions now mastering his face made it a dull dark red, and he was almost frothing at the mouth.

"This is abject tomfoolery!" he persisted. "I shall see to it that the young jackanapes goes nowhere in the bank, and *then* we shall see how much you love each other!"

A thought occurred to him. *And why the devil can't he come and ask me properly for your hand, like any decent, self-respecting man, instead of sneaking around and getting you to come to me first?*

Before Emmaline could reply, he continued. "You have always had everything your heart desired. How can this... this... lowly, no-good clerk, this... this... Oh, Emmaline, have you completely lost your senses? Think, really think, for once in your life, what you are about to do!"

He was so agitated, he had to sit down. His heart was thumping wildly, and his hands were trembling.

Concerned, Emmaline decided not to carry on any further. She touched his hand gently. "I am genuinely sorry, Papa, to have upset you so." Then she quietly left the room.

Claude remained in his chair, his brandy forgotten on the mantle, and seethed with frustration and rage.

What's the matter with them all? he asked the world at large, staring unseeing into the flames, which lazily wrapped themselves around the logs. A pretty mess this was!

He sat there for a long while, and his temper abated slightly as his mind went back over the years. To Celeste, to Emmaline's birth, to Celeste running away. He had never got over Celeste's running away. How could she have done that? Then to Zaphira.

He suddenly remembered his earlier resolution. Yes—his little Zaphira! That's right—he had promised himself to let her know once and for all what she was there for. He rose from his chair and went into his dressing room, where another fire burned in the grate.

CHANGED INTO A SILK DRESSING GOWN, he turned the knob of the door connecting his dressing room and Zaphira's. Locked! *Locked!* He tried it again. *It was locked.*

He stood staring stupidly at the door knob. This was the second time in his life that a wife had locked her bedroom door against him. Beside himself with rage, he stepped back, and sweeping his clothing aside, picked up the heavy oak dressing chair and hurled it with all his might at Zaphira's dressing room door, at the same time giving vent to several full-blooded and satisfying oaths.

The lock gave way, and splintered wood fell to the floor. He violently, viciously kicked at the remains of the door to widen the entrance, then stepped through.

Beyond the further door, he saw a wide-eyed, frightened Zaphira, sitting up in her bed, her knuckles white, clutching the covers to her breast. He stepped toward her, hands outstretched.

"Zaphira..." His body stumbled toward her, fell across the foot of her bed, and slid slowly to the floor.

Claude de Garamonde was dead.

❋

EMMALINE WAS DESOLATE. She told herself that she had been the cause of her father's death, and she could not be placated. Her agony was relieved by her papa's physician when he told her that it had only been a matter of time before he had another, final attack. She had told him that she had argued with her papa some two hours before his death, and the doctor, knowing, like many other people, more than a little about Zaphira's philandering, reassured Emmaline that she had been in no way to blame.

She sought comfort in the company of Jeb, and they determined to be wed as soon as a decent interval had elapsed.

The funeral arrangements were made, and the household was in mourning. Emmaline's face was puffy and tear-stained much of the time, and Zaphira tried to look as sorrowful as she could in her widow's weeds. She decided that black suited her very well!

Claude's casket lay on a black-velvet-draped table in the front hall of his Mayfair house, where people came to pay their last respects. A service would be held at the time of his interment in the family vault just outside Paris. Accompanied by Zaphira and Emmaline, the carriage bearing Claude's remains was sombrely drawn to Rotherhythe, where a ship awaited them. Emmaline and Zaphira accompanied the casket to the elaborate vault, opened and cleaned, and his remains were interred, watched by a tearful Emmaline, a grieving Mignonette, a mournful Charlotte and a very relieved Zaphira.

Claude, the last of the de Garamonde line, was with his ancestors, at peace at last.

Zaphira, trying hard to effect the right degree of sorrow, told Emmaline that since she was so distraught, she would stay awhile in Paris and then visit her family, whom she had not seen since her marriage to Claude. So, when Emmaline returned to London, Zaphira remained. But even if she had a family, she had no intention of visiting them. She proceeded to her old stamping grounds and took up where she had left off, promising herself that she would return to London as soon as her grief had abated somewhat.

✳

MEANWHILE, Claude's advocate, a Mr Charles Whittingham, had come to the Mayfair house requesting a meeting with the widow. Advised of her absence, he asked if he could see Emmaline, who was well known to him.

When Charles Alastair Meriweather Whittingham went into the Faculty of Law at his university, he became known as Cam. This was because his peers decided that his full name was too much of a mouthful and declared that he would henceforth be called by his Christian name initials, C.A.M. When Cam first met his wife-to-be, there was great merriment between them because her maiden name happened to be Charlotte Anne Merce. And so it was that the Whittinghams became known as Mr and Mrs Cam to all but Charles' clients and business associates—all clients, that is, except Claude de Garamonde.

Cam had attended to Claude's legal matters for years and was well aware of the changes in his client's life during that long time. Technically, he should only speak to the widow de Garamonde and would do so as soon as she was available. In the meantime, in acknowledgement of the rapport he had enjoyed with his old client and friend, he felt compelled to speak with Emmaline privately and mayhap prepare her for the news she would have to face very soon.

Emmaline greeted him cordially, accepted his genuine words of sympathy, and ushered him into the library, where she thoughtfully had tea brought in.

Cam was very ill at ease and didn't quite know how to start.

"Emmaline," he began, raising his teacup, "I must tell you that your father died intestate."

Emmaline had no idea what that meant but was alarmed by his tone. She waited for him to continue.

"That means, my dear, that he died without making a will."

Still, she did not grasp the full impact until he explained, "To die without making a will means that his next-of-kin will inherit everything. The next-of-kin in this case is your—" he could not bring himself to say 'stepmother'—"your father's wife!" He coughed nervously and could not look directly at her.

Floundering for words, he babbled, "She is the sole beneficiary of your father's estate and will inherit everything!"

Emmaline's jaw dropped, and Cam mistook this for a sign that she now realised that she was a pauper. But that was not the case. It had simply never occurred to her that her life would ever change in any way at all, and now, it suddenly struck her that, at a single blow, it would change overnight.

No mother, no father, no home, no means of support, no... no nothing!

Her mind reeling, she looked at the kindly face of her father's old friend, sitting opposite her.

"I understand. Thank you, Mr Whittingham, for coming to explain it to me."

Cam's heart turned over. How could Claude have done this, so that that wife of his, that harlot, should have everything?

"Have you thought what you might do, my dear?" enquired Cam.

"As it happens, sir," Emmaline replied, "I'm about to be married, so my future is assured!"

This came as a complete shock to Cam, since he had no prior knowledge of any such plans. Her intended husband could not have been a member of the society in which Claude moved; the engagement would have been on everyone's tongue. Could she have met someone in France, perhaps, when she was staying with Claude's sisters?

"May I enquire who is the lucky gentleman?" he asked.

"Yes, of course! His name is Jeb Abeles. He works—worked—for Papa in the bank."

Cam wondered how well-off this fellow might be, but good manners prevented him from asking. "Well, my dear, I wish you every happiness! And if my wife and I can be of any assistance, you have only to ask! I hope we shall one day have the pleasure of meeting your husband-to-be!"

He rose from his chair and waited for Emmaline to precede him to the door, then bowed stiffly and tipped his hat.

"Good morning, Emmaline. I hope we shall meet again soon."

And off he went, making a note to himself to find out more about this Jeb Abeles fellow. If, as Cam suspected, he was some good-for-nothing gold-digger with an eye on Claude's fortune, he would make damned sure the blackguard knew that Emmaline was penniless! He became so cross about the possibility of his old friend's daughter getting hurt, that he appointed himself her unofficial guardian there and then. He felt he owed Claude that, at the very least.

Then there was Zaphira! The law said she was the sole legatee. How the devil could he make sure that Emmaline would be looked after? Cam had only met Zaphira once, socially, and was appalled at her lack of breeding. What, everyone had asked, was Claude thinking of?

"Well, Cam, my dear," said Mrs Whittingham later, as they made ready to retire for the night. "As they always say—there's no fool like an old fool!" Then she affectionately gave him a quick, soft pat on his bald pate.

❦   9   ❦

Jeb Abeles lived in the house in which he had been born—at least, the remains of it. He had two rooms, together about eight feet wide and some twelve feet long. The stairs to another two rooms on the upper floor had long ago become so rickety that he thought it prudent not to attempt to climb them. In any case, as one could see from the outside, the birds flew in and out of the top windows, from which the glass had long since disappeared, and the old slate roof looked in imminent danger of collapse.

Shorefields was the unofficial name of the leafy area about halfway between Shoreditch and Spitalfields, where there was a short, narrow street called Raleigh Lane. Number 7 in the lane was about one mile from the bank where Jeb worked, and he walked the distance daily, almost always happy and whistling.

The yellow plague had taken his parents from him some ten years ago, leaving the young Jeb to fend for himself. What little furniture they had, he cherished and kept in very good order. It was all he had to remind himself of them. He kept his two rooms in spick-and-span order and cooked for himself in a pot suspended on a long chain over an open fire in the corner of what he liked to call his "drawing room." The other room housed a three-quarter-sized bed, a cupboard for his clothes and a small table beside the bed, on which stood a candle in a glass holder. Adjacent to the candle holder was a small, flat plate, decorated with roses, on which were his father's pearl-shell shirt studs and his mother's ivory hair comb.

If Jeb stood at the front door of Number 7 with his back to the house, he could look across the few feet of laneway to the back garden fences of the big new houses on Church Road. The opposite side of Raleigh Lane had been cleared of all the ancient wooden houses, exact copies of the one in which Jeb lived, their grounds incorporated in the back garden area of the new houses on the neighbouring street.

Jeb sometimes looked wistfully at those houses and daydreamed that one day...! It was to Number 7, Raleigh Lane, he nervously brought Emmaline de Garamonde to show her where she would live if she married him.

He need not have worried; she would have happily lived with him in purgatory! Emmaline was so much in love with him, she was frightened he would no longer want to marry her when he learned she was now a pauper. She told him she had no family, no home, no means of support, and no prospects and asked him if *he* still want *her*! Jeb assured her that all that meant nothing to him, and they were quietly married at St Michael's, with the Mr and Mrs Cam as witnesses and three other guests.

Zaphira had not been seen since Claude's interment and was presumably still in France, reconciling herself to her widowhood. Weeks had gone by, and nobody knew how or where to contact her. The household staff had not been paid, and though Emmaline used up what money she had to pay them, and one by one they had left. The great Mayfair house was locked up, vacant. It still contained all the furniture and furnishings, and all the ghosts, along with Alfred Goodapple, an old retainer Emmaline asked to stay on as caretaker.

From her own room, Emmaline removed the chest that Celeste had bought her at birth and a small painting of her mama and papa. Her elaborate gowns, she left hanging where they were; she took only the very plainest she could find. She left a note addressed to Zaphira on a silver salver on the hall table, just inside the front door.

She had kept Charles Whittingham informed of her situation, and he regularly visited to enquire whether she had heard from Zaphira. Cam always left feeling upset at her married surroundings but amazed at how happy she seemed to be. He was the first to know when Emmaline and Jeb announced that they were expecting their first child.

FROM TIME TO TIME, Emmaline was visited by Miss Amelia Lightfoot, her old governess, who, sad though she was to see her dear girl in such circumstances, had been one of the few guests at her wedding. She brought little treats when she came, including tiny garments she had lovingly made for the expected baby's layette. And it was Miss Light-foot who discovered Emmaline, with only six weeks to go before her confinement, lying at the bottom of the broken stairway in her "drawing room." She had seen a cobweb in a corner of the room, and, to reach it, had stepped up to the fifth decayed timber stair. The old wood had given way, bringing her and the other steps below her crashing to the floor.

Emmaline then prematurely delivered a tiny, perfectly formed son, who, despite a valiant struggle, succumbed after only a few days of life.

She and Jeb were consumed with grief. Weeks went by before they were able to think of picking up the pieces of their lives. Time helped to lessen the depth of their pain, and they slowly came to terms with their loss. But Jeb was weighed down by their financial doldrums and felt the full weight of responsibility on his shoulders. He kept his depression to himself, lest Emmaline should be further upset.

Unbeknownst to Jeb, a possible answer to his woes came in the person of Miss Lightfoot, during one of her regular visits to Emmaline. She had been asked by a friend, a relative of a wealthy merchant and his wife, if she knew of anyone who could teach French to their two little girls. Knowing that Emmaline was fluent in the language by dint of her years with her aunts, she had wasted no time in coming to see her. Miss Lightfoot thought, privately, that it would be good for Emmaline's emotional health, and the extra money would not do any harm, either! Best of all, the merchant and his family lived within a short walking distance of Raleigh Lane.

Emmaline had confronted Jeb that evening with the proposal. She was very enthusiastic, but it still took some time to wheedle a reluctant acceptance out of Jeb. Once she began the work, the extra money it brought to the house was very welcome, and when Jeb saw how lively and smiling Emmaline had become again, he was happier than he had been for a long time. To top it all off, Jeb had been granted a raise of five shillings per week, and suddenly, life seemed to have taken a turn for the better.

Little did they know that, through the efforts of a scheming Charles Alastair Meriweather Whittingham, their lives would, very shortly, take a monumental turn.

ONE OF CAM'S clients was the rich owner of the largest house in Church Road, and he had consulted with the lawyer about the prospect of extending his current grounds. The trouble, he explained, was that the only way he could accumulate more land was to extend his small back garden. He pointed out to Cam that there was a narrow lane behind his garden wall, along one side of which was a row of derelict cottages. Only one was occupied: Number 7.

It took Cam about half a second to see that this could help him realise a dream he had nurtured for some time. He told his client that he would look into the matter in detail and suggested a meeting with the other three Church Road owners. This was arranged forthwith, and it was at that meeting that Cam put forward the idea that all four owners could enhance the value of their properties tenfold if they incorporated the land upon which the cottages were built into their own properties. The four owners, none of whom wished to have a smaller landholding than the others, agreed to leave the legal matters to Cam.

After some weeks searching the musty remnants of records saved from the Great Fire, Cam established the ownership of the Raleigh Lane cottages. It appeared that the lane had once been a part of an ancient tanning works and the cottages had housed some of the master tanners. The laneway, together with its cottages, had been left to successive generations after the original tannery owner,   Jeb's great-great-grandfather. It seemed that that gentleman had been a victim of the Black Plague. Jeb's father had therefore ultimately became the owner, but he was an illiterate man of slow wit, and it had meant nothing to him. He was simply happy to live in the house in which his forefathers had lived for as long as he could remember and thought himself fortunate that he never had to pay rent. It had never occurred to him that he might own it, but even if he had, he had neither the means nor the intelligence to turn his possession to account.

It followed that Jeb, though ignorant of the fact, was the rightful owner of Raleigh Lane and its cottages, and Cam had no intention of enlightening him. Cam had always been a man of high principles, who prided himself on the fact that he had never done a dishonest deed in his life. Yet here he was, he told himself, doing such devious acts as he could hardly believe himself. And, even stranger, he was enjoying it all. It was exciting, so different from his mundane everyday life—and all because some clients wanted to amass more money. Well, if there was any amassing to be done, Cam thought, it wouldn't be his clients doing it!

Cam hatched his plan over many weeks. He had called another meeting of the four Church Road owners and sat behind his large desk to acquaint them with the result of his investigations. Ever mindful of his professional oath, taken many years before, it was totally inconceivable that he should tell a lie, so he chose his words very carefully.

"Good afternoon, gentlemen," he began. "I have some news for you. I have located the owner of Number 7, Raleigh Lane, the only occupied cottage in the lane." *So far, so good.* "The gentleman in question is with the Bank of England." He felt a deal of satisfaction at that one. Well, it was the truth, wasn't it? Could he help it if they thought he *owned* the bank? "And in fact, he is the owner of the whole of Raleigh Lane, and the cottages in it!" *True.* "This makes the negotiations much easier, having one owner instead of several." *True.*

The four gentlemen present exchanged smiles.

Bending the truth just a little, but not so as to change the outcome, he continued, "I have taken it upon myself to approach the owner." Well, he did visit Jeb and Emmaline quite frequently. "He would be prepared to entertain any offer." Cam felt sure that, if Jeb knew about it, this would be true. "But I must warn you that, since he had not previously thought of selling—" *Definitely true!* "—the price will be high!" He would personally see to that!

The four men excused themselves while they had a whispered consultation in the corner of his office. When they came back to the desk, their spokesman, Herbert Fitzherbert, the man who had originally approached Cam, cleared his throat.

"Will you please convey to the owner our offer of one thousand pounds?" To drive home the magnitude of their offer, he added, "That's one thousand pounds from *each* of us, you understand!" And, in case Charles' arithmetic was not up to the mark: "That's a grand total of four thousand pounds, sir!"

Cam was well used to the wily ways of greedy men when it came to matters of property, and he was more than a match. He had correctly guessed that they would agree on a figure among themselves before they had come to his office.

"Gentlemen, gentlemen!" Cam started, feigning a look of shock. "I could not possibly go to the owner with such an offer! He would not believe it!" *True.* "Any offer he would consider would be far in excess of the one you have put forward. Perhaps you will remember Dr Johnson's recent words on the sale of the Thrale Brewery. He said they were not selling a parcel of boilers and vats but the rather potential to grow rich beyond the dream of avarice. Well, sirs, we are not here to talk of mere inches of land!" Since he deemed it entirely appropriate, he included the bit about avarice.

Cam took his courage in his hands and concluded, "I appear to have misled you all and regret the inconvenience I have caused you. Good day, gentleman!" He began to rise from his chair.

Mr Fitzherbert put the palm of his hand up to stay Cam's rise.

"A moment, Whittingham, if you please, sir!"

Cam sat down again and looked expectantly at Fitzherbert.

"A thousand pounds each, sir, as a gesture of our intention to proceed – a *deposit*, if you will!"

"Oh!" said Charles, trying to look shamefaced enough to give the impression that he had not understood. "I do beg your pardon, dear sirs! Pray continue."

Before the end of the meeting, each gentleman had agreed to commit himself to seven thousand five hundred pounds, and every man was happy. But none so happy as Charles Alastair Meriweather Whittingham, who had thirty thousand pounds that he didn't have yesterday.

As he closed the door after the four men, he smiled to himself. That was probably the most satisfying piece of negotiation of his whole career, and only his rheumatism prevented him from dancing merrily around the room.

As always, caution was his companion. Before getting too excited, he would start drafting the deeds that very day. He would see that the entire moneys were in his hands with the least possible delay, and, when that day came, rheumy joints or not, he promised himself that he would dance all the way home!

$$\maltese \quad 10 \quad \maltese$$

An emblazoned, ornate carriage clattered its way through the cobbled streets and stopped at Number 2, Grosvenor Street, Mayfair.

The coachman pulled his horses to a halt and waited. With alacrity, a servant jumped from his stand at the rear of the coach, let down the four steps, opened the door on the side of the coach nearest the house, and stood smartly to attention with one hand on the couch door. After a second or two, a rustling came from inside the coach, and an elegant silver-buckled shoe at the end of a gentleman's leg, encased in green velveteen, emerged and placed itself on the top step.

Then followed the rest of that personage, the late-middle-aged Count Henri de la Salle, a rare dandy! Peeping from within a buttercup yellow coat was a heavily embroidered waistcoat in precisely the same shades of green and yellow as his coat and trousers. He wore fine, hand-stitched dogskin gloves, and a froth of white lace escaped from his coat sleeves. His well-curled and powdered hair was in perfect condition, since, oddly, he wore no hat. He reached the bottom of the steps, ignored the servant, and stood with his back to the coach, twirling a gold-rimmed eyeglass in his pale, manicured hand. He took two steps forward, put his glass to his eye, and looked up at the house with more than a little interest.

The coach swayed and moved up and down a little; another person was inside. Very soon, an absurdity of petticoats and skirts emerged, followed closely by the tip of a parasol and a slim waist encased in a tight, cream-velvet bustier liberally sprinkled with pearls. A gloved hand held the side of the coach door, the top of an elaborate hat emerged, and as she raised her head, the closely veiled face of the Countess de la Salle appeared.

The lady proceeded daintily down the steps to stand beside her husband and joined him in looking up at the great double doors of the house, guarded by four massive white pillars. Behind them, the trunks were unloaded and placed on the bottom step of the house, and the coachman awaited his instructions to proceed to the stabling at the rear of the property.

Zaphira, Countess de la Salle, raised the veil of her ostrich-plumed hat, a look of annoyance passing across her face. She was at a loss to understand why their arrival had not been noted and met. She crossly picked up her skirts and ascended the wide marble steps, closely followed by Henri who, at her bidding, rapped very loudly and sharply on the front door with his silver-topped malacca cane. Henri had to knock a second time, even louder, before they heard the sound of a heavy iron bar being slid back behind the door and the grating of a large key being turned in the lock.

Zaphira and Henri exchanged satisfied glances that turned to astonishment when one of the heavy doors was opened and there stood, or rather stooped, Alfred Goodapple, the ancient caretaker.

Alfred's eyesight was poor, and he did not immediately recognise his mistress. Zaphira pushed past him, almost knocking the old fellow over, and, followed by Henri, stood in the middle of the great hall, her gaze darting from one place to another in disbelief. It was clear that nobody was living there. Dust-covers shrouded the furniture, the shutters were drawn tight shut, and the whole place was dim and musty.

The Countess de la Salle whirled around and demanded to know what was happening. Where was everyone? All the servants?

Without a word, Alfred handed her the salver which held Emma-line's note.

Zaphira snatched it up, tore it open and read:

Zaphira, if you will be so good as to call upon me, I shall endeavour to explain all to you. I am to be married and will reside at No. 7 Raleigh Lane, behind Church Road, Shorefields. Emmaline"

The date was some seventeen months earlier.

Zaphira could not bend her mind around the fact that there was no-one to do her bidding except the decrepit being before her, standing first on one foot and then the other, stooped over and wringing his hands nervously. Sensing, correctly, that it would be futile to order Alfred to do anything for her, she rounded on her husband, who had absolutely no idea what was happening.

"Come, Henri!" Zaphira demanded.

"One moment, dearest!" replied her spouse, and continued his ascent up the stairs of the hall.

"*Now,* Henri!" shrieked Zaphira, losing control, panic in her voice.

The Count, knowing better than to continue his climb, faltered, turned and descended.

"Where to, my love?" he enquired mildly.

Zaphira, so agitated that she was almost incapable of speech, thrust Emmaline's note in his hand, and, skirts swirling, stormed through the front door to the top of the steps.

Henri, unable to read without his spectacles, thought it prudent not to delay and followed his wife down the steps.

As they reached the bottom, they heard the door being firmly closed, the heavy bar being replaced.

Alfred Goodapple, who had not uttered a single word between opening and closing the door, smiled a secret toothless smile to himself and returned to his comfortable room, downstairs at the rear of the house.

❋

On reaching Raleigh Lane, the coachman called to Zaphira.

"It ain't no manner of use going down there, madam, I wouldn't be able to turn me 'orses 'round!"

Zaphira took one look at the narrow lane, and the derelict houses therein, and baulked at putting a foot down in the dusty laneway.

"How on Earth can Emmaline be living in such a place?" she asked Henri. "There must be some mistake!"

She instructed the coachman to make haste to the nearest and best inn, where they would stay until she sorted out what was happening. They put up at the Golden Lion.

Next morning, a light breakfast of lamb cutlets, kidneys and sausages, accompanied by muffins and copious quantities of hot coffee, put the Countess in a better frame of mind, and, despite her doubts, despatched a messenger to the address in Raleigh Lane, with the request that Emmaline visit her, without delay, at the Golden Lion.

She was much surprised when a note came back to say that Emmaline would call on her later that day. Even more surprised was Emmaline when she first received news of Zaphira's appearance. She was looking forward, though not without reservations, to the afternoon's visit when, perhaps, she would be able to sort everything between them.

In her very short stay at the Golden Lion, Zaphira made herself very unpopular with the landlord with her constant demands. The landlord had remarked to his wife that if that was the way foreign nobility behaved, he wanted none of it. Nevertheless, he had set aside a private room for Zaphira, and, at her request, arranged the furniture so that a single hard chair was placed across the room, isolated from Zaphira's soft one.

"It looks like she's going to hold a bloomin' audience!" he said to his missus a little while later. It was just such an atmosphere that Zaphira intended. She felt that it would put her visitor at a disadvantage, which it normally would have.

Upon her arrival at the inn, Emmaline was shown to the room. A servant indicated her chair and said that the Countess would be with her shortly.

"The *Countess?*"

Zaphira made a stately entrance in a grand gown, with spectacular jewels at her throat. She was confident she would be in complete command of the whole meeting.

Before Emmaline could utter a word, Zaphira indicated with a dismissive hand, "May I present my husband, Count Henri de la Salle." Then she sat, taking great care to rearrange her voluminous skirts to the best effect.

The gesture had just the desired effect on Emmaline; Zaphira was pleased to note a flash of stunned surprise on her face.

Her good breeding rising to the surface, Emmaline regained her composure. She offered a polite nod and tiny bow in Henri's direction. "Good morning, sir! And how are you, Zaphira?"

Zaphira made not the slightest attempt to return these pleasantries. "What has happened at the house? When I arrived yesterday, it was locked up! And where are all the servants?"

This last question was asked with an angry glare at Emmaline, and the Countess tapped her jewelled fingers on the arm of her chair, waiting for a reply.

Emmaline stole a sideways glance at Henri and thought that he appeared more nervous than she was herself.

"There was no-one to pay them, Zaphira. They left months ago!" replied Emmaline.

"Well, re-engage them!" demanded the Countess. "And have the house opened up and aired immediately. The Count and I will take up residence straight away."

Struck almost speechless, Emmaline replied quietly, "I'm sorry, I no longer have anything to do with my father's house. I am now married and live elsewhere."

"Yes!" sneered Zaphira, "I'm aware of where you live. I saw it yesterday!" Fighting the feeling of her authority slipping away, she stamped her foot on the floor so suddenly and so hard that Henri visibly jumped and his eyeglass fell into his lap. This lack of control was a new experience for Zaphira. She had noted the reference to Emmaline's "father's house," and this made her ever angrier.

"I'm sure you are aware that the house is now mine," she asserted, "and since you are being so difficult, I have no alternative but to consult with an advocate."

Emmaline now met Zaphira head-on. "Mr Charles Whittingham is the lawyer dealing with the matter," she offered, rising from her seat, "together with, I understand, some of the people from the Bank of England in Threadneedle Street. I suggest you contact him. He will, I'm sure, bring you up to date with the position at Grosvenor Street. I have not been there myself for many months, and I am completely out of touch."

The confidence in her own voice surprised Emmaline. But Zaphira was more surprised to hear anyone, especially Claude's daughter, standing up to her.

Emmaline wanted to ask where Zaphira had been all these months past and how she had brought herself to remarry so soon after Claude's death. But she thought it best to retain the apparent upper hand and concluded the visit.

"If you have no further need of me, Zaphira, I have much to attend to, and I shall bid you a good day." Without waiting for Zaphira's reply, she left the room, bobbing slightly to Henri as she passed, and quietly closed the door.

Enraged, the Countess turned on her husband. "How could you let her address me in such a manner, Henri?" she spat. "I am her social superior, and I'll make sure that she is soon well aware of it! I shall have this... this... Whittingham fellow call on me on the morrow, and I'll be back in my rightful residence! And *you*," her voice was heavy with sarcasm, "my dear Henri, can think about how to get yourself out of *your* bottle of pickles!"

Henri, frightened, stood while his Countess gathered her skirts about her and offered his hand to help her rise. She brushed it aside with great disdain and flounced from the room, leaving Henri standing, at a loss for how to deal with his wife's latest outburst of temper.

From experience, he decided that a discretionary absence from her presence while she recovered her humour was the best course and, to that end, he summoned the landlord and asked him for a large glass of brandy with which to settle his nerves. He soon followed this with another, while he pondered his future.

HENRI CONCLUDED that his future was in a very parlous state. Things weren't quite working out as he had planned. Plagued for years by mounting debts, he had joined the ranks of many of his peers and found himself a wealthy heiress to wed. This seemed to him a very good arrangement: a title in exchange for enough money to pay his debts and to keep himself in the manner to which he was accustomed.

He had convinced his new Countess, as well as his many creditors, that a legacy, a very large legacy, was due to be paid to him very shortly. This, he knew, was a blatantly fraudulent claim. "Very shortly" stretched into "eventually." Renewed demands from his creditors, and a general reluctance by the fashion houses to supply more dresses and jewels for his Countess, had prompted him to suggest to Zaphira that he take her to England, where she could continue the lifestyle she now enjoyed. And, along the way, he thought, she could sustain the lifestyle he himself wished to maintain and help him avoid the distinct disadvantages of poverty.

This idea had been met with much pleasure from Zaphira. She could scarcely contain her anticipation, and eagerly awaited the arrival of the several hats, dresses and necessary accessories she had ordered for her return to London. She had been aware for some time of Henri's perilous financial position and thought that, after a suitable time back in London, she would rid herself of the old fool.

She would then have a grand house full of servants and Claude's fortune to maintain her desired position in society. And a title, to boot! Things were looking up for Zaphira. Delighted with it all, she threw her arms around her spouse and proclaimed that he was the best husband ever!

Henri had stepped back, blinking, and ran nervous hands down his ample front. Despite being married, he was unused to such close contact, especially with a female, and didn't quite know how to react.

He could not remember his mother ever having held him close or showing any outward sign of affection. She seemed forever too busy maintaining her position in the noble circles to which she belonged, and his upbringing was left in the hands of a succession of nannies, nurses and governesses. Until his marriage, quite late in life, he had been a bachelor disinterested in the opposite sex and consequently not attracted to the physical side of marriage, which he thought of as "all that beastly business."

The arrangement, any way she looked at it, suited Zaphira admirably. Young bodies were infinitely more athletic than older ones, and she was free to satisfy her desires anywhere she fancied. She looked forward to energetically distributing her favours all over London—and showing the stuffy English what style really was! She immersed herself in daydreams of endless riches, titles, parties.

But, for Zaphira, as for Henri, events were not quite turning out as they would wish!

CAM WHITTINGHAM PRESENTED himself to the Count and Countess de la Salle at the arranged hour the next day.

Zaphira got straight to the point, demanding to know why she could not gain entry to Grosvenor Street, the house that, she pointed out quite forcefully, was rightfully hers and following with an angry disquisition on the general state of affairs.

Cam listened to this tirade with a show of professional interest, waited politely for her to finish.

"Yes, madame, the house would certainly be yours—*if* it were totally unencumbered!"

Zaphira had no notion of the meaning of 'unencumbered,' but she didn't like the ominous emphasis on it.

"What d'you mean, *'if'*?" she demanded, her eyes kindling.

"Mr de Garamonde left debts. These will have to be paid."

At the mention of debts, Henri's heart did a double somersault, and, for a moment his normally ruddy complexion turned deathly pale. In an attempt to cover up his discomfort, he produced a very large handkerchief and, after shaking it out into a voluminous burst of the finest white linen fabric, held it his nose and generated a very loud snort.

Cam Whittingham startled, and the Countess glowered at him.

"How many debts?" demanded Zaphira, turning back to Cam in anger.

"A great many, madame," he answered. "I doubt that even the sale of the house's contents would defray them completely. Then, of course, there is the house itself!" He left the remark hanging in the air, like an enormous storm cloud, and took on the most sombre look he could muster.

"What do you *mean?*" persisted Zaphira.

"The house, madame," Cam repeated solemnly, "is encumbered with a very large mortgage. The mortgagees are pressing for payment now."

This brought an audible gasp from Henri, and Cam asked him if he was feeling well.

"Oui, oui!" replied Henri, so agitated that he momentarily forgot what language they were speaking.

By this time, Zaphira was caught so off her guard that she was almost breathless. She sat immobile, her bottom jaw dropped unattractively, staring blankly at the man of law in front of her.

Cam took advantage of her silence. "As you are doubtless aware, Mr de Garamonde was an habitual gambler!"

Zaphira gasped. She was *not* aware.

"And," he continued, "It is as well that you have come back to settle his affairs, since the bank, as well as several of his creditors, is about to put in motion the machinery by which these debts will be paid. Debts which, I may add, you, madame, have inherited!"

Pale as a ghost and unaware that she was repeating herself, Zaphira hissed, "What d'you mean, I have inherited the debts? *I* didn't incur them!"

"No, Madame, possibly not—but Mr de Garamonde would have borrowed to maintain his position in the community. You may not be aware, madame, but when you inherit the estate of a deceased person, you inherit the debts as well."

Cam derived a deal of satisfaction in delivering this news and had correctly gauged Zaphira's reaction. She was almost at the point of hysteria.

"What about his daughter?" she shouted. "Why doesn't *she* have to pay them?"

Cam sighed, trying to look sorrowful. "Miss Emmaline? Well, no! Mr de Garamonde died without making a will, and when that happens, the spouse, if there is one, inherits everything." He paused, then delivered the *coup de grace*. "After taxes, of course. She inherits property, *and debts*, if any. In fact, by law, Miss de Garamonde is entitled to nothing at all!"

This last statement would normally have left Zaphira elated, but the enormity of the situation had left her speechless, totally bewildered. In a vain attempt at gaining some sort of support, Zaphira looked at her husband, but he only stared at the floor.

"I sincerely regret, Madame," said Cam, insincerely, "that I have been the bearer of such bad news."

"Humph!" snorted Zaphira.

"*However*," he continued, noting that he now had her full attention, "anticipating just such an inevitable situation, I have thought of a possible way out of your dilemma."

At this, Henri looked up sharply, and Zaphira glared with angry eyes.

"And what, pray, is that?" she pushed.

"Well", answered Cam, with agonising deliberation, "I shall have to work out the final details, but you may be able to sign a waiver—that is, a document to say that you will waive all your rights to Mr de Garamonde's estate."

"And what will *that* do for me?" asked Zaphira, seeing a faint glimmer of hope but not quite sure how or why.

"It will mean," explained Cam, "that everything, house and contents, will be sold, and you will have no claim on the proceeds."

Zaphira almost exploded. "*What?* And who gets all the money?"

Aha! thought Cam. *Her true colours revealed.*

"Why, the creditors!" he said smoothly. "And they include the major one, the Bank of England, who all but own the Mayfair house."

Cam thought he could almost see her mind working. She seemed suddenly to have grasped her true situation.

"May I suggest, madame, that I leave you to reflect on your position? In the meantime, I shall go draft a waiver for you to consider."

Without waiting for a reply and remembering the existence of the Count, who had not uttered more than two words during the entire meeting, Cam rose and bent slightly from the waist in Zaphira's direction and tipped his hat to Henri. "Your servant, madame! I shall return in one week for your instructions"

He extracted his card from a silver case, placed it gently on the table, and left the room.

Zaphira sat immobile, staring unseeingly at her husband. Henri decided that it would be a good idea to blow his nose again, and, with a trembling hand, raised his crumpled, damp handkerchief to his face and blew so hard even the candle on the table some feet away swayed.

He wasn't quite sure which way his wife was going to jump, but jump she surely would, and he didn't want to be in the vicinity when she did. He had seen similar signs before and hardly dared to contemplate the extent of her fury. But to his immense relief, she rose and left the room. He thought he saw a look of deadly intent pass over her face, but she merely complained of a headache and said she would retire to their rooms for a while.

Knowing to make himself scarce until his lady recovered her good humour, Henri patted his inner breast pocket and was comforted to find his cigar case reposing within. He withdrew the case, ran his fingers ruefully over the old crest on the front, shook his head sadly, and put a cigar in his mouth, asking himself what the world was coming to.

And that is where the landlord of the Golden Lion Inn found him some twenty minutes later: shrouded in a cloud of expensive cigar smoke and staring at the opposite wall. The landlord, not entirely unhappy to have a titled gent from over the Channel as a guest, enquired whether the gentleman required anything.

Henri decided that a large brandy or two—or maybe seven or eight —just might allow him to see the world in a much better light.

❄

Zaphira, meanwhile, slowly made her way upstairs, thinking, thinking. She opened the door to their rooms, closed it softly, and, not caring if her gown was crushed—there was no need to impress anyone at the moment—threw herself face down onto the bed, her chin in her hands.

Forced into a corner, Zaphira knew she needed all her wits about her. She realised that, although she derived much pleasure from it, screaming, crying, stamping her feet and wringing her hands was futile. What she needed was cool, hard thinking.

To this end exclusively she applied herself, and she spent the good part of a couple of hours in a welter of indecision.

Over and over, she turned things over in her mind. How dare Claude spend all his money? How dare Emmaline not let her know that he was a gambler? At least she was getting nothing! Any satisfaction derived from that thought was quickly replaced with fear that she might be in the same position herself. Henri was useless; he was bankrupt and probably had been before she met him.

She groaned aloud when she remembered that the Grosvenor Street house was likely beyond her reach. She had pictured herself descending the graceful, curved grand staircase before the enchanted gaze of a field of admiring upturned faces. Oh, it was too dreadful to contemplate! But what to do?

See if Henri had a solution? No, no, don't relinquish control! Anyway, he'd be gone soon enough. But in the meantime, how to manipulate him, and the situation, to her best advantage? And the bank! How *could* they? Who to take on? Emmaline was clearly of no use; she had nothing and, from the look of where she lived, never would! The bank? No—too big for her! Mr Whittingham? No—he'd be more slippery than an eel, being a lawman! He'd know all the twists and turns. That only left Henri

Yes, that was it! Henri! Whatever he had left, it would be *something*, and something, *anything*, was better than the nothing she set to inherit now. Now... how to accomplish it?

Henri must have *some* credibility in London. He had never had any dealings in the town, and his title must surely count for something! There was no way she could personally approach the bank. They would recognise her from the social occasions she had attended with Claude. But Henri could!

No, wait—how could he then say that he wanted to reside at the Mayfair house? She herself would have to do it. She smiled. For once, she would be quite honest. They'd go together, and she'd say yes, she had no idea things were in such a sorry state, but that she had made a new marriage—she'd play up the Countess angle—and she and the Count had come to London to take up residence. They would sort out the debts as soon as Henri could realise some investments in Europe and have the necessary funds transferred! Then she would look pretty, flutter her eyelashes a little and ask if it would be in order to have those considerable funds transferred to the Bank of England?

The more Zaphira thought about her plan, the better she liked it. They would dress in their most sumptuous wear and accoutrements. She could easily convince Henri to go along with her scheme, since he was in the same boat she was. She could also easily persuade him that, once they settled in Mayfair, everything would come right again. He would have to accept that—where else would he go? Then she would bleed Henri dry and leave him to pick up the pieces.

Zaphira sat up, her face calm now. She had a new course of action. All would be well very shortly!

The Countess de la Salle patted her face with *eau de cologne* and tepid water, powdered and painted it expertly, and awaited the return of the Count, as she had some wheedling to do.

Some little time later, muffled murmurings and stumblings on the stair outside their rooms brought her to the door. She opened it to find the landlord standing there, supporting her very drunken husband, who had, since she had last seen him some two hours prior, apparently acquired legs of rubber.

Henri's prop grinned apologetically at Zaphira, and she, with lightning skill, sized up the situation. She smiled a watery smile and murmured, "My poor husband—he's had some very bad news. A tragic death in the family! Please, do forgive us! Come, my dearest." She put her young shoulder under Henri's arm, her arm around his waist, and relieved the Landlord of his millstone.

She closed the door very gently, then unceremoniously dragged Henri across the floor and dumped him in a large wing chair, where he immediately sunk into a sublime oblivion.

Bending down to look at him with utter disgust, she hissed, "Ugh! You are a truly odious creature!"

Another day wasted! Now she would have to wait until morning, when hopefully his head had cleared, to begin her campaign.

❧ I I ❧

The Count and Countess de la Salle took up residence at Number 2, Grosvenor Street some two weeks after the meeting with the Bank of England. As a posthumous gesture to their late superior, the directors agreed to allow the widow to resume occupation, though they covered themselves by seeking Henri's signature on a short-term second mortgage. This, Henri had willingly given, signing his name with a great flourish. He then impressed his seal in the hot blob of red wax adjacent to the signature.

Within hours of the occupation, maids and servants were employed. A great flurry of activity saw shutters and windows thrown open, dustcovers removed, furniture polished, cobwebs brushed off chandeliers, pantries stocked, and fresh flowers brought in and arranged. Zaphira saw to it that Emmaline's wardrobes were emptied of their gowns and ordered these to be burnt. She also had the entire suite of rooms redecorated so that no trace of their former occupant remained.

Once again, Number 2, Grosvenor Street, Mayfair looked like one of the great houses of London. Zaphira was ecstatic. She assumed complete control of the reopening and delighted in ordering staff and tradespeople to do her bidding. No expense was spared, and accounts were run up far and wide, with suppliers happy to have a Count and Countess as customers.

Henri, on the periphery whilst all the activity was going on, settled in with a deep satisfaction and decided that life should always be lived like this.

There was to be a grand ball to mark the reopening of the house, and elaborate gold-embossed invitations had gone out. An eight-piece orchestra had been hired, and Zaphira set the menu. Parting with tradition, she decided to have a long buffet table instead of the usual dinner and imagined guests coming and going for exotic tidbits. Russian caviar and champagne would be served as the guests arrived, and a never-ending supply of nibbles would be available all evening. These would include morsels of smoked salmon specially brought down from Scotland, asparagus, tiny pieces of succulent lamb, Greek olives, French plums in old brandy, and plover's eggs. There would be pigeon breasts set in aspic, delicious trifles piled high with sugared cherries and cream, and plates of the choicest Tunisian dates. Clarets and wines would be served non-stop, and a room would be set aside for the gentlemen to enjoy their cigars and brandy and tiny cut crystal cups of very hot, very strong Turkish coffee.

Zaphira then turned her attention to her gown for the evening. There was no time to have one made in Paris—the fittings always took several weeks, and, in any case, she remembered, tight-lipped, that she had worn out Henri's credit in that city. She decided to wear the grandest gown in her wardrobe, a gown which she had never once worn. It was a very expensive creation of French silk, with laboriously handsewn Bohemian crystals and tiny river pearls cascading down its front and handmade Belgian lace froths at the sleeves. She still had time to have a high and most elaborate wig made. It would be in the palest shade of blue to complement the deeper shade of her gown, and she would wear the sapphires Claude had given her in her first marriage.

The big night arrived. Fires were lit in the great fireplaces, and perfumed logs burned in each one, for the winter chill had set in. A long line of carriages drew up in front of the house. Steam poured from the nostrils of the horses, and all the coachmen donned greatcoats and capes. Gentleman guests, anxious to meet the Countess whose reputation had preceded her, wore their best evening wear, and their ladies, curious in spite of themselves, dressed with the greatest care.

The invitations, when they had been received, had evoked a great range of comments. The gentlemen who accepted did so mostly out of a desire to meet the hostess, having heard of her particular skills. Most of the gentlemen from the higher order of society, however, declined, as their ladies made sure that they had a prior engagement that evening. Those ladies were nevertheless eager to hear the gossip which was sure to follow the ball. Zaphira read the 'apologies' and made a mental note to return the insult at the earliest possible opportunity.

The first rumblings of discomfort began a few weeks after the ball, as unpaid suppliers of food and services rendered their accounts, for the second and third times, for payment. Anxious reminders followed, and when the threat of legal action could no longer be ignored, Zaphira had asked Henri what he was going to do about it all.

Henri had initially been surprised at the extent of his wife's extravagance. Having little interest in day-to-day affairs, he had always left domestic affairs to others and assumed that Zaphira's arrangement with the bank would cover everything. He savoured the lavish lifestyle which he had always enjoyed and which he expected to continue uninterrupted.

But after the ball, he realised with a considerable shock that it was all coming to an end yet again. Life really was tedious, he told himself. His creditors on the other side of the English Channel had managed to locate him and pursued him vigorously. This knowledge, he successfully kept from Zaphira. Poor Henri! What was happening to him? He thought he might go to his club and think about it all.

Zaphira, for her part, staved off the most pressing demands in her usual fashion. It had never mattered to her who she teased and trifled with, so long as her animal cravings were satisfied. But now, she thought, it was time someone paid for the pleasure of pleasuring her. This decision put several of her playmates out of contention, but her horizons had expanded considerably since the ball.

That night, no fewer than two very well-heeled gentlemen had, in covert terms and out of earshot of their wives, signalled to their nubile hostess their desires, and it was they, together with several lesser beings, who were the source of an income sizable enough to defray her most immediate expenses. These were to her, in order of importance: her dressmaker and perfumer, the servants, and, to a much lesser degree, the household food.

Henri saw that a certain amount of money was still coming in steadily. He did not ask its source, being fairly sure that he would not like the answer even if he got an honest one. He was no fool—after all, where was his wife most afternoons? What was more, he suspected that she sometimes stayed out the whole night, not coming down to breakfast or answering her maid's knock at her door. Zaphira had refused his every attempt at conversation about their situation and continued to do what she always did, which left Henri in much of a dither.

One day, he finally sent a servant to fetch a hackney carriage for a visit to his club, the Sussex Hunt in Sussex Gardens. A soft snow was falling gently from a leaden sky, and the light was fast fading. The street gas-lamps had just been lit, and the church steeple threw a ghostly shadow across the gardens. The evening was bitterly cold, but Henri had donned his Paris-made greatcoat and capes. The carriage windows were steamed up, and the clip clop of the horses' hooves was muffled by the two inches of snow already settled in the roadway.

Henri was unaware of his surroundings, deep in thought. He had to be told twice that he had arrived at the Sussex Hunt. He stepped down, burying his ears in the turned-up collar of his coat and thrusting each leather-gloved hand up its opposite sleeve, and passed through the heavy oak door of the club.

Stamping his feet to remove most of the snow, he saw through the bevelled glass inner doors that it was a quiet evening, with few patrons occupying the deep leather chairs. Handing his overcoat and capes to the porter, he proceeded through the heavy glass double doors and headed for his favourite chair in a corner.

Henri was not in the habit of engaging in conversation, frivolous or otherwise, with people he didn't know intimately and normally spoke to no-one apart from the steward. This steward now set a glass of

Henri's favourite brandy beside him, together with the daily newspaper ironed and perched on a polished brass stand.

"Good evening, sir, a very cold one! We hope you find yourself well."

A grunt from Henri assured the steward that he did, and he helped himself to a cigar from the humidor the steward held before him.

Cigar lit and brandy in hand, Henri sank into an unseeing reverie, searching for some reason or conclusion to his predicament. But the more he reasoned, the more elusive became any conclusion.

IT WAS two and a half hours after midnight. Outside, the cold had become even more bitter, and the snow had frozen into a thick hard crust. Sheltering in an unlit doorway, at the edge of a dark lane off Sussex Gardens, stood two of the worst ruffians it was possible to meet.

Harold Parker was a tall, gaunt man with a loose, phlegmy laugh and thin lips capable of bestowing curses and threats cruel enough to curdle the blood. Thomas Hunt was a short, stocky man with blood-shot eyes, a pock-marked face adorned by a week's whiskers. A coal-whipper by trade, Thomas had fallen on hard times, no longer able to lift the heavy loads he had managed for years. A chance meeting with Harold Parker in the tank room of a tavern whilst watching a cockfight had set him on a dishonest but mostly lucrative path.

It was an odd pairing. Harold, by far the worst of the two, was the vicious man with a propensity to settle differences and drive home his point of view with violence and bloodshed. Thomas, on the other hand, was the milder and more easily led.

Thomas pulled a worn, patched greatcoat about his frame, cupped his hands together and breathed into them to keep warm.

"Gawd, 'Arry! 'Ow long d'ye reckon we'll 'ave to wait ternight?' It's bleedin' freezin' art 'ere! I should be 'ome, cuddlin' up ter me missus on a night like this!"

"Ah, shut yer marf, Tom!" replied Harold. "It won't be long now, I reckon! I've 'ad me peepers on a right toff for quite a while, and it's abart now 'e comes art, and 'is legs is all over the place. 'E's well and truly tanked by the time 'e passes 'ere. Comes by carriage but walks 'ome, I dunno why! Lives in one of them big 'ouses in Mayfair, 'e does, and... Ssh!"

As a faraway clock chimed the hour of three, Harold cocked his head to one side, listening intently.

"'Ere 'e comes!"

Henri made quite a comical picture as he lurched and swayed along. He put one foot in front of the other and expected the second one to do the same, but somehow the instruction was never received. The second foot stayed where it was, and the first one went forward again. This unusual attempt at progression had exactly the opposite result, and Henri fell against a lamp-post which appeared at just the right moment. Henri's arm hooked around it, and with his free hand, he raised his hat.

"Thanksh! Very shivil of you, shir!" Then he steadied himself, let go of the post, and lurched forward two steps. But one of his feet slid along the roadway while the other stayed where it was, resulting in an inelegant and quite painful splits.

He lay there for a moment, willing his legs to sort themselves out, then thought he might as well go to sleep, since everything would be all right when he awoke. He was just surrendering to the beckoning blissful nothingness when he was rudely pulled up by two pairs of hands.

"Now, now, Guv'nor," a raspy voice said, "you've gorn and got yourself in a bit of a pickle! Let us 'elp you to brush yourself orf! Hit won't do for you to go 'ome looking like that!"

Henri vaguely felt himself being half-dragged and half lifted into the unlit laneway.

"Now, jest you lie darn 'ere for a while, and we'll look art for you!" the voice coaxed.

Henri was more than willing to allow himself to be laid down in the snow by these two very kind new friends, and this time he couldn't resist the urge to sleep. He raised his eyebrows, hoping they'd drag his eyelids open enough so he could see where he was. They didn't, and he gave up. His lids remained closed, an overwhelming euphoria spread throughout his body, and he sank into a happy unconsciousness, content in the knowledge that the two wonderful friends would look after him. It was far too difficult to bring himself to the surface. How gracious they were, to tuck him up so comfortably. Ah, life was good!

"This is gonna be easier than I thought!" said Harold Parker, "H'it gets a bit messy when they struggles. You 'ave to 'it 'em really 'ard sometimes! Now, since this one was my mark, I'll 'ave his watch and chain!"

So saying, he unhooked the chain from around Henri's large paunch and held it up for closer inspection, grunted in satisfied appreciation, and bent down again to the task in hand.

"I 'ave'nt lost me touch! You was sayin' as 'ow you wanted some new boots, Tom. How'd these be?" He picked up one of Henri's feet, turned around, threw his leg over his victim's, and pulled and tugged until a soft, handmade leather boot and stocking came off, and he unceremoniously dropped Henri's bare foot back in the snow.

"Nah!" said the ungrateful Tom. "Remember I got them ones orfa that mark last week—but I do fancy 'is coat! Me missus keeps tellin' me she's fed up with patchin' the patches on this one!"

"Then you shall 'ave it!" said his companion magnanimously, and dropped the unwanted boot back on the frozen ground, the stocking hanging limply.

"Giss a 'and, will ya, Tom!" said Harry. "'E's a 'eavy cove! Been eatin' too many good dinners, I reckon!" He laughed heartily at his own joke.

Between them, they managed to haul the unconscious Henri into a prone position, extricate both his arms from the greatcoat, lift it from his comatose bulk, and leave him face down in the snow.

"Don't reckon 'e'll be needin' this where 'e's at right now!" laughed Tom. "'E's sleepin' like a babe!"

He donned the greatcoat and capes, spread his arms out like a scarecrow and twirled around

"'E's *warmed* it for me!" he laughed. "Thanks, 'Arry, this's a good 'un!"

"Good!" replied Harry Parker, pleased to have his generosity acknowledged. "Now, giss a 'and to turn 'im over again, will ya? Let's see what else 'e's got!"

Puffing and grunting and slipping in the snow, the two felons managed to turn their victim over once more.

"Lor! 'E looks like a big fat slug, only uglier!" said Tom. "Let's see what 'e's got in 'is pockets!"

Hurried hands, rifling through Henri's remaining grey velvet coat and matching grey silk embroidered waistcoat, drew forth a fine linen handkerchief, into which Harry blew his nose before he discarded it; an embossed silver snuffbox, from which both extracted enough snuff to inhale, leaving them sneezing and coughing uncontrollably for a few satisfying moments; a smashed eyeglass, which they quickly threw aside; a soft calfskin purse containing a few gold coins, which Harry very swiftly pocketed; and a fat leather cigar case that, upon opening, yielded two large hand-rolled cigars.

Harry generously donated these to Tom. "Smokin's no good for yer! It killed me old man at the age of thirty-three."

"'Ow was that?" asked the grateful Tom, not really wanting to know.

"If 'e 'adn't been smokin', 'e'd of seen the 'ole." replied Harry.

"What 'ole?" inquired Tom, now with some interest.

"'E' fell down a coal pit on 'is way 'ome! It was a terrible shame 'cos 'e was very 'appy when he left the tavern!"

Not at all daunted by the prospect of an early demise, Tom pocketed the cigars and withdrew from Henri's pocket the last item: a slim gold, ruby encrusted card case.

Upon discovering several copperplated cards inside, he threw them on the ground with only a disgusted glance—neither of them could read—and was about to pocket the case when Harry snatched it from him.

"Tom, Tom! Aint I taught you nuffin'? Do you want us *both* to get dead? Leave 'em 'ere on the grarnd, and the 'ole *world*'ll know 'oo 'e is! We don't leave no evidence for the runners to find arterwards! You'll 'ave us both at the end of a rope 'angin' orfa the tree at Tyburn! Gawd, Tom, you'll be the end of us if I ain't careful!"

Tom looked properly contrite, biting his bottom lip with his two remaining top teeth. 'Sorry 'Arry, I keep fergettin'."

"Well, pick 'em up again!" commanded Harry, putting the case in his pocket, "Every last one of 'em, while I just git this orf! Allus fancied meself in a posh weskit!"

Whilst Tom was attempted to gather the cards, Harry removed the waistcoat and proceeded to pull the remaining boot from Henri's left leg to facilitate the removal of his trousers.

"And pants to match, 'n all!" he said, and Henri's black corded trousers were unceremoniously dragged from his floppy legs. "These is worth five guineas of anybody's money, these is!"

At that very moment, Henri's left arm lifted and threw itself involuntarily across his chest.

Tom almost fainted. "Oh Gawd 'Arry! That give me a fright! Is 'e comin' to?"

"Not if I can 'elp it, me lad," soothed Harry, holding up a huge clenched fist, "I've got the right medicine right 'ere if 'e do! But—oh ho! What 'ave we 'ere?" He spotted for the first time the crested golden ring on Henri's fat finger.

Picking up the limp hand, he twisted and turned, turned and twisted, but the ring was stuck.

"Fat pig!" swore Harry. "Shoulda brung me knife! I'da 'ad it, finger 'n all!"

Tom froze in horror. "Gawd 'Arry, don't! I 'ates blood! Ain't we got enough? Let's go, *please*, 'Arry."

"Listen! Ssh!"

They heard footsteps approaching.

Flattening himself against the dark wall as he had done so many times before, Harry poked his head out just far enough to see the unmistakeable form of a constable as he strolled, in no great hurry, towards the alleyway.

"Strewth! The watchman!" Harry whispered urgently. "Let's git!"

Picking up the waistcoat and trousers he had carefully laid aside, he grabbed Tom's arm, and the two of them silently melted into the dark of the laneway.

Henri was left lying on the snow-covered ground, dressed only in a thin silk shirt and his cotton underwear, one bare foot crossed over the other, one boot and stocking beside him, the other under his legs, his broken eyeglass nearby, and several of his calling cards scattered in the snow, their white backs merging into the freezing snow.

The Night Watchman strolled slowly past the entrance to the laneway on his way around Sussex Gardens, twirling his staff in one hand and his moustaches in the other, thinking that, thankfully, it was even too cold for the bad 'uns to be out tonight.

Some four hours later, a costermonger taking a slithering, sliding shortcut through the laneway on his way to his pitch came upon the cold, stiff dead body of Henri de la Salle, a stalactite of frozen spittle joining his open mouth to the icy laneway.

❧ 1 2 ❧

Zaphira's immediate relief, elation almost, on hearing that her semi-naked husband had been found frozen to death in a laneway, was quickly replaced by a violent anger that he had been fool enough to leave his cards lying around everywhere, allowing himself to be identified.

These emotions were nothing compared with those she felt when, several days after the death and before Henri's funeral, she was awoken at ten o'clock in the morning by a maid's insistent knocking at her bedchamber door, advising her that three gentlemen had come to see her. She assumed they were on a visit of condolence, the notice of Henri's demise having only appeared in the newspapers the day before, and had them shown into the library when they insisted on staying until they had seen her.

She had slept later than usual, having exhausted herself the previous night. In his sustained effort to "console" her, her gentleman visitor had also worn himself out and was now snoring loudly and contentedly in Henri's bed, his moustaches still at every snorting intake of breath then quivering comically in time with his loose-lipped exhalations.

The Countess was none too pleased at being rudely awakened so early in the morning. By way of retaliation, she kept her visitors waiting as long as possible.

She performed her toilette in as leisurely a fashion as she deemed appropriate and took considerable time in the selection of the right gown for a grief-stricken widow, one which would properly reflect her heart-broken desolation at being left so alone.

Just after noon, Zaphira slowly entered the library, looking as sad, pale and lonely as she could in her mourning weeds. The gentlemen stood up.

The Countess's eyes moved slowly across the three and settled on the form of Mr Charles Alastair Meriweather Whittingham. A sudden bolt of foreboding shot through her, and her heart missed a beat.

"Charles Whittingham, madame," said Cam, with a slight nod in her direction to acknowledge that they had already met. He continued without preamble. "This is Mr Humphrey Fortescue from the Bank of England." He indicated a tall, impeccably dressed gentleman who watched Zaphira with a stern expression, black bushy eyebrows drawn down in a disapproving frown. "And this," his open palm indicated the third man in the room, "is Mr Horatio Catchpole, a court bailiff."

As Cam said this, Catchpole stepped forward and extended a document to Zaphira, who absently took and began to unfold it. Expecting something different but not quite sure what, she had yet to grasp what was happening. She had only vaguely heard the word "bailiff."

Before she could gather her wits, Catchpole, who always loved this part of the job, drew himself up, put out his chest, and, in his most official voice, said:

"This is a summons, madame. In essence, it requests that you forthwith discharge all debts owing to the Bank of England by your former husband, namely Claude de Garamonde, now deceased, and yourself, and of your second husband, namely Count Henri de la Salle, now deceased, and yourself..."

At the word 'deceased,' Zaphira managed to emit a tiny cry of desolation.

"... or show just cause why you should not be evicted from No 2 Grosvenor..."

What was happening? Words swirled around her head as the bailiff went on: "evicted—bailiff—debts—Claude—default—court—husband —bank—deceased..." Her head was spinning.

No! This could not be! *Claude, Henri, what have you done to me? The injustice! They* were getting off scot-free. How *dare* they? Everything was collapsing, sinking, down, down... Her hand reached for the back of a chair to steady herself, and the room was silent as the men watched her.

"*There* you are, my little princess—" said Judge Mortimer Wood-house, stopping dead in his progress into the library towards Zaphira, his hands outstretched to clasp her around the waist. In the silence following the delivery of the bailiff's summons, and Mortimer's descent of the stairs in stockinged feet, neither party was aware of the other.

Poor Mortimer! In a state of semi-undress, his shirttails poking out of his trousers, his cuffs hanging loosely, no day-wig and bloodshot eyes, he was hardly recognisable. It took the banker and lawyer a split second longer than usual to identify him as one of their most illus-trious equals, and it took less than the usual time for the judge to recognise his banker and lawyer. An electric charge seemed to freeze the three gentlemen into speechless immobility, and time stood still for a moment before the three intelligent brains decided, as one, to pretend that the confrontation wasn't happening.

Mortimer turned and left the room as decorously as he could, given his state of dress.

Zaphira had no way of guessing at the charade that had just taken place. But realising that *something* had just happened, she looked from Cam to Humphrey, Cam looked at the carpet, Humphrey looked at Zaphira, and Catchpole nearly went cross-eyed trying to look at the departing Mortimer and the other three. The term "pregnant pause" never had greater meaning.

"Under the conditions set out in that document," Cam continued, recovering himself magnificently, "you have one week from today to assess your affairs and present yourself, together with any proposals, at the Court of Petty Sessions at..." Zaphira's head spun again. All was moving far too fast for her.

Through a fog, she heard Cam reiterate words he had said to her not so long ago, "inherited your husband's debts," along with disjointed words and phrases.

"Court... one week from... just cause why... debts... debts... *debts*!" The word screamed at her. She seemed unable to move, the hand holding the summons hung listlessly by her side, the other, knuckles white, clasping the chair back. She didn't even notice her three visitors quietly leaving the room, and it was some seconds before she realised she was alone.

Zaphira turned and slowly, heavily, ascended the great staircase, entered her boudoir and sat absently on her *chaise lounge* at the window, the summons lying on her lap.

Then the dividing door between her dressing rooms and her late husband's opened, and a now fully dressed and bewigged Judge Mortimer Woodhouse crossed the room toward her.

She wordlessly handed him the piece of paper and looked up at him helplessly. Taking it, he fumbled in an inner pocket for his eyeglasses, raised them and inspected the all-too-familiar document.

"Ah!" he said, and clamped his lips tightly together, frowning a little to give the impression that he was considering the document in minute detail. He was an expert at judging just the right moment to deliver his thoughts.

He was not quite sure whether Zaphira knew, or even cared about, his exact profession. After his exit from the library, he had had a little time to collect his thoughts, along with his wig and his coat, and decided that he would distance himself from any problems she might have, especially now that he knew the extent of her worries. He felt he could rely on the discretion of his banker and his lawyer. After all, what gentleman didn't have a little frolic from time to time, eh? Catch-pole, he wasn't worried about; he was only there to serve the summons. But Zaphira... Well, he had the beginnings of an idea in his mind, and he would formulate it properly when he was away and on his own.

Pity! She really knew how to tickle the senses. Her staying power was truly remarkable, and in her bed he had tasted exotic delights he had never dreamed of. Now, just when he had found her... A great pity indeed!

"Well, my dear!" he said, having quickly scanned the details of the summons, "You'll have to present yourself next week, as directed. There's no way out of that. It's the law, I'm afraid! However, I have a little influence amongst the legal people, and I am sure I will be able to *smooth your way through*." By dint of many years of practice, he was a master of the *double entendre* and had chosen his words very carefully.

Mortimer patted Zaphira's hand. "I'll be on my way now, and I'll see to it that these tribulations will soon be behind you!"

Before she could say a word in gratitude, he was out of the room and down the stairway.

Looking carefully to left and right, satisfying himself that no-one would see him leaving the house, he stepped out and made his way to the Court of Petty Sessions, where he waited for the magistrate to finish the morning's session. He then invited this old friend of his to join him in a temperate lunch at the Mitre in Chancery Lane.

Over the Dover Sole, Mortimer outlined his idea, firmed it during the Pheasant in Madeira Sauce, and by the time the Apple Charlotte and Cream arrived, the plan was laid.

True to his word, being a judge, he kept his promise to the Countess. He did smooth her way through the court process. No-one ever had their case dealt with so speedily and so finally. With a swift dip of a quill pen in an inkwell, and a signature dashed off with a flourish, before she knew where she was, the Countess de la Salle found herself in the debtors' prison. An order was made for the immediate sale of Number 2, Grosvenor Street, Mayfair, together with its entire contents and the personal possessions of the late Count de la Salle and his widow.

Zaphira was still in a state of shock. Events had moved so fast she had barely time to draw breath. Without warning, she had been seized, told there was a warrant for her arrest and been bundled unceremoniously into a holding room at Newgate prison, pending her court appearance.

The following morning, just after the water cart had washed the streets and the first glimmers of dawn were dusting the wet cobblestones with sparkles, she was given a meal of thin gruel and told to look lively.

"I can't eat that!" Zaphira said, turning up her nose at the grey mass swirling around in a battered tin bowl.

"Suit yerself, hoity-toit!" replied her tormentor. "When they finds you guilty, and they allus do, you'll not see the likes of anything as good as this for a long time!" He dropped the basin with a bang on the wooden table, the contents splattering the surrounding area and dripping through the slats onto the stone floor, and the door was slammed and bolted from the outside.

Since it was a holding room, the furnishings were a little more generous than those in a cell: a wooden slatted table and a chair, a small square of polished tin framed in wood and bolted to the stone wall as a mirror, and a small waist-high cupboard containing a metal chamber-pot.

Very shortly, there was the grating sound of a bolt being withdrawn from its barrel, and a grizzled face appeared in the doorway.

"This way, *hif* you please, your ladyship!" invited the man, heavy with sarcasm, and before Zaphira could stand, a rough hand clapped a handcuff around one wrist, yanked her to her feet and hauled her through the door.

"Your carriage awaits!" In the yard outside, stood a rough wooden cart hitched to a dejected, tired-looking old nag, one leg bent, patiently waiting. In the cart stood five prisoners, each with a wrist handcuffed to a rail running around the outside edge of the cart.

Zaphira was not going to give anyone the satisfaction of watching her struggle or be pushed and pulled. So, head held high, and in as haughty a fashion as possible, she picked up her skirts with her free hand and mounted the two steps at the rear of the cart. Her manacled wrist was clamped to the railing.

"All in!" was the shout, the tailgate was slammed shut, and the cart lurched suddenly and settled down to a rhythmic bumping and swaying as the old nag was led out of the gate to start on the mile and a half journey to the courthouse.

It was very unusual for a woman to be arrested for non-payment of debt, so Zaphira was the object of quite a few stares and sidelong glances, not only from the other five prisoners, but also from people in the streets, ordinary folk about their daily business—tradesmen, dogs, children, beggars. A cart conveying prisoners was a common enough sight, but one containing a lady—a young lady at that, and so finely dressed—was a cause for much ribald comment and conjecture.

Always ready to size up a situation to turn it to her advantage, Zaphira coolly took stock of her five male companions. Two trades-men, she guessed by their attire, obviously unable to pay their suppliers—no use to her. A cheeky fellow who, when he wasn't whistling, grinned at anyone who caught his eye—also no use. A stout, red-faced, puffing fellow, having great difficulty overcoming the disgrace of his situation, dressed clothing that, when it was in fashion, was of the very finest—no use. And the last... Ah! Now, *that* was different!

A young dandy, tall and handsome, long lean legs shown off to advantage in his tight, buff-coloured buckskin trousers and polished black leather calf-high boots. He was expensively dressed in a blue velvet coat with a turned-up collar, and his frilled white silk shirt was open at the neck, where he loosed--and lost—his grey silk cravat the night before.

When he was arrested, he had been losing a great deal of money in a card game and, thoroughly out of his depth, was feeling very hot and uncomfortable. At an acceptable interval, he had excused himself from the table... and been nabbed by two runners on his way away from the house.

Zaphira, lost in thought, absent-mindedly pressed her free hand to her corset, reassuring herself that the three gold coins she had hidden there were still in place. As she stared at the young blood, he suddenly became aware of her and met her eyes full on.

Clear blue eyes locked onto fathomless green ones, and a thousand unspoken words between them hinted "another place, another time" and left the conclusion to each other's imaginations. A faint suggestive smile played across his sensuous mouth, and Zaphira, to her astonishment, found herself looking demurely downward. But the sight of the rough wooden floor of the cart sobered her at once, and she recognised the futility of pursuing these signals.

She was still standing stiffly erect, looking straight ahead, when the cart suddenly stopped. Its occupants lurched and bumped into each other.

"Debtors this morning, thieves and pickpockets this afternoon! Out you go!" The manacles were freed from the cart railing.

Zaphira was pushed through the door of the courthouse anteroom and into the presence of a stout, sweaty, muscle-bound man, who leered at her lecherously and contrived to brush his hand across her bosom.

Slapping his hand away and glaring at him only made his grin more salacious.

"Debtors this mornin', thieves 'n pickpockets this afternoon!" announced a clerk again.

"Ladies first!" said the lewd one, bowing sarcastically, having been ordered to see that the Countess was arraigned first. He was enjoying his work particularly this morning. He didn't often get to feel a woman's breast these days, especially a young, upper-class one. The nearest he got was the baker's wife when her husband was off baking in the early hours of the morning, and she wasn't *that* special, though better than his own wife who was worn out looking after their eleven brats.

A large hand on her bottom, Zaphira was shoved into the courtroom and motioned up two steps onto a raised wooden platform with a railing all round.

The dock, into which she was guided, was at one end, a box for witnesses in the middle and a bench for the magistrate at the other end. The magistrate's bench was partitioned off so that the common herd could not stare. A bored jailer stood, leaning against the railings and swinging his keys from his forefinger, and a clerk read out a list of the debts owed by an unrepentant, scheming Zaphira, who was mildly amazed by the extent of the list. Two clerks bent over a desk, writing furiously, trying to keep up with their record of the debts.

Two large green eyes, moist with tears, looked imploringly at the magistrate who thought that if Judge Mortimer Woodhouse hadn't been his friend and superior, he would have been far more lenient. It was a pity, a great shame. She was a beauty. He wouldn't mind some of that himself. But a bargain was a bargain, and you never knew when you might need a favour yourself.

Ah, life was cruel sometimes! He didn't know where the judge managed to find them, but this one was a real eyeful. He might have to have a quiet word with the jailer... No! Don't get mixed up. He pulled himself up with a sudden resolve. He wasn't doing too badly, really. He had recently married a much younger lady, following the death of his first wife of yellow fever, and her appetite very nearly matched his. Yes, don't get carried away—this one would only cause trouble. He congratulated himself for having such good common sense, banged his hammer down hard and delivered the verdict.

"And there you shall remain until such time as your debts shall be fully discharged!"

Those were the last words said to Zaphira before she was taken away by the jailer. It crossed her mind as she was led out that she should have asked how it was possible to repay debts while one was incarcerated. But she had been given no opportunity to utter a word. It was almost as if there was some sort of conspiracy against her!

Later, she looked around her cell. Draughty, cold stone walls with messages of love, longing, revenge, despair, and hopelessness scratched into them by former inmates; a miserable stub of a candle stuck by its own drippings onto the wooden table; and a tiny barred window, unreachable without standing on a table, which allowed a tiny amount of light to enter during the daytime. Zaphira sat on the wooden bench, which doubled as a bed at night, her feet on the damp slate floor. She looked with disgust at the thin, patched blanket provided and pushed it aside. There was a lot of thinking to be done!

Zaphira had always had the ability to accept any situation she found herself in, all the while scheming and conniving to either make it better or escape. She was in jail, that was a fact, but staying there for a moment longer than was absolutely necessary was just not an option. Now – how to get out? One assessed one's situation, weighed up the pros and cons, took stock of the liabilities and assets, and sought a solution. She had never been beaten before, and she would not be beaten now. It may take a little longer this time, given her lonely position, but it would happen!

Well, there were plenty of liabilities. Ignore them. Fasten onto the assets. She had only two: three gold coins, and the perennial one, her body. The purchasing power of the former was finite, but the latter was often infinite.

Now, how to put those assets to the best advantage? And when— not *if*—she got out, where to go? London was no longer an option, for obvious reasons. Probably France, where she knew her way around, or even her native Tunisia. Yes, that was it! There, she would be amongst people whose ways, customs and beliefs she understood, where the language was no problem, and where there were plenty of men with more money than most people ever dreamed of!

But all that was a way off yet. She was in jail, had to get out, and get away over the Channel. It was the getting out that had to be sorted; the last bit would take care of itself.

She was, for the moment, in a cell by herself, so no possible accomplice. Perhaps she would wait until someone else was put in with her. But perhaps no-one would be, and she wasn't going to wait around just in case.

Who came by? Only the jailer, twice a day with her disgusting food. Well, he'd have to be the one. There was no other possibility. She considered him. Not one single redeeming feature, as far as she could tell. A thick-set, squat man with greasy hair, small pig-like eyes, and pudgy hands, who smelled of sweat and alcohol. Ugh! But if that's what it would take, so be it!

She'd watch him for a couple of days to gauge how receptive he was, then she would decide how and when to act. Probably money would be the best approach, but from that angle she would have only three opportunities, and preferably fewer. She would like to keep at least one of her coins for the outside. She weighed up many options and possibilities, some ridiculous and impossible, some far too risky, and some even dangerous. By the end of her second uncomfortable day, she formulated her plan.

For the first time in her life, Zaphira met with a full-on opposition to her most powerful weapon. No matter what she did, what she said, how she teased, toyed and trifled, or how much or how little bare flesh she contrived to show, it was of no use. Dick Mullens was not in the least affected by her many and varied efforts. He had seen most of it all before, though this one even came up with a few he'd never seen or even imagined!

What was the matter with the man? He wasn't human, he couldn't be! Thoroughly demoralised, Zaphira became all the more determined. She tried a totally different tack. She had tried being brazen, even lewd. Now, it was time to try being coy.

But even that failed against the impervious Mullins. He didn't know her name, didn't need to know, didn't want to know. She was just another prisoner like all the rest of 'em, although he had been ordered by the magistrate to keep this one alone and separated from the others. He didn't know why, didn't need to know, and, in fact, didn't care. The only company he ever needed was his bottle of liquor. When he ran out of money for the hard stuff, it was a jug of porter and, after that, the cheapest ale to keep going until payday. Why any man ever needed more, he had no idea. everything else was far too much trouble, especially women! Even though this one was better looking than the usual, they was all nothin' but trouble!

He did the job he was paid for—gave 'em their food, saw that they emptied their chamber pots into the bucket which he placed every second day outside a small flap at the bottom of the cell-door and occasionally looked in at 'em through the door grille to see they hadn't done themselves in. It was too much trouble when they did that, trouble he didn't need.

Faced with such unyielding, immoveable resistance, Zaphira's frustration went from disbelief to dislike, then from anger to rage, and finally to despair. She had never been beaten like this. She was beginning to believe that she would spend the rest of her days in prison, as many had before her. She knew not a soul to help her, and there was no possibility of her discharging her massive debts, let alone those she had inherited from her husbands. So obsessed with eliciting a response from her captor and consumed by grim visions of her future, she entirely forgot the coins she had secreted under the legs of the bench.

"You have ten minutes!" Mullins' voice rasped outside, and Zaphira heard her door being unlocked.

When it opened, a tall stranger stepped inside. As the door was locked behind him, he extended his arms towards Zaphira and said, "My dear sister!"

❧ 13 ❧

The sale of the de Garamonde mansion, together with all its contents, was attended by a great many people: a few to acquire some of its treasures, but most to satisfy their curiosity and see inside the grand home of some of London's most notable people and one of its most lascivious. Afterwards, the ghosts of Claude de Garamonde, who had loved too much, Celeste de Garamonde, who had died giving birth to a lover's child at a late age and Henri de la Salle, who had only wanted an easy life, roamed through the empty rooms of the once-great mansion, remembering the loves and tragedies played out there over the years.

Once-treasured possessions were dispersed among the many buyers. Every picture, plate, chair and book had gone to a new owner. The house itself was acquired by the Bank of England to defray its loans, then sold on to a wealthy tea merchant. The merchant later pulled it down, after odd thumpings and moanings during the nights convinced his family and servants that some dreadfully tortured ghosts had never been properly laid to rest in that house.

After the Bank of England had been repaid every penny owed to them by Claude, Henri and Zaphira, Cam Whittingham made it his business to track down every creditor and ensure that they were properly recompensed. He was ecstatic—at the end of it all, there was a sum of seven thousand pounds left. Since he held a document signed by Zaphira waiving all rights to the de Garamonde estate, he added that sum to the thirty-thousand pounds he already had in a special account.

All his plans, so carefully laid long ago when his Claude de Garamonde died, had finally culminated. He had even kept his plans from his wife, wanting to give her a special surprise when the time came.

MR AND MRS CAM lived in Trumpeters Way, a road leading off Chancery Lane between Covent Garden and Lincoln's Inn Fields. When the charred ruins of the Great Fire had been cleared away, the town planners had thought fit to reconfigure some of the road systems, and new, wider roads had been laid around the city. Trumpeters Way was one such road, and its houses were constructed of the red brick used so extensively at the time.

When he was twenty-six, he had wed Charlotte Merce, and it was eleven years later, in 1759, when he had made a name for himself in the world of law, that they had moved into the Trumpeters Way house. Through no choice of their own, they had remained childless, and Charlotte had assuaged her maternal hunger by doing volunteer work at the Foundling Hospital. For many years, she had walked the three quarters of a mile there, six days a week, through snow, wind, rain and sunshine, and swore she enjoyed every second she spent with the hapless children there. Many was the time she would like to have brought a child home as her own, but she judged that she could spread more happiness to more children if she remained at the hospital.

Cam was approaching his sixty-seventh year—and was getting tired. He said to Mrs Cam one night:

"Charlotte, I am ready to retire. I've just finalised something I've been working on for a long time, and I am now ready."

"And about time, if I may say so, Cam!" she replied. "I truly was beginning to think that the only roof you would have over your head shortly would be a coffin lid! It will be lovely to have you at home, all to myself, for however long we have left. My prayers have been answered!"

"Since it's summertime, what do you think about us spending my birthday having a picnic by the Serpentine?" asked Cam. "We haven't done anything like that in a long time, have we? We'll take a hackney down there, and just to celebrate my retirement, we'll have Fortnum and Mason prepare a hamper for us!"

"Oh, Cam, that would be lovely!" She threw her arms around him and kissed him soundly. Then she stood back, watching him. "And what, pray, are you smiling at so secretively?"

Cam was enjoying himself. "You'll see, my darling! I have a special surprise, but you will just have to contain yourself for a few days!" He loved to see the excitement in her eyes—it made them sparkle so. He caught her around the waist, and they danced a little jig around the room.

"Cam Whittingham," said Charlotte, out of breath, "I wonder what you are up to now?" She laid her white head on his shoulder and smiled a happy smile.

SUNDAY, 7th July 1789 was Cam's sixty-seventh birthday—and also the date he had set for his retirement.

He and Charlotte sat at home, dressed and waiting for the carriage to arrive. A large open coach, complete with four matched greys, arrived, and Cam handed his Charlotte into it.

"Cam!" she said, flushed with pleasure and excitement. "A hackney carriage, you said! You are very extravagant—and naughty! This is lovely!"

Cam bowed from the waist. "Well, m'lady, if we are to ride down Rotten Row today, we can't go in anything but the best! One never knows whom one will meet, does one? I had asked their Majesties to bring their own picnic if they cared to join us, but George said affairs of state may prevent him, and he couldn't let *his* Charlotte come on her own in case I got the two of you mixed up and kissed her instead! Also, he is worried about the situation in America and the French starting a revolution, and he doesn't much like the look of things on the other side of the Channel!"

Charlotte's laughter was cut short by Cam's last sentence. "Is that true, do you think Charles? *Is* there a likelihood of a revolution?" she asked, a concerned look in her eyes.

"It does sound like it, I'm afraid," replied Cam soberly, then clasped her hand tightly. "But we are not going to worry about any of that today! Today is a *special* day, and not even the French can spoil it!"

The horses clip-clopped into Chancery Lane and turned right by St Clement Danes, into the wide carriageway of the Strand, then past the church of St Mary-le-Strand. A little further on, Cam pointed out the unusual design of St Martin-in-the-Fields.

"Yes, if it didn't have a cross on it, I wouldn't believe it was a church!" said Charlotte. "It almost looks like a theatre! Most unusual, and I think it was very brave of Gibbs to build it like that, especially since he was a disciple of Sir Christopher Wren!"

Right into Regent Street, then left along Piccadilly, they trotted to Hyde Park Corner which was officially the end of the City of London, and where the country started. The coachman slowed his greys to a walk so that they could enjoy a look at Lord Apsley's new house, built for him about twelve years before by Robert Adam, with an official address of Number 1, London.

"Do you know that a lot of the distances to England's towns are measured from this point?" said Cam. He pointed northwards. "And if we went to that corner up there, we would come to the Tyburn tree where they did all the hangings until six years ago."

Charlotte shuddered.

"Look!" cried Cam. "We are now on Rotten Row! We shall stop just a little way along here, by the grass at the water's edge, and await our guests."

"Guests!" exclaimed Charlotte, alarmed, adjusting her hat and smoothing down the lace at the front of her dress. "Who, Cam? You didn't mention any guests! Do I look presentable?"

Cam laughed and gave her a quick peck on the cheek, which made her blush and become all the more flustered.

"Cam! In public!" she admonished.

"You look perfectly adorable, my darling!" Cam said, laughing harder. He was already enjoying the day immensely. "If I didn't see our guests arriving now, I would give you another one!"

Charlotte turned to see a young man holding the hand of a young lady, guiding her as she daintily trod the grass toward them.

"Charlotte," said Cam, "may I present Jeb and Emmaline Abeles!"

Before Charlotte could catch her breath, Emmaline made a little bob, and Jeb bowed.

"Very pleased to meet you, Mrs Whittingham" the young man said.

"You're just in time, Jeb," Cam interrupted. "Will you please give me a helping hand with this hamper? Over there, I think!" he said, indicating a spot close to the water's edge, "Then we'll spread this rug down to sit on."

"Come, my dear!" said Charlotte, tucking a hand under Emmaline's arm. "I'm so pleased to meet you at last. I rarely get to meet any of Cam's clients or acquaintances, and he has spoken of you and your husband many times. I feel I know you quite well already! Oh, isn't this just a perfect day?"

Emmaline was immediately put at ease. Before long, one young head with its curls poking out from beneath a pretty bonnet and one white head in a blue picture hat were nodding and bobbing quite like those of old friends.

"I've never been to the Serpentine!" said Emmaline as they stood at the water's edge. "This is wonderful!"

"Yes, considering it's only about fifty years old, it looks like it's been here for ever, doesn't it?" asked Charlotte. She continued, "I think Queen Caroline did astonishing work forming this lake from the Westbourne River!"

Charlotte took a great interest in history, especially the rebuilding of London after the Great Fire some one hundred and twenty years before, and, with an attentive and captive listener, warmed to her subject.

"And do you know, King Henry VIII may have ridden or stood in this exact spot, when it was a deer park. Henry appropriated the park from the Abbey of Westminster, who'd had it for some six hundred years. He was naughty, wasn't he? The odd duel is still fought here at dawn, too!"

She waved a hand to their left. "You see Kensington Palace over there? That used to be the Earl of Nottingham's country house! Well, King William III purchased it about a hundred years ago and laid out the gardens at the front. Then Queen Anne came along and extended them, and then Queen Caroline made them even bigger. Somewhere in there, Sir Christopher Wren built Queen Anne's orangery. I would love to see that, but the whole palace and gardens are private. One day, maybe, like Hyde Park, it'll be—"

"Enough of your history lessons!" interjected Cam. "Come, both of you, and sit down and enjoy what Messrs Fortnum and Mason have packed for us!" He carefully handed to each lady a square napkin of the finest white linen, with "F & M" embroidered in a corner. "For you, Emmaline. And one for you, Charlotte."

Charlotte took hers, and a glittering object fell from it into her lap. She picked up an exquisite enamelled brooch, set with emeralds, rubies, diamonds and three pearl drops. She held it in her palm and looked enquiringly at her husband.

"To celebrate my retirement—and my love," said Cam simply, smiling and looking into her eyes.

"Oh, Cam, it's so beautiful!" cried Charlotte, bright sparkles suddenly appearing in her eyes. "I don't know what to say!"

"Just be a good girl and start your lunch," replied Cam, "in case F and M's will think you don't like it, and my third day in retirement will see me with pistols drawn, in the mist of dawn, somewhere over there by the trees!"

Quite overcome with emotion, Charlotte pinned the brooch with a trembling hand to the front of her dress, then helped Emmaline to some of the delicious food in the hamper.

"I haven't quite finished yet," ventured Charles. "We can't leave out our guests! Jeb and Emmaline, this is for you both." He handed to Jeb a large white envelope.

Perplexed, Jeb broke the seal on it and extracted a draft on the Bank of England, made to the order of Jeb and Emmaline Abeles, for thirty-seven thousand pounds. An absolute fortune!

Jeb's mouth dropped open, and he stared wordlessly at the paper in his hand. He handed it to Emmaline, who looked at the draft and broke the tension by dropping it in her lap as if it had scalded her hand.

"We can't accept *that!*" said Emmaline.

"Why not? It belongs to the two of you!" said Cam.

"How so?" asked Jeb. "I think I would know if the Bank of England had been robbed, and I'm not aware that it has!"

Three pairs of eyes glued themselves to Cam's face, waiting for his explanation.

"No!" he laughed. "I haven't robbed anyone. But if I hadn't made a few enquiries, driven a few hard bargains, and attended a sale, *you* two would have been robbed!"

The contents of the hamper forgotten, Cam's audience of three listened to his account. When he had finished, Jeb and Emmaline looked at each other, wordlessly, tears of gratitude glistening in their eyes.

Charlotte took hold of her husband's hand and said quietly, "That was a wonderful thing you did, Cam. I'm so proud of you!" Tears spilled unashamedly down her soft old cheeks.

"Now!" said Cam. "Jeb, Emmaline, you'd better hurry up and buy a house somewhere. I can't stave off the buyers of Raleigh Lane for too much longer!"

❧ 14 ☙

Cesare and Isabella Bellini sat looking at each other down the length of the highly polished surface of their dining table, waiting for their servant, Salvatore, to finish serving their dessert. When he had done so, and gone to stand over by the wall, Cesare looked disconsolately at the exquisite viands placed with reverence before him, then at his son, Matteo, seated in the middle of one long side of the table. He had waited until this moment; one did not spoil good food with unpleasant business.

Sighing deeply, with sorrow and resignation in his voice, he ranted, "Well, I don't know what we are going to do with you, Matteo! Again I've been forced to rescue you from your own trouble. A debtors' prison! I can't believe it. We've never had the slightest breath of anything like that in the family. What possessed you? It's not as if you have nothing going for you! Your grandmama would expire all over again if she knew what you've been up to!"

Matteo sat silently, the long, elegant fingers of one hand curled around the stem of a hand-cut crystal wineglass, his deep blue eyes watching as the candlelight caught the ruby liquid inside and sent a bright dot dancing across the tabletop. He tilted the glass and tried to aim the dot onto the side of a silver serving dish.

He'd heard it all before, tried to look as if he was listening. He thanked his stars that he had a good story ready for his father, his best story yet, concocted on his way back to Naples from London. He was vaguely aware of his father's voice and decided he would wait until he was asked what he had to say for himself.

He quickly stole a glance at his mother. She was looking at him mournfully, and he had the grace to quickly cast his eyes downward again. He was the apple of her eye, as he had been to his grandmama, whose considerable legacy he had gambled away in the best clubs of London. He was even a little sorry that she appeared upset.

"What have you got to say for yourself, Matteo?" asked his father.

"First of all, Father, I want to thank you for helping me. The truth is, I was where I was," and here he hesitated, and his gaze fixed on his mother, "because of a lady!"

His father looked at him with a renewed interest. This was a new one! Isabella stared her son with the faintest smile on her lips and looked as if a great weight had been lifted from her elegant shoulders.

Four different sets of thoughts flew around the room.

Isabella Bellini thought, *Maybe the darling boy is going to settle down at last and give us a grandson!*

Cesare Bellini thought, *That's my boy! At last!* and decided not to pursue any details. He didn't want to upset Isabella further, especially not after she had recently discovered him in a somewhat compromising situation.

Matteo thought himself a very clever fellow, latching on to such an excuse.

Salvatore thought he knew who would be sharing his bed tonight, now the young master was back in Naples.

"It was all a dreadful mistake," Matteo went on, "I won't go into the details, they are too embarrassing for me! I will say that I am presently courting the most beautiful young lady—a Countess, in fact. With your permission, I would like to go back to London to collect her. She has no family herself, having been orphaned at an early age." A sudden brainwave struck him. "She has been brought up by the nuns. She is all alone, and I was protecting her!"

He hoped no-one was going to ask him to elaborate, since he hadn't quite worked out the rest, but when he saw his mother's countenance soften at the very thought of his Countess being all alone, he decided he was very clever indeed.

"We have spoken of marriage, and I was preparing to bring her to meet you when an unfortunate set of events landed me where... where I never, ever want to be again!" He thought a deep sigh and a shudder would go down well at that juncture and convincingly executed them.

"Well, well, well, my boy!" exclaimed Cesare, forgetting all about having extricated Matteo yet again from a long line of escapades. "This does call for a celebration! And to think, I was despairing of your ever coming to any good!"

Cesare and Isabella beamed at their only child.

Matteo beamed back at them and waited for the inevitable.

"At last, I shall have someone to carry on the business, to carry on the name of Bellini. On the day of your wedding, Matteo, I shall sign everything over to you, as I have promised. As I have said before—" *Yes, Father...* thought Matteo. *You* have *said it before, at least ten thousand times. Just be patient and hear the old man out...* "It will all be yours. It has taken me many years..."

Here, Matteo thought he could join his father in a duet. He knew word for word exactly what was going to be said. His thoughts strayed first to his plans for the return trip to London, then to the delights awaiting him later that night in Salvatore's warm bed.

"... sailing in three day's time." He was aware of his father finishing speaking, rising from the table, and coming toward him.

Putting his arm across his son's shoulders, Cesare said, "I can't tell you how happy we are! It gives us just enough time to make some arrangements to welcome your little Countess."

At this apparent, and unexpected, total acceptance of his story, Matteo managed to smile at his father, though not quite sure what he had said whilst he was daydreaming. He hoped Salvatore had been attentive, so that he could tell him later in his quaint Spanish-Italian. As he succumbed to his mother's perfumed embrace, his mind was racing ahead, putting the finishing touches to his plans.

Extricating himself from a froth of lace and ribbons, he turned to leave the room, winked at Salvatore, and made his way to his quarters, which were set at quite a distance from those of his parents. He was just in the right frame of mind, and Salvatore's duties would be finished with the meal, meaning he would be along within the hour. Matteo had brought him a small trinket from London and couldn't wait for him to express his gratitude.

AND SO IT WAS, three days later, that Matteo embarked on one of his father's vessels sailing for London. The day after his arrival, Matteo presented himself at the debtors' prison in Newgate, pressed a coin into the palm of Dick Mullins' outstretched hand, and asked to see his 'sister.'

As Zaphira's cell door opened, she saw a tall, handsome young man advance toward her. He was dressed in a dark blue *frac*, light knee breeches, polished brown boots and a silk cravat, knotted in the latest fashion.

To her astonishment, he advanced toward her, arms outstretched, and said "My dear sister!" With his back to the door grill, he pursed his lips and made a sign for her to be silent.

"I had no idea," he continued. "I've only just heard! I've been home and arrived back in London yesterday."

He took her hands in his, pulled her to her feet and clasped her to his chest. Then he whispered softly, urgently, "Be quiet! I'll get you out!"

He held her at arm's length, and Zaphira recovered her senses enough to recognise the young man with whom she had exchanged glances on her way to prison some weeks before. Again she noticed his handsome face, his long, dark side-whiskers, and the black hair curling down his neck and behind his ears, and again her green eyes locked onto his blue ones.

"Father and I are making arrangements to have you freed, and I shall visit you again in a day or two."

Zaphira said nothing, for fear she should undo whatever it was that was happening.

"Try to keep cheerful, dear sister, until I return," he said, stooping to kiss her lightly on her cheek.

He turned to signal to the jailer, who he knew had been suspiciously observing everything through the grill.

Mullins didn't trust anybody, especially "them wot 'as a foreign accent and is dressed like a toff!" The door was opened to allow Matteo to pass through and clanged shut again, leaving Zaphira to wonder who he was and why it was that he was promising to help her.

It took three more visits, each a couple of days apart, for Mullins to leave them without observation. It was after the first of these visits that Matteo discovered the jailer's strong addiction to alcohol and began providing him with a steady supply of spiritous liquor at each visit. Delighted by these gifts and bored with standing at the grill every time, Mullins gladly allowed Matteo much more access to the prisoner than the rules allowed.

Matteo promised to bring Zaphira some fresh clothes on his next visit and promised that her freedom was not far off. He gave her no details of his plan, instead limiting his conversation to general 'family' matters and managing by a word or gesture to intimate that his plot was progressing well.

Though not daring to pry and upset anything, Zaphira even managed on occasion to ask a vague question or two. "How was Father? Was he well?"

Matteo had judged Mullins well—the man was getting mighty thirsty. On one visit, he smiled at Mullins, apologised and handed him an extra-large bottle, which he had doctored with a sleeping draught.

Entering the cell, he greeted Zaphira in his usual brotherly fashion. "I thought you might like some new clothes, Sister." He placed a *valise* on the stone floor. Standing by the grill so that he could observe Mullins, and with his back to her, he indicated to Zaphira that she should change as quickly as possible.

It had been three days since Matteo's last visit, and Mullins had quite a bit of catching up to do. He took a long and satisfying guzzle from the bottle. Then, sitting down, smiling and patting his belly, he took another long swill. Ah! That was mighty good! He had been worried that he would have to go back to buying his own grog, but this was much better! He closed his eyes, and a nice warm feeling started to creep up on him.

A voice came through the grill of Zaphira's cell. "Mr Mullins, I have to go now. This was just a short visit to bring my sister some fresh clothes."

Mullins' legs felt like lead. He must have had a drop too much! His head was a bit muzzy too. Better do as this fellow asked, for he was the generous bringer of the bottle and Mullins wanted to make sure that the supply lasted as long as possible.

Oh! He *was* dizzy! Reaching the cell door, through a blur he managed to locate the keyhole and shakily inserted the key. As he opened the door, his knees started to buckle.

Matteo quickly grasped the jailer's arm. "Oh dear, Mullins! Are you not feeling well?" Catching hold more firmly as Mullins stumbled forward, he guided him to the bench.

Looking up in a sort of hazy light, Mullins watched as Matteo moved toward him. Well, that was all right. Somebody was going to look after things for him, make sure everything was all right. One hand waved heavily around. Where was his bottle? Another swig might fix everything.

All too much effort. His eyelids closed and reopened with the greatest effort. God! How tired he was. Better nod off for a bit and sort things out later. He felt very happy, actually, and inhaled deeply, waved his arm wildly around, flopped it uselessly across his great paunch, and with a long, deep sigh he sank into a wonderful dark place where everything was all right.

"Hurry! Hurry!" urged Matteo, casting a quick look at Zaphira, then turning his attention to the comatose Mullins.

He deftly and quickly extracted the keys from the chain around the fat bulk of the sleeping jailer and, firmly seizing Zaphira's arm, threw a large silk shawl around her shoulders and across her bosom, half-dragged her out of the cell, slammed the door shut and turned the key in the lock.

"That'll keep him quiet for a while!" Matteo said. He passed the bunch of keys through the grill of the next cell.

"A present from me!" he called to the unknown behind the door. "Pass 'em on when you're free! Mullins won't come looking for you for quite a while. He's having a bit of a rest!"

Turning to Zaphira, he said, "Come—act normally. Don't be in too much of a hurry. Take my arm!"

In a daze, she did as she was bid and was guided past Mullins' table with his half-empty bottle, through two more doors and out to a hackney carriage waiting outside.

Giving the driver instructions to make haste for the docks, he settled Zaphira and himself inside.

"Please finish dressing yourself," he said, nodding to her front.

Looking down, Zaphira was startled to see that, under her shawl, none of the buttons on the front of the chemise-style dress had been fastened, and the rest of her clothing was in some disarray.

Drawing the shawl across her, she fumbled with the fastenings and smoothed down the front of the dress. She was aware of her rescuer looking at her with a half-amused smile.

He was thinking that, surely, this must be the first time she had been commanded by a male to get dressed—and been so modest about her state of undress. Well, that was all to the good; it would give the right impression in the right place when it was necessary.

Zaphira suddenly became aware of her own breathing. It felt as though she hadn't drawn a breath since their escape from the prison. She closed her eyes to gather her thoughts and told herself that it was probably all a dream. Willing herself to open them, she was half surprised to find that, indeed, she was in a carriage with a total stranger, and they were travelling at a great speed.

When she opened her mouth to ask the first of many questions, her companion put his fingers to his lips and signalled her to be quiet. She sat looking at him, trying to weigh up his motives. She'd better do as she was told, in case the whole thing became undone and she found herself back in the cell. There would surely come a time for questions. In the meantime, she didn't think that she would come to harm—the man didn't look dangerous!

For the rest of the journey, she busied herself tidying her hair and clothing and, from time to time, looking at the man seated opposite her. Whenever she looked at him, he was sitting quite still, looking directly back at her, as if considering every aspect of her. As the minutes passed, she grew a little agitated at this constant appraisal and determined that, at the first opportunity, she would demand to know his course of action. All she knew was that they were headed for the docks, and by the time they had almost arrived, her agitation had turned to anger.

She was about to throw all caution to the wind and insist he tell her everything, when the carriage came to a stop at the docks.

At the sight of the vessel they were to board, Zaphira's anger was replaced by surprise. Her companion was obviously someone who commanded a considerable degree of respect. They were taken up the gangplank and shown along to the door of a cabin. The door was opened, and, with a cursory nod to the escort, Matteo stood back to allow Zaphira to enter.

"Refreshments will be along shortly, sir!" Matteo was told as he shut the door and threw himself down on a sumptuous leather chair, closed his eyes, stretched out his long legs and emitted a long, long sigh. It had been a long, long day!

Zaphira was left, ignored, standing by the closed door. She looked around at her new surroundings. This was no ordinary ship's cabin. It was far more luxurious. Stealing a quick glance at the man in the chair, she slowly walked around the cabin, running her eyes along the polished mahogany woodwork, gleaming brassware and opulent furnishings. She turned to find her captor looking at her with one eye open, and a half-smile upon his lips.

"Is it to your liking?" he asked, heavy sarcasm biting his words. Her surprise vanished, and her anger flared once again.

Eyes blazing, hands on hips, she whirled on him.

"Who are you? What ship is this? And where are you taking me? You owe me an explanation!"

Overwrought from the activities of the day, he rose from the chair like a shot from a gun. Almost pouncing on her, he brought his face within an inch of hers.

"I owe you nothing. *Nothing!* On the contrary, *you owe me*. I got you out of that place, and be assured, I can much more easily get you back in again."

Surprised at his vehemence, she recoiled, and he was tempted to throw her into a nearby chair.

"I will tell you when I am good and ready. But for now, I'll say that I have gone to considerable trouble to find out all about you, so don't come the innocent with me! I can assure you that I will not harm you —in fact, in your present state, I wouldn't *touch* you!" He wrinkled his nose as if he couldn't stand the odour.

Then he strode to the door, turned the key and pocketed it. "Please avail yourself of the toilette facilities in there." He indicated a polished door to his right. "We shall speak when I have rested, and when you smell better... and have a better attitude."

So saying, he turned and disappeared through another door, leaving a bewildered Zaphira standing alone, her cheeks on fire.

❧ 15 ❧

"It would give us the greatest pleasure if you'll stay with us whilst you look for a suitable house."

The Abeles and the Whittinghams sat in the garden of Trumpeters Way, taking tea. It was a soft spring day, and the warm sunshine painted a glow of love on the dear old faces of Cam and Charlotte Whittingham. It was Charlotte who spoke as she lifted the blue Wedgwood teapot with white classical figures adorning the bowl.

"I can't tell you how grateful we are for your kind offer," said Jeb.

Emmaline agreed. "It would be wonderful—and solve a big problem for us!"

"Well, that's it, then!" Cam joined in, passing a matching sugar bowl to Emmaline. "Just say the day!"

Charity was not the only motive for Cam's generosity. Truth be told, he and Charlotte very much liked the idea of having young people in the house.

"We think we've finally found just the place," said Jeb. "I enjoy walking to the bank in the morning and wanted a place where I could continue to do so. Where we have found will mean a walk over the bridge, but I'd like that!"

"Ah! I expect you mean Southwark Village," said Cam. "A very nice place, near enough to your place of employment, but far enough away from it as well—which is also important! A man should be able to close the door on his work at night and have enough time to contemplate the pleasure of opening the door to his own hearth a little while later." He paused to smile lovingly at Charlotte. "Southwark sounds just the spot!"

"I'd have liked to go a little further out into the countryside of Lambeth, but even though there's a road running out westwards along the river, it's still mainly market gardens and orchards, as well as being a little too far to walk to Threadneedle Street. We did try turning left at the other side of the bridge, off the turnpike road to Kent, but we didn't like the area toward Bermondsey. It's very old and quite marshy out that way. On the right, however, and just past the clink, and south of there, we found just what we wanted!"

He was quite breathless, explaining it all, and the others could see how excited he was by the prospect.

"A little while ago" he continued, "it would have been beyond our wildest dreams, but thanks to you...! Truthfully, I'd have liked to put Emmaline in a mansion—which is, as you well know, not in any way beyond our means—but she would have none of it! She says that big houses mean nothing to her—"

"They don't," interjected Emmaline. "I lived in one once and have only unhappy memories of it all. I have a different life now, and I need nothing more than what I have." She spoke so simply, so calmly, and so certainly that there was no doubt in the minds of the other three that she meant exactly what she said.

A short silence followed while three pairs of eyes fastened themselves on her delicate frame. Emmaline blushed, and her long lashes lowered as she cast her eyes down to her hands, nervously clasping themselves together in her lap, embarrassing without really knowing why.

Suddenly, she realised that her words could have been misconstrued. "Oh! Please, I didn't mean—I don't mean—oh dear! I—we—would love to come and stay with you. It's not that your offer isn't appreciated. I didn't quite mean what I said in the way that I said it—and now I'm making a dreadful mess of this and..."

Her words were interrupted by Cam and Charlotte laughing heartily at her discomfort and Jeb catching hold of her hand.

"Of course we know what you mean!" he assured her. Turning to Cam and Charlotte, he said, "And when we are settled, we hope you will do us the honour of paying a visit!"

"We shall be delighted!" replied Charlotte.

"When do you think you will remove to Southwark?" asked Cam.

"Well," said Jeb, "That brings me to another point. Will you please see to the legalities for us?"

"Of course! It will be an honour" His professional side took over. "Has a price been agreed?"

"Yes," replied Jeb. "And the bank's valuers have inspected it and agreed that it is a fair price!"

"Ah! A very good idea to have it inspected!" said Cam. Young Jeb's stock had just gone up considerably in his estimation

"So all is agreed," said Jeb. "And it only remains for the legal work to be done. In a strange sort of way, it will be quite a wrench! Raleigh Lane is the only home I've ever known." He felt the pressure of Emmaline's hand as she gently squeezed his. "But I am looking forward immensely to a new start!"

Knowing of the paucity of furniture in Raleigh Lane, Cam said, "One of my clients—indeed, a very good friend—is an excellent furniture maker. He has made several pieces for us over the years. Would you like me to put you in touch with him?"

"Oh, yes please!" replied Jeb. "That is going to be one of the most exciting parts of our new life." And he suddenly seemed to come to a realisation. "You know, that's how I look at it. I can't help feeling as if something immensely important is about to happen. I don't know what it is—I feel a sort of bubbling up inside!"

He suddenly stopped, aware that the others were looking at him, amazed to see the usually subdued Jeb so animated.

"It is exciting, though, isn't it?" Charlotte said. "I'm excited myself, just watching you two with all you have in front of you. I think we should have another cup of tea to celebrate!"

❄

WHILE JEB and Emmaline were settling in to their new cottage in Southwark Village, Zaphira tried to sort out her bizarre situation.

Looking at Matteo, his handsome face, his tall, slim but muscular build, not to mention his obvious wealth, she mused that, again, her life seemed to have taken a turn for the better. When he told her to take herself off to the bath, she had been embarrassed and furious. But, left alone, she had no choice but to do his bidding. She was amazed and somewhat mollified by the wonderful toiletries and clothing available to her. Someone, perhaps the young man's mother, had thought of everything. No sooner had she entered the room than a knock came at the door, and Matteo's personal servant entered and filled an enamelled hip-bath with hot water, then left her alone.

Luxuriating in the bath, her first in many a long day, she took stock of her surroundings. On a dressing table were silver-backed brushes and combs, a lidded tortoiseshell container of powder, several crystal bottles of lotions and perfumes, a chased silver-backed hand mirror, and a small selection of hair ornaments. Two wall-mounted oil lamps had been lit and their rich glow gave a wonderful feeling of warmth and security to the small room.

Wrapped in luxurious towels, her hair hanging in wet tendrils, she opened a mirrored door to examine in closer detail the few dresses of various sizes which hung inside.

Then, after donning a pale green printed chemise dress—the neckline, a low décolletage, trimmed in lace and the girdle set high just under her breasts—she stood and admired herself in the mirror, twirling and turning to see all angles. She thought that the simple style suited her admirably, made her look almost girlish—virginal, even! She decided to let her long curly hair hang loosely down her back.

She gave a long deep sigh and felt her old instinctive cravings come to the surface. By the time she was bathed, dressed, coiffed and powdered, her anger had subsided.

It was time she set about thanking her deliverer, her rescuer! After giving herself an extra puff of perfume, she opened the door into the main cabin to see Matteo sitting once again in his chair, his long legs again stretched out before him.

His eyes slowly swept her from head to toe and back again.

"That's better!" he said. He motioned to a table set for one. "Help yourself! I expect you are hungry." This was said flatly, with no apparent interest in her wellbeing, but it struck her that this was the first show of any kindness toward her since her arrival on board.

Without a word, she advanced toward the table. He made no move to pull out her chair for her, so she did it herself and sat down.

"Eat!" he commanded, waving an indifferent hand in the general direction of the table. Before Zaphira was a large white plate, gold trimmed, in the centre of which, all in gold, the letter "B" surrounded by a border of elaborate flourishes. All the fine porcelain on the table bore the same decoration, and the cutlery was the finest. Blue Venetian glassware complemented beautifully the simple and graceful lines of the porcelain, and a selection of tidbits was on a salver in the centre of the table.

"I'll have some wine," Matteo said, holding out his glass.

She looked at him without moving. He had, by the moisture in his glass, already imbibed and, seeing her immobile, he shook the glass impatiently in her direction.

She rose, brought the decanter to him, and refilled his glass, the ruby liquid catching in the light of the lamps as it swirled around.

Without looking at her, he managed a cursory "Thank you" and took a sip.

I can't quite make you out, thought Zaphira. *But if that's the way you're going to be, I'll soon change it! Wait 'till I've eaten, had a glass or two of wine, and we'll soon see how quickly you will melt!*

Finishing her food, she picked up the decanter, along with her own glass, and moved toward him.

Before she got halfway, he pointed to a chair opposite him. "Leave that on the table, and sit down."

Rarely coming across someone so impervious to her charms, she obediently returned the glass and decanter to the table and sat down. It was only then that Matteo outlined his proposition.

MATTEO'S PARENTS greeted Zaphira cordially on her arrival—with mixed feelings.

Isabella Bellini took an instant dislike to her. Some sort of intuition told her that this strange woman was a threat to her own position. *Ridiculous*, she told herself. *A soul left all on her own in the world, with no family and no means of support. Poor little thing!* And Matteo loved her. For the sake of her darling son, she would make every effort to embrace Zaphira.

Cesare thought he would reserve his judgment. He couldn't quite put his finger on it, but there was something—*something*—about her. She was certainly very beautiful, and he could quite see how Matteo had fallen for her. But she reminded him of a spider—a woman like her could seduce a man with her beauty and allure then gobble him up!

But at least Matteo had found himself a lovely woman, and that was a blessing in itself. He'd been worried about his son's predilections for some time, but it appeared his worries were unfounded. He realised every young man should go out and enjoy himself before he settled down. After all, he himself had done so, though not as long and as expensively as Matteo. And he never had to ask *his* father to bail him out. The old man would never have done so anyway. Times certainly were different; he really didn't know what young people were up to these days!

Well, for Matteo's sake, he would make this woman welcome. Perhaps marriage to the little Countess would help him to settle down and become capable of heading up the Bellini merchant shipping house, the successful business that Cesare's own father had started. Cesare had made it clear that he would remain at the helm until he felt comfortable about bowing out and leaving it all to Matteo.

Matteo, for his part, thought that if the only way he was going to get his hands on the old man's money was to marry, well, that's what he was going to do!

He knew he had to find someone whose antecedents were respectable, who knew how to comport herself in the circles in which his family moved, and beauty wouldn't go amiss either! The fact that he was not even slightly interested in the female gender was well known to all Naples, though only suspected by his father and strongly denied by his doting mother. This naturally put the local ladies out of contention. He had to find someone far from home, who would never be recognised in Naples but who met the requirements.

Even in London, his preferences were becoming known, so when he saw Zaphira as they were both carted off to the debtor's prison, he knew he had found the answer. Her dress and comportment said everything, her beauty was absolutely not in question, and when he heard her title in the court, he knew his fortune was secure.

His release from prison was a foregone conclusion; he only had to get a message to his father. It only remained for him to get her out, and he worked on that plan for some time.

After her initial confusion, it hadn't taken Zaphira long to sort out what was what. After her advances on board ship had been so definitively repulsed and she observed Matteo in his own home, it quickly became apparent where his preferences lay.

Well, he didn't want her, that was certain. If that's how he was, she certainly didn't want him either, though it still irked her that such a beautiful man was denied to her. And if she did marry him, it would be only a matter of time before she was cast aside in favour of his preferred companions. Then where would she be?

And surely, they'd be expected to have a child. Unthinkable! Anyway, how would she ever conceive one, with Matteo the way he was? She could get someone else to father it; that would be easy! No—then she'd be stuck with the brat. Anyhow, her natural antipathy to bearing a child overrode all other considerations. The very thought of a swelling belly was unthinkable.

Where to go, then? How could she keep her hands on the fortune and not marry?

Old Cesare—*that was it!* The more she thought about it, the more sense it made to her. She'd done it before, and she would do it again. There had never been a wife in the picture before, but that would only make it more interesting!

THE DATE of the wedding approached.

Isabella swallowed her natural reluctance and accompanied her future daughter-in-law on various outings to introduce her to Naples' society, where Zaphira was greeted again with mixed reactions. Who on earth was this Countess nobody had ever heard of? Where was she from? No one knew. Yet here she was, marrying into one of the wealthiest families in all Italy! At this point, all the mothers with marriageable daughters decided the rumours that had circulated about Matteo's love life were not true, and some even berated their offspring for not ensnaring the young man. Now he had been snatched from them by this *foreign* girl.

Matteo reassured his special friends that nothing would change with his marriage. It was only a marriage of convenience for both sides, he said, which would give him access to far more wealth. With that in mind, everyone agreed: the sooner, the better!

Zaphira set her sights on old Cesare—very, very subtly at first, and, when that failed, more blatantly. Her advances only convinced Cesare that his earlier reservations were correct, so much so that he made it his business to find out all about her from his many contacts in London and beyond. He kept this information to himself, waiting for the chance to make it work for him.

Getting nowhere with Cesare, Zaphira now concentrated her efforts and resorted to blackmail.

She left Cesare in no doubt that his suspicions regarding his son were correct and that she wouldn't marry him unless it was made financially advantageous for her to do so. Given enough money, she assured him, she would never utter a single word to anyone.

Cesare countered this deal with his knowledge of her and her sordid background, right back before Claude de Garamonde.

Cesare had her beaten, both she and he knew it, but he now had to be rid of her. She was never going to go quietly. For one mad, insane moment, he toyed with the idea of arranging her demise. Then, ashamed of his own dreadful thoughts, he proposed a compromise.

For a certain, very large sum of money, she would join his next ship sailing for the Americas, there to disembark and seek her fortune, never again to return to Naples.

At the mention of the sum of money, Zaphira seized the proposition as a way out of her dilemma and a ticket to a new life, in a place where her reputation had not preceded her.

As agreed, and without another soul being told, Zaphira embarked on her next journey, leaving Cesare and Isabella to dream up all sorts of plausible excuses for the continued single state of their son.

⚜ 16 ⚜

Benjamin Ainsley's business interests seemed to grow by the day. He was now a very wealthy man. He had everything he wanted except a wife with whom to share it, and there was only one woman he wanted: Gemma Gallimore.

He'd wanted her ever since he first set eyes on her, years before, when, as a frightened young woman, she'd been assigned to him as a convict. Her service in his household had been exemplary, and when Mrs Dainty, his housekeeper, returned to England and Gemma took her place, he had set about trying to break down the barrier between them.

Gradually, very gradually, he attempted to lift the restraints of an employer-employee relationship. Now and again, he made her smile, and, once, she even laughed outright. His heart did a double flip when he saw her throw her head back, her eyes sparkling.

Ben had taken to coming home each evening and telling her what happened during his day. He even asked her to join him at dinner every evening, reminding her that there were plenty of people in the kitchens to attend to all that was necessary, and anyway, he didn't like to eat alone!

It had become a ritual between them, and she always changed into one of the dresses she had sewn from fabrics he brought back from his many trips to England and brushed her hair back into a shining knot. Occasionally, a curl would escape down the back of her neck or over her ear, and Ben had to stifle the impulse to grasp her to him, pull the combs out of her hair and bury his face in it.

Gemma always sat at the opposite end of the table from Ben until he insisted she move closer, telling her that it was far too taxing for an old man to converse the length of a long table.

Old man, indeed, thought Gemma, as she smiled and moved to a position on one side of the table, and nearer to him.

Gemma herself was now thirty-four years old and judged correctly that Ben must be about thirty-nine or forty. An easy, but still restrained, rapport had developed between them, and she often wondered why such a personable man was still alone. She had heard rumours of an earlier marriage and that he was a widower. She supposed that a lack of suitable ladies in the new land must be the reason why he remained unmarried.

Governor Phillip had encouraged free settlers from England during the last days of the 1790's, specifically asking for farmers to remedy the continuing food shortage. These duly arrived, with most often their wives and generally with small families. They had been granted quite large tracts of land to work, and they regarded the convicts as social inferiors.

Gemma was painfully aware of her background and ever mindful of her position at Hillingdon. She had been at great pains to take no liberties nor seek favours of any kind.

The only problem was, she was desperately, hopelessly in love with Benjamin Ainsley. Gemma wondered how long it would be before she let down her guard and destroyed her relationship with him.

Ben also agonised over how long he could keep her at arms' length. His longing was painful, and at times seemed to put itself between reason and his business judgments. He often daydreamed that she was his, to have and to hold at the end of each day, and knew that it could not be long before he made his love known.

The year after the first landing, Governor Phillip had decreed that the citizens of the new country should be given a public holiday to honour the birthday of King George III, to be held on the first Monday of June each year.

That day was approaching. Ben had racked his brains to contrive a situation where he could declare his love gently, without frightening Gemma off forever.

He decided that a picnic by the river would be a good opportunity and thought he had the perfect excuse to get her there. Not far from Hillingdon, on the same side of the river and adjoining his land, he had been commissioned to construct a mansion for the governor. So, he asked Gemma if she would like to see the almost-completed mansion. She was delighted at the invitation and readily accepted.

On a wonderfully warm, clear autumn day, the King's Birthday holiday arrived, and Ben arranged the picnic. Over a long period, Gemma had heard Ben speak of this new building whose design was to set the trend for the great London houses of the time, a style later known as Georgian. Built by convict labour from handmade bricks and hand-cut blocks of local stone, all from quarries set up and owned by Ben, it was a most imposing construction, one which vied for excellence with Hillingdon itself.

Ben settled them close to the river's edge, on a little hillock with an ideal view of the mansion.

Seated on a large plaid rug, the picnic basket between them, he said, "A far cry from Governor Phillip's official residence, don't you think?"

"What was that like?" asked Gemma. "Did you ever see it?"

"No," he replied. "But apparently, it was only a canvas shelter erected by the sailors from the *Sirius*. When you think of it, they had shelter unless they brought it with them!"

"It must have been awful," said Gemma, "to come here to an unknown land, with no homes, no food and no means of getting any until the next ship arrived or until someone could grow some. I'm glad I came later."

Ben looked directly at her and said quietly, "I'm glad you did too, Gemma." On an impulse, he reached out and grasped her hand.

Just as impulsively, she quickly withdrew it, high colour suffusing her cheeks, her heart fluttering wildly.

"Damn!" he swore aloud. "This is not how I meant it to be!"

Ben saw the fright in her eyes as memories came flooding back to her, memories of a long-ago incident in a dark lane in London.

"Gemma—please, please—I didn't mean to frighten you. I don't know what came over me. Please forgive me." This he said so sincerely, so seriously, that Gemma regretted her reaction.

She looked down at her hands and said, very quietly, "I'm sorry—I am glad, too, truly."

"Sorry and glad, all in one breath!" Ben said, smiling. "That was a bad beginning to what should be a wonderful day. Let's start again, shall we? Are you hungry?" Without waiting, he began to unpack the wicker basket of food. "Did you ever go on a picnic in England?"

"No, I never did," she replied very quietly, her heart now slowing.

"Well, you missed something wonderful. But this picnic is not like any picnic anyone ever had in England. You have only to look at the trees!"

Gemma turned to look at the evergreen eucalyptus gum trees; their long leaves hanging limply in the autumn sun.

Ben painted a vivid word-picture of red and gold leaves falling softly from the beech, elm and chestnut trees of England, of those leaves lying on the ground, waiting for someone to walk through them, ankle-deep, just to hear the sound of their soft rustling, of them waiting to be blown up in drifts against the fences and hedgerows by the winds, the harbingers of the winter to come.

He described a sort of time that she had never known, and for all she knew, never would. She was now in another land, a world away from the country of her birth. In her old world, all she had known was a very short time of love and warmth before that had been snatched cruelly away from her, then poverty, sadness, cruelty and terror. She thought of Isaac, her long-lost brother. Where was he? What was he doing? Was he still alive?

"Gemma? Where'd you go, Gemma?" Ben's voice filtered through the veil of her memories, and she focused her eyes on his anxious, smiling face.

"Ah! I'm sorry. You made such a lovely description, it made me think of my brother."

"You miss him." It was a statement, not a question.

"Yes, I do, almost daily, still. It's the not knowing that's the most painful. We never even got to say goodbye." She said this with quiet resignation, sure that that last sight of his back as he walked off on his chair-mending business would have to sustain her for the rest of her life.

Anxious to stave off any sad thoughts, Ben cast around desperately for something, anything, to bring a smile to her face. He spotted a trail of ants climbing up the side of the wicker basket and down inside, then dozens of them marching across the rug.

"We have company!" said Ben, pointing. "I think we'd better move!" He sprang to his feet, bending toward her and offering both hands to help her up.

With both her hands firmly in his, he gently pulled her up until they were standing face to face, only inches apart. He could not—was not physically capable—of releasing her hands.

Neither could she.

An invisible force held them as they stood, not breathing, aeons of repressed emotions about to be released, and they could see into the very depths of each other's souls.

Releasing his breath in a long, long sigh, he closed his eyes and gathered her to him.

"Gemma! Gemma! Gemma! Oh, my Gemma!" he whispered, his voice catching as he held her to him.

Silence, a long, long silence as they rocked gently together, the tall strong man and the small soft woman.

She melted against him. At last! At long, long last! It felt so right. This was not like before. These were two arms which held her so tightly, yet so reverently, so lovingly. She was home!

"Gemma, I have loved you for such a long, long time. Since the very first moment I saw you, I've loved you! I need you, I want you, I love you. Do you think you could love me, just a little?"

In answer, Gemma lifted her head from his chest, stood on tip-toe, pulled his head down and kissed him hard and hungrily.

"How else can I show you, Mr Ainsley?" she asked.

He held her at arm's length and laughed, joyous. "Call me Ben—and give me another one!"

He caught her to him, and this time planted a much more tender, lingering kiss on her mouth, followed by dozens of little kisses on her eyes, her cheeks, her hands and the top of her head, both of them crying and laughing at the same time.

Lifting her easily in his arms, he moved further up the mound, under the trees, away from the world, and there, while time and the world stood still, two people became one in a wild, gentle, abandoned, hungry, raw, timeless space, a spinning, swirling, deep, soaring, flying, floating ecstasy.

❧ 17 ❧

Their move into the large cottage in River Lane, Southwark, was the beginning of a new era in the lives of Jeb and Emmaline Abeles. Set on a wide plot with two pear trees and an apple tree in an overgrown garden, it had leadlight casement windows in a diamond pattern at the front. After the honeysuckle had been cleared, windows in the rear enabled them to see the garden gate at the end of a long path. Through the gate was an open field, which belonged to a local farmer, and in which his cows grazed contentedly on the rich grass.

It was the end of summer, and Mr Proudfoot, the furniture maker, had received an order for almost a houseful of furniture. At Charles Whittingham's urging, he had given the job top priority and set his apprentices to work, having learned that Jeb and Emmaline had almost nothing with which to furnish their new home. As each new piece was completed, and every precise detail of its construction having passed the eagle eye of Proudfoot, it was delivered and carefully placed. Gradually, the house began to look like a home.

Every day, Jeb walked down the cart-wheel rutted lane to the Kent Road, turned left and crossed London Bridge. He mused that the many times Mr Proudfoot's horse and cart had travelled over the lane had done little to improve its condition.

He and Emmaline were glad that the furnishing of their house had occurred during the long summer months. In winter, under the relentless drizzle, the lane would be turned into mud, as would the hundreds of roads, lanes and streets throughout the country. Only the squares and streets of the rich had been paved and cobbled. The marvellous roads which had crisscrossed the country, laid down by the Romans many centuries earlier, had long since disappeared under many layers of foot- and wheel-compacted mud and dirt. Seeds of weeds and other plants flourished in a rich diet of ordure laid down over the years, and hedgerows planted by farmers to mark the boundaries of their holdings were sometimes been laid over the now-invisible Roman roads. The setting out of country fields and lanes had almost obliterated all but a few of the old roads.

Jeb and Emmaline had brought with them their most precious possessions from their old lives, and one small cart had been sufficient to hold all their belongings. Jeb brought the small bedside table which had belonged to his parents, along with the mementos on the rose-painted plate. Emmaline had brought the portrait of her mother and father and the chest purchased at birth, by her mother, Celeste, these being the only two items she had taken from the Grosvenor Street house on Claude's death. Their clothing and the contents of the kitchen made up the bulk of the load.

As Jeb closed the door of the Raleigh Lane house for the last time, he held Emmaline's hand tightly. It was a strange feeling for them both, leaving the only home they had known since their marriage, where their tiny son had been born and died.

As they turned to leave, one of the dozens of ancient slates slid slowly, gratingly from the collapsing roof and crashed to the ground, a couple of feet from where they stood.

They looked at each other and laughed.

"Well! That settles it!" said Jeb. "Something is trying to tell us it's time to go!" He tugged Emmaline's hand and led her down the lane to follow the man with the horse and cart.

At the end of Raleigh Lane, they didn't even turn around; they only looked forward, knowing that, in a matter of weeks the old house, the whole row of derelict houses and the laneway would be swallowed up by the rich owners of the large houses in Church Road, as they enlarged their already-handsome landholdings.

Within a few weeks of their move to River Lane, Emmaline visited Paris for the interment of her beloved Aunt Mignonette de Garamonde, and she returned to London with the collection of beautiful family heirloom jewellery which Aunt Charlotte had passed on to her.

"I am too old and too wrinkled to do this justice!" Charlotte had said. "Mignonette hadn't worn it for years, and she wanted you to have it! You are the last of the de Garamonde females. It's right and proper that you should have it!"

It was 1790, and the Abeles had resided in River Lane for just over a year. During that year, Jeb had been elevated to the position of Chief Clerk. The directors of the bank had decided in their peculiar way that it was not quite right, unseemly almost, that a lowly clerk should own his own house, in addition to having such a large credit balance in the books of the bank. It would be quite different, you know, had he been a director's son, or even remotely related to one, but he wasn't! In fact, nobody had been remotely interested in Jeb or his background until he deposited a large amount of cash in the bank one day.

Suddenly, he became very interesting, and someone might even have to treat him with a degree of deference! From an employee not even important enough to be even smiled at, he became a valued member of the bank, greeted with a reserved cordiality whenever he came face to face with a director. This situation was avoided as much as possible, but now and again it was necessary. Still not important enough to be in the physical presence of the bank's customers, he nonetheless enjoyed the benefits of a substantial wage increase.

In 1792, the great painter Sir Joshua Reynolds passed away, and his will stated that Emmaline was to receive the large portrait of herself which he had painted many years earlier at the behest of her father. Cam Whittingham, in his capacity as Emmaline's self-appointed, unofficial guardian, was present when Sir Joshua bid for the portrait at the sale of the Grosvenor Street house. He took the opportunity to apprise the artist of the background to the portrait and how it came to be included in the auction. Sir Joshua had always reckoned that the portrait was one of his best and, knowing the story attaching to Claude and his second wife, Zaphira, made an effort to retain it, lest it should disappear into oblivion.

In that same year, in the early hours of a wonderful, warm spring morning, a daughter, Sophie Celeste, made an uncomplaining entry into Jeb and Emmaline's loving world. Sophie was the darling of her parents and spoiled dreadfully by Charlotte and Cam Whittingham.

When Sophie was five years old, Emmaline again crossed the Channel. She remembered when, seven years earlier, she had made the journey to say a final goodbye to Aunt Mignonette, and now it was Aunt Charlotte's turn. Charlotte managed to hang on long enough to tell Emmaline how much she had been loved by her and her sister, and how happy they were that she and Jeb had found each other. Charlotte passed peacefully away as Emmaline held her soft old hand in hers, tears splashing down. The last of the de Garamondes had gone. She was now an Abeles, and her former name faded away into history.

Before she left Paris, and after the de Garamonde vault was sealed for the last time ever, Emmaline was summoned to the presence of Monsieur Bouchier, the lawyer acting for the last remaining de Garamonde. She was handed a bundle of letters, tied with ribbon. They were the letters she had written to her aunts over the years since she had left their care. They had hungrily devoured the details of her life, and each new letter was a light in their lonely lives. Monsieur Bouchier also informed her that she was the sole beneficiary named in the last will and testament of Charlotte de Garamonde. Emmaline inherited Mignonette's and Charlotte's combined wealth, which was considerable.

In the closing days of 1797, a bleak and menacing winter set in. Jeb continued to walk across London Bridge, setting out in the early hours and making his way to Threadneedle Street, more often than not arriving wet and muddied. On those days, he contrived to arrive earlier than usual so that he had time to make himself presentable before the workday began. At the end of the day, he would hail a hackney to take him home. Anyone unfortunate enough to be standing or walking within five feet of the horse's hooves or the cab's wheels would be rewarded with a spattering of mud. It was an unusually wet, cold winter.

During those long dark days, Charlotte Whittingham succumbed to a particularly vicious attack of the pneumonia which plagued her almost every winter, and, in the early days of February 1798, just when spring promised to warm the world, she passed peacefully in the arms of a devastated Cam.

Shadows filled his world. His only relief was an increasing reliance on his friendship with Jeb and Emmaline. He visited them frequently, during which times they could only sit and listen to his reminiscences. He was unable to detach his mind from the fact that his love was no longer with him. His life was on the wane, and he made no attempt whatever to prolong his stay on this earth. He was very comfortably well off, but it meant nothing to him without his Charlotte, and Jeb and Emmaline increasingly worried about him. He was allowing himself to sink into a decline from which there was no release.

His agony ended when he finally relinquished his painful hold on his empty life.

Having not heard from him for a couple of days, which was unusual, Jeb visited the house in Trumpeters Way. He found his old friend and mentor, peaceful and smiling in his final sleep. He was sitting in Charlotte's favourite chair, her rug around his knees. Upon the rug was his last will and testament, leaving all his worldly goods and chattels to Jeb and Emmaline Abeles.

The year was 1800. In some eleven years, the Jeb and Emmaline had gone from poor as church mice to very, very wealthy. Altogether too wealthy for a senior clerk, according to the directors of the Bank of England. It was embarrassing—demoralising, really!

By the time the Whittingham and de Garamonde estates had been wound up, there was close to four hundred thousand pounds in cash in Jeb's bank account. As his bank balance increased, so did the consternation of the directors, some with accumulated wealth that could not match Jeb's. It was unthinkable that he should be made a director—men who started out as lowly clerks just didn't ascend to such lofty heights. But what else could be done?

Jeb thought it unnecessary to reveal the source of his funds, and polite protocol dictated that he should not be asked. The several arrivals of such large funds gave rise to much conjecture and frustration amongst the most senior staff. Nothing like this had ever happened before, and jealousy made some of the Threadneedle Street gentleman quite contemptuous. After all, Jeb was many years the junior of most of these men, and it was unthinkable that he should be wealthier than they.

At last, a compromise was reached. Jeb, at thirty-seven years old, would be put in charge of the accounts of several wealthy merchants and landowners. Their balances were very high, and their accounts active. Since they were not often in London, their visits to the bank were infrequent. Some were domiciled in the Americas, some in India, and one in the new colony of New South Wales.

It was, therefore, inevitable that Jeb should make the acquaintance of Ben Ainsley on one of his annual visits to London. The two men developed a relationship marked by concord. Years of diligent work had made Jeb the consummate banker, and this, Ben admired. Anyhow, he personally liked the younger man.

One day, Ben suggested that the settlement in the new colony of Australia, now some twelve years old and expanding rapidly, was in great need of a bank. And he thought he knew just the man for the job.

Jeb and Emmaline thought long and hard about the proposition. In front of Jeb was another winter of walking through an impenetrable murk of fog as he crossed the bridge on his way to Threadneedle Street, mists that swirled around him at night, shrouding the world in gloom, and cold rain falling sluggishly.

Ben had painted an honest picture of the colony and had been at pains to point out the many problems which he saw, both entrenched and developing. He had extended an invitation to Jeb and his family to stay at Hillingdon until a suitable house and bank premises could be built and offered his services in their construction.

So, in the year of our Lord 1802 and in the fortieth year of the reign of His Majesty King George III, Jeb and Emmaline Abeles, accompanied by their ten-year-old daughter Sophie, set sail for the town of Sydney, named after the British Home Secretary, Lord Sydney, in the new British colony of New South Wales.

PART 2

❧ 18 ❧

In 1770, Captain James Cook found and claimed the east coast of the great south land for King George III. He named it New South Wales. Joseph Banks, the botanist who accompanied Cook, reported to the British Parliament that it did not appear to be the barren, useless wasteland that earlier explorers had said it was.

This was perhaps the answer to a problem! No longer able to send their lawbreakers to the cotton fields of the American colonies, the jails in Britain and Ireland were overflowing. Miscreants of every description filled the prisons, from petty thieves jailed for stealing half a loaf of bread with which to feed themselves or their starving families to hardened criminals, and the politicians listened when Sir Joseph suggested that the newly discovered land in the southern seas would be a good place to send these convicts.

Seventeen years later, under the command of Arthur Philip, a first fleet of eleven ships, with seven hundred and fifty criminals and a similar number of free civilians sailed for Port Jackson on the east coast of the new continent, and many of those people played a large role in establishing the new colony. On board were supplies of food calculated to last them about two years, together with cattle, goats, sheep, pigs and poultry. Plants and seeds were purchased during a month-long layover at Table Bay at the Cape of Good Hope.

The early arrivals faced a frightening time. A great deal of the food had been lost or destroyed during the long months of the voyage. There were no native food crops. They had to grow what they could from the supplies they had brought, and many of the settlers reached starvation level.

When a supply ship was delayed or lost, salt pork and rice was the staple fare. The soil around Sydney was poor, and pests, flood, fire and droughts often wiped out months of planning and waiting. The only clothing they had was what they had brought with them from Ireland and England, which turned out to be far too heavy and hot for the new climate. To shade their heads and faces from the relentless southern sun, they often made hats from the large leaves of the cabbage palms.

Crude houses and shelters had to be made from whatever the land had to offer, and this was, more often than not, only bark slabs cut from the native trees. There was no window glass available for the square holes cut into the bark; hessian and canvas, if available, did the honours. At least the convicts were housed and fed, although frugally, in return for their sweated labours, and in this one respect they were more fortunate than the free settlers. But all suffered great hardship and loneliness.

Two totally opposite cultures, one unchanged for thousands of years, the other changed by thousands of years of conquering invaders, met each other head-on in those early days. For millennia, the Aboriginal peoples had roamed the vast southland, surviving on whatever the land, the sea and the rivers had to offer. Semi-nomadic, their tribes roamed from place to place over limited areas, moving on only when the food was exhausted. They were expert at knowing what was available in any season within an area and were strong and healthy.

Where the newly arrived white settlers starved, they flourished. Nuts, flowers, honey, shellfish, turtles and their eggs, flying foxes, reptiles, kangaroos and emus, some cooked and some raw, made up their diet. Only in the south did they shelter in caves or cover themselves with furs and skins during the short winters. They lived mostly naked and slept in the open for most of the year. Theirs was a culture of burial customs, tribal beliefs, marriages and medicine men, and punishment systems practised since time began. They knew of a time called the Dreamtime, the beginnings of their world, lost in the dim misty past, and told their children wonderful stories passed down to them through the ages.

The two peoples could not have been more different, and there were many skirmishes and incidents where naked black men with spears faced heavily clothed white men with guns. For the most part, at least until the black men obtained guns, the weapons of the white man won, and dozens of natives were massacred. Of those who survived, some left for the vast lands of the interior, some stayed to become drifters around the white man's fast developing settlements, and a few integrated with the new arrivals. But for a long time, the mutual slaughter went on, whites murdering blacks, blacks murdering whites.

Governor Phillip's men captured an Aborigial man named Arabanoo, who was installed in the governor's house as an interpreter. When smallpox claimed him very shortly thereafter, two more, Colbee and Bennelong, were captured. Colbee escaped, but Bennelong stayed to become a favourite of the governor, and some settlers built him a small house on a tiny finger of land jutting out into the harbour.

In 1791, by the time the Third Fleet had arrived from Britain, there were some three and a half thousand convicts in the colony, along with a handful of free settlers, most of whom were struggling to survive. On occasions, wheat had to be brought from the island of Tasmania, where Captain Bligh had planted fruit trees, seeds and potatoes a few years before.

Philip's Royal Marines objected to their role of prison warders; they were sailors, they said, not nursemaids to a load of wrongdoers. They were soon sent home, and a specially recruited infantry division replaced them. These new soldiers were called the New South Wales Corps.

Philip had always battled ill-health, and at the end of his three-year term, he resigned and returned to England, taking with him the Aborigine Bennelong. For the next four years, until a new governor could be appointed, two officers of the Corps acted as lieutenant governors.

This was in the same year, 1792, in London, that Gemma Gallimore and her son Sebastian were sentenced to transportation for pickpocketing, Gemma's loved brother Isaac was left behind ignorant of his sister's fate, and Sophie was born to Jeb and Emmaline Abeles.

ONE OF THE officers of the New South Wales Corps was the paymaster, Lieutenant John Macarthur. His wife, Elizabeth, and young son, Richard, had accompanied him on the long voyage from England. Along with many others in the Corps, John had been granted a parcel of land, and he worked very hard, with the help of convict labour, to clear fifty acres of bushland. He built a house on the land and established a farm, which he named Elizabeth Farm. As employers of convict labour, he and Ben Ainsley often met, and they became fast friends, despite the difference in their characters. Both men treated their convict servants firmly but well.

"I can't understand the attitude of the British government!" fumed John one day. "They just want to leave New South Wales as a penal colony. Can't they see that it should—*must* be developed? They are blind."

Ben listened, nodding.

"Look what I have been able to achieve in just a short time," John continued his rant. "The farm is doing well, and I am employing people and feeding them."

By now, he was becoming quite agitated, as he usually did when he started on his favourite subject. He was a great fan of Governor Philip.

"The governor had the right idea, you know," he said, "when he asked for more free settlers with farming and building skills. Most convicts are lazy, and they have no skills. They have to be taught to be of any use! They're not all Ruses, are they?" He was referring to an ex-convict, James Ruse, who in two years had been able to support his family on an acre of land granted to him by Philip. "There's a world of untapped labour right here on our doorstep, and we're not making use of it! We've got to have more farmers. We simply do not have enough, and people have to eat. This country, one day, will be rich beyond our dreams, and nothing is being done to achieve it!"

John Macarthur hardly drew breath. "The possibilities are endless! Look at the area between here and the mountains. There's miles of it! Then there's that river, north of here—what's its name?—the Hawkesbury—that the governor found. I don't think we have the faintest idea of the prospects there are."

John never lost an opportunity to expound his theories, whenever he found an ear into which to pour his ideas.

"Don't let that fellow Macarthur get on his soapbox!" a settler was once heard saying. "He won't listen to your point of view—gets almost hysterical should you dare to differ. Take my advice and steer clear of the man. He's made enough enemies already!"

But Ben shared Macarthur's ideas entirely, although not so vociferously. He quietly continued to expand his own empire and remained one of John's true friends till the day he died.

Another good friend of Ben's was the army chaplain, Mathew Johnson. Mathew had originally asked Governor Philip for funds and labour to build the first church in the colony. This request had been refused on the ground that it was an unnecessary expense and use of convict labour. Mathew fell out with the governor over the issue and, within a year of the governor's departure, built a church at his own expense, with a great deal of gratuitous help from Ben Ainsley. A year later, a chaplain's assistant arrived in the person of Samuel Marsden, a Yorkshire-born clergyman. Marsden, a very ambitious, often cruel man, soon overtook the milder Mathew and was promoted to chief chaplain, leaving Mathew to pursue his interest in setting up a school.

Both John Macarthur and Mathew Johnson were concerned about the recent change in leadership of the colony.

"Now the Governor's gone home, the commander of the Corps has been appointed to act as lieutenant governor for two years," said Mathew.

"Who's that?" asked Ben, during one of their frequent get-togethers.

"His name's Grose," interrupted John, "and I don't like one bit what he's doing!"

"Neither do I," agreed Mathew.

John continued, "He's handing out good land to his cronies at a most alarming rate. The quicker a new governor gets here the better, I reckon. God knows—sorry, Mathew, but God alone knows what damage he'll do in his two years."

Mathew nodded, acknowledging his friend's reference to the Lord and agreeing with his point at the same time.

"Yes, and he's also using convict labour off the government farms for himself. He's not paying them properly, and half the time they're drunk!"

"So I hear," said Ben. "We don't have a problem with liquor here at Hillingdon, but the quarries are a different matter. Where's it coming from?"

Before Mathew could answer, John jumped in. "Rum! Grose and his offsider, Paterson, are providing it. Plus, the other officers are in on it—not all of 'em, though. They're trading in everything, but especially rum. They're selling it to the men and using it to pay them as well!" He twisted his face into an expression of disgust. "There's going to be trouble, I can smell it!" he finished, clamping his lips together, and frowning.

BEN KEPT A VERY close eye on his workers. The ones at Hillingdon were no trouble: they were well fed, kindly treated and generally happy. But those at the quarries were the lowest order of Irish and English criminals. It seemed there was always a seething undercurrent among them. Fights broke out, injuries were inflicted, and, to Ben's horror, one bloody murder had occurred. Not intelligent enough to cover their own tracks, the two perpetrators were quickly identified, put in irons and despatched to the penal hell-hole of Norfolk Island, nine hundred miles off the coast.

Several months later, in 1794, Captain William Paterson took over from Francis Grose as acting governor. But instead of improving, matters became worse.

The three friends were stood on the grassy slope toward the front of Hillingdon and looked down to the river, the heavy grey-green water turbulent and fast flowing. The sun slanted through the trees, and the shadows were dancing madly on the grass.

"Well, I thought Grose was bad," mused Richard, "but Paterson is worse. Far worse!"

"Yes," agreed John. *"I've* asked for and received another one hundred and fifty acres, but I've done it through the proper channels. I've put in an official request, and it's been granted. Paterson knows better than to refuse me. He knows I know too much! He's living his role as governor to the full. It's gone to his head, I reckon! Without even being asked, he's dishing out land to his favourites, same as Grose did. As far as I can tell, about fifteen thousand acres of prime land has already been given away to a select few. Thank God, though, that some of it is on the Hawkesbury River. It's absolutely beautiful soil up there, just perfect for crops."

"And along the south bank of the river at Broken Bay," interjected Mathew, "there's some wonderful stuff. All out of this area. Y'know Tom Reiby and his little wife, Mary? Well, they've been given land up there. Tom's a canny fellow when it comes to the land. If *he's* got acres there, you can bet on it that it's good. He hasn't accumulated his wealth without having a nose for the stuff. He can see a future, at least. A few more like him farming up there, and we'd soon have good food crops going. I've approached Marsden to see if this indiscriminate handing out of prime land can be stopped, but even he's in on it and doesn't want to listen. When's it all going to end?"

"When we have a new governor, who's not bent, can throw Paterson out, and can see what's what, that's when!" snorted John.

"Hear! Hear!" said the other two in unison.

"Ben, you're interested in building," said Mathew, changing the subject while there was a chance to divert John from his ravings. "Have you seen what the settlers are using now?"

"Do you mean the timber they're cutting from the black wattle trees?" asked Ben.

"Yes," replied Mathew. "They're building their houses with the green timbers and sticking it all together with mud and twigs. They're calling them wattle and daub houses!" He laughed, amused.

"And what do you think'll happen when the timber dries out?" asked John.

Mathew continued, ignoring the question. "I must say, bringing people from Europe to a new land like this, where there has never been a house, a piece of sawn timber, a roof tile, or even a cooking pot has brought out the very best in people."

"Yes, and the worst!" John muttered darkly.

"Now, now, John," Mathew said, "try to look at the world with a generous spirit."

"Humph!" snorted John. "You sound like my old vicar back in Plymouth."

Ben laughed and said, "Well, what do you expect. He *is* a vicar!"

"Yes, yes, of course!" John spluttered. "I didn't mean it quite like that. My apologies, though how you can have a generous spirit when you have to work with that Marsden fellow, God alone knows. I believe he's going to be appointed the magistrate now!"

"Yes," replied Mathew, his voice heavy with resignation, "that is so."

"Well, I pity any poor devil who crosses his path. He's got a cruel streak, that man, and I don't like him!" growled John.

"Not many people do," said Ben mildly.

"Well," Mathew said, trying to head off another burst from the quick-tempered John, "he leaves me alone. As you know, I'm just trying to set up a school. There are so many children here, and there is little for them to do."

"I'm with you, Mathew," said Ben. "A capital idea!" And the general conversation turned to the difficulties of the project.

THE SECOND GOVERNOR arrived some months later in the person of the Scottish-born John Hunter, captain of HMS *Sirius*. Hearing through Philip and others returning to England of the corruption in the New South Wales Corps, the British government had commissioned Hunter to restore order and discipline in the colony.

Accompanying Hunter was Bennelong, the Aboriginal man whom Governor Philip had taken back to England some four years earlier.

Bennelong had caused a great sensation in London, and a concerted effort had been made to anglicise him. He tried his best and was well treated, but the land of his birth, his roots, forever beckoned, and he became homesick and withdrawn. He was taught a great deal of the English language, and in return his captors were able to build up quite a lexicon of Aboriginal words and their meanings.

On his return, dressed in the English fashion, and speaking the language, he was as much an oddity to his own people as he was to the people of Britain. He quickly resumed his old life, returned to his own clan, the Cadigal tribe. The remnants of that clan still lived by the river which the settlers now knew was called the Parramatta, an Aboriginal word meaning "plenty of eels." Bennelong always remained friendly with the white invaders.

"HUNTER'S BEEN HERE A YEAR," said John Macarthur to Ben Ainsley, as they sat comfortably ensconced in horsehair-stuffed leather armchairs in the library at Hillingdon, enjoying a large glass of brandy and each other's company. "A whole year, and nothing, absolutely nothing has been done!"

He looked into the flames licking the logs in the grate, for it was July, the day was on the wane and a chill was in the air outside.

Ben puffed contently on his pipe of sweet Virginia tobacco, watching the smoke curl up and away, to be lost in the beams overhead. He sensed one of his friend's bitter verbal attacks approaching. He knew there was more to come and that nothing could deter John once he launched into a diatribe. Wherever he went, he created controversy. Ben settled back and listened.

John continued, "And I... am resigning as Inspector of Public Works!" he said, as if the idea had suddenly occurred to him.

Ben looked up quickly, startled at the determined defiance in his friend's announcement.

Before he could comment, John said, "I've had enough! I've always been, and I hope I always remain, a proud army officer." He squared his shoulders and straighten his back as if to emphasise his military training, but his shoulders drooped again. "But I am sickened by the immorality, the—the—the *dishonesty* I see all around me. Even most of the superior officers, as far as I can see, are as bad as the convicts they are supposed to control."

"Very strong words, John!" Ben said, looking his companion straight in the eye.

"Yes, I know," he agreed, "but true! At least Paterson is out of the way. He's gone home sick to England. I don't doubt his own activities made him sick—they made me sick!"

A wry grin escaped Ben's lips.

John, really wound up, continued. "I just can't understand the new governor. He's so ineffective! As soon as he landed, he ordered his men to stop their trading activities. And what did they do? They just continued as if he wasn't there. He's like a toothless tiger with its claws removed! I tell you, Ben, things could not be worse!"

Macarthur looked into the fire again, and another thought seemed to suddenly leap out of the flames and strike him. "Then there's Marsden!"

Ben was long used to his irascible friend and his outbursts and aware that he had alienated himself from most people around him. He wasn't nicknamed "the perturbator" for nothing! He'd quarrelled with almost everyone he came in contact with, from Governor Hunter down.

"Marsden? What's he done?" asked Ben, already knowing the answer.

"He's cruel in the extreme. He'll have someone flogged at the drop of a hat. I truly think he enjoys it. The Senior Chaplain! He's supposed to be a Christian, for God's sake! Bah! He's managed though, hasn't he, to amass land and wealth. One wonders how. Well, I may just beat him at his own game." In his agitation, he hadn't realised the incongruity of his statement.

In the middle of knocking the ash from his pipe on the unburnt end of one of the logs on the brick-laid hearth, Ben looked up.

"Game? What game?" he asked.

"Merino sheep!" John shot the reply.

"Merinos? Which merinos? I didn't know we had any!"

"We didn't, until about three months ago," answered John.

"Where from? How did they get here?" Ben asked, now more than a little interested. So busy with his other activities, he had little time to think of much else and so had heard nothing of this news.

"Waterhouse!" said John, as if that explained everything.

"What d'ya mean, 'Waterhouse'?"

"Probably the only good thing our new governor has ever done," replied John, "was to send a couple of ships to the Cape to buy cattle. He knows we have to have beef for food."

"Well, that's one thing he's got right!" Ben smiled.

"The only thing!" snorted John, not easily appeased. "Anyway, Waterhouse, the Captain of the *Reliance,* as well as bringing back cattle, brought back some Spanish Merino sheep for himself. I know that they're not much good for meat, but they can even stand the worst weather. I've bought three rams and three ewes from him, Marsden's bought some, a few others have got a few, and Waterhouse has kept the rest for himself. I hope to breed mine for wool."

"I wish you good fortune," said Ben, "and that reminds me. Do you know anything about some fellows finding coal somewhere? I've heard a rumours."

"Not thinking of mining coal as well as stone, are you?" enquired John, raising an eyebrow.

"Well, you never know, do you?" replied Ben succinctly.

"Yes, well," said John, "from what I've heard, and I don't know what truth there is in it, a ship must have foundered somewhere south of here, and some poor devils swam ashore and reckon they've found some coal! Apparently, the powers that be reckon it's too inaccessible to work—and we all know who those powers might be!"

"Oh, well," said Ben, choosing to ignore the reference to the governor, "if you hear some more, perhaps you'll let me know?"

"Of course!" replied John. "What I know now is that one of our lieutenants, John Shortland, was looking for some escaped convicts *north* of here, and he says *he* has found some deposits."

"Really!" said Ben, his interest growing. "And what's being done about it?"

"Nothing, if I know Governor Hunter! But he damned well should do something about it! Shortland also found another river up there, and guess what he's named it? The Hunter River." He snorted.

"Did he find the escapees?" Ben asked casually.

"No, and he probably never will. Shortland said he had to go over some pretty big hills, and there's nothing but trees and bush everywhere." The two men lapsed into a companionable silence, each with his own thoughts, dreams and realities all mingled together.

SOME MONTHS LATER, on his return from a journey to England, Ben visited the Macarthurs at Elizabeth Farm, and he and his hosts were seated at the dinner table. As always, they were very anxious to hear of events "back home," and in turn they brought Ben up to date with events in the colony.

"Dare we hope that you have found a lady for yourself, Ben, dear?" asked Elizabeth, smiling across the table at him.

Elizabeth was very fond of Ben and nursed the private hope that he would find someone with whom he could share his life. By now, it was quite clear that he had recovered from the loss of his wife at sea years before. Elizabeth thought it was a great waste for such a man to be on his own for so long, and every time he had returned from one of his frequent trips away from the colony, she hoped that he would bring back a new wife. Occasionally she had tried to pair him off, none too subtly, with an unattached lady she thought suitable, but always Ben managed to avoid a meeting.

He had his heart set on one woman, and one woman only, and he would not rest till she was his.

"Elizabeth, you will be the very first to know when I do!" he replied gravely, and his eyes twinkled.

John, more interested in the day-to-day affairs of life, brought the conversation around. "Things here have gone along at the usual pace. The governor's been recalled, and Paterson still hasn't been able to stamp out the corruption in the Corps, especially the liquor trading. Can't see, myself, why they ever brought him back here from England!"

"I wonder if he had anything to do with Governor Hunter's recall?" asked Ben.

"Dammit Ben, Hunter's been just as useless as Paterson! He's fallen out with most of the Corps officers, and most of 'em by now have got very large landholdings for themselves. And the liquor trading goes on bigger and better than ever! Did you know that I personally wrote to the Secretary of State for the Colonies, telling him exactly how ineffectual Hunter was?"

Ben stared at his friend. "No! Good God! I didn't know you felt *that* strongly about it!"

"Well, I did, and I do! They must've listened, eh?" said John, with a sardonic grin.

"Who's going to replace him, do you think?" asked Ben.

"He's on his way already," answered John. "Fellow by the name of King—Philip Gidley King."

"I haven't heard the name before," Ben mused. "What's his background?"

"He was the Captain of the Sirius in Philip's first fleet and commanded the settlement at Norfolk Island for about four years, I think. He had some dealings with convicts there, so maybe, just maybe, he's the man to sort things out here!"

"Let's hope so!" Ben agreed, though he privately wondered how long it would be before John and the new governor were at odds.

IT WASN'T long before Ben's misgivings were justified. Governor King set to with a vengeance. Upon his arrival, he set in train some moves to stabilise the money of the colony, keep food within reasonable prices, and actively encouraged exploration. He then turned his attention to the New South Wales Corps and its officers. He had been made aware of the problems but was surprised at how deeply entrenched they were. Despite his orders to the contrary, the activities of the Corps continued unabated.

One afternoon, John rode over to Hillingdon in a great hurry and asked the housekeeper, Gemma, if he could speak to her master on a matter of some urgency.

Observing his flushed face, and his manner in general, Gemma showed him straight to the library, where she knew Ben was completing some records at his desk.

Ben looked up in some surprise at the sudden and unannounced entry of his friend. He stood quickly. "John! What is it? What's happened?"

John threw himself into a chair. "I've come straight here! I haven't even told Elizabeth!" He hesitated, drew in a deep breath and looked squarely at Ben. "I've been challenged to a duel!"

For a moment Ben could not quite grasp what had been said. "You've *what?*" he almost shouted. "Dear God, man! By whom?"

"My commanding officer!" John replied, almost with resignation.

Ben was appalled. "In Heaven's name, John, how has this happened? Tell me it's not true!"

It's true all right!" replied John, then a new energy, a new anger took hold of him. "I tell you Ben, he's as weak as the governor!"

"Who?" asked Ben.

"The commander!" John spat. "A blind man could see that King is weak." For a second, Ben was confused as John leapt from one name to another.

"Oh yes, he's made a big noise sorting out the food prices and the currency, but the corrupt officers of the Corps are doing what they have been doing ever since they arrived!"

So impassioned he hardly paused for breath, he continued, "Well, I tried to get the commander to see some sense and join with me against the governor, but he refused. He *refused*! I tell you Ben, this'll never get sorted out, y'know! I worry about us all."

He suddenly seemed to run out of breath and passion, and he looked down disconsolately at his hands lying listlessly, hopelessly in his lap.

"But a duel, John? It's *illegal!*" Ben said.

"I know, I know, but I'm not about to let that stop me making my point. He's challenged me, and, legally or illegally, I shall meet him!"

Ben was aghast. "John, what happens if you are wounded—or killed? Think of Elizabeth, man! And your sons! What will happen to them?"

"They'll be fine!" John answered, almost impatiently, as if they were a minor irritation. "The farm is prospering, and I'm a rich man, Ben—not in your league I know, but through my own efforts here, I've made a small fortune in my few years here. What I *don't* seem able to do is convince others..."

Oh, no, Ben thought. *Here he goes off again, on his favourite theme.*

"... that trade and agriculture will make this colony rich beyond the dreams of most men, and a lot of people will be able to share in the wealth, not just a few unprincipled ones!"

Ben's emotions were in turmoil. He knew that John was arrogant and uncompromising and had utter contempt for those who did not share his views. He was sorely tempted to give John a piece of his mind.

But what if he is killed and I never see him again? And Elizabeth! How could he ever face her again, knowing that he had fought with her husband on the very eve of his death? It was unthinkable. She was such a soft, tender creature, who loved her husband without reservations. It would wound her mortally. Ben could see that John was not to be deterred. As usual, he was so intransigent he would not listen to reason.

"John, I see I cannot persuade you to abandon this wild idea of a duel. I can only hope that both you and your superior will satisfy your egomania in a way that neither of you will be hurt."

"I mean to meet him, and I will have my satisfaction!" John said. "And please say nothing to Elizabeth until it is all over!"

"All over!" exclaimed Ben. "All over for whom John? You, your commander, Elizabeth, your children—*who*, John?" He was now getting angry. "I tell you, John, it is only the fact that we have been friends, good friends these past few years that's preventing me from telling you exactly what I think of you and your foolish rigidity!"

Both men rose from their chairs, knowing that anger and frustration between them were of no possible use, that there was nothing more to be said.

Ben extended his hand and made a last appeal. "John, I sincerely hope that you will not proceed with this. I only wish the very best for you."

John took Ben's hand, shook it very firmly, turned on his heel and left the room without further words, closing the door quietly behind him in what seemed a final gesture of defiance.

Ben was left standing, staring unseeing at the closed door. He suddenly realised that, in his agitation, he hadn't even asked John when or where the duel was to take place. He hoped that both men would realise the futility, the stupidity, of it all, and perhaps agree, like mature human beings, to bury their differences for the good of everyone.

Forty-eight hours later, Elizabeth Macarthur drove her gig at a great speed to Hillingdon and fell into Ben's arms, sobbing.

"Ben! Oh, Ben! John's been arrested!"

"What? Why?" demanded Ben, holding her at arm's length. "How?"

"Oh! You know how pig-headed he is!" she cried. "He apparently could not make his commander see his side of things, and they fought! The commander's been wounded, and John's been arrested." Her tears came anew and spilled down her cheeks in great streams.

No amount of pleading John's cause could deter Governor King from sending him back to England to face trial before a military court. While he was awaiting passage, in recognition of his long and exemplary military service, he was allowed back to Elizabeth Farm on several occasions, under escort, to brief Elizabeth and his son Richard on the running of the farm. He was particularly anxious that his successful sheep-breeding program should continue uninterrupted.

He told Ben, "I shall take some sample fleeces with me, and if I can't convince the British government of the importance of New South Wales as anything but a penal settlement, it won't be for the want of trying! I have some good friends in high places and I'm sure they will help."

He's never going to give up, Ben thought. *He'd rather die in the attempt.*

"My dear friend," said Ben. "We've had some good times together

—and some not so good—and I'll miss you. Rest assured that I shall be in touch with Elizabeth from time to time until your return.

He turned to Elizabeth. "You've only to ask and I will do anything to see that she is well and as happy as she can be. But there's one thing I would like both of you to do for me before you leave."

"Name it!" John said.

"I would like you both to witness my marriage."

If a musket had been fired close behind her, Elizabeth could not have been more startled.

"Ben!" she cried, a wide smile spreading across her face. "How wonderful! When? And to whom? Tell me quickly!"

She was so excited, Ben thought he would trifle with her a little.

"Well," he drawled slowly, prolonging her agony of anticipation, "I *had* arranged a spring wedding, but since John will be away, I will bring the occasion forward."

Elizabeth was fidgeting, and Ben decided to tease her a little longer. "I have asked Mathew to perform the ceremony in his church."

"Ben Ainsley," Elizabeth lost her patience, "if you don't tell me *who* this very instant, I don't know *what* I shall do."

Ben thought he had played with her long enough.

"I have asked Gemma to do me the honour of becoming my wife," he replied, softly and seriously. He felt he ought to play down his happiness a little, considering John and Elizabeth were soon to be parted for an unknown period but couldn't help himself. "And she has accepted!" he beamed, and his eyes shone very brightly.

He still could not contain his excitement, his wonderment, every time he thought about her. His heart almost jumped out of his chest every time her image came into his mind.

"Of course we will witness it. It will be an honour!" John said. "And congratulations." He grasped Ben's hand very tightly, and almost shook his arm off.

"About time too, Ben. She's been in love with you for years," Elizabeth said. "She's a very lovely person, and I shall look forward to spending many happy hours with her." Her face became solemn. "It will help me to pass the time until my dear John comes home."

Tears sprang to her eyes for the hundredth time since her husband's arrest. She tried to dash them away, not wishing to spoil Ben's joy, and John reached for her and held her in his arms.

"Come now, Elizabeth, don't cry. It won't be too long. Richard and the little ones are here and Ben will see that you get up to no mischief. Who knows, after a little while, you may be *glad* I'm not here!"

His attempt at humour fell flat, and it started another great flood of tears.

Ben thought it a good time to leave them, and he quietly motioned to the military escort to accompany him out of the room.

"Come on, man! Surely you can stay out here and leave them alone for a while?" he asked. "I will vouch for him."

The sergeant nodded, and Ben walked quickly away.

19

Ben and Gemma watched as the three arrivals stepped off the gangway of HMS *Resolution*, and Ben grasped Jeb's hand and shook it vigorously.

"Welcome to New South Wales!" he said, beaming widely. "This is my wife, Gemma." He gently put his hand on the small of her back, treating her like a goddess the way he always would. "And Sophie, you've grown into quite the young lady since last I saw you. You must have had a birthday?"

"I did, sir, on the ship. And Captain Joseph made me a special cake!"

"He made it himself?" asked Ben, smiling and winking at Emmaline.

"Oh yes!" enthused Sophie. "It was lovely, but it was so big I couldn't eat it all by myself, and I shared it with my friends. Their names are—"

"Sophie, dear," chided her mother, "you can tell Mr And Mrs Ainsley all about your friends later on."

Looking towards Ben and Gemma, she said, "She's so full of her adventures since we left England that I don't think we'll ever stop her chattering."

"We would very much like to hear about all your adventures a little later, Sophie," Ben said kindly. "But for now, we must see you properly settled. Gemma, will you please help Emmaline and Sophie to the big gig and go on home? Jeb and I will see about unloading the luggage. We'll be along as soon as we can."

"Come this way, Mrs Abeles," invited Gemma as she set off in the direction of a gig standing a little way to the side of the wharf.

"Oh, please call me Emmaline!" she begged. Following Gemma, she gathered up her skirts, and they picked their way through the stacks of large wooden boxes, coils of rope, bales of wool, kegs of rum and barrels of water and salt pork ready to be loaded for the return trip. Stray dogs, horses, carriages, workmen and children all mixed and mingled together to create an animated picture of subdued excitement.

"Thank you; please feel free to call me Gemma," she smiled gratefully. "We're so happy you've arrived safely. It's such a long voyage, isn't it?" She well remembered her own journey, over ten years before, an experience awful beyond words, being imprisoned below decks for much of the four months of the voyage.

They arrived at the gig to find a very tall, good-looking young man untying the reins. His face broke into a wide smile the moment he saw them approach.

"This is my son, Sebastian," said Gemma. "Sebastian, this is Mrs Abeles and Sophie."

Sebastian gave a very tiny bow and extended his hand to Emmaline. "I'm very pleased to meet you, Mrs Abeles, and you, too, Sophie—hello!" He looked down at the long red curls hanging down her back, the blue satin ribbon, crisp no longer, vainly trying to restrain them. A shiny film of perspiration bathed her face, and she waved her hat in an attempt to cool herself.

"Hello, Mr Ainsley," Sophie responded. "It's hot, isn't it?"

"I'm not Mr Ainsley, I'm Sebastian. Sebastian Gallimore! We'll soon have you in the shade. Mrs Abeles." He held out his hand for Emmaline to grasp as she stepped onto the sideboard.

"Mamma?" he continued, and he handed his mother up.

Both ladies settled themselves and their skirts on the wooden bench seat, their backs to the horse.

"Come along, Sophie," he said easily, "hop up, and we shall drive the ladies home." With his hand under one of her elbows, she quickly jumped aboard.

Sophie seated at his side, Sebastian gently flicked the reins, and they made a soft slapping sound on the horse's rump.

"Off we go, Horace!"

Sophie lurched backwards as the horse started off at a brisk walk. She let out a squeal of delight and laughed, "Horace? What a funny name for a horse!"

Sebastian smiled broadly, and before he could respond, Sophie announced, "I've never been in a gig before. This is great fun. I think I like New South Wales!"

Both Gemma and Emmaline laughed, and Gemma produced three parasols from under the bench, saying, "I think you'll find the heat is a little more than you're used to."

"Yes," Emmaline nodded, "and I understand that it will be a lot warmer later on."

Before Gemma could explain that it was early summer and that it would get almost unbearably hot a few weeks later, Sophie looked up at Sebastian and asked, "How old are you?"

"*Sophie!*" her mother scolded her. "It's very rude to ask people their age. Apologise to Mr... um..."

"It's Sebastian," he reminded her, then turned to Sophie. "Seventeen. And how old are you?"

His eyes twinkled, and a deep dimple appeared in his right cheek as he smiled crookedly.

"I'm ten, and I've just sailed all the way around the whole world," she said, bouncing on her seat.

"Oh, dear me!" said Emmaline hopelessly. "Sophie, *please* mind your manners!"

To Gemma she said, "I do apologise for my daughter's bad manners. She's been so excited from the day we left home and was in such a hurry to get here. She asked everyone she met on board whether they had ever been here. Eventually she found a very nice gentleman who was returning to New South Wales, and he kept her enthralled for hours."

"Please don't apologise," Gemma said kindly. "It's refreshing to have such exuberance in our midst. Sebastian, will you please take the track along the river? It will be shadier and cooler for us all."

There was a dual purpose in Gemma's instruction. The narrow track she referred to had been earlier cleared by Ben for his sole use. When he had built Hillingdon years before, the track ran alongside the river from where the early supply ships landed to the bottom of the hill on which his mansion stood. Since then, another track had been made to the front of the house, and it was now being widened to accommodate the increased traffic now that settlers had moved in on either side of Hillingdon. A chained gang was working on the roadway as Gemma spoke, and she wanted to spare Emmaline and Sophie the sight. Rough men, their feet chained together, stripped to the waist, covered in a lather of sweat and dust toiling away in the midday sun, a government overseer strolling languidly up and down the line, a whip hanging loosely at his side, ever ready to be laid hard across the back of any man he thought might be malingering.

Plenty of time for them to see such things, Gemma told herself grimly. *Hard to avoid.* Wherever you went these days, gangs of convicted men were clearing trees and bush or splitting sandstone and rock to build roads.

The river was running high and wide, green and swirling. Up ahead, just as the watercourse took a bend, a large mansion set on a high point came into view. Down from the house to the edge of the water was a blanket of bright green grass. Large patches of dappled shade dotted here and there were cast by a handful of huge old gumtrees, judiciously left when the land was cleared. The track on which they travelled turned and led up the side of the hill, and Horace slowed to a walk as he took the gig and its occupants around the side of the house to the front entrance.

"Whoa, Horace!" Sebastian commanded needlessly as the horse came to a gentle stop. Sophie watched as his ears and tail flicked constantly to be rid of the flies, which settled on him the minute he halted.

"Welcome to Hillingdon!" Gemma smiled, and Sebastian helped

the ladies to alight. Sophie couldn't wait to be helped and jumped out of the far side

"Oh, Mamma! Isn't this beautiful? Is this where we are going to live?"

"Hush, Sophie!" her mother said, looking at Gemma, embarrassed.

Gemma volunteered, "You'll be staying here until your papa builds your own house. And we shall be delighted to have you!" she smiled.

Sophie spun around, arms outstretched, her long skirt swirling around in a bell shape, red curls flying madly.

"Please, do come in out of the heat," Gemma said, leading the way into a high, wide hall and through to a large room at the rear of the house, from which one could view the green slope, the river and part of the track they had just travelled.

Gemma threw open the windows. "Please settle yourselves, and I'll arrange some refreshments for us."

"Where is Sebastian?" asked Sophie, who had apparently claimed him as her own.

"He will be here shortly," replied Gemma as she left the room. "He has to look after Horace."

"May I go and watch?" asked Sophie.

"Sophie!" her mother chided. "You must not be so forward. Please do remember that we're guests, and behave like a lady." she instructed.

"Yes, Mamma," Sophie murmured, looking down, suitably chastened.

At that moment, Sebastian arrived, and Sophie forgot all about her mother's admonition.

She jumped up and asked, "May I see where Horace lives?"

"*Sophie!*" her Mamma cried despairingly. "At least let poor Sebastian draw his breath."

"Of course, you may," Sebastian replied, "but there's plenty of time. Remember, you will be staying with us for quite a while."

Gemma returned. "Tea will be along shortly. It's odd, isn't it, that despite the heat, we still cling to our English cups of tea? Even in the hottest part of summer, we still have it! A cool drink is on its way for you, Sophie."

"When is the hottest time?" asked Emmaline.

"Probably December and January. But I still find it a little too warm for me at other times. Ah! Here's the tea. Thank you, Maureen," Gemma addressed a young girl of about sixteen years.

Realising that the girl was a servant, Emmaline surreptitiously grasped Sophie's hand very firmly, conveying an unspoken message. Never having employed any, she was unsure how one spoke to servants.

"When you have rested," continued Gemma, "I shall show you to your rooms. Sophie, we've put you in a room next to your Mamma and Papa. You'll be able to overlook the side gardens and probably see Sebastian sometimes. He works very hard out there, keeping us well supplied with flowers and vegetables."

BACK AT THE WHARF, Ben and Jeb completed the arrangements for the storage of the Abeles household goods and the conveyance to Hillingdon of the boxes containing supplies for their immediate needs.

They started the drive home. Ben drove the gig along the new road being constructed, and in front of them was a dray taking goods to a house further along. Despite its slow progress, the dray left behind it a cloud of dust and grit. The gang of convict workers stood aside to let the vehicles pass, and, as Ben's gig passed, a convict looked Ben squarely in the eye and spat contemptuously on the ground, the back of his hand then sliding across his bottom lip, leaving a dirty smear of spittle and dust across his face.

"I've brought you this way on purpose," said Ben, ignoring the man's gesture and blinking to rid his eyes of the dust. "Gemma's gone the other way to spare your wife and daughter on their first day in New South Wales." As he said this, he turned to look behind and assure himself that another gig was following some distance away.

Satisfying himself that it was so, he continued, "You may remember when I saw you last year in London, I mentioned this was an everyday sight here. Things have moved quickly over the last five or six years, and the government is pushing roads through everywhere. And I think we've still only scratched the surface. To the west of here is a range of mountains—the Carmarthen Hills and the Landsdowne Hills—and just this year, a fellow called Barrallier, an ensign from the New South Wales Corps, managed to get quite a way up into them. He says it's very rugged country. The government is trying to find a way around the mountains to see what the country is like on the other side, but it looks like they will have to try and find some way over the top. From all accounts, there's a bit of a strange phenomenon up there. When you are in the mountains they are as you would expect, but from a distance, they look blue!"

Again, Ben turned to look at the gig following behind and nodded his head in that direction. "He's still with us! Did you see much of him on the voyage?"

"Not very much," replied Jeb, "He seemed a friendly enough fellow, but mostly kept to himself, I think. Didn't mix much at all. Actually, he seemed to spend a great deal of his time reading. I should think he's brought more books here than anything else. Why, he even bought some during the stop-over at the Cape!" He hesitated. "For obvious reasons, we kept Sophie right away from him."

Ben laughed. "That must have been difficult. She seems such an exuberant little one."

"What exactly is the New South Wales Corps?" asked Jeb.

"Well, they're our policemen, really," Ben replied. "They were originally sent here at Governor Philip's request, to keep order after the Royal Marines left. But the activities of some of the more senior officers leave a deal to be desired. As it happens, I have two very good friends in the Corps. One has just... gone back to England for a while, and the other is the chaplain. But don't let us influence you; you must make up your own mind about the Corps, Jeb. You may need their services at one time or another. And you'll certainly be employing the convicted men."

"Some of those men back there looked pretty tough," Jeb said, gesturing with his thumb over his shoulder. "Don't they give you any trouble?"

"At the quarries, yes, but back at the house, never. They're quite a different kettle of fish altogether. And of course... I'm hoping to have a new man in charge soon."

Both men laughed conspiratorially.

"Here we are!" Ben said. He stepped down from the gig and handed the reins to a servant standing by the door, murmuring a quiet thanks. "I expect the ladies have already had a cup of tea. I'll wager you're thirsty—I know I am!" They walked side by side through to the rear of the house.

"Papa! Papa!" called Sophie, jumping up and throwing herself at her father. "You should see where my room is! It's lovely. It's all so pretty, and I'll be able to see Sebastian in the garden!"

Jeb caught her in his arms and looked at his wife. "Emmaline, can you not keep your daughter under control?" Then he smiled indulgently at his little girl. "What are we going to do with you, Sophie? Now, come and sit by me and behave yourself, do!"

"I hope it was not too onerous for you to arrange for our belongings?" enquired Emmaline.

"Er—no, no—not at all!" Ben replied.

Gemma looked at him quickly. He seemed distracted, and he paced from one side of the room to the other and back again for no apparent reason. He stood with his back to the room, gazing out the window, then, realising his rudeness, he turned and sat in a vacant chair.

Gemma kept looking at him, concern on her face. It was so unlike him to be fidgety.

Jeb turned his eyes to Emmaline, and back to Ben. The silence was strange! Six people in the room and no-one was speaking.

Suddenly, Jeb and Emmaline started to say something at the same time, and it broke the awkward pause.

Sebastian realised that something odd was going on and, to break the silence, he asked, "Mr Abeles, would you permit Sophie to come and see where Horace is kept?"

Before Jeb could reply, a servant tapped on the door and said, "Excuse me, ma'am. There's a gentleman at the door asking to see you."

"To see me?" asked Gemma. "How odd! I'm not expecting anyone." She puckered her brow and looked enquiringly at Ben.

"Aha! Is it your gentleman friend calling because he thinks I'm not here?" Ben asked, looking lovingly at her.

"*Ben!*" Gemma said, feigning shock, but relieved to see him acting normally again. "Please excuse me."

Ben watched her go, and his eyes shot across first to Jeb, and then to Emmaline. There was a palpable tension in the room, and Sophie, for once in her life, kept silent, sensing that something strange was happening.

Sebastian looked at Ben, his eyes silently asking for an explanation. In reply, Ben put a finger to his lips to signal silence.

"Oh! *Oh!*" A high-pitched cry from Gemma echoed through the house, and Sebastian froze.

"It's all right, Sebastian. Your mother's fine!" Ben jumped instantly from his seat, and threw his arm protectively around Sebastian's shoulders, restraining him gently.

"Ben! Sebastian! It's Isaac!" Gemma came flying into the room, wildly pulling the beloved brother she hadn't seen for over ten years. "Sebastian, look! It's your Uncle Isaac!"

She was so excited, she stood holding Isaac at arm's length, then pulled him fiercely to her and tightly wrapped her arms around him, tears spilling unashamedly down her face.

"Oh, Isaac! It's been so long. How did you find us? We've never stopped thinking of you!"

Isaac looked across at Sebastian and held one arm out to enclose him. "You were seven when I last saw you. I can't believe how tall you are—taller than me!"

Gemma extricated herself from Isaac's embrace. "Ben, I'm so sorry! Isaac, this is my husband, Ben."

Isaac smiled. "I know."

"And this is Mr and Mrs Abeles and their daughter, Sophie—wait, *what* did you say?" Gemma looked up at her brother, her mouth open.

"I said 'I know'," Isaac replied. It was only then that Gemma noticed that they were all smiling at her knowingly.

Ben came across the room and put his arms around her. "Isaac's arrival is my belated wedding gift to you!" he explained gently.

Gemma almost collapsed against him. She could not trust herself to speak, and another lot of tears tumbled down her cheeks.

Unnoticed by the others in the room, Jeb held Sophie's hand

tightly and beckoned to his wife to follow him. They walked through the opened French windows, across a wide terrace, and down on to the grass.

"Let's go down and look at the river." said Jeb.

"So that's it!" said Sophie, understanding. "That man is Mrs Ainsley's brother! Why wouldn't you let me speak to him on the ship?"

"Because you're such a chatterbox!" her father replied. "You might've let the cat out of the bag and spoilt the surprise for Mrs Ainsley and Sebastian the minute you got here!"

"Oh, I wouldn't have! I can keep a secret!" Sophie replied indignantly. "But isn't it exciting? Mrs Ainsley's found a brother, and Sebastian's found an uncle. How did they lose him, I wonder? Why didn't he come with them when they came here? And why...?"

"Enough questions for one day, my lady! Come and sit here by me and watch the river go by!" Jeb commanded, trying in vain to sound stern.

"Look, Sophie, a pelican!" said Emmaline. "And there's another. Aren't they graceful?"

Sophie wandered off to the edge of the water, while Jeb and Emmaline sat watching her.

"Well, that was certainly a wonderful surprise for Gemma!" said Emmaline.

"Gemma?" queried Jeb, faintly shocked.

"She asked me to call her Gemma, and I have asked her to address me by my Christian name," explained Emmaline. "I think she is a lovely person. She's very warm, isn't she? I'm glad Ben told you all about them before we got here. It would have all been very confusing, especially Sebastian having a different surname. Can you imagine the questions from Sophie? I think, perhaps, we should speak to her before she embarrasses everyone."

Ben agreed laughing. "A very good idea. Now's as good a time as any."

By the time they had explained the circumstances to Sophie and answered a thousand questions, an hour and a half had elapsed since they had left the house.

Ben came strolling down the grassy slope toward them. "I'm so sorry you have been left on your own. Do come up and join us again."

"We've thoroughly enjoyed just sitting here," said Jeb. "It's been such a long time since our feet have touched grass, it seems like forever."

Emmaline joined in, "It's a truly beautiful, peaceful place, Mr Ainsley."

"Oh please, don't stand on any ceremony. My name's Ben!"

By the time they walked back to the house, things had settled down a little. Gemma sat on a settee with her arm linked so tightly in Isaac's, it looked as if she would never let him go again, and Sebastian sat opposite them, smiling broadly.

"How could you all keep such a secret?" Gemma asked incredulously. "Oh! What a wonderful day—and what a coincidence that Ben found Isaac! If he had never gone to those brickworks at St Albans, they would never have met!"

There was a knock on the doorframe, and the housekeeper announced that dinner was ready.

"Thank you, Martha," Gemma said. Holding her hand out towards the open door, she told her guests, "Please, come and eat! And now I know why Ben was taking such an unusual interest in tonight's dinner... He insisted on Martha making it especially special!"

Later that night, in Ben's arms, Gemma said, "Just fancy! If you hadn't wanted to know the latest developments in brick-making, if you hadn't gone to that precise brickworks, if Isaac hadn't mended that chair for the man from the brickworks, and if Isaac hadn't mentioned his old apprenticeship, and if the man hadn't taken a liking to Isaac, and if his manager hadn't died—poor man—and if—"

Ben stopped her with a kiss. "And if," he said, "you hadn't come here I would never have found you, and if you don't stop 'iffing,' I'm going to keep kissing you till you do. And I think I'll keep kissing you anyway!" and he held her tenderly at first, and then fiercely.

After a while, Gemma murmured sleepily, "Ben, I've cried many tears in my life, but I don't think I have ever cried tears of happiness. Thank you. I love you."

"If you don't stop talking, I'll start kissing you all over again," Ben said. "In fact, come to think of it..."

$$\maltese \quad 2\,0 \quad \maltese$$

"John! Welcome home—'tis so good to have you back!" Ben exclaimed, grasping the hand of his old friend and shaking it vigorously.

Elizabeth Macarthur had invited her closest friends to Elizabeth Farm to celebrate the return of her husband from England, and she quickly introduced Isaac and the Abeles family.

"Jeb has established a bank since you left, and Emmaline and I have spent many happy hours together," she elaborated.

"And did I hear aright?" asked Ben, when they had finished their meal and were sitting out on the large wide veranda. "You are no longer a military man?"

"Yes, that is so," replied John, stroking the hand of Elizabeth, who sat close to him and linked her arm tightly in his. "I've resigned my commission, and I'm going to concentrate on breeding sheep for wool. As I said I would, I took some of my fleeces to England, and they were most impressed. Said they were every bit as good as the best from Spain! And I've brought back with me some very rare Merino rams from the king's flocks"

He looked fondly at his wife and continued, "Elizabeth has done a magnificent job of running the farm over the last four years in my absence, and thanks to her, our stock has increased threefold. With the new rams I have brought back, I see no reason why we should not build up a very impressive flock."

"Ah! Do forgive me," he said, turning to Jeb, "for being so discourteous! I have been so wrapped up in my own affairs. I'm very glad that at last we have a bank set up here, and as soon as my affairs have been settled, I'll be along to see you."

Ben closely observed John as he spoke.

Hopefully, he's not so quarrelsome. Maybe his arrest and four years in England have had a sobering influence on him. Maybe.

Emmaline looked around. "Where have Sophie and Sebastian gone? They disappeared as soon as we all got here!"

"Richard is showing them the telescope John brought back for him," Elizabeth replied. "He couldn't have thought of a better gift! Ever since Richard went to the observatory Governor Philip set up on Dawes Point, he's been fascinated with the night sky."

"Well," Emmaline smiled, "at least she'll be giving poor Sebastian a rest for a while. She never leaves him alone."

"I wouldn't worry about Sebastian," Ben laughed. "He loves the attention. They get on very well together."

Not much given to enjoying light banter, John brought the conversation around, his face serious. "Now, tell me, Ben, Jeb—what has happened since I left?"

"Well," Jeb offered, "I've been so busy building my house and the bank that I've had little time to take in the affairs of the colony. I think I'll let Ben bring you up to date—and maybe me as well."

"Yes, well, where to start?" Ben reflected, tamping down the tobacco in his pipe and locating his tinder box in his waistcoat pocket. He drew the flame into the sweet tobacco and let a lazy cloud of smoke rise and dissipate in the warm air. "I think, just as you left, they were trying to settle a colony in Tasmania."

"Where?" asked John, confused.

"Van Diemen's Land to you!" Ben clarified. "They've re-named it, and they've done it having first made sure that it belongs to Britain and not to France!"

Ben thought he would leave it as long as possible before

mentioning the governor's name and continued, "And Paterson's been made administrator."

"Humph!" snorted John, and before he could volunteer any further comment, Ben continued.

"There's a pardoned convict by the name of Redfern who looks like he's going to be a bit of trouble."

"I thought he'd gone to Norfolk Island!" Isaac said.

"He has, but I don't think we've heard the last of him by a long shot." Ben replied. "Anyway... oh, yes! We've actually had the first book printed here!"

He glanced at Isaac and smiled. "Poor Isaac! He's a regular book-worm, and he's been starved in this place. I think he's read every book ever brought here and then some. He got quite excited when he heard that George Howe was printing a book. You should have seen his disappointment when he learned the title! 'New South Wales General Standing Orders.'"

"I read it, just the same!" Isaac laughed sheepishly.

"Well, I had enough of standing orders to last me a lifetime during my military years," John said. "I'm going to make my own from now on!"

Ben stole a sideways glance at John. *He hasn't changed after all.*

"We still haven't crossed the mountains," Ben continued, "but a certain George Caley got a long way up into them. Reckons they're impassable. And..." said Ben, hesitating before delivering the biggest news, "we had our first armed uprising last year."

"Good Lord!" John expostulated. "I thought I'd heard the last of that sort of thing for a while. England is full of Admiral Nelson's battle with the French. Can't think that it'll be long before there's a resolution to that conflict, though. Been going on for so long, too long. I think it was actually coming to a head just as I left. But what happened here?"

"Oh! It was dreadful!" Elizabeth shuddered. "Those poor men!"

John looked lovingly at her. *Elizabeth would say 'poor men' no matter whose side they were on,* he thought.

"About thirty miles west of here," said Ben, "a place called Second

Ponds. Some two hundred or so convicts, mostly Irish it seems, and a handful of free settlers revolted."

"Against what? Who?"

"The usual..." sighed Ben. "Anyone or anything in authority. It was on a government farm, and one night a fellow lit a fire in a hut to signal the start of the uprising. It was quite a bloody battle but over fairly quickly. One of the leaders was hanged without trial, and I'm told his body was hung from the staircase at the Windsor General Store, as a lesson to everyone. A few of the rebels were killed, some were court marshalled and hanged—nine of 'em I think—and quite a few were flogged and sent off to a chain-gang at the Coal River coalfields north of here."

"I have to say, however," Ben ventured with a drawn-out sigh, "that I do have a deal of sympathy for the rebels. The first shiploads of convicts were mostly pretty hardened criminals, but the second wave was different. They were more political, with their minds set on sedition. It seems the legal system back in Ireland leaves a lot to be desired, since they often arrive with no papers and nothing to show what crime they had committed or even what sentence they had been given. And when you come to think on it, most of 'em only spoke Gaelic anyhow, so how could they understand? Even one of the priests who came had served a prison sentence back home! Amongst the rebels, there was a smattering of Chinese and a few others. And our friend Marsden hands out the most severe penalties, barbaric at times, for quite minor infringements. A thousand lashes is not uncommon for him, especially to the Irish, whom he hates with a passion! After that, if they still live, he sends 'em off to Norfolk Island, and that's a hellhole if ever there was one."

John had been listening intently and from time to time nodded his head. Though he had no time for those intent on maintaining the criminal activities which brought them to the colony in the first place, like Ben, he treated his convict labourers well and, in return, expected a fair day's work in return for their keep.

"Anyhow, the rebels were an ill-assorted, rag-tag bunch, with little or no direction. And when the soldiers arrived, they didn't stand a chance."

"I'll wager Marsden was delighted—a few less Irish to hate," John said bitterly.

"Well, yes, I suppose," Ben mused, "but he was also pretty disturbed that four of the condemned asked him for the rites of the Church of England before they were hanged. Anyway, the rest of 'em realised they'd lost the battle and gave up. They were allowed to go back to their work. If the rebellion hadn't been so poorly organised, God knows what would have happened."

He paused and decided it was inevitable that Governor King's name needed mentioning. "The governor proclaimed a state of insurrection and declared the area under martial law."

"Humph!" John said, predictably. "Took his mind off what he *should* be doing!"

Ben jumped in quickly. "You know, his posting is almost at an end, and we're to have a new governor, man by the name of Bligh, coming out from London. Did you hear anything of him over there?"

"Not much, really. Naval man. It seems his men mutinied somewhere or other a few years back, and he was set adrift in a long boat. Must be a very competent sailor, though!" said John with admiration. "Apparently, he navigated some thousands of miles of open seas and ended up on a South Pacific island somewhere. He's now back in London."

"Well, he's due to take over from Governor King in a few months," Ben said.

Before any further conversation could be pursued, Elizabeth interjected, "It's getting very warm out here. Would anyone like to go back inside in the shade?"

Gemma and Emmaline stood, glad of the invitation. Emmaline could feel her long undergarments sticking to her stockinged legs.

"Oh, yes, please!" she murmured, and the gentlemen rose as one and followed the ladies inside.

On their way in, Jeb said to John, by way of friendly conversation, "I have a customer at the bank who's a successful sheep breeder. It might be useful to you to get in touch with him; I'll arrange an introduction if you wish. Strangely enough, his name is Marsden—don't think it's the same one you've just spoken of."

Ben winced and stole a sideways glance at Gemma. John's jaw stiffened.

"It is, and thank you, no," John spat. "Marsden and I have met before, and I personally would be very happy if I never set eyes on the man again!"

"Oh!" Jeb said, quite deflated, knowing nothing of their past history.

Trying to salvage some of the good humour of the day, Ben asked Jeb, "Do you have Simeon Lord as a customer?"

"I do," Jeb replied gratefully.

"Now *there's* a man!" Ben said, turning to John. "Only a year after he received his pardon, he bought a trading ship—nobody knows how, but he did! And in the last four years, he's been bringing in all sorts of stuff. He's trading in coal, cedarwood, sealskins, rum from Mauritius, even! He's now a very wealthy man."

Jeb nodded in agreement. "He's set up some weaving mills at Port Botany, and he's always looking for wool. Has a good market for it overseas. You may wish to get in touch with him?" Jeb suggested hopefully, looking at John.

Nobody thought to mention that most of Marsden's wool was being woven at Lord's mill.

"Well, I shall certainly be using his services!" John said. "I want to build up a good export trade. After all, the colony *needs* to send goods away so that it can earn enough money to buy the goods it needs."

Ben looked despairingly at Gemma. *He's never going to give up! He's been back here five minutes, and he's on his favourite topic already. We are all in for a lesson in economics, unless I can head him off again.*

Before Ben could gather his thoughts, John said, "I've been granted five thousand acres of prime land for my sheep, and I don't want to add it to the farm. Where's the best land available now?"

"Large parcels are being developed in the Hawkesbury River area," Ben said eagerly. "Very rich land, I believe."

"Too far!" replied John. "Anything closer?"

"I've heard that there's some prime grazing land in the high country, southwest of here," offered Jeb.

"That sounds promising; thanks, Jeb," John said. "I'll certainly inspect that area. Mmm, this lemonade is delicious, my dear. I'd forgotten how good it is on a hot day!" He smiled at Elizabeth.

BEN SLAPPED Isaac on the shoulder. "There's been a noticeable decrease in trouble at the brickworks. It was a very difficult task for you to come to, and you've done a damned good job!"

"Well," Isaac responded, smiling, "I can't say I enjoyed it in the beginning, but things are definitely getting better. I can't thank you enough, Ben. In fact, all we Gallimores will be forever grateful to you."

"Do you feel like a long day's ride tomorrow?" Ben asked. "John Macarthur's been telling me how lucrative the wool business is. Now he's been granted that large acreage, I thought I'd go and have a look at the area myself, but a bit to the east of him. There's plenty of space out there, but I must say, I'm personally attracted to the high country."

Ben had a faraway look in his eyes and added, almost apologetically, "You know, I feel good when I'm up high! It's strange, since I'm not a religious man, but I feel close to God up there!"

Isaac looked at him and thought, *He looks like he's already up there! He's got a strange peace about him somehow, and I couldn't possibly intrude on something that made him feel and look that way.*

Ben came back to the present and said, "I've been into the Illawarra area once before, and I thought I'd take another look now that the summer's nearly gone, see if the grass is still as lush. It'll be a hard day's ride. But I'll be on Samson, and he's done it before."

"Thank you, but I can't," Isaac replied. "I've promised to go with Sebastian over to the Abeles' house. It's Sophie's fourteenth birthday. Sebastian's grown a special rose for her, and Gemma and I are giving her the telescope you sent for after she was so interested in Richard's."

"Are you sure you're not going over to see the Abeles housekeeper?" teased Ben. "She's a very handsome girl!"

"Yes, but she's still got four years to go before she's free," Isaac replied, colouring slightly.

"I waited twice that long for your sister, and I would have waited a hundred years!" Ben replied with feeling. "But that's fine. I'm going anyway."

As he began to turn away, he stopped and, looking straight at Isaac, said sincerely, "Don't wait too long. You're how old? Forty-one? Life is short, and happiness is fleeting. Grasp it with both hands, man, while you have the chance. And you may take that as good advice from one who knows! I thought I was happy once, but I didn't know what happiness was until I married Gemma."

THE FOLLOWING MORNING, Ben was up and ready in the early hours.

"Samson and I have a long ride ahead of us," he told a sleepy Gemma. "'Bye, my darling! I hope to see you tomorrow evening, but if it's too late, I'll put up somewhere along the way."

"Please be careful, Ben," Gemma said, raising her arms to embrace him.

"If you do that again," he laughed, "I won't be going at all! Now, tuck yourself up like a good girl, and I'll see you soon." He kissed her again and was away.

The big black stallion was waiting in the stable, ears pricked, and a soft whinny greeted Ben as he walked in. Samson had been his favourite for a long time, and he knew it. When Ben mounted him, man and horse became one. They loved nothing better than a long, hard ride. Away from the house and on the track, Ben let him have his head, and Samson lengthened his stride, his long black tail flying straight out behind him, the wind stroking horse and rider.

After a full-out gallop, Samson slowed to a walk, nostrils flaring, white foam frothing around his mouth. Once they came across a small creek and Ben dismounted, he wound the reins around the pommel and let Samson go free.

Ben leant against a tree, watching the stallion thirstily draw the cool, crystal water and waited for him to come back and nuzzle his shoulder. He caught a handful of black lustrous mane and rubbed his face against it, tickled Samson behind his ear and asked, "Are we ready to go again, my beauty?"

Up and away again—sometimes the exhilaration of a full gallop, sometimes the exquisite pleasure of a stately canter, and sometimes the companionship of a slow walk. Sometimes on the old, worn wagon track, sometimes through the trees at the side. Samson knew exactly what was required of him, and it was rare for Ben to ask for something different. He had slowed to a walk and Ben looked around. With a slight start, but not entirely surprised, he realised he was not where he had intended to be. Something had drawn man and horse up and away from the flatlands and into the hills.

Strange, he thought. *But this is where I am meant to be. It feels right. It is right!*

They had been climbing steadily since they left the town and followed the track up and around the gullies and ravines. Here and there, little waterfalls splashed and tumbled as they had done for thousands of years, now past a stand of magnificent cedar trees not yet violated by the cedar getters. By mid-afternoon, Ben reached the top of the escarpment.

To his left and far below was the ocean—blue and calm, sparkling and flaunting a white lace edge as it caressed the beaches. The scene held no attraction for Ben. It was the savage grandeur of the wind-scoured bluffs and the rolling hills away to the mountains on his right which held him. He was elated. There was a mystery, a magic in the area, and he felt a prickling sensation run up his spine and raise the fine hairs along his arms.

Shielding his eyes from the westerly sun, he saw a great grey shadow advancing toward him, clothing the earth and draping itself over the trees, outcrops and gullies as it came slowly, slowly forward. Above the land, he watched a massive bank of dark clouds rolling and billowing like a storm-tossed sea, coming up and over the distant horizon and soon covering half the sky. As it came slowly, majestically, deliberately toward him, Ben marvelled at the sight. Where he stood, the grass was bright green and sparkling in the sun, and yet ahead of him, the earth was dark and menacing.

I'm standing on top of the world, Ben thought. *I'm witnessing the making of a miracle. I feel like God!*

As he watched, the sky was suddenly split in two by a great shaft of lightning, spearing itself into the ground ahead.

Samson flinched, but Ben reassured him, saying, "Looks like we're in for a bit of a storm, my boy!" He patted the stallion's neck.

Another bolt of lightning was accompanied by a great clap of thunder, and Ben felt the hair rise on his head, neck and arms.

Samson reared on his hind legs, snorting and pawing the air.

"Whoa, Samson! It's all right," Ben soothed. "Let's make for cover." And he wheeled the horse around and made for a large old ghost gum, fifty yards away.

As they fled, a ferocious gust of wind caught up with them, taking Ben's hat with it. It tumbled and turned ahead of them, and Samson's tail was whipped along his flank.

Ben guided his mount behind the vast trunk, smooth and white in the weird half-light, and he had trouble pacifying the terrified animal. Samson pawed the ground, nodding his great head up and down, pulling on the reins as he trampled around and around.

As the storm raced toward them, each new thunderclap and lightning bolt made Samson flinch and draw in his hindquarters. The wind picked up and lashed the leaves violently against each other, sending showers of them tumbling and glittering and flicking through the air, and it rolled twigs and small stones along the ground after them.

Strange, no rain, Ben mused. *Just a dry storm and the heavens letting us know how puny we are! This is what the birth of creation must have been like. A maelstrom, a holocaust.*

He was exhilarated, felt immensely privileged to witness it. Fiendish blasts of wind swelled the storm into a roar, which wrapped itself around the massive tree, enveloping man and beast.

Ben had an overwhelming feeling of exaltation. He let go of the reins, stood high in the stirrups, and held his arms aloft. He felt he was nearer to the heavens than he was to the earth. A sense of unutterable excitement overtook him. He was omnipotent!

A deafening crack of thunder shook the earth, and a great spear of exquisite blue lightning rent the giant tree clean down the middle. The terrified Samson reared on his hind legs and a primeval shriek escaped him.

Ben was thrown to the ground, and, in his euphoria, he made no attempt to escape the falling tree. He watched as it descended slowly, slowly, closer and closer, until it was over him, on him, crushing the breath, the life out of him, and an everlasting blackness, a blessed peace, enveloped him.

Samson, in his terror, bolted for the trees, the whites of his eyes shining madly. Away from his master, away from the storm, away through the bending, cracking, thrashing trees, he thundered and crashed as if the very Devil was after him. Along the top of the ridge and down into a gully he flew, smashing and crashing, long brown spiky fingers tearing at his legs, his body, his bridle. He stopped dead, steam coming in fast bursts from flaring nostrils.

He stood trembling, exhausted, the silence around him strange and unreal. Away in the distance, he heard a rumble of thunder as it rolled around the heavens and slowly faded away and a shaft of weak sunlight filtered in a speckled beam through the canopy overhead.

The great black stallion lifted his head, knew the danger was passed and began to make his sad, weary, lonely way home.

THE LIGHTS of Hillingdon were extinguished one by one as Gemma decided that it was far too late for Ben to make it home. She had a feeling of unease, of foreboding, as she retired for the night.

Silly, she told herself. *Ben said he would put up for the night if it got too late, and that's obviously what he's done. He's found a settler's hut somewhere or other, yes, that's what he's done.*

Nonetheless, it was only in the early hours of the morning that she managed to close her eyes, sitting propped up in the pillows. She was still asleep when the first rays of the coming day filtered through the curtains, and a frantic knocking on her door brought her instantly to the surface.

"Mama! Mama! Wake up, Mama!"

"What is it? Sebastian! Come in, what is it, what's wrong?" Alarmed by the urgency in his voice, she sat fully upright, clutching the bedclothes to her as her son rushed to her bedside.

"Mama, Samson's back! He's alone! His legs are badly cut and bleeding, and he's exhausted." Sebastian was breathless, and he watched his mother's face blanch a deathly pale.

A dizziness swirled through her head, and she closed her eyes. She filled her lungs with a sharp intake of breath, held it, biting her bottom lip to prevent it escaping.

No, no! she screamed silently. *It cannot be!*

She let out a long breath, slowly opened her eyes and looked at Sebastian. Summoning every atom of resolve, she said, "Samson's probably been spooked by something and run away. Ben knows him too well. He's let him go somehow."

Sebastian grasped her hand and said softly, "Mama, his bridle is half off, and the reins are broken."

"Yes, well, take Delilah and go and meet Ben. He's probably been walking for miles. You ride Delilah, and take the big bay with you," she said, businesslike, detached. "Go!"

She could not, would not accept that anything could possibly happen to Ben. Not Ben, no, not Ben. Yet a dread feeling had gripped her, and she felt her heart thump wildly.

All day she waited, never losing hope that she would see him riding up on the bay, jumping off, smiling at her, holding her. Sebastian arrived home after dark, forlorn and dejected.

"No sign, Mama! And nobody's seen him."

Gemma stared at her son, her anxiety increasing. "I've sent Isaac to try and find that black tracker who found the little boy who was lost that time. Ben gave Isaac the impression that he was probably going to make for the high country, so maybe that'll be a guide."

Sebastian nodded, thinking. "Willy. That was his name. The tracker, I mean. Good idea! Now, Mama, there's nothing more you can do. It's too dark." He put his arm around her shoulders. "You look worn out. Come inside and sit down. Everything that can be done *will* be done as soon as it's light."

Gemma sighed. "I'll be all right. You go in and rest. I'll stay out here a while."

Sebastian could see that he could not change her mind. He went inside to fetch a shawl and brought it out, wrapping it gently around his mother's shoulders.

"Don't stay out here too long, Mama. It's getting chilly." Getting no reaction from his mama, and expecting none, Sebastian slowly went inside after casting one last worried look at her. He had a dread thought that maybe Ben would never come home again and feared for his mother.

Gemma looked up at the sky. Cloudless blue, vast and empty during the day, and now, moonless and black, the uncountable stars of the Milky Way sprinkled from one side to the other.

Ben, where are you? Come home. I love you so. Where are you? She closed her eyes tight, and tears squeezed from under her eyelids and slowly made their way down her cheeks.

Gemma had no idea how long she had been out there, and the air was getting colder. At some point, Sebastian and Isaac came out and, one on either side of her, wordlessly took her arms and gently guided her inside the house. She offered no resistance and allowed herself to be guided to her bedroom. She lay on the bed, the shawl still around her, and stared unseeingly at the ceiling, her mind meandering in and out of a maze of memories and maybes until a fitful sleep overtook her.

And that's where she was when the housekeeper woke her, late in the morning, with a tray of breakfast. Still fully dressed from the day before, the shawl still around her, she came to and looked blankly at Martha.

"Ma'am, they found the tracker, and the men left before dawn. Please try and eat something. It will make you feel better."

"Which men?" asked Gemma, ignoring the tray.

"Mr Sebastian, Mr Isaac, Mr Macarthur and Master Richard, Willy the black tracker and some other men. They'll find him, ma'am, don't you worry, and he'll be safe and sound. Now, please try and eat a little."

"Thank you, Martha," Gemma whispered. She lifted her hand listlessly, hopelessly, and Martha withdrew.

Gemma had no appetite for food but gratefully took a few sips of hot tea. She rose from the bed, put the tray to one side, and went outside and sat on the veranda. The river below meandered past, green and silken, a fish now and then disturbing the surface and leaving ever widening circles. But Gemma saw none of it.

At midmorning, Elizabeth Macarthur and Emmaline Abeles drove over to offer some comfort. Noting Gemma's crumpled clothes and undressed hair, they gave up trying to make any sort of conversation and, after a while, left, shaking their heads and wondering with alarm what the effect it would have on their friend if her husband was lost.

By dusk, Gemma had not moved from her place on the veranda, and she looked up as she saw Sebastian, Isaac, and John come slowly toward her.

Isaac and John took their hats off and stood in front of her, their heads bowed, twisting their hats in their hands, and Sebastian came and knelt at her knee, taking both her hands in his.

"Mama." he said, choking. He could say no more, and Gemma froze, knowing her worst nightmare was now real.

"Where?" she asked, her voice dead as she looked up at her brother and her husband's best friend.

"Up in the high country," Isaac said, and his voice broke.

"It must have been a storm—a lightning strike," John added, looking down again. "A tree..." He could not finish.

"He must be brought home," Gemma said, a quiet resolution in her voice, "here to Hillingdon. It's where he belongs." It was a statement not to be questioned.

"He's on his way," Isaac said, almost whispering. "We've sent a dray up as far as we can, and he'll be here the day after tomorrow."

From that precise moment, Gemma put her grief on hold. She knew what had to be done. No time for falling in a heap now, time for grieving later. She set to with a cold, hard efficiency. A coffin had to be made. A site had to be selected. It had to be a special place, somewhere at Hillingdon, which had a special meaning for Ben. A funeral—a big funeral—had to be arranged. Refreshments, flowers, carriages. And clothing – yes, she would have to make some black weeds of course. And there wasn't much time.

She rose from her chair, put her hand to her hair and, looking down, was amazed to find her dress crumpled and wrinkled. She'd have to change that straight away! There was such a lot to be seen to.

"Thank you." she said crisply. "Please make sure that the tracker is well paid. If you will excuse me, there is much to be done." One hand drew the shawl around her, the other picked up her long skirts, and she walked inside, her back as straight as a ramrod.

One of the three men left outside turned slowly, sadly, and went on his way back to Elizabeth Farm. One got up from his knees and followed his mother inside. The third stood there, motionless, as memories of a long-ago time came flooding back, a time when his and his sister's mother died in the workhouse and their father never recovered from his grief. He could still see the swollen corpse, dragged through the Thames mud at the end of a grappling iron, and he and Gemma running away as fast as they could, lest they should be discovered wearing the workhouse clothes. Oh, yes! Gemma and he had already experienced death at close quarters. But there were *three* Gallimores this time, Isaac thought: Gemma, Sebastian and himself, all older and much wiser! They had survived before, and they would survive again, better and stronger.

❧ 21 ❧

Following Ben's interment beside the river and within sight of Hillingdon, Gemma gave way to her sorrow. She withdrew into a silent and uncommunicative world, spending day after day sitting, staring at the mound covering Ben's remains, and nothing or no-one could coax her out of it.

Sebastian and Isaac wrung their hands and despaired. Against his will, Isaac again remembered his father's unending grief when their mother died, and he feared for Gemma. Sebastian knew nothing of that and could not understand how his mother could change so—how could she turn from the warm loving mother he had always known into this pale, disinterested and devitalised shadow?

Gemma spent the rest of the summer, the autumn and all of the winter trying to come to terms with her pain. Often, she went down to the railings surrounding Ben's resting place and spoke aloud to him, begging him to come back, telling him how much she loved him. Sitting on the veranda above, she could see the headstone, and knew the words by heart:

Here lies Benjamin Ainsley
Died 1805, aged 49 years

Beloved husband of Gemma
Rest in Peace

As autumn came and went, she remembered Ben recalling his childhood in the old country and telling her about the autumn leaves falling thick on the ground, golden and red and brown, waiting for the wind to play with them, and how he loved to walk ankle-deep in them and hear them crackle and whisper. She had no wish to go back to the place of her beginnings. She belonged here at Hillingdon, here with Ben. Why wasn't he here with her?

The winter arrived, and the sky was leaden, the river grey and swollen. Great sheets of rain, driven almost horizontal by the blustering southerly winds, drenched and ran down Ben's headstone in rivulets, made the ground soft and the mound over his remains become flatter, and softer and less menacing. Sometimes, Gemma could not even see the grave through the rain-spattered windows, and once she thought she saw his blurred outline coming toward her from that direction. And still he did not come back.

Gemma slept little, ate less, and spoke not a word, and the inevitable happened. Her defences down, she caught a chill and developed pneumonia. Hollow-eyed, thin and weak, her breath ragged, she was carried to bed, helpless to protest. Voices edged with fright and worry washed over her. Isaac and Sebastian kept daily vigils and despaired.

Gemma gratefully allowed herself to sink into unconsciousness, and she began a descent from the top of a long, winding flight of steps. At the bottom, she blissfully entered a soft, warm, blue pool, and Ben spoke to her.

"Gemma, my darling, my love. Why do you weep so?" He wrapped his arms around her, held her close and safe. She could feel his heart beating and his lips in her hair.

"My dearest, you must not grieve for me. I'm at peace, and nothing can harm me. But it is not yet time for you to come to me. Sebastian and Isaac are waiting for you above. Go up into the light and do what you must. Hillingdon is waiting, and there is such a lot for you to do. When it is time, I will be waiting for you here in eternity. Now,

Gemma, take my hand, and step on the first stair and keep climbing back, one at a time. Gemma, my darling, my love, don't look back. I shall always be here. Climb, Gemma, climb. I shall wait for you, I love you."

Gemma let go of his hand, their fingers caressing each other as they slowly separated, and she climbed, climbed, up into the light, and opened her eyes.

From under heavy lids, she saw Sebastian and Isaac standing near and felt Sebastian hold her hand. Why were they looking so sad? There was nothing to be sad about. She gave a tiny smile, a deep sigh, and closed her eyes again. Everything was all right. She knew exactly what she was going to do. Ben had told her.

"The fever has passed," Dr Millward said softly, wearily, having sat by her side for many hours. "She must now have lots of rest. I will call again tomorrow." As he quietly slipped from the room, he shook his head and marvelled. He had felt sure that they had lost her! He told himself that she must be made of something very strong, and that when his time came, he hoped he could summon up some of the same.

"I HAVE DECIDED," Gemma announced, "that the brick and stone works are to be sold."

Sebastian and Isaac looked at her, then at each other, and then back to Gemma. Something had happened to her in the weeks and months following Ben's death. Buried deep within her was a strength which surprised Gemma herself. She had somehow emerged from her deep, dreadful grief a different person, someone with a purpose—and the nature of that purpose was soon to be revealed.

Isaac and Sebastian, with the help of the loyal Martha, had managed between them to maintain the quarries and the house, they could not go on indefinitely. Ben's will had left to Gemma all his worldly goods, and those included not only Hillingdon and the brick and stone works but also the remains of his shipping and other interests in England.

"I am going to consolidate!" Gemma said.

Neither Sebastian nor Isaac understood precisely what she meant.

"I have booked passage to England to settle the estate there," she went on. "During my absence, I expect the sale of the brick and stone works here to be completed. I have retained the services of Mr Julius Templer to attend to all legal matters for me here, and the accounts are with Jeb Abeles." Gemma baulked at saying "Ben's" or "my" accounts. She still could not bring herself to refer to them in any way but the general.

Isaac and Sebastian continued to stare.

Gemma looked from one to the other and smiled, "Well! I don't know what reaction I expected, but I wasn't expecting *no* reaction—that is—wait, I've confused myself..."

The tension broken, the three of them laughed, and Isaac was the first to speak.

"Gemma, of course, you must do exactly as you wish. It was a surprise, that's all!"

Sebastian asked, "Mama, how long will you be away?"

"About a year, I should think," Gemma answered gently. "The length of the voyage there and back won't leave much time in England to see to the affairs, but I shall be back as quickly as I'm able. I have sent my instructions ahead and matters are already being attended to. I have no wish to be away from either of you for a moment longer than necessary."

A bitter thought crept into her mind. *I've only ever loved five people in my life, and three of them are gone, Mama, Papa, and Ben, and I want to hold on to the other two for as long as I can.*

"When do you go?" Isaac asked.

"The ship leaves in about six weeks," she replied.

Seeing the forlorn look on her son's face, she took his hand and said, "Sebastian, you may not think it now, but the time will go quite quickly. You will have a lot to do while I'm away, and," she tucked his hand beneath her arm and took Isaac's hand under her other arm and said, "we shall be a lot busier when I come home."

She looked from one to the other, and her eyes sparkled. "We're going to be sheep breeders and farmers!"

❋

SOME SIX WEEKS LATER, Sebastian and Isaac waved goodbye to Gemma as the *Voyager* sailed out on the morning ebb tide. A fair wind blowing from the southwest pushed little puffs of cloud across the late summer sky, and the sails filled immediately, taking the ship majestically out of Port Jackson and into the Pacific Ocean.

By a fortuitous coincidence, Governor King was returning to England on the same ship, having handed over the office of governor to William Bligh. Governor King was accompanied by Mrs King. Gemma was, of course, known to Governor King, Ben having built the first government house and been responsible for several additions at the behest of successive governors. Very soon after they had left the harbour, Governor King made it his business to express again his sincerest regrets to Gemma at the death of her husband. He invited her to join him and his dear wife for their evening meals and on various other occasions that might arise during the voyage. By the time they reached England some four months later, the three had developed a firm friendship.

During her stay in England, Gemma managed to complete the legal matters of Ben's estate and left as a woman of considerable wealth. Thanks to Governor King's representations in the appropriate quarters, she was granted two thousand acres of prime land of her choosing in the Southern Highlands of New South Wales. This, she was told, was in recognition of Ben's contribution toward the establishment of the new colony, in both his buildings and his employment and housing of government labour.

While arranging her return journey to New South Wales, Gemma made it her business to stipulate that any ship on which she travelled would not be carrying convicts. She remembered the conditions in which she and her little son had travelled to the colony years before and thought that no being, good or bad, should have to endure such suffering. She could not sleep if she knew that below decks held such a cargo of human misery. She wanted to be able to wander the deck, feel the wind in her hair and the sun on her face, be free.

During the voyage, a gentleman of obvious means actively pursued her when he saw that she was travelling alone. She gave him not the slightest encouragement, and he finally gave up, shaking his head and asking himself how she could possibly resist him so easily.

Oh well, he'd just have to make do with his wife, who was mostly confined to their cabin, sea travel not agreeing with her in the least. But, dammit, a little diversion might have been very agreeable now and again, especially with such a good-looking woman as that young Mrs Ainsley. Don't know what her husband is up to, allowing her to travel such a long way on her own. By Jove! If she was his, he'd be keeping her busy, all right. Ah, life was cruel, was it not?

✻ 22 ✻

On Gemma's return from England with a grant of land, John Macarthur, along with Elizabeth, offered his help locating a suitable site and setting up the farm. He suggested the Highlands, where he had established Camden, as a starting point.

"I don't know whether to keep sheep or cattle," Gemma said, "but it does seem that I should do one or the other at first."

"Yes, indeed," John replied, "though I know nothing about dairy cows or cattle. For that matter, I'm still learning about sheep! I'm happy to help you in that direction, and for that reason, I suggest you start with sheep. Later on, if you want to breed cattle or have a dairy farm, you can annexe more land. And as you will see, there's plenty of it to be had! Go for the outskirts of settled land. It's less picked over, and fences don't have to be erected so soon. Then any adjacent unoccupied land can be used. Choose both high and low land—high for the wet season and low for times of drought."

Gemma was taking in as much advice as possible before she, Sebastian and Isaac set out to scour the countryside in the general direction of the Macarthur sheep station at Camden Park.

"Look for good timber, you'll need a great deal of that, and also plenty of water in a river, creeks, or, at the very least, good deep waterholes that look like they won't dry out in a long dry spell. And," the advice continued, "the very first thing you do after you've got your animals and men there is to plough about ten acres of good flat land and leave it for a couple of months while you are getting settled in. Then cross-plough it and sow most of it in wheat and a bit of maize for your horses and put in some potatoes and other vegetable seeds."

"You have convinced me, John," Gemma said, "and I am immensely grateful. Thank you. As you can imagine, I'm anxious to begin as soon as possible, but where *do* I start?"

"Well, once you've decided on your land, before you buy a single animal, you must, of course, set up buildings to house yourself and your help, and you must build hurdles to enclose the stock. You know, Gemma," John said, scratching his head, "I have to say, it's pretty unusual for a lone woman to embark on such an undertaking, and..."

"I can do it, John," Gemma interjected. "I know I'll have a lot to learn, but I can and will do it! I have Sebastian and Isaac to help me, and I cannot imagine anything that will stop us."

John laughed. "Oh, I'm sure you'll do it, all right." Suddenly, his face took on a serious, intense appearance. "Pity more people don't have your determination. You and Elizabeth are damned fine people, Gemma, and New South Wales is a better place for the likes of you. You are made of the right sort of stuff, and it's people like you who will make this country great." His eyes shone. "Pioneers! That's what you are, we all are."

Gemma could sense the almost fanatical drive which had made him so many enemies over the years.

He scowled, and his mood changed again. "Let us hope," he said darkly, conspiratorially, "that with our newest governor, things will be better for all of us! In the meantime, let's get down to business, shall we?"

Gemma and Elizabeth exchanged glances at this point, and Elizabeth looked quickly down. *Dear Elizabeth,* Gemma thought,. *She looks very uncomfortable. I wonder why?*

"HERE! Right here, on this very spot!" Gemma announced, excitedly and with finality. She was standing with Isaac and Sebastian atop a rise, against a backdrop of dark green wooded hills and valleys, their horses pulling and tugging at the reins as they nibbled and munched on the lush grass.

She shaded her eyes from the glaring mid-afternoon sun and lifted her face to scan the countryside around her. In front of her was an unending panorama of gently undulating hills, some tree-covered and some grassy with a lone tree here and there. To her right was the vast acreage of John and Elizabeth Macarthur's sheep farm at Camden Park and, beyond that, the pale blue haze of the mountains. To her left was a deep valley, on the other side of which was the great escarpment of the Illawarra where Ben had met his death.

One day in the future, when she felt she had mended enough, she resolved to go onto the escarpment and see for herself what it was that had drawn Ben so strongly. It must have a special magnetism, a malevolent force, which could draw a man away from his intended destination and all that he held dear. She hated it, was frightened of it. What if she went too close, and it drew her and destroyed her as it had destroyed Ben? She shuddered and made a conscious effort to bring herself back to where she stood, flanked by her son and her brother.

What would she call it, this two thousand acres which she could now claim as her own? John had called his large acreage 'Camden Park' to honour Lord Camden, the English bureaucrat who had convinced the British Government not to pursue Court Marshall proceedings against him following his illegal duel. Camden had also been instrumental in the granting of land to John and his acquisition of Merino rams from the King's flocks.

'Hillingdon'? No! There could only ever be one Hillingdon, just as there could only ever be one Ben. Hillingdon was Ben's, and only now hers, and she would not, could not, share the name.

Macarthur had named his original farm at Parramatta 'Elizabeth Farm' after his wife.

'Gemma Farm'? No, didn't have the right sound.

'Ainsley's Farm'? Maybe.

Think—who would own it and work it? She, her son and her

brother, that was who, and after she had gone, her son and his sons. All Gallimores.

That was it! Gallimore. Just Gallimore. She set her lips and nodded.

"This," she spread her arms to encompass the land before and around her, "is Gallimore." She drew a deep breath, held it, and let it out in a long, satisfied, purposeful sigh, smiling.

"And on this rise," she pointed a finger downward, "we build the house."

Her eyes were shining, and she was filled with such an excitement as she had never known before. Strange, she couldn't put a name to it, didn't know what it was. A feeling so deep, so overwhelming that tears came to her eyes. She could not speak for the lump in her throat, and Sebastian somehow understood. He grasped his mother's hand so tightly, her wedding ring bit into her finger, leaving a bruise that was visible for days afterwards, and Isaac, sensing the enchantment of the moment, turned away lest Gemma should see the moisture in his eyes.

For five full minutes, Gemma stood, silent, motionless, lost in her dreams, her eyes open, misty. She saw nothing, only Ben—smiling at her, nodding, agreeing with her: yes, this was the place.

Finally, the image of his face faded, the landscape slowly came back into focus, and Gemma brought herself back to the present. She smiled, contented, radiant. She was at peace with herself and the world. It had been a long, sad journey from the past. But now it was ended, and another journey was about to start. An exciting awakening, a quest—for what? Her heart pounded, and she had to make an effort to speak normally.

"Let us go and tell John," Gemma said, quietly, seriously.

The three mounted their horses and went down the rise, turning toward Camden Park in the distance. Sometimes, they rode in silence, each lost in thoughts of times past and to come. Sometimes, they cantered contentedly. And sometimes, they raced each other over open country, laughing, breathless, exhilarated, warm wind kissing them; horse hair, mane and tail flying; hooves pounding in dull thuds on green earth—then slowing, walking, winding in and out of trees and scrub, stopping now and then to drink at one of the creeks which criss-crossed the land, small, icy, pure, crystal-clear, babbling and

gurgling over smooth stones. Then they rode across Macarthur terri-
tory and up to the big house surrounded by scattered farm buildings.

At the sound of their arrival, John emerged from the farmhouse
and helped Gemma down, clasping her hand affectionately and
nodding cordially to Sebastian and Isaac.

He took one look at her flushed face and said, "I can see you've
decided on your land, Gemma! Come inside and tell me all about it."

At the end of her description, as a gift to Gemma and a mark of his
long standing friendship with Ben, John offered the loan of two of his
convict workmen to erect a couple of bark-slab huts on her chosen
land and suggested that she return to Hillingdon to begin getting
together the long list of supplies he had written out for her. Over the
next weeks, Gemma planned the movement of supplies and labour to
Gallimore and registered with the governor's office her ownership of
the land.

ON A FINE, sunny day in mid-September 1807, two six-bullock teams,
drawing fully laden drays, left Hillingdon on the first leg of an expected
four-day journey to Gallimore. Terrain that could be easily traversed in
a hard half-day's ride by a man on horseback, proved slow and difficult
for bullock teams. Large rocks and stones, deep, dark gullies and steep
inclines, sometimes flooded creeks, broken wagon wheels and
unhitched bullocks straying during the night made the journey
arduous.

Accompanying the train, under the ever-vigilant eye of its overseer,
Isaac, were two bullock drivers, a night watchman of the animals, a
cook-cum-hutkeeper, a storekeeper and sometime personal servant for
Isaac, a general handyman-labourer, two wood splitters and two
natives. These last two men proved their worth several times during
the trip, including their discovery and killing of a large black snake
that had curled itself up under the log on which several of the men sat
by the campfire, taking their evening meal of salt beef, damper and
large tin mugs of hot sweet tea. Aboriginal skill in reading the country
was invaluable, and, more than once, Isaac was rewarded with the sight

of startlingly white teeth surrounded by black shiny faces, when they smiled in recognition of his thanks.

When gathering together the supplies, Isaac had forbidden the inclusion of rum or any other form of alcohol, having seen the bloody fights its use had wrought during his days at the stone quarries. So far, he had no need for convict labour. The men accompanying him, with the exception of the two Aborigines, were either free settlers or ticket-of-leave men, all glad of the opportunity of earning a living in return for long days of hard labour.

Isaac knew it would not be too long before he had to employ government labour and with it would come, despite his instructions to the contrary, the heavy use of rum and the inevitable quarrelsome drunkenness. He already knew that the source of supply was the corrupt element in the New South Wales Corps and that wherever government labour was used, there would be rum—and plenty of it.

A sudden rainstorm turning their track into heavy mud at one stage caused quite a long delay while drays were hauled out and a leading bullock was slaughtered because of a broken leg. The band of eleven tired, dirty and bedraggled men arrived at Gallimore on the seventh day after their departure from Hillingdon. As Isaac and his weary company emerged from the trees behind the intended site for the new farmhouse, he was gratified to see two newly constructed bark-slab huts, ready and waiting, and he breathed a silent thank you to John Macarthur.

A note in John's handwriting nailed to the door informed Isaac that John was unable to greet him, as he had to go back to Elizabeth Farm, but hoped it would not be too long before they could meet.

Meantime, John had written, "If you have need of any assistance, my own overseer, a good and trusty man by the name of Tobias Bull, has been informed of your arrival and intentions, and he may expect a call from you."

In the next two days, a flurry of activity saw the unloading of the drays and the setting up of the quarters for seven of the men in one of the huts. The two Aborigines opted to erect their own bark *gunyah* at a small distance from the white men's huts and, on occasion, brought a snake or possum to be cooked on the white men's fire. The second hut, partitioned into two sections, housed Isaac, his servant-storekeeper and the stores.

The running of the camp soon settled into a weekly routine. The two splitters were kept busy chopping down and splitting green timbers into posts, palings and railings. The bullocks and drays carted and hauled timber and great logs to wherever they were needed. The nightwatchman set the animals free at the end of their long hard days and watched them overnight as they grazed, rounding up and harnessing them ready for the next day's labouring. The hutkeeper kept the fire burning, cooked the meals, hauled from the nearby creek a never-ending supply of water for drinking and cooking and generally kept the hut as neat and tidy as it was possible considering its occupants and their lifestyle. The handyman did everything that everybody else didn't.

In the larger portion of Isaac's hut, the storekeeper slept, guarding the stores until proper wooden walls could be constructed and a door made so that the room could be locked. For the moment, the only thieving done was that by marauding possums and, one night, by a large goanna, which ended up as the evening meal for the two blacks, who got tired of the white men's salt beef.

$$\text{\quad 23 \quad}$$

"I just don't know where it's all going to end!" wailed Elizabeth Macarthur, a worried frown creasing her once-youthful face. At thirty-nine years of age, younger than both Gemma and Emmaline, she looked far older. The birth of her seventh child some months earlier and the years of working outdoors at Elizabeth Farm, especially at Camden overseeing her husband's sheep breeding during his lengthy absences, had exacted a hefty toll. Lined leathery skin, broken nails on calloused hands and a worn-out body went unnoticed by John, but not by her two friends.

Gemma managed to persuade Elizabeth to come on a rare visit to Hillingdon, and Emmaline Abeles had joined them.

"Are the older boys helping you at Camden?" asked Gemma gently.

"Of course," she replied, her bottom lip trembling slightly. "Poor Richard, in his nineteen years I think he has put in a lifetime of labour —and the others are following suit. But no, that's not it. It's *John!*"

By the year 1807, Elizabeth had shared so much with Gemma, and lately Emmaline, she was not afraid to speak frankly. "He's getting worse! There seems no stopping him. There's some sort of a devil that keeps driving him on and on and on. Not content with Camden Park, he's bought into a whaling ship, he's trading in all sorts of things and he quarrels and has quarrelled with everyone who crosses his path. Even now, he's right in the middle of another dispute with the governor—something to do with a ship... I think. I've lost track!"

She paused and smiled crookedly at her wide-eyed friends. "Well, you did ask!"

"Yes, and I did want to know!" Gemma said earnestly. "We haven't seen you in ages. I admit I've been very busy with Gallimore. Thank heavens for Isaac, though. He's invaluable out there. And Sebastian is virtually running Hillingdon.

"That's if Sophie leaves him alone!" Emmaline said, rueful. "Poor Sebastian! She idolises him."

"And he loves having her around," Gemma laughed. "They get on so well. It's lovely to see them together."

Just as she finished speaking, the muffled sound of a galloping horse pulling up outside and the ringing of the doorbell interrupted their talk, and a maid came to the door. "Beggin' your pardon, ma'am, but there is a messenger to see Mrs Macarthur urgently."

"Thank you," Gemma said. "Will you please ask him to wait?" Elizabeth's hand had flown to her mouth, and her eyes were wide and pleading.

Gemma and Emmaline stood quickly, each offering her a hand to help her to her feet.

Elizabeth stood, closed her eyes, breathed out and said softly, "What now?" It never even crossed her mind that it might be one of her children who was in trouble.

At her request, her friends accompanied her to the front hall, where a uniformed man of the New South Wales Corps stood, shako in hand and looking as if he had ridden quite a distance in a great hurry.

"Mrs Macarthur, ma'am," he said, looking at her and nodding politely to the other two, "I've come to tell you that the governor has arrested your husband. He wishes to see you."

"The governor wishes to see me?" asked Elizabeth, half in a dream.

"No, ma'am, your husband."

"Oh," Elizabeth replied lamely. Gathering her wits about her, she said, "Please tell him that I shall be along shortly."

"Ma'am" the soldier replied, saluted her, turned on his heel and left.

The three women went back into the sitting room, and Elizabeth almost fell into an armchair, her face ashen, while Gemma and Emmaline fussed over her.

"Would you like one of us to accompany you?" asked Gemma.

"Oh, no, thank you," Elizabeth stammered. "But I'll go straight away. I'm so sorry to bring such a lovely visit to a sudden halt." Recovering somewhat, she continued, "It was so nice to see you Gemma, and you too Emmaline. We must all visit again very soon. I'll let you know what's happened."

After they had farewelled her, Gemma and Emmaline resumed their afternoon tea, and Sophie came into the room, followed by Sebastian.

"Is everything all right, Mama?" asked Sophie. We saw a Corps man ride up in a hurry, then Mrs Macarthur left so suddenly!"

Gemma replied, "She had to go and see Mr Macarthur about something urgent."

Sensing one of Sophie's interminable question interludes coming up and trying to head it off, Emmaline asked, "And what have you two been up to?"

"Oh," Sophie said casually, "I've just been proposing to Sebastian."

"Sophie!" her mother exploded, aghast. She looked at Sebastian, who had a huge grin spread over his face.

"Apologise at once!" she admonished her wayward, incorrigible daughter.

"And what did Sebastian say?" Gemma asked, her eyes smiling.

"Oh!" Sophie said in a disgusted tone. "He said to ask him again when I was twenty-one and one day, for Heaven's sake!" She sighed loudly. "But that's years away."

Emmaline sat with her head bowed, her hand to her brow and her eyes closed, almost too shocked to continue.

"Gemma," she said, looking up, "and Sebastian, I do apologise. I am yet again embarrassed by my daughter's bad manners. And Sophie, you're far too forward for a young lady. I don't know what your father will say!"

She turned to Gemma and continued, "I think I'd better take her home before she humiliates us all any further. Come, Sophie, get your bonnet on and thank Mrs Ainsley for a lovely day."

Dutifully, Sophie came toward Gemma, gave her a kiss, and thanked her. Then she turned to Sebastian and said, "I'll be counting the days, you know!" She blew him a kiss.

Poor Emmaline was so outraged, she grabbed her daughter's arm and yanked it so forcefully that Sophie's long red curls flicked across her shoulder and bounced up and down her back.

Gemma and Sebastian waved their farewell, and as Emmaline's gig turned a corner and disappeared from view, Gemma turned to her son, linked her arm in his and looked up at him with an unspoken question in her eyes.

"I love her, Mamma," Sebastian said, "and I intend to ask her to marry me."

"But why twenty-one and a day?" Gemma asked.

"Because I shall ask her on her twenty-first birthday, which is one day before she asks me again. I want to get in first!"

Gemma hugged her son fiercely. "I couldn't be happier, Sebastian. She's a lovely girl, and you're so right for each other. But why wait so long?"

"Well," he answered slowly, "I think Richard Macarthur might be going to ask for her hand sooner or later, and I know she's very fond of him. I want to be sure."

"Oh, Sebastian, you're so serious. Too serious sometimes, I think—and a little blind, as well," Gemma said. "She's been in love with you since before she was old enough to know what the word meant!"

"I hope you're right, Mamma, but I'm prepared to wait. I'll only be twenty-eight, you know."

"Well, my dear, don't end up like Uncle Isaac. He's well over forty now, you know, and I'm sure will never be wed."

AS IT HAPPENED, Richard was far too engrossed in his father's affairs to be interested in romance. After John's arrest, the governor refused to grant him bail, and he was kept in prison. The Corps Commander,

Major George Johnston, then arrested Governor Bligh, appointed himself Lieutenant Governor, released John and made him Colonial Secretary.

Elizabeth was horrified when she found out that her husband had been arrested by Bligh for importing stills for the illegal manufacture of rum.

"How could you?" she had asked, appalled. "For years, you've been ranting about the use of rum by the Corps, and all this time you've been as bad. You're as corrupt as they are." She removed to a separate bedroom from that day and a strained relationship was maintained between them.

In the course of the next year, while Bligh was in prison, the British Government sent to the colony a new governor, one Lachlan McQuarie, a Scottish soldier. Johnstone was recalled to England for a trial. John Macarthur decided to follow and speak for him in Court. In the event, Johnstone was dismissed from the army, and the Court ordered that since it could not try a civilian of New South Wales, John be tried for treason in the criminal court of New South Wales.

To avoid arrest on his return to the colony, John wrote to Elizabeth that he would be remaining in England for some time. He sent instructions about the sheep breeding at Camden, exhorting her to be especially careful with the Merino flock.

"It is extremely valuable," he wrote, "and must be your first priority. It should not be too difficult for you. You have our sons to help you, together with a labour force of some thirty-odd convicts. I shall send you further information as I learn the latest developments in the production of fine wool and what the English market requires. I will also be touring the European wine-making countries to learn what I can in that direction."

Reading his missive, Elizabeth could only shake her head. It looked as if the whole sheep breeding programme now depended upon her, but she felt she could cope. But wine-making?

It would be nine long hard lonely years before John returned to Camden.

❄

DURING THOSE YEARS, Gemma completed the construction of Gallimore and its surrounding farm buildings. Sheds for shearing, wool-washing, sorting, pressing and baling were built, sheep yards erected and stocked, crops planted and more and more convict labour hired. Gallimore thrived.

Gemma had purchased a further five hundred sheep from Camden Park, and Elizabeth drove along to oversee the delivery, but mainly as an excuse to catch up with her two oldest friends. Gemma had invited Emmaline Abeles and Sophie along, and they all looked forward to a three-day visit to Gallimore.

While Isaac took in the animals, which were brought over by a drover and Richard Macarthur, the three women chatted together excitedly, bringing each other up to date. Gemma explained how she divided her time between Hillingdon and Gallimore, and the running of Gallimore was left to Isaac.

As soon as Sophie heard that Richard had accompanied his mother, she wandered outside to catch sight of him. Through a rising, billowing red dust, she could see the three horsemen: Isaac, Richard and the drover, shepherding and counting the sheep into the hurdled yard. Sophie stood at a short distance away, swatting the flies as they settled on her in dozens and squinting in the bright sunlight. As the last animal was shut into the yard and the drover instructed to join some of Gallimore's men in one of the huts, Richard and Isaac came over to Sophie. Dismounting, and wiping sweat and dust from their faces with the backs of their hands, both men smiled and greeted her.

"Hello, Mr Gallimore." She smiled, "And Richard, it's nice to see you again."

"I'm off for a drink of water," Isaac said. "I'll see you in the house later."

Slightly crinkling her nose as she surveyed Richard's dusty, sweat-soaked and smelly clothing, Sophie said, "I've never seen you look like this before. You're always dressed for visiting when we meet."

"Yes, well, these are my 'visiting while working' clothes," Richard replied, slightly put out. "I'm a sheep farmer, not a bank clerk, you know!"

"Do you really, truly enjoy it, Richard?" asked Sophie, ignoring the unintentional reference to her background.

"Yes, I do actually," Richard answered slowly, as if thinking about it for the first time. He'd never been asked before, and it took him a little by surprise. "I never thought I would, but yes, I do. There is something exciting about all the wide-open space that I truly enjoy."

"What about all the biting and slithering things? And the dust and the dirt and the flies? And the *smell?*" she queried.

"That's all part of it," he said. "I don't even notice 'em." A sudden idea entered his head. "Why don't you let me show you what I mean? Ride back over with us the day after tomorrow and stay a day or two!"

"Ooh, I'd really like that! I'll ask Mamma."

"That's done, then," Richard announced. "I'll get cleaned up and join you in the house in a while."

Every time he set eyes on Sophie, Richard's heart turned over. At sixteen, she was a beauty. Those flaming red curls, those brilliant blue eyes, they were enough to make any man weak at the knees. And that bubbling personality, with an undercurrent of something untamed and wild... Who could resist her?

He envied Sebastian, who saw her a lot more often than he could, then felt instantly ashamed. He was pretty well promised to another!

He turned, stripped to the waist and leant over a trough in the shade of a hut, splashing the almost-cool water over his head and shoulders and washed off as much of the dust as he was able. He donned a clean shirt from his saddle bag, slapped his trousers hard to get rid of more dust, raked his fingers through wet hair and went around the side of the house, where he found everyone settled in the shade of the wide veranda, a jug of cool lemonade on a table nearby.

"Mamma said I may stay, Richard!" Sophie said excitedly.

Richard grinned and extended a hand to Emmaline. "Thank you, Mrs Abeles. We shall take great care of her, won't we, Mamma?"

"Of course," Elizabeth murmured.

He then shook Gemma's hand. "All in prime condition and counted."

"I presume you mean the sheep?" Gemma smiled crookedly.

He reddened. "Yes, the sheep—of course!"

"Elizabeth," Gemma said, "Isaac and I would be at a complete loss without your help. You have been a godsend! John was quite right when he suggested we look in this area for land, to be close to Camden when we undertook something as foreign to us as a sheep farm. Isaac's taken to it like a duck to water."

Looking fondly at her brother, she said, "I think you'd be lost without it now, wouldn't you Isaac?"

"I would," he answered. "I find it very exciting—demanding but very satisfying, quite uplifting, in fact."

"See!" Richard put in, looking meaningfully at Sophie. "That's just what I was saying to you."

"I think I'm a very fortunate person to have you all," Gemma smiled. "Shall we go and have some dinner? I thought you might like beef, as a change from lamb and mutton. I brought some over from Hillingdon."

THE MEAL ENDED, oil lamps were lit, and Isaac suggested a game of cards.

"But there are six of us," Gemma protested.

Richard seized the chance and said "Sophie and I will sit and chat —if that's all right with you, Sophie?"

"Oh yes! Let's go out on the veranda," she agreed. "I just love sitting out in the dark, under the stars."

Outside, the air was warm and still, tiny insects flitted around, moths fluttered and banged mindlessly against the window, lit from behind, and the bleat of a restless sheep rose up now and again.

Overhead, a sky so black it seemed endless was the backdrop for countless thousands of stars. Sophie was standing with her back to the house, her hands on the railing which ran the length of the veranda from both sides of the wide entrance.

She sighed deeply. "Do you know what a sky like this reminds me of, Richard?" She tilted her head and looked skyward.

Standing a little to one side behind her, Richard saw the red gold of her long curls in the soft glow of the oil lamps and again felt a sudden stirring of desire. The feeling had come upon him so fast, he was bewildered. This wasn't the way it was meant to be, he thought, and struggled to bring himself back to reality.

"Richard?" Sophie repeated, turning around. In his turmoil, he had not replied.

"Sorry!" He gathered his wits about him as best he could. "No —what?"

"I imagine I'm in a great big barn, all closed in, the doors shut, and it's all black and silent and lonely inside. In the tin roof there are hundreds and thousands of nail holes, and I can see the daylight twinkling through them. And I'm not alone or lonely anymore. It looks just like the sky and the stars out there, and I feel as if I'm a part of it."

She stopped, suddenly, her eyes shining. "Does that sound silly?"

"Er," Richard said, collecting himself, "I've just never thought of it that way, I suppose. It's just the sky and the stars to me. Represents the end of another day's work, time to eat and sleep and get up and start all over again." He was aware that he sounded flat, uninteresting, banal, and wondered how he could make up for it.

"Richard," Sophie almost whispered, "You know, you are really missing something, thinking like that!" She hesitated. "It's the sky, it's heaven, it's the stars, it's the magic, the unknown. What's up there? Oh, I wish I could fly up there and find all the answers. Richard, did you never wonder when you used to look through your telescope? Don't you still look through it and wonder what's up there?"

Glad of the opportunity to answer a straight question, Richard laughed. "I think your head's up there in the clouds, that's what I think!" Then, soberly, he added. "I suppose I did once, but I haven't looked at it for years. Been a bit too busy!"

Sophie suddenly felt selfish, and she laid a hand on his arm. "Oh, Richard. I'm so sorry! Of course you have! How thoughtless of me. Sebastian always says that my imagination runs away with me sometimes."

A short silence, an awkward pause, and they both started to speak at the same time.

Another pause.

"Ladies first!" Richard said, bowing slightly, and the tension was broken.

Did she have to mention Sebastian? he wondered.

"Oh," Sophie said brightly, "I was just going to say that in the next couple of days, while I'm here, I'll try and convince you to see beyond the land, beyond what you now see."

He gently took hold of one of her hands. He wanted to tell her that in the depths of her eyes, he could see all that he ever wanted to see. But he simply said, "We shall see!" He was amazed at his own self-control.

Sophie, quite content to let her hand rest in his, smiled up at him. She loved him as a friend, sincerely and unreservedly.

"Where shall we go tomorrow? Could we go for a long ride, a good gallop, over the hills and far away? I'd love that. Could we, Richard, please?"

He looked down at her, patted her hand lightly, and again said, "We shall see! Come on, let's see who's winning." He tucked her hand in the crook of his arm, and together, as old friends, they went back into the lamplight.

SADDLED mounts awaited them next day after lunch, and the two friends chatted amiably as the horses rode side by side away from Elizabeth Farm.

Sophie, in her usual fashion, bubbled brightly on all sorts of topics, and to Richard's slight annoyance, Sebastian's name cropped up repeatedly.

After some twenty minutes, the beginnings of open country spread out before them. Sophie turned to Richard, eyes shining brightly, mischievously.

"Let's go!" she shouted, raising her hands holding the reins. She leaned forward, tucked her elbows in and, none too gently, dug her heels into her mount's sides. "Yaarhh!" She took off, curls flying and straw hat slipping off her head, held at her back by the blue ribbons around her neck.

A good rain the previous week had softened the turf, and eight hooves made a dull, urgent pounding as the two riders thudded at full-out gallop toward a distant stand of trees. Sophie, on a daintier ladies' mount, was easily overtaken by Richard, who was astride a larger faster steed.

Reaching some trees lining a small creek, he dismounted, freed his horse to drink and leaned against a tree. When Sophie drew up, he helped her down and asked, smiling naughtily, "Where've you been? You were so long, I decided you must've turned back and gone home!"

Sophie slapped his arm lightly with the folded reins in her hand. "Oh Richard! That was glorious!"

He took the reins from her hand, twisted them into a knot and let the animal go for a well-deserved drink.

"Come and sit down," he invited, holding out his hand to take hers, and indicating a large old log lying at the edge of the water. Sophie accepted the invitation and gratefully, gracefully sank down in the shade of the magnificent old tree. He sat beside her, both of them relishing the rest from the strenuous ride and lost in thoughts of their own.

Richard leaned back against the gnarled trunk of the tree, locked his fingers together behind his head, closed his eyes and let his thoughts wander where they might. On the one hand, he was exhilarated, and, on the other, asked himself what he was doing there at all. He was surprised at the depth of his emotion the night before, and yet even more surprised that those feelings had not resurfaced in the morning.

Hard working, decent and honourable, he took his role at Elizabeth Farm seriously and knew well that his mother relied heavily on him. Moreover, it was more or less understood that he would one day wed a certain young lady from a neighbouring farm. And yet here he was, on a frivolous ride to nowhere with Sophie. He felt an odd discomfort about it all, and, leaning forward, placed his elbows on his knees and set his sights vacantly on the smooth white pebbles in the shallow depths at the edge of the water at his feet.

His reverie was interrupted by Sophie, who suddenly asked, "Why, on such a lovely day, would anyone be unhappy, Richard?"

He slowly brought his mind around to the present and turned to look at her, surprised to see a forlorn expression on her face.

"What about? Why?" he asked. "Surely you didn't think to beat me, did you?"

"No, silly, of course not! It's Sebastian." This was said with a deep sigh of resignation, and Richard was bewildered.

"Sebastian!" he shot. 'Why? What's he done?"

"Oh! Richard, it's not what he's done, it's what he *hasn't* done!"

Richard had no idea what to say next, and while he was thinking about it, she continued, "I've asked him to marry me, and he just won't give me a straight answer!"

"You've what?" he almost shouted, incredulous. "Sophie!"

Before he could gather any more words together, Sophie continued forlornly, "I love him, don't you see? It's hopeless! How can I wait for so long?"

Richard looked at her quizzically, still struggling for words.

"You're engaged, aren't you, Richard? Did you wait for a long time before you asked for her hand?" A sudden idea struck Sophie, and she grasped Richard's arm, pleading, "Could you talk to him, Richard? Oh, but maybe he doesn't even want me! Maybe he's found someone and already asked her! Maybe..."

"Sophie, Sophie!" Richard said, placing his hand over hers. "I'm sorry, but I can't do that. Men don't speak of such things to each other."

Seizing a wild thought to comfort her, he said, "And maybe if he hasn't given you a direct answer, don't you think that may mean something? If he didn't want you, wouldn't he just say no?"

Not to be placated so easily, Sophie put her head on her knees and cried none too softly.

Richard was at a loss. The oldest member of a family of boys, he was totally unused to such feminine displays. He felt desperately sorry for her to see her in such torment and wanted to put his arms around her to comfort her, but a sense of propriety prevented him. He looked away, thinking it wrong to see her distress, then back again because that didn't feel right, either. He reached for her hand, squeezed it wordlessly between his two to try and transfer some comfort to her.

Then, thinking to let her recover with some degree of privacy, he rose quietly to his feet and moved along the edge of the creek and stood with his back to her.

Sophie stayed where she was, with her head bent over her knees and gave in to the luxury of her misery. Aware that Richard had moved away, she let her tears flow unabated. She was glad to be able to let her thoughts and feelings pour out freely; they had been imprisoned so long.

After some little while, she raised her head and, unladylike, dried her eyes on the cuff of her sleeve and got slowly to her feet.

Hearing this, Richard moved to her. She looked up at him, eyes red-rimmed, nose shining, then sniffed and offered him a watery smile.

"Sorry, Richard!"

Richard stood awkwardly and, still trying to offer her some comfort, said lamely, "I'm sure it'll all turn out well in the end."

His sentiment hung in the air as she sniffed again.

"I hope so. Thank you. And I really am sorry... I managed to spoil a lovely day together, didn't I? Do you think we could go back now?"

Glad of some sort of release, Richard said, "Of course!" He moved to bring the horses around.

Mounted again, and in sombre mood, they cantered most of the way back to Elizabeth Farm, the silence spread between them punctuated by occasional sniffs from Sophie. On the way, Richard resolved to announce his engagement as soon as possible, and Sophie resolved to ask Sebastian again to marry her.

BEFORE SHE HAD a chance to do so, Richard's wedding date was announced.

Sebastian was overjoyed and confided in his mother that he now no longer felt the need to wait to ask Sophie for her hand. Gemma breathed a sigh of relief, knowing her son would now be complete and happy, delighted even when her thoughts wandered back to Ben and how she had loved him.

Sebastian's feelings for Sophie were so intense he found it painful to be in her company. He could no more stop loving her than he could stop the sun from shining. Whenever she was near, he wanted badly to seize her, spin her around and kiss her roughly, madly, until she was breathless and limp.

Not long after Sebastian had spoken to his mother, an ecstatic Sophie threw herself into his strong arms so forcefully she nearly knocked him over.

"Steady on there, Sophie! I've only asked you to marry me!" he laughed, holding her at arm's length and looking deep into her eyes.

Gathering her to him, he was surprised to see tears coursing down her cheeks, and he kissed them tenderly away. Looking down at the top of her shining red curls cradled against his chest, he marvelled that he had waited for so long and ever doubted that she might not be his.

Sebastian knew that there was now nothing he couldn't do, nowhere in the world he couldn't go—no mountain too high, no valley too deep, no ocean too wide. At last, he had his Sophie, and his heart overflowed with joy.

The happiness of Sebastian and Sophie's first year of marriage was blunted by the sudden and premature death of her father, Jeb. Sophie missed him badly, and she was brought even closer to her mother by the anticipated arrival of a first grandchild early in the following year.

By the end of 1816, after a protracted and painful labour, Sophie had been delivered stillborn twin boys. The great dividing mountains of Australia had been crossed and a road built. Bennelong, the tragic aboriginal taken to England by Governor John Hunter nineteen years before, had returned and been killed in a tribal fight. Bushrangers roamed the roads, thieving and murdering. Boxing and horse-racing had been introduced to the colony. New South Wales had its first coinage, in the form of the holey dollar. Shorthorn cattle had been brought into the Illawarra area, and great stands of ancient cedar trees had been found and felled for timber. There were established industries in whaling, sealing, sandalwood and pork. And Napoleon had been defeated at Waterloo.

Convicted felons were still arriving by the shipload, but the colony was no longer purely penal. As word got around abroad, the ships also brought from far and wide many hopeful souls, enticed by the promise of free land and great wealth, mostly good and some bad, some with money and status and some with neither. These arrivals were the free settlers. And the colony was not yet thirty years old.

By the end of the second year of her marriage to Sebastian, Sophie was again pregnant and gave birth to Hannah, followed over the next five years by Alice, Charity and Nicholas. Tobias and Grace came along in 1827 and 1830, and finally Edward was born in 1833, when Sophie was forty-one and Sebastian forty-eight.

❧ 24 ❧

Septimus Arion Cavanagh was a bachelor, set in his ways and in his law practice at a good address in Dublin. The only son of a classical scholar, he was a good Catholic man, an upstanding citizen—good-looking and very well-to-do, although somewhat prosaic.

Until the day fifteen-year-old Anna Allison had tearfully employed him to administer her widowed mother's estate, he had never had much time or thought for the fair sex. His new young client was left alone in the world, and, as the sole beneficiary, had been left a sizeable fortune by her mother, who had appointed Septimus the executor of her estate. Devastated from watching helplessly as her beloved mother faded away from the world, Anna leant heavily on Septimus for advice.

Very soon, his forty-one-year old heart dissolved, and his association with his young client became less than professional. So much so that, by the time she was almost sixteen and to his utter surprise, Septimus found that he was head over heels in love. Anna returned his feelings and, to the consternation of them both, she discovered that she was pregnant. To avoid a local scandal, Septimus swiftly married Anna, and, before her condition became obvious, they set sail for the other side of the world. The year was 1835 and Anna gave birth to their first child, William, before the end of the voyage. A year later, Noah was born, followed ten months later by James. Then, at twenty years of age, Anna had the daughter she had always wanted, Eliza.

Life in Sydney was pleasant for the Cavanagh family. Anna's fortune, coupled with the past wealth of Septimus and his ongoing legal practice, afforded them a relatively luxurious lifestyle. A large house was built for the family, and they were quickly accepted into the so-called "exclusives" of the colony.

It was not long before the Cavanaghs and their four children and the seven children of Sophie and Sebastian Gallimore became fast friends and frequent visitors in each other's homes. Their close association was cut short, however, by Sebastian announcing that he and Sophie, who were still mourning the loss of their son Tobias, were removing to Gallimore and that Hillingdon was to be torn down.

Anna and Septimus, whilst sorry to see their closest friends in the neighbourhood move away and promising to exchange visits regularly, immersed themselves in everyday life—Anna in raising their young children and Septimus in his practice. He was busier than he had ever been in his life. Before his arrival in the colony, a great deal of the country had been opened up. Years before, Blacktown, Bankstown, Liverpool, Penrith and Fairfield had been settled and named. Van Diemen's Land had been settled by Britain in an attempt to prevent the French from claiming the island, the Great Divide had been crossed, the rich country of southern Queensland and the Brisbane River had been discovered, and free settlers had established themselves in Western Australia, South Australia and Victoria, as had squatters everywhere.

Legislative councils were being set up here and there, and the ensuing legal matters had to be attended to, convict transportation to the colony was being halted due to public outcry, and corruption and crime were rampant. Berrima Jail was full to overflowing with the worst dregs of society, control of Sydney was in the hands of three police magistrates, and there were many campaigns for legal reform.

John Macarthur, earlier declared insane, had died in 1834, leaving the widow Elizabeth and her children in charge of some two hundred and forty thousand acres of land at Camden Park. Sheep like theirs were introduced into New Zealand. Francis Greenway, convicted forger turned architect, was designing churches, schools and public buildings, the great Conrad Martens was making a name for himself painting scenery such as had never been seen in Europe, and John and Elizabeth Gould were writing about and painting birds such as had never before imagined.

SEPTIMUS WAS THOUGHTFUL, even a little excited. The often dull routine of his legal life was to be relieved. He was required to attend, in an official capacity, the colony's first trial by jury, to be held at Berrima Court House. He would be away for several days and took leave of Anna and the children.

"Anna, my dear," he said. "I hope to be back by the end of a week, but one never knows how long these matters will take." He didn't relish the thought of leaving them for so long and still marvelled that he had found love and contentment at such a late age.

With his beard freshly close trimmed and a cravat elegantly tied at his throat, he cut quite a handsome figure, and Anna, looking at him, wondered at her occasional feelings of discontent. His carriage was waiting at the ready, and he waved goodbye as he mounted the steps, closed himself in, and began to look at his papers.

The journey to the southern highlands took up most of the day. He had stopped at the Wollongong Hotel for a hot lunch of mutton, onion sauce and roast potatoes, and a jug of refreshing Cascade ale brought up from the brewery in Tasmania. He put up at Berrima for the night and was quite comfortably prepared when, next day at precisely midday, Mr Justice Burton opened the proceedings with the usual ceremonies.

The Berrima trial heralded the beginning of the end of Septimus's life as he had known and enjoyed it. So much happened over the next several years that he grew old before he noticed it. His bright legal mind was in great demand as the various colonies throughout the land expanded and were granted the right to self-govern.

Four long journeys to England and back made matters worse. His children were growing up before his eyes, yet he was missing it, and, even worse, Anna was changing, growing distant. And when, at the end of long days and even longer journeys between and around the colonies, he came home tired and sometimes irritable, Anna was disinterested in his advances and more often than not rejected them.

Anna, for her part, grew weary of having no attention paid to her or the children for long periods and succumbed to the overtures of one Adam Tennant, a barrister who occasionally worked with Septimus and was much closer to her age. They conducted a brief clandestine affair which lasted until her fifth child was conceived.

Septimus, ignorant of the circumstances and thinking that life was on the improve, eagerly awaited the birth and was desolate when Anna miscarried at three and a half months. He convinced himself that the fault was his: at sixty-six years of age, he was certainly too old to sire a healthy child. From that day forward, to Anna's relief, all relations between them ceased.

From then on, Anna applied herself exclusively to the upbringing and care of her four children, but especially that of her daughter, never again having another dalliance.

IT WORRIED Sophie that she had difficulty in stopping the bleeding whenever her two older boys cut or scraped themselves.

In particular, Tobias seemed to be the more delicate. At the age of eight, as young boys will, he climbed a tree and stood on a branch not strong enough to take his weight. Both it and he plummeted to the ground, the boy striking his head on a stone. Despite Sophie's successful attempts to stem the relatively small flow of blood, he slipped into a coma, and a distraught Sophie held him to her as he passed away two days later.

On a wet, miserable, dark July day, Tobias was interred in the grounds of Hillingdon, not too far away from Ben. The burial was witnessed by Toby's two wide-eyed brothers, one-year-old Edward and ten-year-old Nicholas, who missed his younger brother dreadfully.

Sophie, supported by Sebastian on one side and Gemma on the

other, stood bowed, grief suffusing her face, dry vacant eyes staring unseeing as the soil covered the small coffin.

Gemma, who had driven over from Gallimore, held herself erect, tears coursing down her face, quietly remembering a day twenty-nine years earlier on the same turf, and found it very difficult to come to terms with the fact that a young grandson had gone so early. The doctor had told Sebastian and Sophie that it was most likely an inherited problem which had caused Tobias's intracranial bleeding. This was the catalyst for many sleepless nights and hours of soul-searching and blame-laying. Grief and disbelief alternated with unanswered questions, regrets and guilt. Had it not been for the presence of her surviving children, Sophie would have sunk into a bottomless depression, but for their sake, dull and disinterested, she carried on.

Both Emmaline and Gemma, privately and individually, looked inward for a possible answer. Each thought they were personally to blame for the inherited condition. Emmaline remembered the child she had borne before Sophie's birth and chose to forget her fall through the rotten stairs in her first home with Jeb all those years ago in London. She thought also of Sophie's stillborn twin boys and her surviving children.

But why was it only the boys who seem to be affected? An anxious meeting with Dr Caldicutt did nothing to persuade her that the fault was not hers. All he could offer was that he thought he had read somewhere that there was some obscure disease affecting only the males of a family and most likely passed on from the mother, But without recourse to further study and consultation back in London, he was unable to submit any further explanation or solace.

Rather than add to her daughter's misery, Emmaline kept her thoughts to herself, just as Gemma reserved hers. What about Sebastian, the son she held so dear, and who was the product of her rape some forty-nine years previously? Though she would never forget the face of her attacker, she knew nothing about him. Did he carry the dreadful disease which was now affecting Sebastian's sons? Two stillborne sons, poor little Toby now dead, and ten-year old Nicholas having to be so careful not to hurt himself. What was happening?

Thank goodness baby Edward, at least so far, showed no evidence of anything untoward, and she hoped that Sophie, at almost forty-two years had no thought of having any more children.

Sebastian comforted his four daughters as best he could, clung tightly to his two remaining sons and mourned the loss of not only his three young sons but of his bubbly, effervescent Sophie. She was now bent and bowed, her once glorious red-golden hair was dull and greying. He saw the pain in her eyes and wept for her and didn't know what to do to make things better for her and them all. Resolving to seek advice from his mother, he rode over to Gallimore.

Gemma didn't need her son to say a word. She felt his anguish and, embracing him lovingly, took his arm and led him into the shade of a large old pepper tree at the side of the house. The soft buzz of a summer afternoon surrounded them, and Gemma spoke earnestly, quietly, choosing her words carefully.

"Sebastian, I'm not getting any younger..."

Sebastian had not expected these words and caught his mother's hand, looking at her with concern. Death and sorrow had not been far from him of late, and a sudden fear gripped him. Seeing this, Gemma put her other hand over his and drew in her breath.

"Would it be too much to ask of you to come over to Gallimore and help me—us—Isaac and me? Isaac is also tired these days, though he won't admit it. He's seventy now, you know, and refuses to let up."

Sebastian's thoughts were racing. How could he leave Sophie and the children alone? But how could he not help his mother? What would happen at Hillingdon?

Before he could put any of these concerns into words, Gemma continued, "Gallimore will be yours one day, Sebastian, and it needs you. It needs a younger body and mind to take it to where it must go."

Surprised at the suddenness of all this, Sebastian spoke as if in a daze. "What will happen to Hillingdon?"

Gemma's voice grew even more grave, more serious. "We will knock it down. We don't need it anymore. The house itself, I mean. I couldn't bear to part with the land." She knew he understood.

Sebastian took his mother in his arms and held her very close. For a few moments the silence between them spoke volumes. Eventually, Sebastian's body relaxed, and he gently put Gemma away from him.

Taking her hands in his, he looked into her eyes and whispered, "Mama..." He could hardly speak through the dryness in his mouth and the lump in his throat. "Every time Sophie looks out the window..."

"I know, I know," Gemma replied softly. "That's why we must keep the land." Her voice grew strong. "There are three Gallimores next to Ben, and they must all be allowed to rest in peace and quiet where we may forever go and visit them. For my part, I have a great need to go there and sit quietly, just now and then, to remember, to be sad, to smile, to weep, to dream." Her voice trailed off, but she gathered it together again, her eyes and mouth smiling a little. "What do you think?"

"I think, Mama," he said slowly, thoughtfully. "I think that would be the best thing for all of us."

Nothing further needed to be said, planned, promised or deliberated over.

Sebastian silently rose from his seat, raised Gemma to her feet, held her hands to his lips, gently released them and made his way back to Hillingdon.

Hillingdon, the great house where Ben and Gemma had lived and loved for such a short time so long ago, was razed to the ground, and the land on the slope down to the river was fenced off. The graves of Ben Ainsley and the three little Gallimore children, all with their white marble headstones and intricate iron railings, were joined in 1842 by Nicholas, who, at the age of eighteen, did not survive a fall from his horse, and, only seven years later, by another—Gemma Gallimore Ainsley. And there they remain to this day.

It is said that a soft sigh can be heard there every once in a while. Nobody can tell from whence it comes or whether it is sad or serene, languid or lazy. Maybe it's the river, maybe it's the wind, or maybe it's only in the imagination. But it is definitely a sigh. I've heard it myself.

❧ 25 ☙

Anna held her wriggling daughter close as her three sons marched off, long fishing sticks in hand. Giving in to the pleadings of the boys, she had fashioned three fishing rods from sticks, string and bent pins and gave them a chunk of bread each for bait. This would keep them busy for some hours, and she could have Lizzie all to herself.

The boys would be in one or other of the many rivulets which flowed into a larger stream, dubbed the Tank because of the several tanks earlier built into the sides to store fresh water for the young colony. The Tank itself was now so filthy and polluted, it was deemed unusable as drinking water and only used for the enjoyment of the local cattle and pigs. A new clean supply had been found in the swamps close by, and a bore was being built to drain water towards the town. While this was under construction, the streams and swampland surrounding the area afforded little boys magical places in which to swim, fish, play Bobbies and Robbers, and generally have all the adventures their imaginations could conjure up.

"Shush! You're too little to go fishing. Besides," Anna chided, cajoling, smiling and stroking Lizzie's fair hair, "you're a young lady, Eliza Cavanagh, and young ladies don't do such things!"

Lizzie's mouth drooped, and Anna knew she was about to cry.

"I know!" she said quickly. "I'll go and make some paste, and we can draw some pictures. We'll colour them and cut them out, and you can paste them into your scrapbook. How does that sound?"

This was one of Lizzie's favourite pastimes, and she ceased her twisting and turning. Gathering together paper and chalks for her daughter and settling her down to commence her drawing, Anna mixed flour and water together in a pot, and set it on the stove to boil and thicken into paste.

Absent-mindedly stirring the mixture lest it become too lumpy to use, Anna looked over at Lizzie. What a dear little soul! What an easy child to rear! A pleasure! Always happy to accept whatever is offered. Lizzie would cope with whatever life will bring.

What a contrast between her and the boys, but maybe that was just the difference between boys and girls. Not for the first time, she thanked Heaven for sending her a daughter. She always felt very close to Lizzie and thought that they would be friends always. Not like with the boys.

A sudden rush of guilt overcame Anna. Maybe she just didn't like boys. They were certainly different. Always dirty, hungry and demanding something. She mused that, one day, they would be gone, and she and Lizzie would be able to enjoy each other's company and do all the things that mothers and daughters did together.

Septimus was no company. He was away often, and even when he was at home, he had neither time nor energy to give to his family. Good thing there were three boys to amuse each other so that she could give most of her attention to Lizzie. Not that she was a bad mother to the boys, she consoled herself. She looked after their essential needs, and the rest took care of itself. And, anyway, girls needed their mothers a great deal more than boys did. Anna felt better after she rationalised her feelings toward her boys, dismissed the whole issue from her mind and got down to the much more pleasurable business of helping Lizzie.

WILLIAM, at almost eight years of age, was a strong sturdy boy, quite capable of taking care of himself—and, under protest, his two younger brothers, the last of whom he regarded as nothing more than a nuisance and a useless baby. He was being progressively asked to look out for six-year-old Noah and five-year-old James, and he was increasingly resentful.

James, in an often-futile attempt to keep on the right side of his big brother, either kept out of his way or, failing that, tried to do his bidding exactly.

Noah was torn between the two. He was a little frightened of his older brother, who sometimes didn't hesitate to hand out a painful cuff on the side of the head if he thought he could get away with it. But at the same time, he felt sorry for and was protective towards little James.

Out of sight of their mother, William roughly prodded James ahead of him with the end of his fishing stick.

"If you have to come, get a move on will you!" he spat. "It'll all be your fault if someone's taken our spot." He prodded again, and James did his best to keep a good distance between himself and the end of the stick.

A foul temper had descended upon William. Why he had to be bothered with two younger brothers was quite beyond him. By way of asserting his dominance, he wordlessly handed his fishing rod and the bait to Noah to carry.

Noah knew he would never have been allowed to do something as exciting as fishing on his own and so silently, though resentfully, accepted the burden. It was a small price to pay for the privilege of accompanying his big brother.

William, now without his prod, grew impatient at having to wait for the others to walk fast enough. He overtook them and, for good measure, gave the littlest fellow a hearty shove on the way past.

Striding ahead and exhorting the other two to hurry up lest the day be wasted, William came upon a narrow log fallen most of the way across a shallow but fast-flowing stream. Jumping on, he easily ran the length of it and took a running leap to breach the space between the end of the log and the opposite bank.

Noah, next in line but hampered by the three rods, took two

wobbly steps backward before attempting to run forward to bridge the gap. He fell short and landed up to his ankles in the muddy water near the bank. In an attempt to keep his balance, he dropped the rods and watched as they began to rapidly float off downstream.

"Imbecile!" William shouted. "Quickly, get them. Get them!" Noah floundered and splashed his way along the stream and managed to capture two. It was his great good fortune that he'd earlier given the bread to James to carry. There'd have been the devil to pay if it got wet and useless!

William now turned his attention to young James. Standing with hands on hips, he shouted, "Are you coming or not?"

Having witnessed what had happened to Noah and always intimidated by William, poor James stood frozen to the spot at the other side of the creek.

Noah, meanwhile, had clambered out of the creek with the two rods, the larger of which William grabbed.

"Where's the bread?" he demanded. "You haven't lost that as well, have you?"

"James has it in that bag," Noah replied, pointing.

"Are you going to stand there all day? Come on!" William glared at the frightened five-year old.

Now too terrified to even begin to cross the log, James stayed where he was.

William threw his rod to the ground, easily jumped the gap back onto the log, bounded across it and so roughly grabbed the bag of bait that the little fellow was thrown off balance.

James stayed where he was and began to cry. Now exasperated beyond reason, William ran back across the log, shouting, "Stay there, cowardly custard! Stay there until we get back! Come on, Noah! Leave him there. He's only a baby anyhow."

Noah hesitated. He didn't want any harm to come to James, but he didn't want any harm to come to himself, either, for not obeying his older brother.

James sat where he was for quite some time, crying hard and watching his two brothers disappear around a bend and in and out of the trees. He really did want to go fishing with them, but that was a huge gap to jump, and he didn't want to fall in the water like Noah. Mamma would be cross with Noah for getting his boots all wet and muddy.

After a while, he stopped crying, wiped his eyes and nose on his shirt-tail and considered his position. The thought of staying where he sat was not an option. He would be lonely and frightened. He really had no idea of his exact location. He had just followed the others. And what if they came back another way and left him there all night? There'd be horrible creatures lurking everywhere in the dark, just waiting to come and get him! All things considered, he thought that the best thing would be to try and catch up with the others, and he slowly, tentatively started to cross the log.

SOME WAY further down the creek, a totally unproductive fishing foray catapulted William into an even worse mood. All the bread had gone, and in a fit of pique, he had smashed his rod against a tree, broken it into three pieces, and hurled them into the water.

"Come on, Noah!" he snorted. "Let's go home. This is a waste of time."

Without waiting for a reply, and in any case not interested in one, he turned on his heel and started the trek back to the fallen log.

Noah had to almost run to keep up with him, but he also managed to stay well clear just in case. When they reached the spot, William jumped across the gap, sprinted the length of the log and started on his way home, giving no thought whatever to James.

"We're back, James!" called Noah. "Where are you?"

When there was no answer, he yelled after William, who was already far ahead.

"William! I can't find James!"

Not much interested, William replied, "He's probably gone on home." He was hungry and didn't want to waste time looking for a pest of a young brother.

Noah hesitated, casting his eyes around for any sign of James. Was he hiding? He often did that.

He called again. No sign. William must be right.

"WHERE'S JAMES?" asked Anna when the two boys arrived, noting with distaste Noah's muddied legs and wet boots.

"We thought he had come home," William replied, quick to spread any blame that might be forthcoming.

"I've told you before, William," Anna scolded, "Look after your little brothers. You're the oldest and must learn the responsibility of that. Please, both of you, go back and look for him."

William's mind raced ahead. Back at the fallen log with still no sign of James, he knew he had to protect himself.

"You know, Noah," he started, his voice very serious, "if we can't find James, it'll be your fault."

He waited for his words to sink in, and before Noah could protest, he continued.

"You were the last to see him. If you remember, I went on ahead, so I didn't see him."

Wide-eyed, terrified, Noah listened.

William noted with satisfaction the effect of his words. Conspiratorially, he went on, softening his voice. "It's better we stick together. I won't tell anybody you were the last to see James. We'll say he told us he didn't want to come and he was going home. And you must always stick to that. Do you understand?"

Noah's mouth was dry, and he tried hard to swallow.

"This will be our secret. Do you understand, Noah?" William repeated, his voice now stern.

Thoroughly alarmed, Noah nodded, glum, silent, petrified.

"Spit on your hand and swear it!" demanded William.

The swearing accomplished, a cursory glance around satisfied William that James was nowhere to be found.

"Well, he's not here, is he?" William stated rather than asked, a note of finality in his tone. He started back home. The whole business was rather a nuisance, really.

Speechless with fright, Noah followed.

A subsequent search by the menfolk of the neighbourhood failed to find James. It was the construction gang working on the drainage system nearer the town who fished from the water the drowned body of the little boy some twenty-four hours later.

ANNA AND SEPTIMUS marvelled at how well William coped with the loss, but their grief was compounded by its apparent effect on Noah.

"He's hardly uttered a word since..." Anna said, her voice trailing off. She could not bring herself to complete the sentence.

She was guilt-ridden herself, remembering her thoughts about her sons on the very last day little James was alive. God was punishing her, she knew, but why Noah as well?

Septimus could find no words of comfort for his wife. As the days went by, he withdrew into his legal world, glad of an escape, and Anna and he grew even further apart.

William seemed to have completely recovered, Anna mused, and Eliza was too young to comprehend it, but Noah was different. He seemed to be caught in a sad, lonely place of his own.

She could not know that he was imprisoned in a world of fear and guilt. He was tormented day and night. Was it really his fault? Yes, it was! He could have, should have, stayed with James to look after him. The more he thought about it all, the more he believed in his responsibility for the loss, and the more he remembered the secret William had made him swear to.

PART 3

❦ 26 ❦

Sebastian took the spectacles from his nose and laid them gently on the latest issue of *The Sydney Gazette*, spread across his knee. The faint aroma of whale blubber which served to light the newspaper office reached him as he leaned back in the chair and closed his eyes. He inhaled deeply, held the breath and let it slowly escape. The item on the "Society" page of the newspaper read:

> *The marriage took place last Saturday at St James Cathedral between Eliza, only daughter of Mr And Mrs Septimus Cavanagh, and Edward, son of Mr Sebastian and the late Mrs Sophie Gallimore. Among the many distinguished guests was the new Governor of New South Wales, Sir John Young. The happy couple will reside at the Gallimore property outside Camden.*

It was a short paragraph—too short really, Sebastian reflected. And it was awful to see the words "the late" in front of Sophie's name. Tears stung his eyes. If only Sophie could have been by his side. His beloved Sophie, who never came to terms with the pain of losing their sons, her grief so corrosive it had almost eaten away her sanity. She had been gone a year now, but it seemed like yesterday. He looked down again at the newspaper and thought how odd it was, improper even, that a whole lifetime could be condensed into a few words of print on a page.

Sebastian re-read the item and thought bitterly that it could have said "only son" as well. Of five sons born, only Edward survived, and of his four daughters, only Hannah and Grace had attended the wedding.

Alice, now forty-two years of age, was living in England with her husband and their offspring, grandchildren neither he nor Sophie had ever seen.

Charity had point blank refused to attend the nuptials. She had long ago fallen out with Edward, left home, refused the generous allowance offered by Sebastian, and remained unmarried. She lived a frugal life, eking out an existence as a companion to an elderly genteel spinster lady. She had attended Sophie's funeral but kept very much on the periphery, opting to speak to neither Sebastian nor Edward. Her deep-seated antagonism toward her brother always simmered just below the surface and she had no wish to meet him face to face. She had never forgiven him for being instrumental in separating her from the love of her life, a man she cared for deeply and with whom she was making plans for the rest of their lives together. Charity regarded her young brother as a manipulative, grasping ne'er-do-well, and nothing he could do would ever change her opinion.

THOUGH THEY DID NOT KNOW the precise reason, Sebastian and Sophie were long aware of the icy relationship developing between the two siblings. Their love for the two was the same as for the other children, but even then, they had some reservations, though never shared, about Edward's character. As their only remaining son, he had been spoilt and protected throughout his childhood, especially by Sophie, who always feared that he would succumb to the dreaded blood disease which had taken away his brothers. As he progressed through his early years it appeared that he had escaped it, and he was allowed ever more freedom.

He took full advantage of this, and his arrogance got him on the wrong side of most of his peers. The Gallimore wealth provided him with just about everything he desired and, in the early days of his adolescence, bought him out of many scrapes.

By the time Edward was twenty-one, Sebastian had had enough. Yet again, he'd come to his son's rescue and saved him from a certain spell at Her Majesty's pleasure. Edward was advised that unless he changed his ways, he would no longer be supported.

"Furthermore," Sebastian said, "you may take it that your inheritance of Gallimore is no longer a foregone conclusion. I've changed my will in favour of your sisters. I'll of course ensure you're not left penniless, but you won't have control of the estate. I've taken this step with great reluctance, I can assure you, but your behaviour is causing your mother and me much anguish." Sebastian relaxed his voice a little and he looked Edward square in the eye. "Nothing would give me greater pleasure, Edward, than to reverse my decision at some time in the future. It's up to you entirely. You won't think so now, my boy, but one day, you'll see that this is for the best."

I'll be damned if I will, Edward thought. He'd started the meeting in a sullen mood, and as his father's speech progressed, his reaction swung between disbelief and belligerence.

He scowled at his father in silence, knowing he had no defence, let out an impatient snort and swaggered from the room. Hands dug deep in his pockets, eyes straight ahead, teeth clenched together and lips set in a line, he turned the corner at the end of the passageway, into the hall and toward the outer door. Though it was open, he kicked it viciously on his way past.

Out on the gravel terrace, he continued down the slope, and across to the stables. Slinging a bridle on his favourite mare and without wasting time saddling up, he threw himself up onto her back, dug his heels hard into her sides and aimed at the railings surrounding the yard.

Mare and man sailed over, and he bent down along her neck.

"Yaaarh!"

She knew what was expected and where they were going; she'd done it many times before. As fast as she could, she raced down the hill away from Gallimore and across open country, never stopping until she reached the trees down by Three Mile Creek. In and out of the trees along the banks of the water she went, forest and bush getting thicker now, until she reached the place.

It was always a surprise when this place appeared so suddenly. Nobody else in the world knew it was there. It belonged to Edward. It was his and his alone, ever since he found it as a child when they had first come to live with Grandma Gemma at Gallimore.

He jumped off the mare's back, tossed the reins across her neck and threw himself down in the long grass of the little clearing. Sometimes, if he came to this place wanting to be alone, he would lie on his back and would lose himself in the clouds drifting overhead. Other times, if he was angry, he would roll over and twist and tear at the grass with feverish fingers. This is where he always came, to be alone, to hide, to scheme, or if he was frightened or angry.

And he was angry now. Very angry. And frightened. Angry at his father for catching up with him, and frightened because, in the deepest, darkest corners of his mind, he could see Gallimore slipping away from him. After all, his father wouldn't live forever, and he had plans, big plans, for what the wealth of Gallimore could do for him. And sheep and cattle had nothing to do with any of them.

Well, he'd just have to change his ideas for the moment. Things hadn't turned out the way he was expecting. He fleetingly thought of killing the old man and just as quickly discarded the notion. Ridiculous. Stupid. He'd end up in jail, and the girls would get Gallimore anyway.

He already had a few projects rumbling around in his mind, projects that would show everyone—everyone—what he was made of. Pity though! He was on the brink of asking his father to loosen the purse strings for a sizeable loan to fund a never-fail investment he'd come across. Dammit, that well was dried up, at least for the present.

He had some weighing up to do. Think of all the alternatives. He could walk away completely—no—Gallimore was meant to be his, and he was going to make damned sure it was. He could marry some-one—someone with money of course. He knew plenty of well-to-do families. Put that option aside for the moment.

He could go to the goldfields out west. That's where fortunes were being made almost daily, by all accounts. Might strike it rich. But then again, might not. Too much like hard work, anyway. Discard that one.

Could get on a ship and disappear somewhere. England? America? No. Too many unknowns.

No, he was going to stay right where he was. Not let Gallimore out of his sight and reach.

Ideas, ideas. He was always good at ideas. Why couldn't he come up with a good one this time?

A wry thought struck him: he was in a pickle now precisely because one of his ideas hadn't worked. He'd better come up with a good one this time. His anger was beginning to subside a little, and he was thinking more clearly.

Responsibility and respectability. That was all the old man ever thought of. Well, if push came to shove, he could—no, *would*—grovel. He would be interested and involved in the running of Gallimore. That would take care of the responsibility thing. The respectability, he supposed, would come along with it, but how to fast-track it? He came back to the marriage idea. But to whom?

In order to satisfy the old man, it would have to be somebody *respectable*. Someone highly regarded socially and, even more important as far as he himself was concerned, someone with financial substance. A great deal of financial substance, he smiled to himself.

Dorothea Arkwright had plenty of money but was *too* damned respectable. Hoity-toity. A man had to have some enjoyment in life.

Daisy Faulding—very respectable but absolutely no money, and he was going to need plenty if Gallimore didn't work out.

Mary Skillings—lots of substance, but hardly respectable. He half grinned to himself, remembering when he had, on more than one occasion, tasted the delights she freely offered to anyone who asked.

Frances Burge—moneyed, very respectable and very, very pretty. But far too young.

What about Eliza Cavanagh? Now there was a distinct possibility. Respectable Irish family, and extremely wealthy. Father a lawyer. That might come in handy. Brother a banker. That too might be useful one day. Apparently, there was another brother somewhere. Somewhere down in the southern goldfields or something.

Lizzie Cavanagh... That was it! She was the obvious choice. He'd met her a few times. Not what you'd call beautiful—pleasant, really. Yes, she'd do. She fitted the bill perfectly. He thought she was about eighteen or nineteen years old. Always seemed to be with her mother. He'd never met the father. Had met her brother William a few times here and there, and he seemed a pleasant enough fellow, although quiet.

Edward decided that the best course of action would be to charm Anna first, before starting on Lizzie. And if it was old world charm that was required, he knew exactly how to go about it. His mother had seen to that. It was all a bit of a boring nuisance, really. But if that's what it was going to take, that's what he was going to do. The effort would be worthwhile.

He felt a lot better now. It was all going to be so easy. He would have the respectability so important to his father, but more to the point, he'd have money to burn—at least, when the old man died, and that couldn't be too far off. He was nearly seventy-five already. And—another pleasant thought—he'd still be able to have Mary Skillings whenever he wanted. And with no strings attached.

What was it the old man had said? "You've more often than not shown very little wisdom in the choices you've made, Edward, and it's time you began living with the consequences."

Well, he was going to start living, all right, living like he'd never lived before. He'd be a man of wealth and leisure. He was so impressed with his afternoon's planning, he allowed himself a crooked smile, closed his eyes and went into a deep satisfying sleep.

ELIZA WAS SO flattered by Edward's courtship, she fell head over heels in love with him. She knew she was not the most beautiful creature on earth, so it was a pleasant surprise when Edward came calling. And he was such a gentleman, especially to her mama. Anna relished the attention as much as Lizzie did, and Edward was welcomed with open arms. Both women wouldn't hear a word against him, shrugged off the odd rumour that was whispered about his character and couldn't possibly see how any man who was so close to his father and who worked so hard alongside him, could be found wanting. They took him as they found him, and they found him not lacking in any way.

It was not long before Edward approached Septimus to ask for his only daughter's hand in marriage. Septimus was mildly surprised at the speed of events but could see nothing that would cause him to withhold his consent. In fact, it might not be half bad to have a decent young man in the family, a son-in-law.

His own sons didn't give him much pleasure. He wistfully wondered what sort of a man little James would have been, had he not drowned all those years ago. He hadn't seen or heard from Noah for several years—he could be dead for all they knew—and William and he didn't have much in common.

William remained unmarried and still lived with Anna and himself, but he kept out of their way as much as he could. A very private person —almost secretive, Septimus often thought. At least the boy had made something of himself with a good position at the Bank of New South Wales and from all accounts was set for greater things. That much could be said for him.

And Lizzie had done extremely well for herself, too, about to marry into the Gallimore family.

Lizzie was beside herself with happiness, and she and Anna set to with great gusto to make plans for the nuptials.

Sebastian's wedding gift to his son and new daughter-in-law was a handsome sum of money, a house on Gallimore land for them to live in, and, most importantly, the reversal of his last will and testament, leaving the bulk of his estate, after making provision for his daughters, to his "sole surviving son, Edward, and his heirs and assigns."

Five years had passed since the drowning of his younger brother, James, yet Noah relived the tragedy almost daily. He could not escape

the idea that it was he who could have prevented the death, and William saw to it that he remained in his mental prison. Noah withdrew from the family, speaking only when spoken to. Apart from thinking that he was a quiet child, his parents thought little of it.

Septimus knew there was enough capital to ensure that his family would want for nothing, and, barring some unforeseen catastrophe, there always would be. Otherwise, he had very little interest in their welfare. He and Anna had become distant since the loss of their youngest son, and, in any case, he was kept ever busier with the formation and introduction of new laws in the developing colony.

When a reluctant Noah, at the age of fifteen years, was employed by him, Septimus allowed himself an unaccustomed smile of satisfaction when he added "& Son" to the firm of Cavanagh Lawyers, George Street, Sydney Town.

Anna, never much interested in boys and their habits, which she perceived as dirty and disgusting, thought only of the delights of bringing up her only daughter. Eliza was the apple of her eye, and she relished every moment spent with her. Apart from ensuring that her sons were provided with their basic needs, Anna was quite content to let them go their own ways.

This made it very easy for William to maintain his hold on Noah. Noah was now convinced that he not only could have prevented James' death but also caused it. Though he was tortured by guilt, every once in a while, some tiny inner voice told him that something was not quite right.

By the time he was seventeen, he concluded that, unless he was prepared to submit forever to the relentless hold his brother had over him, his only salvation would be to get away. Right away. Far, far away from the place, his family, and most of all, William.

But where would he go? He had the glimmer of an idea but was not quite sure how to go about it. Though he spoke little, he listened well, and tales of gold strikes and great fortunes being made in Victoria held his attention. But how would he get there, and what would he do when he did? He'd have to bide his time and wait till the right opportunity arrived, as it surely must. It *had* to! A small prick of his conscience reminded him that he had a family, but he rationalised his plan by telling himself that he had nothing to do with his sister, little affection for his parents, and none whatever for his brother. He had more of an odd sort of respect for William, really—respect borne of fear, he realised, and his anger surfaced.

He was surprised at the depth of his own emotions. He wasn't an angry person, yet here he was, feeling the worst kind of anger. What a turmoil! He had to get away. He hated being cooped up inside in his father's offices every day, he loathed the tedious tasks of a legal clerical worker, and he despised himself for allowing his life to be in the mess it was.

A surprising development a few months into 1851 provided a possible answer.

"I'll be travelling to Melbourne within the next fortnight," Septimus announced to his family one evening, "and Noah will accompany me."

Four pairs of eyes looked up suddenly from the evening meal.

Anna smiled inwardly. That would be very pleasant; Lizzie and she would go visiting.

William's immediate thought was that it would be very good not to have to put up with his father's insufferable stuffiness but felt slightly uncomfortable that Noah would be going. He didn't quite know why but the idea of his brother being so close to their father was not entirely to his liking.

Eliza looked toward her mother for guidance on how to react, found nothing and so ignored the news.

Noah was completely dumbfounded. Being a very minor clerk in the law office, he could not remember a time, ever, when he had been included in any of his father's plans.

He felt a sudden excitement. Maybe this was what he had been waiting for! Septimus had not asked him whether he would like to go. It was a statement. He was going, and there would be no argument. Noah looked at his father, an unspoken question in his eyes.

Septimus, unaccustomed to sharing what was in his mind, deliberately put a silver forkful of meat and gravy into his mouth and chewed it slowly.

Swallowing and wiping his mouth on a crisp damask napkin, he said, "There's trouble brewing in the goldfields down in the Victorian colony."

Before he could continue even if had he thought to, William jumped in. "What sort of trouble?"

"Nothing of interest to anyone in a bank," Septimus replied dismissively. Pointedly turning his eyes away from William, he sighed heavily and reflected that perhaps he should have educated his family in the ways of the world outside the cosy existence he had provided for them all.

"When gold is found," he went on, "and men of all nationalities and characters converge in their thousands like bees around a honeypot, there's bound to be conflict. Crime is rife down there, there's robbery on and off the diggings, the new jail's already overflowing and the constabulary hasn't yet got any legal clout. Half of them have gone off to the diggings themselves! There have been one or two small finds of gold in New South Wales. Before the situation here becomes out of hand, it would be a good idea to have some laws in place."

That was quite a long speech at the dinner table for Septimus, and he immediately looked down and continued his meal.

The discussion was at an end. Anna had said nothing at all, keeping her thoughts to herself. William and his question had been dismissed, and Lizzie was not interested.

"Thank you, Father," Noah said, "I shall look forward to that."

Septimus looked sharply at his son. "Don't get the idea that it will be anything but a lot of hard work, Noah," he growled, his expression full of its usual severity. "You will be by my side at all times. It will be good experience for you, and you should learn some valuable lessons.

He lowered his head and looked over the top of gold rimmed spectacles down the length of the long dining table, at nobody in particular but everyone in general. "Now, I have a great deal of thinking to do. Please do me the courtesy of allowing me to continue my meal in silence." So saying, he resumed his eating, the quiet only interrupted by the subdued clatter of expensive silver cutlery on the finest English china.

Noah could hardly conceal his excitement. He had no idea how he was going to accomplish his severance from his family, but he knew that if he didn't take the opportunity just handed to him, he may never get another one. He resolved that, until their departure for the southern colony, he would do everything in his power to keep on the right side of his father, giving him no reason to change his mind.

THREE WEEKS LATER, on a cool, wet September morning, a bad tempered Septimus and an excited Noah set off on the Great South Road. Apart from a cool handshake and a half-hearted wish for the success of their journey after dinner the evening before, William made sure that he was required to be elsewhere at the actual time of the departure, which had been delayed a few days due to stormy weather. Anna offered a cool cheek to her husband and son, and any interest Lizzie might have had was purloined by her new pet puppy, which ran around madly, yapping at the excitement of all the activity.

In the days following their arrival in Melbourne, father and son were kept very busy. The previous month, the British Parliament had turned the colony from a penal settlement into a self-governing community by passing the Australian Colonies Government Act. The society as a whole was now in a state of turmoil.

Septimus growled, more to himself than to the assembly of lawyers he had gathered together in an office behind the Melbourne Courthouse.

"This is why I advised against the act! I knew there'd be trouble. What do they expect, when a society containing a great number of people who came here as convicts less than fifty years ago want to rule themselves? Disaster, that's what. And disaster is what we've got!"

Noah listened with mounting feelings to his father railing about the failure of the people in the new colony, who had left their British beliefs and institutions behind. It was clear that there was not, never would be, nor should there ever be, as far as Noah could see, a ruling class like that in the home country. Men would be judged on their abilities rather than on their positions in society.

He could suffer it no longer. Completely forgetting his position, he asked, "But why should not all men be equal?"

There was a stunned silence, and eight whiskered faces turned toward him. Eight pairs of eyes and eight mouths opened in shocked surprise as they tried to grasp the enormity of what had just happened. Surely, they had not heard aright?

Noah continued to look straight at his father, waiting for a reply.

Septimus was beside himself, and his face boiled into a suffused red. He was the most senior advocate in the room, and it was unthinkable that his junior clerk, never mind that the junior was his own son, should stand there and speak at all, let alone question any statement made in the room.

He struggled to compose himself as best he could, glowering at his son. "You are privileged to be here to listen and to learn. It is not your role to venture any sort of opinion. You are forthwith dismissed from these proceedings." He waved his hand in curt dismissal.

Noah went back to the lodgings less than happy. He had for days been close by his father's side, listening, watching and thinking. He didn't at all like what he was hearing. His father complained that the British way of doing things was not being recognised, the old traditions not being adhered to. Noah couldn't think why they should be.

SEPTIMUS SUMMONED his son at the hotel later that evening. When Noah arrived, he was almost frothing at the mouth.

"How dare you?" His furious face was within a hand's width of Noah's. He waited a second or two and repeated the question, this time with more force. "How *dare* you? You have caused me great offence, and your ideas and your company are no longer tolerated here. Get out of my sight!" He pointed a shaking finger toward the nearest door.

Noah had been prepared to defend himself but now realised that nothing he could say would be of any use. He stood his ground for a few seconds, looking directly at his father, then turned and left the room.

Back at his lodgings, he collected the few clothes he had and the almost thirty shillings he had saved and walked out into the road. He had a strange sense that this moment was the end and the beginning of something and was surprised that he felt a suppressed excitement.

Did "Get out of my sight!" mean forever? Or just now? Noah had no idea and didn't waste time wondering. He had no thought of what he was going to do, only knew that he had to put as much distance as he could between his father and himself.

Earlier that year, the first railway had been opened, joining the town of Melbourne with the Port of Melbourne, and Noah decided to board the train when it left the next morning. He walked to the departure sheds, selected a quiet corner, put his bag down and sat on it, leaned against the timbered wall and closed his eyes. He drifted in and out of sleep. Stiff, cold, hungry and cramped, he came to early in the fog of the morning, purchased a mug of steaming tea and a thick slice of bread and dripping from a makeshift stall outside the shed, and made his way to the train.

Among his travelling companions, separated into two classed carriages, were several sailors returning to their ship, most trying to get over the effects of an inebriated night in the town's brothels; a man, his wife, two children and luggage going to join the same ship to Cape Town; one or two settlers removing to Adelaide Town to try their luck there; a fat, well-dressed gentleman with a gold ring on the little finger of each hand; a sad-looking elderly couple dressed all in black; and a boy carrying a brightly coloured parrot in a cage.

Noah amused himself watching the comings and goings, and at one point idly wondered if his father had even noticed his absence, then quickly realised that he cared not a jot. He was interrupted by the ticket collector demanding one shilling and two pence.

At the port, two vessels were at dockside, one with sails up and ready to leave, and one just arrived. Hoping for a passage to somewhere, anywhere, he gathered up his bag and ran, arriving just in time to see the last ropes let go and the sails softly billowing as the *Scarborough* gently left the quayside for the open sea.

The second vessel was one of the new steamers, just arrived from America and not due out for another week or so. Noah had never seen anything like it and stood wide-eyed, dreaming. It was disgorging its passengers and cargo, and he could feel the air of excitement and expectancy among the men, women and children of all nationalities, as they stepped onto land for the first time in many days. There were Chinese, Spanish, Americans, Italians and Canadians, all fresh from the Californian goldfields, unlucky there and hoping to make their fortunes at the deposits found at Bendigo and Ballarat. Noah was swept along with the tide.

A line of drays loaded with picks, shovels, buckets and billies, rolls of canvas and blankets, sieves, pannikins, and tea, salt and flour was drawn up a little distance from the dockside. It was kept clear of the barrels, kegs, crates, ropes, trunks and household chattels being unloaded from the holds. The wagoners were soon negotiating to sell their wares and take fortune-hunters out to the goldfields.

Seeing them being readily filled with people and starting off, Noah hastily strode down the line to one still available.

"How much to take me?" he asked.

"Where are you going?"

"Wherever you are!" grinned Noah, with little thought as to where that might be.

"One pound three shillings to you," replied the wagon master. If the young fellow didn't care, why should he?

By the time Noah realised that he was on the way to the goldfields, owned only what he stood up in, plus a few extra clothes and exactly twenty-five shillings and ten pence in cash, he was sat atop some bags of flour, dried mutton, corn and tea, mail, books and newspapers, and the small tin trunks and rolls of his fellow travellers' belongings, including four chickens and a cockerel in a cage. He was surrounded by two families and four single men, all piled onto the dray and a linked wagon pulled by eight draught horses yoked together.

The wagoner, a smile on his leathery face, cracked his rawhide whip, and the wheels jerked and jolted into life as the horses strained to get their load rolling.

Day after endless day of bumping and wobbling, squeaking and grinding—along a track well rutted by the wheels of hundreds of wagons gone before; in and out of forests; over small bridges roughly made with tree trunks and cut slabs of timber; along creeks, some muddy, some crystal clear; up and over hills; and in interminable heat, flies and dust—allowed Noah plenty of time to think. He had no regrets at all about his decision. He had a very keen view about what was right and what was wrong in his world, and what he was doing now felt right.

During the first couple of days, as the distance in front of him became ever more of the same as that behind, he listened to the other travellers talking. Two of the single men had come directly from the Californian diggings with stories of crime, back-breaking work and dashed hopes. The two families and their children sat in a group, as they listened and hoped for a golden future and promised to stick together come what may. One of the other two unattached men was a shady looking character, sullen and dishevelled and apparently quite content to be left alone. The other was a twenty-something-year-old, and he and Noah naturally gravitated toward each other. Animated talk between the two soon took over from the awkward discourse of strangers.

At night when they camped, the two wandered a little away from the fire and exchanged hopes and dreams.

"Well, Noah, if what we hear from the two men from California is true, there'll be a need for us at Ballarat," mused Beau Edwards. "You being a lawyer's clerk and me being a policeman—well, an ex-policeman."

"Mmm," said Noah, "I'd hoped to leave my former life well behind. I don't think I'm cut out to be a lawyer."

"A goldminer, then? An extremely rich goldminer?" ventured Beau, laughing.

"We shall see!" Noah said, "Who knows what awaits us at the end of this journey."

"Well, I'm not afraid of hard work! And I fully intend to make my fortune in a short time and go back to Melbourne Town and ask a certain very pretty and charming young lady for her hand in marriage." Beau lapsed into silence.

Noah felt quite comfortable under the night sky, alive with a trillion stars, the odd bark of the wagoner's dogs and the quiet clink of harness sounding somewhere out in the dark. As the convoy settled down for the night, he felt the silence, the blackness and the loneliness of the outback.

THEY MADE GOOD PROGRESS, about twenty miles a day, occasionally passing men pushing wheelbarrows or pulling hand-carts behind them, piled high with hope and their goods and chattels. By the end of the eighth day, with a red dusk just beginning to settle over the land, the wagoner's passengers and his cargo were off-loaded without ceremony outside a low wooden building with a bark-slab roof.

"This here is Bill Turner's General store," they were told. "He will rustle up almost anything you will need. Goodbye and good luck— you're going to need it!" The wagoner smiled his crooked smile, tipped a forefinger to the brim of his battered, dust-laden hat, turned his exhausted horses around and rumbled and swayed off along the dirt to the creek.

Noah and Beau picked up their belongings and made their way into the store, where they purchased a small second-hand tent, some salt beef, a damper, some tea, a billy, and—the most basic implements with which to find their fortunes—a set of sieves and a wide shallow pan. They erected their shelter and hoped it wouldn't rain through the large roughly cobbled-together tear in one of the sides. Then they tore pieces of damper off the loaf, shared the salt beef, made a fire under the billy of creek water and eventually sat on a fallen log sharing a steaming pannikin of tea.

Tomorrow, they would move a little way upstream and claim a place to start panning, but for now they were just tired but happy that they had arrived. Dotted here and there around them were the dark outlines of tents, sometimes just a piece of canvas slung between two trees or poles with a sleeping figure beneath wrapped in a blanket, his head propped up on a bundle of something; a dog or two roaming and sniffing around; a thin spiral of wood-smoke curling up into the black sky; a babe crying somewhere; a man and a woman yelling at each other; a thin, reedy concertina being played off in the dark; the light of a digger's lamp casting a soft glow up the trunk of a lofty gum; a woman nursing a child; and a small group of miners sharing a yarn and a pipe of tobacco, carved off the plug with dirty calloused fingers.

Neither Noah nor Beau notice the hardness of the ground as they settled down to sleep, fully clothed and exhausted. For his part, Noah had just enough time to think that this was a long way from his previous life with a soft bed and clean linen, food prepared and served by staff and nothing whatever to come between him and a carefree, cosseted life. He smiled to himself and curled up, contented, knowing that he was at the beginning of something big, exciting and fulfilling.

From that very first night, for the first time in his life, he felt he was where he belonged. He quickly learned how to kill snakes and spiders and got used to seeing kangaroo and emu coming down to drink from the creek and hearing the screeching of galah and cockatoo overhead.

OVER THE NEXT TWO YEARS, an advancing tide of people from all walks of life saw huge changes in the area. Hundreds and hundreds arrived at the diggings, most with nothing more than they could carry on their backs. Fuelled by stories—some true, some embellished and some wholly invented—of instant and immense wealth, they left their former lives in droves. The big towns were emptied of butchers, carpenters, blacksmiths, policemen, farmers, bakers, tinsmiths, farriers and even some doctors, and the social structure of the deserted towns was dislocated. Some brought their families along with them, some came alone. Some had slipped through the government ban on ex-convicts in the goldfields, and some were hopeful itinerants, and there were people of every nationality you could think of.

Some built stores, hotels, bakeries, butcher shops and brothels. Many, many more suffered the trials of back breaking work with no reward. And a few—a very, very few—made their fortunes. There was theft, forgery, drunkenness, prostitution, murder and mayhem, births, deaths and an occasional marriage. There was happiness and helplessness, desertion and desperation, profiteering, penury and lost dreams. Law and order were rare, and miners often dispensed their own brand of justice. Claim-jumping disputes were frequent, and bushrangers roamed the roads, holding coaches and miners to ransom, plundering and stealing from settlements along the way.

Over time, Noah and Beau built a more substantial dwelling for themselves in amongst the stringy barks. Men from every trade and profession, now turned miners, helped each other to cut and strip planks of timber and to erect, cover and plug walls. Since nails were scarce, everything was held together with wooden pegs. Spaces between cut wall-timbers were filled with mud to keep the weather out. There was no glass available, so a rough wooden shutter was fashioned and attached to a single window opening. Huge bark slabs made a good roof, and, at the beginning of their second winter, they added a sod chimney. The rain fell down it and hissed and spat in the fire below.

The hut was comfortable enough, a single room with a floor of dirt tamped to a hard iron surface. They needed nothing more than a room to sleep in and somewhere to eat at the end of a long day when the weather turned sour and prevented them building a fire outside. Any furniture they had, they built from whatever the bush had to offer. Stools were made from cut logs, and a table was made from green tree branches overlaid with slabs of pressed bark. By the end of the second winter, a wooden floor was installed, and finally the ground stopped turning to mud every time it rained.

As the creek-beds gave up their precious grains and specks to the hundreds of panners, those who had the fortitude moved to digging deep shafts to access the reef gold. Consortiums of miners were formed, but some went it alone, and some simply gave up and returned, bent and broken, to the towns.

Among those who decided to try their luck at digging a shaft were Noah and Beau, who moved to an area recently named Eureka. Beau was destined never to leave the town of Ballarat.

NOAH'S JOURNAL

I came back to Sydney permanently in 1864, and today is the anniversary of the death of my friend, Beau. All these years later, it still affects me deeply. To think that we were well short of twenty years of age when we first met on that old dusty bush track on the way out to Ballarat, I to escape from my family—no, from my father if I be truthful—and Beau to make his fortune so that he could ask Catherine to marry him.

How odd it all is! Beau is dead, I made the fortune, and Catherine and I are now man and wife.

I remember it all as if it were yesterday. Beau and I had moved away from the creek and dug our first shaft at Eureka. It was weeks and weeks of backbreaking slog in heat, mud, rain and cold. All autumn, winter and into spring, we dug and crushed rock to find gold. We were very lucky. All around us were shafts dug by others which proved, after months of hard work, to be duffers. We found a good vein only about thirty-five feet deep and had begun to bring up some significant amounts, including one quite large nugget and a few smaller ones.

We decided to save time by not moving our hut, so we walked the two miles or so each day to our shaft and wearily back again when it was too dark to see beyond the dim light of our lanterns. We had a couple of minor cave-ins and were flooded once, but, all in all, our hard work was paying handsome dividends.

When we first built our hut, we dug a small hole in the hard ground in one corner. I remember we had laughed together and said that soon we would have to dig a much larger hole, then maybe start our own bank in which to store our finds. We then constructed a sort of rough chest to stand over the hole, and on this we placed all our other belongings. It did not do to let anyone know of a decent find. Trust was hard to come by on the diggings, and many a good man had his skull cracked, or worse, by another intent on relieving him of his hard-won treasure. Men took risks but guarded their finds as well as they could.

Every twenty ounces, if you had the sense, you took to the gold commissioner's tent, where it was weighed, sealed in a leather pouch and sent off to the treasury in Melbourne to await your claim on it at some time in the future. Even then one ran the risk of the gold coach being held up by bushrangers, who saw to it that your bit of cargo, along with that of many others, never reached its intended destination. This happened in spite of the presence of the men from the 40th Regiment, formed especially as an escort for the gold transfers. Actually, during the sixties, these robbers became such a scourge that a law was passed allowing a recognised bushranger to be shot on sight, and a few actually were. Beau and I were very lucky; we only ever lost one shipment that way, and over time the treasury held several hundred ounces for us.

Right from the start, Beau and I agreed to share everything we found. We worked very hard, he and I, side by side, as much for protection as companionship. We forged a very close friendship, cemented at the end of each day as we sat under the stringy barks, smoke drifting up lazily from our fire and our pipes of tobacco. We enjoyed our meals of mutton, damper, tea, and, if we were lucky, a potato or two and an onion from the latest bullock-dray arrival from Melbourne. As we became successful, we celebrated by allowing ourselves a small swig of brandy in our billy tea.

Mining on Sunday was prohibited by law, and once a tiny Methodist church and an even smaller Catholic one were established, many miners attended. We even had a theatre, the Adelphi, and on a Saturday evening, we could enjoy a spot of Shakespeare, opera, or comedy. On Sundays, we sometimes joined our neighbours in a game of cricket. Sunday was looked forward to as a reward for a hard week's work, and, if they had them, some folk even dressed up for the day in their best clothes.

How can you not get to intimately know a friend when you spend every waking minute with him?

It's hard to put a finger on when exactly the rumblings started. When I think on it, there were probably three major events which were responsible for where and who I am today. Well, four, I suppose. My life is happy now, but there have been some intensely sad events along the way.

In the early part of '53, there were the beginnings of unrest among the men. The colony was in a great deal of debt, and all sorts of plans were developed to raise money. Licenses were issued to cover just about everything and everyone, including storekeepers, hotelkeepers, brothel keepers, traders and hawkers, panners and diggers. And of course, wherever there are rules, there is always someone trying to find a way to break or at least get around them. Anyone who was so disposed and could afford to bribe the government men and police to look the other way did so.

Beau and I were extracting about forty-five ounces of gold to the ton of crushed rock, so we had little difficulty in paying the thirty-shillings licence fee every month for our six-foot square patch. But some of the men were unable to pay, and a lot of them point-blank refused. All manner of ruses was devised to thwart the efforts of the officials, who fairly regularly went around to check if licences were up to date.

Then a situation arose which further fanned the flames. Sir Charles Hotham replaced LaTrobe as Governor of Victoria. Hotham was a member of Her Majesty's Royal Navy and came with a reputation for being a harsh disciplinarian. Despite this, high hopes were held that this fellow would realise the hardship that the payment of licence fees was creating for many men.

But the opposite occurred. Hotham soon concluded that the small amount of money collected had no relevance to the number of men on the diggings, and he stepped up the number of checks to twice weekly. This move engendered more hostility among the diggers and fostered a great antipathy toward anyone who represented the authorities.

Beau said one day, "You know Noah, I don't much like the feeling around the fields these past few months. There's tension building. It's a cloud, an unease. There's something afoot and I don't like it at all."

I too wondered where it would all lead, and I have to confess that I was far too immersed in our own activities to take much notice of the bigger picture.

Beau was clearly agitated as he looked me in the eye and continued: "Before things become uncomfortable—and I think they will—I'm giving serious thought to calling it a day and going back to Melbourne to ask a certain Miss Catherine Donnelly to be my wife."

For a moment, I was at a loss for words. It somehow had never crossed my mind that our association might one day end, but of course, if I had been honest with myself, I would have seen that it must.

Gathering my wits, I said, "Of course, Beau, you must do what you wish. It goes without saying that I shall miss you. We have become tight friends over these last two and a half years, haven't we? I wish you every happiness. Will you go back to being a policeman?"

"I've thought about that," Beau said sombrely, "and I think I must. With my share of our gold, which I understand is selling at about a pound an ounce and a policeman's wage of about seventy-five pounds a year, I think I'll be very close to being able to purchase a cottage."

I asked him when he was thinking of leaving.

"Well, it's now almost March, and I thought I'd like to go before the winter sets in, which makes it about three months from now. I hear that there's a stage coach company due to start running between here and Melbourne in the next month or so. It'll be bringing mail and passengers in and out of here. I'd thought of booking a passage on that."

He paused and grinned, I thought, a little apologetically. "A better way to leave than on the wagon we came here on, eh?" All of a sudden, he brightened. "Why don't you come with me? You can afford to! We've done very well, you'd have to agree."

I think he was caught up with the excitement of leaving behind forever the never-ending hard work of the mines—with the dirt, dust, flies, heat, snakes, cold, the isolation—and of course the prospect of a future life with Catherine. And who could blame him?

"Thank you, but no," I replied. "I'll stay for a while longer. I'm happy here, where I'm a free man, answerable to no-one but myself."

"Well, think on it," Beau said. "I can tell you, there's trouble brewing here. If you change your mind and go back with me, and I can arrange for you to stay with me until you get yourself sorted out. Then I can present Catherine to you, and you'll see for yourself what a beautiful creature she is."

One month later, almost to the day, something happened which altered the course of our lives.

I came into our hut and found him staring into space, his eyes focused on something into the beyond, yet seeing nothing.

"Man! What's wrong? Are you ill?" It was so unusual to see him acting strange, and I was quite taken aback.

He looked up slowly, and I was shocked by the look in his eyes. He was ashen, shaken to the core, hollow. He had been reading a tattered copy of the *Melbourne Argus* dated the previous October and handed me the newspaper, folded into four.

I took it and quickly scanned for anything that could have affected him so. It didn't take long.

The engagement is announced between Miss Catherine Donnelly, only daughter of Mrs Frances Donnelly and the late Mr Clarence Donnelly, and Mr Jonah Burge, second son of Mrs Henrietta and the late Mr Thomas Burge. Mr Jonah Burge is a member of the Victorian Constabulary and has recently received a promotion to the rank of Sergeant. The marriage is expected to take place in June of next year.

You have to remember, of course, that in those days, newspapers from Melbourne, when they arrived, were devoured by those of the miners who could read and were handed from one to the other until they were unreadable. This meant that we usually received our news very late.

Beau turned a desolated face to me, his lips white, eyes tortured.

"Mr Jonah Burge!" he spat. "Jonah! He's well named, isn't he?"

Up to this point, I had been speechless. What does one say when one sees a man so totally destroyed? I offered a few lame words and stood looking down at my friend, my hand on his shoulder in an awkward gesture of sympathy.

After a pause, Beau said softly, "I suppose it *would* have been unfair to ask her to wait all this time. I suppose I should have said something to her before I came out here." He explained that he had ever only worshipped her from afar, waiting until he had made his fortune before he made his feelings known. He reasoned that his courtship would have a greater chance of success if he had more than a policeman's wage to offer her.

From that day on, Beau was a changed man. I watched helplessly as he turned from a happy and dependable friend into a sad and remote being. But what alarmed me the most was his change of lifestyle. He began frequenting the newly and hastily erected Eureka Hotel, which the government built only eight months before, having lifted the ban on the sale of alcohol on the diggings, thereby putting out of business the sly grog places which seemed to flourish everywhere. Often, he came back inebriated and fell onto his bed without a word.

I thought that his agony would pass and that he would come to his senses. How wrong I was! Some days he would not even get up and go down to our mine, and when I would get back after my day down there alone, he would be gone again, back to the hotel. On one or two occasions, he stayed out all night. I continued to hope that he would see what he was doing to himself.

Gradually, he seemed to come out of his depression. He still regularly visited the hotel and kept the same poor company there, but his drinking as suddenly ceased as it had begun, although June was a bad month. The hour of day and the date had little relevance to the diggings. We went to bed with the sun and rose by the sun, and the days just kept rolling around, one after the other without much to distinguish one from the other, apart from Sundays.

I wondered why he became so withdrawn as June drew near and soon realised that it was the month of Catherine's intended nuptials.

Life is cruel, isn't it? If we had known then what I know now, Beau's life and doubtless mine, would have been entirely different.

As I say, June was not a good month, but it came and went, and as the winter wore on—and it was a particularly harsh one that year—he seemed to recover somewhat and came back to work. But things were never quite the same. He increasingly expressed resentment toward the imposition and collection of the licence fees, and I have to say, I more than once saw instances of bullying tactics at collection time. Of course, none of us liked having to pay part of our hard won gold for a licence, but I always kept mine up to date.

So you can imagine my utter astonishment when, one day, one of the Commissioner's men came to check on our papers, and Beau swore roundly at the man.

"You can go to perdition before I'll show you any paper!" This was said quite quietly, but with fervour, and he turned his back on the officer whilst informing him that he was every sort of a fool.

Before I could intervene, Beau was arrested and chained to a tree with three other prisoners. My protestations and offers to find his license and present it were to no avail, and the four men were later that day taken to the government jail. I was even more shocked the next day, when I paid the five pounds fine to have him released, to find that he indeed did *not* have a license and, he announced, had no intention of obtaining one—ever.

Back at our dig, Beau said, "Thank you, but had I known that you were going to pay the fine for my release, I would have objected."

Before I could ask him what he thought the alternative might have been, he continued ominously, "Things are coming to the boil, Noah. I don't know when or how, but it's going to blow the lid before very long."

What he meant at that moment, I had no idea, but when I think back on it all these years later, I regret that I did not at least try to steer him away from the course he was bent on pursuing. I am torn— could I have prevented the awful happening, or at least Beau's participation? It's a question I don't suppose I shall ever resolve.

Beau was increasingly becoming involved with a large group of men who met every evening to air their grievances about their conditions and the licensing system, the high cost of food, the corruption and, probably above all, the lack of representation in the government. A natural leader had emerged from within the group in the form of Peter Lalor. He was a tall, educated Irishman, having qualified as an engineer at Trinity College, Dublin, and had been in Ballarat for just over a year. He spoke well in public and was an obvious choice as a spokesman. Under the guidance of Lalor, the men formed themselves into a group they dubbed the Ballarat Reform League. It had the stated aim of abolishing the licensing system and seeking the right to vote for members of parliament.

In August that year, we had an immense storm. By then, we were fairly used to the extreme weather, but this particular storm was the worst any one of us had ever endured. Big clouds started rolling in from the west, and the sky looked angry, grey and swollen. A wind had sprung up during the night and was gathering pace fast. Then, with a rush, the rain came together with the lightning and thunder. The noise was tremendous. We could hear tree branches snapping outside, and the wind tried, in vain, to tear the roof off our hut. It was thanks to the expertise of the men who had helped us construct it that it stayed put.

We had battened down as fast and hard as we could, but even so the inside of our hut was lit like daylight with every lightning bolt, and we had to shout to make ourselves heard above the din. All night, the wind howled and raged, but by morning it had worn itself out. The rain continued, however, with renewed vigour. It fell straight down so hard and so fast that it was difficult to see any distance at all outside.

Answering cries for help, Beau and I went out in the downpour and were shocked at the devastation. Trees were uprooted. Branches had fallen on and flattened tents. Bits of torn canvas, blankets and clothing were wrapped around tree trunks, pots pans and billies were strewn everywhere, and soggy bags of flour, salt and sugar leaned sullenly against the remnants of tent poles and hut walls. The rain had gouged out little runnels down every slope, filled every pothole and turned the dirt to mud ankle deep. The creek was running a banker, and all the horses had bolted in fright. Most of the stores were either flooded or destroyed.

Beau and I did the best we could to help out where we could. Neighbours on either side of us appeared to have lost everything and we ended up cramming five other people in our hut for two days.

The rain eventually eased, and a watery sun came out on the fourth day, washing over the devastation. The damage was awful. Many men had lost all their belongings, but the final blow was the discovery that their mine shafts were flooded and unworkable. Humankind being what it is, most pitched in to help where possible, but for a few, the barrage was the last straw, and they left. The majority stayed and stoically tried to get their lives together again.

The storm had the effect of binding the community even closer together—especially the group of angry men of the Reform League. Facing such disaster made them all the more determined, and the situation was really starting to ferment. It was made much worse in October, when James Scobie, who worked the shaft next to Lalor's, was found murdered.

Apparently, although already drunk, he had insisted on being served more liquor at the Eureka Hotel after it had already closed for the night. Scobie, it was said, made some disparaging remarks about Mrs Bentley, the owner's wife, and it appears that Bentley took after him. Bentley was a violent ex-convict from Van Diemen's Land, rumoured to be bribing the local police and gold commissioner. This rumour was strengthened when he was arrested and charged with the murder of Scobie and acquitted just four days later. Bentley was pretty unpopular, and the men of the Reform League were convinced, probably quite correctly, that he had bribed the magistrate.

Incensed, they took the law into their own hands. Despite my misgivings, which I daily communicated to Beau, he was in the thick of it all. He said that he had no life back in Melbourne. Catherine was no longer available to him, and he had no family, his mother and father being deceased. So he might as well put his weight behind the Reform League!

Anyway, a small group of men were so angry at Bentley's discharge that they descended on the hotel and burnt it to the ground. Thankfully, Beau was not among them at that event, but many of the men were arrested and three were sent to jail. A deputation, including Beau, was despatched to Governor Hotham to plead for their release, but it was denied.

Hotham's answer was to order the rearrest and retrial of Bentley and to send in four hundred and fifty extra soldiers in horse carts. When the miners saw the carts arriving, they threw sticks and stones and actually pulled some soldiers from one of the carts and attacked them. One was so badly injured that he died a few days later. The pot was boiling to overflowing, and something had to happen. Even *The Ballarat Times* printed articles in favour of reform.

The next day, Lalor called a huge meeting at Bakery Hill, and the men were told of Hotham's refusal to release the three men. As a strong protest, someone suggested that the miners burn their licences, and, there and then, they built a bonfire. Some five hundred miners threw their licences on the flames.

Next morning, the governor parried by ordering a special licence inspection and arrested about thirty men. Despite the heat of the sun and the blustery wind, the men gathered more supporters, and, carrying a special flag they had sewn, went back again to Bakery Hill. By that time, there were about a thousand men up on the hill, and Lalor asked them to kneel under the flag and swear to protect each other and their liberties. About half the men swore the oath.

The men hardly needed convincing that the time had come for a showdown, and they gathered as many bits of timber, branches and planks of wood as they could and erected a barricade around a large area. They set up camp inside their stockade and waited. That was on the Thursday. Friday came and went, Saturday dawned, and there was no sign of any soldiers. Most of the men left to collect more firearms, and, thinking that nothing would happen on a Sunday, stayed at their diggings, leaving about a hundred and fifty men in the enclosure. These last few men, many of them drunk, settled down for the night.

At about 4.30 in the morning, when they were least expected, about four hundred police and soldiers crept up from their hiding place, fired off a couple of volleys and then charged. They tore down the miners' flag, burnt their tents and took a lot of prisoners. The few diggers behind the stockade managed to kill five soldiers, but the toll on their number was catastrophic. The whole thing lasted no more than fifteen minutes, and those of us who had heard the shots raced in to see what we could do. About thirty miners were lying around, either dead or dying.

I soon found my dear friend Beau, glassy eyes staring sightlessly upwards, half his chest blown away.

I think it was only the second time in my adult life that I have wept. I stood and cried uncontrollably. Poor Beau. What a senseless waste. Do you know that, at the time of the fight, there were about twelve thousand miners at Ballarat, yet only about a hundred and fifty stood against the might of the government?

For a long time afterwards, I was eaten by guilt: why hadn't I been able to dissuade him? But now, I am convinced he was in the right. I am immensely proud of him. As events turned out, miners everywhere to this day owe a great debt of gratitude to those few brave men, especially to the thirty who were slain.

At the end of that dreadful day, the soldiers rounded up the rest of the men, but Peter Lalor was nowhere to be found. Two days later, hundreds of troops arrived from Melbourne and declared martial law. The arrested diggers were sent to trial. Most were later released, but thirteen of them were taken to Melbourne to be tried for high treason, and within a week Governor Hotham appointed a Royal Commission to examine the facts and reasons behind the rebellion.

A couple of months later, the thirteen men were acquitted of high treason, thanks to a jury of local men stating that the uprising occurred as a direct result of the high-handedness of the government men when dealing with the miners. The findings of the Royal Commission were handed down, and Governor Hotham had to admit defeat. He declared an amnesty, and I think the whole thing must have destroyed him, because he died within a year. When the amnesty was declared, Peter Lalor came forward. He had been hidden by friends since the day of the revolt, when he had taken a bullet in the left shoulder and had his arm amputated.

So you see, even though I will forever mourn the death of my young friend, a reasonable man would have to agree that the whole sad business had a good outcome in the long run. Within a year, the licenses were abolished, and the so-called Miner's Right was issued. This cost a mere one pound a year, instead of the iniquitous thirty shillings a month. Attached to the new document was the right of the men to vote in Parliament, take a parcel of land, erect a cottage and garden on it so that he and his family could grow enough vegetables to sustain them. Within a year, Peter Lalor was elected to the Upper House.

The third of December, 1854—will I ever forget? What a momentous time! There is no doubt in my mind that the eleven months afterwards changed the course of this country's history.

AFTER I COLLECTED myself following Beau's death, I quickly realised that working a mine shaft single-handed was nigh impossible. Anyway, my heart was just not in it.

About three months into the new year, on a warm spring day, I was conversing with old Bill Turner, the owner of the general store. You may remember that it was he who provided Beau and me with our basic needs on the very first day of our arrival in Ballarat. Bill mentioned that his good wife was not very well and that he would like to take her back to Sydney, where the climate was more to her liking. Being well past middle age, she was not looking forward to spending another winter in Victoria, especially if it was as harsh as the one just gone. He was selling up and clearing out. I was hardly listening, only thinking that this might be a solution to my woes. To cut a long story short, I sold my mine to a three-man partnership from New South Wales and purchased—lock, stock and barrel—old Bill's store.

I renamed the store Edwards and Cavanagh, combining Beau's and my surnames. As I may have mentioned previously, Beau had no known relatives, and despite my quite thorough enquiries, none came forward to claim his half share of our gold. So it was that I was able easily to purchase the store, and also to acknowledge Beau's contribution by including his name on the store sign.

Going from miner to storekeeper was quite an experience, but I enjoyed it. The goldfield's population was increasing rapidly, and, within a year, I had need to increase the size of the premises. But the land on both sides of our store was occupied by a saddler on one side and a dressmaker on the other. Furthermore, we were on Main Road, which sat on a low part of the area and prone to flooding. I was not looking forward to the coming winter, when the creeks rose again.

As it happened, a fierce fire destroyed almost all the buildings on both sides of Main Road a few years later, so it was as well that I removed. At the time, though, I thought long and hard about it all and decided to take a large parcel of land on the high side of the settlement. On this, we built three adjoining stores. In the first one, we sold everything that a digger could want, from a simple bucket and spade to sieves, winches, saddles, ropes, boots, gold weights and scales. In the middle one, we offered everything for household needs, like tallow candles, tins of herrings, jars of pickles, flour, sugar, salt, bottles of brandy and plugs of tobacco. The third shop was stocked high with fabrics and laces, gloves, babywear, parasols, bonnets and shawls, shoes, stockings and bloomers. There were many wives on the diggings by that time, so we had to cater for the ladies and their children. We also kept blue flannel shirts and other clothing for the menfolk.

In the clothing store, we employed a matron and a spinster lady to look after the needs of our patrons, and four men were kept busy in the other stores. Most of my time was spent travelling back and forth to Melbourne to buy stock for replenishment.

You ask why I always refer to the business as "ours," but I looked upon it as Beau's and mine. After all, it was his half of the gold which enabled me to purchase it in the first place. Anyway, Edwards and Cavanagh was the largest business on the diggings at that time, and we went from strength to strength. Around us, as more and more storekeepers abandoned the flood prone Main Road area, were stores of every description. Just along from us were a printer, a dressmaker, a baker, a butcher, a cobbler and a barber. In the street running at right angles to ours were an ironmonger, a saddler, a wheelwright and a blacksmith. There were several eating houses, all run by Chinese, where you could find a fine pie, a filling stew or a bowl of nourishing soup.

The two doctors were kept very busy dealing with dysentery, accidents in mine collapses, toxic air and machinery mishaps, a frightening outbreak of cholera, scurvy, heatstroke and sunburn in the summer and rheumatism in the winter. A lot of the fevers and such were from the local water, polluted by animals and people cleansing themselves and their cooking utensils. The doctors charged two pounds for a home visit, prescribed Holloways Pills in their hundreds and applied leeches by the dozen. As a side effect, of course, it was not unusual to see the undertaker and his black horses, with ostrich plumes nodding on their heads, drawing his black coach along in front of a mourning family. Often, "death by the visitation of God" was the reason given for the demise, whether it be by snakebite, accident or disease, and "Gone to a Better Place" would be inscribed on the poor unfortunate's wooden cross planted at the head of his final resting place.

Late at night, the air was filled with the jangling of piano-playing and strident singing emanating from the numerous bawdy houses and hotels, and the local constabulary was ever present.

Life was harsh, unforgiving, busy and interesting, and I was very successful.

I had been in Ballarat for about ten years when I was approached by two well-dressed gentlemen from Melbourne, who asked if I had thought of selling the stores. Up until then, I had been quite content to let my life go along from day to day without much thought to the future, but they made me stop and think.

The mix of people in the town had changed. Many of the American and European men had left to try their luck elsewhere, mainly in New South Wales, I thought. Quite a few families had left and turned their hands to farming. There were hundreds of Chinese around the town, mostly from Canton. Since they were often more successful than the locals, there was quite a bit of resentment toward these people, including a frightful uprising in 1855, when the government had to intervene. But I always got on very well with them. I admired the way they kept their families close and how hard they worked, and it was they who provided us with fresh potatoes, onions, beans, and cabbages. Enough fresh vegetables for a family for three or four days could be purchased for a shilling. When they weren't tending their vegetable plots, they were busily sifting through the tailings left by the diggers, making significant finds in abandoned creek beds and mine shafts. I made some very good friends among them, and there was much merriment when we had to resort to gestures to converse.

And it was about this time, for some reason or other, when I started to think about my family. Occasionally, I wondered what my mother and father would have said if they could see what I had accomplished. I also thought about my brother and sister, William and Eliza. I had not had a single word from any of them, nor of course had I made an effort to contact them.

Taking all this into account, I decided to sell. I had not given much thought to what I would do afterwards, but one thing was uppermost in my mind. I would visit my family and try to rebuild a few bridges, so to speak. My buyers and I agreed on a good and fair price, and the business changed hands with the proviso that I kept the name of Edwards and Cavanagh. At the time, the memory of Beau was still too raw, and I did not want to sever myself completely from his name. I had the thought that I might carry it on to another place somewhere, sometime, perhaps in Sydney.

After the formalities were concluded in a lawyer's office in Melbourne, I returned to Ballarat to say farewell to the many friends I had made there and to our good and loyal employees. I also went to Beau's grave to say a final goodbye and pay my respects. I put together my belongings and took the Cobb and Co. coach out of Ballarat for the last time. It was a strange feeling, leaving that place and its happy-sad memories.

But I also had an odd sense of excitement. I was in good physical shape, wealthier than I had thought possible and not yet thirty years of age. I walked around the main roads of Melbourne for a couple of days and had grand thoughts of starting another business. The Edwards and

Cavanagh Emporium sounded good to me. But I decided to put those ideas on the shelf for the moment and headed for Sydney Town, for my father's house.

SEVEN DAYS LATER, after I had settled myself in some comfortable lodgings in the town, I approached the high, ornate wrought-iron gates to my former home. I opened them and walked around the semi-circular gravelled drive to the portico, within which was a set of cedar doors with highly polished brass door furniture.

A carriage was pulled up close to the door, and the coachman was waiting patiently. I had no idea what sort of a reception I was in for, but I was not prepared at all for the one I got.

I was about to raise my hand to pull the bell-rope, when the door opened and there stood my father, a maid handing him his hat, coat and gloves. He shot me a quick glance from under stern, bushy eyebrows, made no acknowledgement whatever as I stood aside and proceeded down the steps and into his carriage.

To be charitable, I could have assumed he simply didn't recognise me. But in truth, I supposed it was inevitable that he would not acknowledge my presence after so many years—and taking into account the manner in which I had left. His nature made it difficult to overcome any offence.

"Is Mrs Cavanagh in residence, please?"

A small, open hand indicated that I should step inside. "Who may I say is calling, sir?" the maid enquired.

"Noah," I said. "Noah Cavanagh." If she had any idea that I was the prodigal son returning, she gave no indication whatever. She politely asked me to wait.

I don't know whether it was the prospect of meeting my mother after so many years, but I felt my heart racing and my face warm. Before I could analyse my emotions fully, the maid returned.

"This way, please. Mrs Cavanagh is receiving this morning."

The formality surprised me—I had forgotten what it was like to have English servants. Anyway, I followed her through an inner hall and into an elegant withdrawing room.

Seated in a high-backed upholstered chair in a bay window looking out onto a green lawn, an elegant silver-topped ebony walking stick by her side, was my mother, a tiny, frail-looking lady wrapped in a large shawl about her shoulders and a fine tartan rug across her knees.

"Noah?" she asked in a small voice, looking up through pale washed out blue eyes. "*Our* Noah? Is it really you?"

"Yes, Mama, it is I," I said and gently took her hands in my own, which were calloused from years of manual work. I hardly dared hold them for fear of bruising them; they were nearly transparent, blue veins just below the surface.

I can tell you, I was really quite shocked. She was not the mother I had last seen years before. She seemed somehow broken, defeated, waiting. "Abandoned" might be the better word. She kept unblinking eyes on mine, and tears welled up and spilled down her soft cheeks. When she closed her eyes and let out a long sigh, more tears squeezed out from under papery lids.

Overcome with sadness to see her like that, I knelt on the floor beside her chair and put my arms around her. How tiny she was! I closed my eyes and felt hot tears stinging. How long we stayed like this, silent, I don't know, but eventually I felt her body relax. I released her, and she gave me a wan smile.

"It's truly wonderful to have you here," she said. "Tell me where you've been and what you've been doing."

I drew my chair very close, sat down and reached for her thin hand.

She looked me up and down. "Are you a lawyer?"

"No, Mama, I'm not a lawyer. In fact, I'm not anything at the moment."

"Oh! Well, you look very prosperous." She lowered her head and looked at me, pretending to be stern. "Are you a bushranger?"

I laughed. "No, Mama, I'm not a bushranger, nor have I ever been. But I'll tell you all about it a little later. First, I want to hear about William and Lizzie."

I made up my mind to ask her about herself a little later, I think because I was afraid of the answer.

"I saw father just leaving as I arrived," I added, "but I don't think he recognised me. He looks quite well."

Mama set her lips in a thin line. "Oh, he'd never admit it, but he would have recognised you perfectly well. He's never forgiven you, and I'm sorry to say I don't think he ever will. He's even forbidden your name to be mentioned. He's a bitter, angry man." Her shoulders drooped, and she set her gaze into the distance with resigned acceptance.

I wasn't quite sure how to deal with this information and decided to deflect the conversation.

"What about Lizzie? How is she?" I said.

"Oh! Lizzie's all right. She's married, you know, and expecting again."

This took me completely by surprise. "Married? To whom?"

"Lizzie did very well for herself, did Lizzie. She married Edward Gallimore! I rarely get to see her these days. And when I do, it's not always a happy occasion." She leaned forward and said in a lower voice, "I don't think she's very happy, though she'd never say so. I think Edward treats her well enough, but he does have a reputation for seeing other women."

"You said she's 'expecting again.' How many children does she have? How long has she been married?"

"They married in sixty-one," Mama replied, "just after old Sophie Gallimore died, and she was with child almost immediately. She miscarried that first time, but then little Charlotte came along."

Again, I decided not to pursue the topic, but before I could change the subject, Mama looked directly at me and asked, "And what about you, Noah? Are you married? Do you have a family, and...?"

"No, and no," I answered. "To be honest, I've been so busy these last few years that I've not given much thought to ladies and marriage."

Mama looked at me very quizzically, as if she thought there was something wrong with me, so I steered the conversation away once more.

"And William? Is he still with the bank?" I ventured.

"Yes, he's now the manager. He's never married, either. I don't think he's at all interested in matrimony. He still lives here with us but keeps himself to himself. Don't expect to have any sort of a conversation with him; it's as much as I can do to get him to be civil. Spends his days at the bank, comes back here to dinner in the evenings, then retires to his rooms."

I looked away from Mama and into the gardens outside. What had I come back to? A bad-tempered father, a sad, frail mother, an estranged sister and a silent, morose brother.

Mama reached for a bell at the side of her chair. "You will stay for morning tea?" she said, more a statement than a question.

Before I could accept or decline, a maid entered, and Mama asked, "Will you please bring tea for us? My son and me." She invested those last words with a great satisfaction, I thought. Within minutes, the small table at my mother's side was covered with a fine hand-embroidered afternoon tea-cloth, and laid thereon was a delicate set of porcelain cups and saucers, a silver tea-service and a selection of cakes and sweetmeats, the like of which I had not seen for many a long year.

"This is a most exciting day. I cannot remember when I was last so happy!" Mama smiled.

I thought that was sad. There she was, with every material thing one could wish for, yet she seemed to have nothing.

"Where are you staying?" she asked. "And you still haven't told me what you've been doing all these years, apart from not getting yourself a wife!"

"I am staying in some very good lodgings, thank you. Well, to make a long story short, I've been a gold-miner and a storekeeper."

She stared at me then, as if those were the last things she expected I'd been up to, then recovered herself. "Well, well! And I'm pleased to note you seem to have been very successful!" She reached over and patted my hand. "Tell me all about it."

She settled back, teacup and saucer in hand, her eyes locked onto mine and ready to absorb every tiny detail.

I assumed that my father had long ago given his version of our parting in Melbourne, and, not wishing to reopen old wounds, started with my life in the diggings. After about an hour, during which time Mama had not uttered a word, so absorbed was she, I could see that she was tiring.

I took the opportunity of leaving, telling her that I had some important matters to attend to in the town. This was, of course, a bit of an untruth, but I wanted to avoid an invitation to dinner, which would certainly lead to a confrontation with my father and possibly William. I was not quite ready for that, and, in any case, I wanted to be in charge of any situation where an unpleasantness might arise. I had to get my thoughts in order.

I promised Mama that I would come back in a day or two and continue with my story. She clasped my hands very warmly and told me that it had been one of the best days of her life. I was glad to have brought her such joy.

The Hotel Carlyle offered a very substantial lunch, which I enjoyed. Thus fortified, I decided to take the bull by the horns, so to speak, and visit my brother. I called at the bank and asked to speak to the manager. A young clerk conveyed my name to an inner room, and I was asked to present myself.

As I approached William's desk, the clerk closed the door behind me, my brother stood up, cocked his head to one side and looked straight at me. "Noah?"

"William!" I replied, extending my hand. As if he suddenly remembered his manners, he put his hand forward and took mine. I saw him wince slightly at my firm handshake.

His was quite soft, which surprised me somewhat, but I was more taken aback by his appearance. To my eye, he looked older than he should have done. Of course, what he thought of my appearance, I shall never know. But despite there being on only a year between us, yet he seemed to have put on many more years.

"It's good to see you, William," I began, and I was quite genuine in my greeting. "How are you?"

"I'm well enough," he began, looking me up and down, but not like Mama had done. "What brings you back?"

It was awkward, almost chilling. He remained behind his desk, and there was no warmth, no depth in his voice as he continued to look at me. He was summing me up—I could almost see his brain working, wondering how to deal with this brother who had reappeared after all the years.

He did not invite me to sit, and I decided quite suddenly that I would not be intimidated by him, then or ever again. So I very deliberately took hold of the carved top of the mahogany chair beside me, turned it to face him square on, and sat down.

With a resigned sigh, he too sat down and kept his gaze fixed on me, obviously waiting for something to happen.

We sat there, my brother and I, like strangers. For his part, he made not the slightest gesture toward friendship. His desk was a huge barrier between us, and there was something in his posture.

I decided to counter this by being very courteous and carrying on as if I had just dropped in for a casual chat.

In reply to his question, I said, "I've been looking forward for some time to visiting the family, and, since I have some business to attend to here, I thought it a good opportunity to combine."

He raised an eyebrow. "Business?" he echoed, his tone disbelieving.

I ignored his question and went on, "I visited Mama this morning."

Again, he raised an eyebrow.

"And I'm pleased to say I left her in good spirits, better than when I found her, I think." In a perverse way, I took pleasure in saying those last few words.

"I've not yet spoken to Father, but I hope to make peace with him soon. And, of course, I'd like to see Lizzie."

"Hummph..." was William's response. He obviously had no intention of extending the conversation. Before the silence became too confronting, I added, "Mama tells me that Lizzie is well and expecting a child."

This information elicited yet another raised eyebrow, as if it was the first time he had heard the news. That may well have been the case. By now, I had realised that mine was a very odd family, with no one member knowing or caring what the others were up to.

I could see I was getting nowhere, so I stood and extended my hand once again across his desk. "It's good to see you're well, William. I expect to be here for some time, and doubtless we shall meet again shortly."

He had the grace to stand and hold my hand in his moist and slack one. I quickly and deliberately left his office, closing the door softly behind me.

I had a strange feeling of elation—I felt I had come off the victor for the first time in my life in an encounter with my older brother. It was a relief, a release.

So engrossed was I in my thoughts that I did not see the young lady looking at me with a bemused smile on her lips. I was standing in the doorway of the bank, hat in hand, smiling like a fool and preventing her, or anyone else, from entering.

Good manners dictated that I should at least acknowledge her presence and apologise for my odd behaviour. I found myself looking down into the most wondrous pair of deep violet eyes. I swear to this day that they were twinkling brighter than any star in the heavens on a dark, dark night, yet it was afternoon.

"I do beg your pardon!" I spluttered and stepped aside to let her pass. I realised too late that I could not raise my hat, as I was still holding it in my hands, and ended up wildly waving it around in the air.

She dropped a tiny curtsy as she daintily lifted her skirts and took the two steps up into the premises.

"Thank you, kind sir," she said, giving a merry little laugh as she passed.

All thoughts of my brother and my supposed victory vanished in an instant as I watched her tiny figure disappear into the building. I tell you, it was the oddest thing. I felt as if I had been hit over the head with something very heavy. It was a feeling so intense and so new to me that I had no idea what to do with it!

I knew, though, that I had to see her again. I was unaccustomed to the way of meeting young ladies, so I decided to walk to the other side of the road and wait until she emerged from the bank. A few minutes later, she came down the steps, turned to her left and walked perhaps fifty yards to a small shop, where she put a key in the door and stepped inside.

I tried to look nonchalant as I walked to get closer to the shop and read a sign in the window. *MILLINER*, it read. Surrounding the sign were perhaps four or five frothy confections of coloured laces, ribbons, feathers and flowers.

Now I knew where she was employed and felt very pleased with my detective work. But how to contrive a way of meeting her again? I remembered that I had intended to visit Lizzie and thought that maybe I could get an idea from her. Females seem to know a lot more about the ways of other females than we mere males, don't they?

I then thought to visit my father. I made my way to his office and, on looking upward at the signage, saw that the words "& Son" had been removed from the name above his doors. Why should I have been surprised? Yet I was.

What with everything that had happened that day, my mind was in a mess. I decided to go back to my lodgings, sort out my thinking and my belongings and arrange a visit to my sister. My father could wait! A few more days after all these years could not make *that* much difference, could it?

I wrote a note to Lizzie and discovered that the mail coach was not due to leave till the following Monday. I don't know whether the young lady I had seen the day before had anything to do with my decision—though I think she must have!—but I had made up my mind to stay in Sydney and establish Cavanagh & Co. I also chose to omit the Edwards name, partly, I suppose, to avoid having to explain why Mr Edwards was not around.

While I awaited a reply from Lizzie, I spent my days looking for premises and eventually found exactly what I was looking for in Hunter Street, running off the larger George Street. I settled quickly and moved myself into the accommodation above the building so that I could oversee the establishment and development of my new emporium. In between times, I made time to visit Mama and keep her up to date with my doings.

I still did not speak to my father and wondered if I ever would.

As you may imagine, I was busily employed for quite some time. But my thoughts regularly strayed to She-of-the-Violet-Eyes. In the midst of all the activity, I received a letter from Lizzie, written in beautiful copperplate, stating that she would be delighted to see me as soon as I could get to Gallimore—and containing the most amazing request.

In one of the most peculiar, fateful quirks of life, she asked if, since her husband was away and she was heavy with child and could not easily travel, I could possibly render her an immense favour by picking up a hat she had ordered from her milliner in George Street!

I could hardly believe my eyes and felt a real surge of something indefinable in the pit of my stomach. I stood there, holding the letter in my hand, staring at it and reading it over and over, as if the words were going to disappear and I would think that I only dreamt it all.

I decided to go to the little hat shop at once to give the young lady as much notice as possible that I would be collecting my sister's hat. The next morning, after taking particular care of my ablutions and trimming my beard especially neatly, I presented myself at the address in George Street.

I was surprised at how nervous I felt, but I need not have concerned myself.

"Oh! Good morning, sir!" Violet Eyes said, smiling easily and looking directly up at me, quite clearly remembering our previous meeting. I noticed a deep dimple appearing in both cheeks as she spoke.

I explained who I was, the purpose of my errand, and that I would be going to visit my sister in the next two or three days.

"Of course, Mr Cavanagh, I shall have it carefully packed and ready for you to collect. I hope you will find Mrs Gallimore in good health. She's a very charming lady, if I may say so."

Having completed my errand, I bid her good-day and left, realising that, although I did not know her name, I still thought she was the most exquisite creature I had ever come across.

In the next couple of days, I had to force my mind back to the job of setting up my premises. It was all going along very nicely, with the cabinet makers and fitters strictly adhering to my instructions. The only big problem I could see was being able to fill the premises with stock in as short a time as possible. I had already approached a merchant who was expecting a shipload from America within the next six weeks and we had negotiated a figure for his entire cargo.

I had intended to hire a horse and ride out to Gallimore, but, acknowledging that I would be carrying a lady's hat, I decided to rent a horse and gig. I planned to stay just one night at Lizzie's, not wishing to spend too much time away from Hunter Street and all the activity there.

ON THE EVE of my departure for Gallimore, a steady, soaking rain had fallen, and at the last moment I exchanged the gig for a covered buggy, not wishing to get either myself or Lizzie's hat drenched. To make an early start, I pulled up outside the milliner's tiny shop almost immediately after breakfast. Puddles of rain lay in the wheel ruts of the road, and the air had a wonderful, freshly-washed feeling.

I had to wait only a short time before I saw the young lady daintily picking her way around the mud at the side of the road toward her shop.

"Good morning, sir!" she said as I alighted and followed her through the door. "Mrs Gallimore's order is all ready for you." She handed me a large rose-pink and white-striped hatbox, tied with a matching pink satin bow.

She smiled up at me with those incredible eyes as I took the box from her.

"Thank you, Miss...?"

She pointed to a white label affixed to the top of the box. "Donnelly."

I read the label. *Catherine Donnelly. Milliner.* read the label.

My heart fairly leapt into my mouth. That name! It could not be! *Could* it?

I was so taken aback, I just stood and stared at her for a long moment. She must have felt uncomfortable and wondered what an odd person I was.

"Mrs Gallimore has already settled her account," she said, attempting to fill the silence.

I almost, *almost,* asked her if she had ever had any connection to Beau, but thankfully remembered just in time that he had never told her of his feelings, and indeed, for all I knew, she might have no knowledge of his existence!

I vacantly mumbled a hasty acknowledgment and took off like a scared rabbit.

What she thought of me, I had no idea. I had met her on only three very brief occasions, and two of those times, I had behaved like a raving idiot.

I had to get my head sorted out, and once I was out of town bound for Camden, spent a goodly part of the morning weighing up my thoughts. By the time I reached the edge of the Macarthur property, I had convinced myself that if ever I had the opportunity, and she was, by the oddest coincidence, the same Catherine Donnelly, I would never, *ever*, tell her of my connection to Beau. To this day, years later, I still believe it was the right decision.

A wooden signpost at a split in the track diverted me along the side of Macarthur lands and on my way to Gallimore. On all sides stretched beautiful green pastures, softened by the overnight rain, and in the far-off background was the magic blurred-blue of the majestic mountain ranges. I could not help but marvel at the beauty of the countryside. No wonder the Macarthur and the Gallimore families had years ago chosen these lands for their sheep and cattle holdings. Twice I crossed the same crystal-clear creek as it snaked and babbled its way around the land, and at one point, I entered a huge stand of magnificent ancient gums. Here I stopped in the shade and drank in the magic of my surroundings. So peaceful, so beautiful! The sun had risen to its midday height and, though it was early spring, was soft and warm.

I had never been to the Gallimore property, although I had of course heard about it when I was a boy. I was not prepared for my first sight of the mansion. From the far side of the river, which I had to cross, it stood like a citadel atop a great green hill. High white columns shone like giant candles in the noonday sun, and the wide verandas surrounding the building promised cool shade beyond. The house commanded views around most of a huge valley where cattle and sheep grazed as far as the eye could see. Outbuildings dotted the area around the house, and, in the distance, perhaps a couple of miles further down the valley side, there stood another large house and its outbuildings.

This house, oddly named The Retreat, was the home of Edward Gallimore and my sister, Lizzie. I took the track down to The

Retreat, and, tired and worn out from my journey and my machinations along the way, I presented myself—and Lizzie's hatbox—at the door.

"Mr Noah!" cried the lady who opened the front door in a thick German accent. "Thanks you are here! *Kommen!* Miss Eliza is wanting to see you now today! *Kommen!*" She almost grabbed the hatbox from my hands.

I could scarcely believe my eyes! The lady who now confronted me was none other than Miss Berthe Metternisch, our old housekeeper, whose name, when we were small, we could not pronounce and therefore became 'Metty.'

"Metty?" I said incredulously to her retreating back. "Is it really you, after all these years? What are you doing here?" She ignored my questions and hurried through a large hall, expecting me to follow her, which of course I did!

She led me under an archway, through a comfortably furnished morning room and out onto a shaded veranda, where sat my sister, looking, I have to say, a little washed-out.

I did not know what to say first, I was so full of questions.

"Noah! Oh, Noah! It's wonderful to see you. Come sit here, do!" She patted a fat cushion beside her on a long wicker chaise. It quickly crossed my mind that I was having far more luck rebuilding bridges with the females of my family than with the males.

It is all so jumbled when I try to remember it now, but I learnt from Lizzie that old Sebastian Gallimore had died the year before, of a broken heart, they said; Metty, who had always had a soft spot for my sister, had followed her to The Retreat after explaining gently to our mother that she preferred a household where there were little children, whose company she enjoyed, never having had any of her own; and that Edward was spending more and more of his time at Gallimore now that he had inherited it.

I thought I detected a sad note in Lizzie's voice when she told me that last bit, and I was soon to discern that all was not well in the marriage. I again learnt that my father had never forgiven me and undoubtedly never would; that my mother was a sad, frail, lonely figure; and that my brother was a remote unapproachable bore, seemingly incapable of forming any sort of a close relationship with either man or woman, much less his own kin.

I was introduced to my one-year-old niece, Charlotte, and tiny Theodora, only eight days old—and was frightened out of my wits when she was handed to me to hold. I had never held anything as precious or as fragile. This caused both her mother and Metty much merriment at my expense!

Later that evening, my sister and I shared a dinner prepared and served by Metty, who hovered and fussed around, making sure we had everything we needed and some things we did not.

Eventually, Lizzie looked up at her and gently chided, "Oh, Metty! Do stop fussing, please. Everything is perfect, as usual, and we're quite capable of looking after ourselves, aren't we, Noah?"

Before I could agree, Metty looked sternly at me and said, "Vell, you don't keep Miss Eliza up too much! She must rest, you know!" With that, she swept out of the dining room, leaving Lizzie and me to smile knowingly at each other and continue our meal.

In my room that night, I stood at the open window and looked out into the night, moonless and glittering with a million stars. A huge, blank silence engulfed the world outside as I tried to make sense of everything, and, in bed, I tossed and turned, remembering that I had not even broached the subject of Miss Donnelly. I decided that I would do so next morning as soon as possible.

Not very artfully, I have to confess, I asked Lizzie if she had a chance to discover whether her new hat was exactly as she expected.

She gave me a curious sideways glance. "She's a very pretty young lady, is she not?"

I have never been very good at hiding my thoughts and feelings. I must have reddened, because Lizzie laughed and said, "I don't think she is spoken for!"

I decided not to bandy words and dived in straight away as if I hadn't heard her last words. "I hadn't heard of the Donnelly name in Sydney before I left. Are they newcomers to the town?" I asked.

"Well, *she* is," Lizzie replied. "I have become quite friendly with her. She told me she doesn't have any family. She arrived about four years ago from Melbourne. She hasn't said so, but rumour has it she was escaping from an unhappy romance, perhaps even a marriage! She's very good at her trade and is becoming quite sought-after, I believe."

This information left me flummoxed. There was no doubt in my mind that she was the same Catherine Donnelly of whom Beau had spoken. But what had happened to her? Had she married that fellow—Jonah something or other? If so, had he died? I needed to know!

I decided there and then to make an ally of Lizzie and confided in her. I had already told her of my adventures and my association with Beau, but now I added the bit about Beau and his unrequited love.

She listened intently. She was as intrigued as I, and I think she was looking forward to having a part in unravelling the mystery.

To this end, she declared that she would do her utmost to glean any information she could about Catherine's background. As she was able to travel, she would order another hat, whether she wanted one or not!

We laughed together at the conspiracy, and our conversation moved to other things—namely, Edward.

Where Lizzie had been on the defensive the day before, there now seemed to be a special bond between us. She freely opened up.

It appeared that Edward was spending more and more time away from the marital home. He didn't even come back to see his new daughter until four days after her birth, citing troubles at Gallimore—troubles bequeathed to him by his father, he said. Even then, he did not stay overnight, and what the "troubles" were, he did not elaborate.

Lizzie said she had not realised that there were any troubles at Gallimore. She had been very fond of old Sebastian and had no idea that everything was not as it seemed. Whilst Edward had always had all manner of ideas of what he was going to do with Gallimore when it became his, she was not prepared for some of the wild notions he entertained. Before old Sebastian passed away, Edward had tried to convince his father that sheep and cattle were too much hard work and that planting vineyards was the way of the future. Sebastian had vetoed this idea, along with some of Edward's other scatterbrained plans. Lizzie suspected the old man had lost his interest in Gallimore and was more than ready to join his beloved Sophie and his mother, Gemma, on the grassy slope in front of where the old Hillingdon mansion once stood.

At the end of my visit, I bade farewell to my sister, one-year-old Charlotte and little Theodora and gave Metty a hug and a quick kiss on the cheek at the door, exhorting her to look after Lizzie and the little ones. With lips set in a disapproving line, yet blushing at the same time, she gave me a look and a conspiratorial nod which told me she was aware that the atmosphere was strained between Lizzie and Edward and I quietly left her with my address in case she thought I might be needed.

THE SCHEDULED opening day of the Cavanagh Emporium was fast approaching. I was busy tying up loose ends, but the image of Miss Catherine Donnelly constantly intruded into my thoughts. I thought up ridiculous schemes to meet her again and discarded every one. My caution was rewarded during my opening-day speech, when, from the first-floor balcony, I spotted her in the sea of faces below.

How could I miss the most beautiful creature on this earth? She was wearing a simple but lovely gown of spotted muslin, with ribbons at the elbows and neck that exactly matched those wondrous eyes. She was hatless, which, when I thought about it later, was odd since she was a milliner. But a hat would have hidden the chestnut hair piled high on her head, little tendrils escaping behind each ear and down the nape of her neck.

I have to confess that my breath caught at the sight of her, and I lost my train of thought to the point where I probably looked slightly foolish. I had to drag my eyes away from her to regain my place, and my words came out flat and automatic. I was speaking one thing and thinking another. I hoped she would not disappear before I could finish, hurry down the stairs and approach her.

At last, I finished speaking and was able to seek her out. I found her balancing a cup and saucer in one hand and a plate in the other. I don't think I was imagining things when I noted that she was not displeased to see me.

I made some inane talk about escorting her around the departments. She declined, however, having sorted them out earlier, and I had to think of something else to say. Diving in like a bull in a china shop, I asked if I may call upon her.

She blushed most charmingly and said that I might. For the rest of the week I was walking about six inches above the floor!

I went out a couple of evenings later and put a note under her shop door, saying that I would call for her on the following Sunday afternoon and that we might have a picnic beside the water down by the harbour. I had recently purchased a horse and gig and asked my landlady if she would kindly prepare an especially excellent hamper.

Every now and again, I wondered at my excitement. There I was, thirty-one years of age, having never had any thoughts of the opposite sex and now behaving like a lovelorn schoolboy.

I performed my toilet with as much care as I could and, dressed in my best, presented myself at her lodgings on a clear, warm early spring day.

As I raised my hat, she came toward me and shyly put her hand in mine as I helped her onto the step and into the gig. Again, I marvelled at her beauty and the fact that she was hatless. This time, her hair was tied in a ribbon at the back and hung down almost to her waist.

We found a good spot under a large shady tree and faced the water. A couple of tall ships were in the bay, and numerous fishermen in small craft dotted the water. It was a magical day, one of those where nature puts on sights and sounds enough to blow all your cares away. It must have had the right effect on us, because we easily and unconsciously slipped into an uninhibited rapport. When I asked why, despite being a milliner, she was hatless on every occasion that I had seen her, she made me laugh by replying that she hadn't yet designed a hat which she herself would like to wear. She then regaled me with details of some of the monstrosities she had manufactured on the precise instructions of one or two elderly clients who thought they still looked like young ladies. And she laughed when I described to her the first time I had set eyes on her on the steps of the bank, walked to the other side of the road and slap bang into a lamp-post trying to see where she went as she left.

We laughed a great deal that day, and I drank in every detail of her: her eyes, her mouth, her beautiful, serene face, her throat, her tiny waist and down to two tiny pointed satin shoes peeping out from the lace at the hem of her dress. We had a perfect day and some hours later I returned her to her lodgings with the promise that we would meet again the following Sunday. It became a regular meeting, and, as the weeks passed, we started telling each other of our families and lives.

I told her about my parting from my father in Melbourne and of my sojourn in the goldfields, but I left out any specific mention of Beau. I referred to him as a friend, never actually mentioning his name, and said that he had died in the rebellion. I confess I was hoping to hear from her some mention of Beau, and it wasn't long before I did.

I learned that she came from Melbourne, both her parents were deceased and she had escaped a disastrous near-marriage. She sat with her hands in her lap, eyes downcast as she quietly related how she had become engaged to a member of Her Majesty's constabulary named Jonah. She said that Jonah had teased her that there was another constable who was madly in love with her but was not willing to make his feelings known until he had made his fortune in the goldfields. She did not know the other man's name, and Jonah would not tell her, so she assumed that he was joking.

By this time, I was absolutely certain that her unrequited lover was my friend, Beau, and I stuck to my decision to never, ever tell her. I never have, and I never will.

Which is not to say that I did not have some misgivings. Can you imagine my thoughts? Was I right in my courtship of Catherine? What would Beau have said had he known? But he was gone, killed in the uprising. How would he react? Well, he could not, because he was not alive. Half of my fortune had started with Beau's contribution. Should that half really belong to Catherine? No—she didn't even know he existed! Yes, she did—Jonah had told her! This jumbled thinking kept me awake into the early hours on many nights, but I was in love. Deeply and inextricably in love. What was gone was gone and should stay in the past, I decided.

I also determined that I would propose to Catherine, and if she would have me, I resolved to cherish her and leave no stone unturned to see that she would never be unhappy again.

Catherine accepted my proposal, and we made plans for our wedding. I started to look for some land on which to build our house, and we settled on a large site on the harbour shore close to where we had enjoyed our first picnic.

ABOUT THIS TIME, I learned that things were going from bad to worse for Eliza and her marriage to Edward Gallimore. He was rarely at home, had a reputation as a gambler, his many scatterbrained ideas for the Gallimore property invariably came to nothing, Gallimore was going to the dogs and rumour had it that he was deep in debt.

Catherine and I tried to comfort Lizzie and her two little daughters as best we could. All this I kept from Mama, though I suspected that she knew something of the situation. I have no idea what my father thought about it all, since I have never been able to break down the barrier between us, despite many attempts at a reconciliation. William was no help, either; he remained a sullen, introverted bore. What a family!

The construction of Catherine's and my house was almost completed just prior to our wedding, and immediately after the ceremony, we sailed off to America for our honeymoon. I had already imported or ordered locally most of the contents to be placed inside during our absence, and all these things were stored in the business premises. We would have a complete home to move into on our return. I combined the trip with forward-buying several shiploads of cargo for the emporium. Life was bliss, and I was never so happy.

Near the end of our ten-month long honeymoon, we discovered that Catherine was with child and made plans to get home as quickly as possible so that we may settle into our new home. We had laughingly decided to call the estate Cathnoah.

What a dreadful shock greeted us on our arrival. Lizzie was there to meet us, and as soon as I set eyes on her, I knew that something was wrong. She embraced Catherine warmly but briefly, then turned to me and burst into uncontrollable sobbing.

"Oh, Noah! Thank God you're home. We have some terrible news!"

It all came out in a rush between sobs. "William has committed suicide, and Mama has died of shock!"

I could hardly believe my ears. I stood staring at Catherine over Lizzie's head, my mouth open in disbelief.

We made our way to some seating, and poor Lizzie's grief was awful. She had had to bear it all on her own, William dead and buried and Mama, too, only a few days afterward. William had left no note and the reason for his suicide was unclear. Father guessed that he had wiped his hands of all of us and simply had nothing to live for anymore. Edward was no help at all, since he was always away somewhere, chasing one of his nefarious schemes. On top of it all, Lizzie had given birth to a third daughter, Sarah, during our absence.

Poor Lizzie! We comforted her as best we could, and she left to go back home to The Retreat at the bottom of the hill at Gallimore. Catherine and I had not the heart to tell her of our happy news, and we sadly made our way to our new home.

THE CAVANAGH EMPORIUM had been trading very well during our absence, increasing turnover almost weekly. Beyond regularly showing my face there, there was little for me to do, since the store practically ran itself.

Catherine's condition was progressing well, and she was happy and healthy. Because of my estrangement from my father, the only way I could glean anything about his doings was from the occasional item in *The Sydney Herald* or *The Bulletin*, where his name cropped up in court reports. It appeared that he was kept quite well occupied.

Imagine my disbelief, then, when I read, "The services of Septimus Cavanagh, Esq., Lawyer, will not be retained by the bank following the suicide of its manager, Mr William Cavanagh, and the discovery of several thousand pounds missing from the bank." It seemed the bank thought it inappropriate to retain Father's services in light of his relationship to William.

Catherine and I tried to keep Lizzie as far away as possible from all the hubbub, and we mulled over the revelation of the missing money and whether William could have been implicated in any way. The item in *The Bulletin* seemed to point the finger at him, but there was no evidence so far. His very ordinary lifestyle gave no hint whatever that he had been stealing such large sums for himself.

All of my family's woes were put on hold for a few weeks when Catherine delivered a healthy baby girl. The baby was so perfect and so beautiful, we named her Arika, the Aboriginal word for Waterlily. I was so proud of Catherine and our tiny girl, and I was only sorry that I could not share our joy with my parents, or for that matter with my brother William. Lizzie was happy for us but had her own troubles to contend with. For too short a while, life settled down for us, and I watched my beautiful Catherine and our little daughter thrive together and forge a bond that was wonderful to see.

Catherine was glowing in her role of mother, and we were planning to add to our family when a distraught Lizzie came to us for help. It appeared that Edward had left her without any news of his where-abouts or money with which to look after herself and their three young daughters.

I rode out to Gallimore and was amazed at the state of the once-great house, gardens and land. I could not gain actual access to the house. It appeared almost abandoned, the gardens and orchards were neglected and overgrown and a few unshorn sheep dotted the fields.

I rode down to The Retreat and asked Lizzie where all the live-stock had gone. She had the impression that Edward had sold them all off over a period of some months, but he had never been in the habit of sharing any details of his ventures with her.

When I was able to get old Metty aside for a while, she wrung her hands and said, "Mr Noah! Vot vill happen to Miss Lizzie now? She so sad. She have no money, and she all the time crying. What to do, Mr Noah?"

I patted her soft, lined cheek, held her hands in mine and told her not to worry. I was there to help, and they were all to come and stay with us until we could find a solution. I held her close until her sobbing ceased, and she rewarded me with a watery smile.

Lizzie, Metty and the three girls came to stay with us a few days later. Cathnoah was very large, and we had plenty of help. Catherine and Lizzie got on very well, and the two older girls loved playing with Arika and Lizzie's tiny Sarah.

Over time, Catherine gleaned a few more details about Edwards's behaviour. Apparently, even before Sebastian's death, Edward had got rid of a lot of the livestock and had spent a great deal of money—on grapevines, of all things! He had imported the rootstock from France but knew little of the cultivation. Of course, the vines failed. He then bought a ship to begin an import/export trade. On its second voyage to England via the Cape, it must have sunk because neither it nor its crew were ever heard of again. Edward then started offering land for sale, land which, it turned out, he did not own. So then the law was after him. Apparently, he was able somehow to bribe his way out of that debacle, and other ill-conceived schemes followed.

All the while, he was gambling heavily. Lizzie often wondered where the money came from to fund one failure after another was concerned by the company he kept. Any pleas from her fell on deaf ears, and he increasingly neglected her and the children as he careered from one mad plan to another.

Despite all of that, she was worried about her husband's health. She said that he had not been looking well, and she feared that he would be carried away one day by the disease of the blood which had in the past affected the male members of the Gallimore family. In their early days together, he had told her of the deaths of his four brothers, all born before him. The affliction seemed to have avoided him as a youth, and, once he got older, he became convinced that he had escaped. When they were first wed, she cosseted him, fearing that she might lose him at any time. As the years went by, she concluded, like he, that he had escaped—but now, she was no longer so sure.

I took it into my head that I would go out and try to find my brother-in-law and knock some sense into him. Of course, I had only met him a few times, when I was much younger and long before he married my sister, so I did not really know the man. I was not at all prepared for the person I was to meet.

I managed to track him down, in the company of some very shady characters in a gambling house in the docks area. He indeed looked very ill, unkempt and belligerent.

His eyes slid around to meet mine. He wanted to know what business it was of mine to look him up and question him, then said I could go to hell as far as he was concerned.

I told him that I was there to make him an offer I didn't think he would refuse,

That calmed him down somewhat. I managed to separate him from his cronies and asked him how much he wanted for Gallimore in its current state. I left him in no doubt that I knew a bargain, as well as a dud, when I saw one.

I could almost see his mind working. After some haggling, his need overcame his greed, and we agreed on a reasonable figure—with two conditions. The first was that, as soon as the property had been conveyed to me, he was never to set foot on Gallimore land again. The second was that a third of the purchase money was to be retained in trust for the upkeep of Lizzie and the children.

To this last condition, he reluctantly agreed. Then he brightened considerably.

"I'll be glad to see the back of the place."

He was anxious to receive the payment, and I arranged this as expeditiously as I could.

To say that I was pleased with my transaction would be to put two faces on it all. On the one hand, the whole thing ensured Lizzie's future wellbeing and that of her children, and Gallimore would be saved from certain destruction. On the other, it did nothing to save Edward himself. He had an unerring capacity to make a bog of everything he touched, and I could see that it would be no time at all before he consumed yet another financial windfall.

Lizzie was aghast when I told her what I had done, but I assured her that she would have a home at The Retreat as long as I was the owner—and I had no intention of ever getting rid of my acquisition.

I did not tell her of the first condition of the sale, but she seemed happy with the second. I hoped that, in time, she would realise that Edward was not coming back to live with her and the children.

I have spent much time mulling over the wisdom of that first condition, along with how I can bring the estate back to its former glory and look after Lizzie and the children so that they will be happy in the only home they have ever known as a family.

The conveyance to me of Gallimore and its lands and all the appurtenances thereon was completed some time ago, and the renovations and restoration are well underway. I hope I will soon be able to move my family to Gallimore as our country estate.

I have, however, some unfinished business with Edward. I aim to track him down in the next week or two, so that we may put a troubling issue to rest once and for all.

CATHERINE'S JOUNAL

I have never kept a journal before. I know it is unusual, and I always intended to when I was younger. But somehow, after the death of my mother and my disastrous engagement, I never quite had the heart. But on finding my beloved Noah's journals, and in particular his last one, I thought I should record my memories of and thoughts on the events which have brought me to this point in my life.

My story starts when I was born in 1841. I had an unremarkable but happy childhood with my parents, Clarence and Henrietta Donnelly. I can vaguely remember my father passing away after contracting cholera, leaving my mother and me on our own. I don't know how she did it, but Mother somehow contrived to clothe and feed us, supplemented by my meagre offerings when I was twelve years old and apprenticed to a milliner.

From time to time, Mother would sigh softly and say that she hoped I would one day find someone to marry, someone who would look after me. She was overjoyed when Jonah Burge came calling when I was sixteen. He was a tall constable in Her Majesty's Constabulary, with a handsome face and good sense of humour that quite swept me away.

Jonah appealed just as much to Mother as to me, and we were soon engaged. We arranged our wedding for the following June, and I busied myself after working for hours on my *trousseau* and collecting a well-stocked bottom drawer. Mama helped me in this last regard, not only by embroidering and stitching into the early hours but by earmarking items in her possession to pass on to me. It seemed that I would have a most bounteous glory box to take into my marriage. I was to be married in Mother's own wedding dress, and she and I were happy.

My joy was brought to a sudden halt when Mother passed away after yet another attack of angina, an affliction which had troubled her for as long as I could remember. Since I had no other relatives, I of course looked to Jonah for consolation.

One of his first remarks was that the question of where we should live after our marriage seemed to have been settled by the death of my mother at a very convenient time. To say that I was put out by these mercenary, unsympathetic words was to put it very lightly.

My feelings toward him cooled, and I began to ask myself some searching questions. The whole issue was settled quickly when, about six weeks before our intended wedding, a knock came at my door. There stood a person—I cannot bring myself to call her a young lady—who, without any preamble, announced the obvious. She was expecting a child, and the father was none other than my intended bridegroom, Jonah Burge!

I confronted Jonah. There was no denial.

I think I experienced every emotion ever invented, apart from joy: shame, embarrassment, anger, sorrow and, for some odd reason, a tiny feeling of guilt. To this day, I do not know why.

Suffice it to say, my engagement was terminated, and I fled—first into myself, until I could come to terms with the sudden end to my hoped-for future, then to Sydney for a new start.

The proceeds of the sale of the house enabled me to set up a small shop in George Street as a milliner. For the first time, I was grateful for the harsh training I had received at the hands of Miss Predicott. I spent many a long hour creating a selection of hats to display in the window and soon built up a small but select clientele.

I found some very comfortable lodgings with a kind, widowed landlady within walking distance of my shop, and I had money in the bank. Mother would have been so proud of me! I was always so busy that I had little time to reflect on how I'd found myself in Sydney, and, apart from missing Mother, Melbourne seemed a long way away. I settled into a daily life of almost nothing but hat-making, eating and sleeping and did not realise anything was missing... until Noah came into my world.

How Noah and I met is described in his journal. They were glorious days, and I was so happy. My dearest Noah—how I long for him! He was so handsome, so kind, so strong yet so gentle; I could not have asked for more. I loved him deeply, right up until the day he left us.

On that dreadful day, a large part of me died with him, and, but for our precious little daughter, barely twelve months old, I think I would have just faded away and joined him. My memories of that period are as painful today, in my fifty-fourth year, as they were then. But, distressing as those memories are, I intend to record as much of the family history as I am able. Perhaps it may afford me some sort of release?

If I sit and reflect on my life, I am amazed at the twists and turns it has taken and how fate has stepped in numerous times to deflect me from a particular course. The revelations in Noah's last journal are naturally a big part of my theorising. I am constantly imagining how, if such-and-such an event had not occurred, I could be in a place totally different from where I am now.

But what point is there to that? My fates have brought me to the place I *am* now, from deep happiness to abject depression and loneliness to, I suppose, some sort of reluctant acceptance.

I WELL RECALL the first day I ever set eyes on Noah. There he was, my gentle giant, standing on the steps of the bank with a satisfied smile on his face and completely blocking my entry.

He seemed a thousand miles away and was quite put out when he looked down and saw me waiting for him to move. He stared a moment, then, quite flustered, apologised, fumbled with his hat and stepped aside.

I have to confess that, as he stared at me with those deep, dark blue eyes of his, my heart gave a little flip, and then it was I who was all at sixes and sevens! I wondered who he was and surprised myself by hoping that we might meet again.

Meanwhile, a new emporium was being set up a little further down the road, and I couldn't wait to see what it could offer me in the way of ribbons, laces, feathers and other such fripperies. My stocks were being fast depleted, and I was having to get inventive in some instances.

A week or so before the new store opened, the handsome stranger from the bank came into my shop and introduced himself as Noah Cavanagh. He was there to arrange the collection of a hat for his sister, Mrs Edward Gallimore, who had recently delivered herself of a third child and was too delicate to travel into town.

A big jolt to my heart left me almost breathless and returned with the same strength days later, when I handed him the hatbox, thinking that it was taking him a little too long to transfer it from my hand to his.

I could feel his eyes on my face and felt a strong flush spread up my neck to diffuse my cheeks. His presence seemed to fill the whole shop, and I felt a real shock as our hands touched.

He looked me directly in the eye, thanked me and strode with purpose out to his buggy. A soft rain was falling, and the light playing on the droplets made a silver sheen on the shoulders of his beautifully cut topcoats. I watched through the window as he mounted the step, carefully placed the hatbox on the seat beside him, bowed slightly and raised his hat to me and gently slapped the reins along the horse's back.

I was all of a dither and had to sit down for a while to collect myself. Then I gave myself a good talking to. Acting like a silly girl! He was probably a married man with a horde of little ones and a fat, happy wife waiting at home.

I vainly tried not to think of him and turn my energies toward creating beautiful hats for my ladies.

❄

Some days later, the new emporium opened, and the whole community was invited to the grand occasion. I was amazed at the wonderful haberdashery there, from as far away as England, America and China, and made up my mind that I would visit again to replenish my almost-empty shelves on the morrow.

A loud gong sounded, and an announcer introduced the new owner, who would say a few words before officially opening the store. You can imagine my astonishment when I discovered that that personage was none other than my handsome stranger, Mr Noah Cavanagh!

He was standing on a first-floor landing, but his and my eyes locked the moment they met. He paused for a moment in mid-sentence, collected himself and without taking his eyes from mine, continued his speech. When the speech ended, a sumptuous afternoon tea of beverages and cakes was served, and I was happy that I had dressed in my prettiest gown.

But before I could eat a bite, I saw him coming towards me. Bowing slightly from the waist, he said in his wonderfully rich, deep voice, "Good afternoon, Miss Donnelly. It's a pleasure to meet you again. May I accompany you to some departments in which I am sure you'll be interested?"

"Thank you, Mr Cavanagh, but I have already found my way," I replied honestly. "You have some wonderful goods with which to tempt us."

"I hope to tempt you far beyond what you may see here," he said, looking me in the eyes.

He smiled broadly, showing a row of perfect white teeth under an immaculately trimmed red-gold moustache, which matched his full head of curly hair. A starched collar topped a pleated white shirt, which peeped over the top of his dark grey silk waistcoat, and a heavy gold watch chain looped across his middle and disappeared under the flaps of his fine English wool coat.

I took all this in, blushing furiously. All I could think to offer was an inane, "Thank you, sir!"

"Noah is my name!" he said. "And I would be greatly honoured if you would allow me to call on you sometime."

I was completely under his spell. Unable to speak, I looked toward my feet.

"I hope you won't be so serious when we meet again. I promise I won't eat you," he said, eyes twinkling. "Though I confess I would like to!"

I had to smile at that, I could not help myself.

"Till then," he said. Gently taking my plate, he raised my hand and brushed his lips across my fingertips. "Now, please excuse me. I am being very neglectful of my other guests." He bowed and turned away.

My heart was fluttering madly, and I was so shaken that I put down my plate, cup and saucer and fairly flew back to the sanctuary of my lodgings. I had just proved that there *was* such a thing as love at first sight: I was totally smitten and nervously looked forward to our next meeting.

WE WENT for a truly delightful picnic on the following Sunday, and it was the first of many similar outings to follow. During these occasions, we got to know each other well. I told Noah about my background, my escape from Jonah and the reason for it and how glad I was that I had landed in Sydney. For his part, I learned of his awful estrangement from his father—who, to this day, I have never met—his ailing mother, his distant brother William and his sister Eliza and her marriage to Edward Gallimore.

Saddest of all, to me, was the drowning of his little brother James many years before. It was odd, but, in his telling of that event, I felt that there was something he was leaving out. Perhaps it was too upsetting for him to recall in detail.

In the summer of 1866, I accepted Noah's proposal of marriage and thought my heart would burst with happiness. After a few months, Noah found a wonderful parcel of land on the foreshore of the harbour and set about commissioning the building of a large house for us to live in after our marriage.

It was during this time that Noah began to worry quite a lot about Lizzie. She was very unhappy with her husband Edward's activities, and Noah didn't like to hear that the Gallimore estate was being neglected, its stock dying or being sold off, its station-hands leaving without notice and a general malaise sitting over it.

In December 1867, we were wed, and Noah surprised me by taking us on an extended honeymoon to America. I had never sailed before and never dreamt that I would ever leave my home shores. What an adventure!

Noah, of course, had travelled to America before, and he spoiled me dreadfully. He took great delight in showing me everything he could, and I could hardly believe my good fortune. Towards the end, we were given the wonderful news that I was with child.

In late September 1868, on a mild spring-like afternoon, we disembarked in Sydney to be met by an almost hysterical Lizzie, who, after a very cursory greeting, imparted the awful news that my brother-in-law William had taken his own life only two weeks before and my mother-in-law had suffered a fatal stroke. These dreadful tidings took the edge off our happy ones.

But oh, it was good to be home! How grand our new house was. Noah had spared no expense. Long French windows, crystal chandeliers, Aubusson carpets on softly glowing black oak floors, polished mahogany furniture, gleaming silver, delicate gilding on ceilings and cornices. Outside, a lagged terrace led through columns and pillars to a low fountain splashing in the sunlight, with intricate wrought ironwork on upper balustrades. Noah treated me like a princess, and I felt like a queen.

Before we left on our honeymoon, I had closed my millinery shop, and I now spent my days awaiting the birth of our first child and sewing an extensive layette. We had a full staff to cater for our every need, and life was truly wonderful.

Noah attempted to make peace with his father, especially since his mother's passing, but to no avail. He was left in no doubt whatever as to the old man's obstinate refusal to meet his son and the only news Noah ever gleaned was from the odd article in the newspaper.

❄

IN MARCH of 1869 our little daughter was born. She was such a perfect little thing, like a flower, and Noah suggested the name of Arika. He had drawn on his friendship years earlier with Aboriginals in the goldfields, who taught him that the word meant "waterlily." It sounded just right to me, and we added the name Henrietta, after my mother.

The following year, 1870, was the year Noah was murdered and I stopped writing this journal. What was there to write about? How can one write about an event so horrific that it alters one's life irrevocably?

Following Arika's birth, I had some small complications and was not very well, but they were as nothing compared to the sudden loss of my husband. Our poor little Arika, not yet one year old, was left in the capable and kind hands of nursemaids and other staff whilst her mother sank into a bottomless depression.

I felt as though I sat on the edge of a giant bowl, its sides slippery and sloping into a black pit at the bottom. I was drawn inexorably to that dark place as I slid down. At the start, I felt such deep peace down there, and I gave in to it. Time stood still, and I savoured the release from my torment.

Gradually, however, the outside world intruded into my unlovely place, and I made tiny, irregular steps up into the light—only to happily slip down again at the slightest hint of anything unpleasant. I was *safe* down there!

After a long, long time, I did get out. And when I did, I found my little daughter well and looking forward to having a mother again. I picked up this journal again, intending to continue the story. But I could not write in the same vein. My earlier ramblings came from the heart of a young mother, in love and loved. I realised I had put my romantic version of events on top of Noah's and was only repeating what he had recorded.

But he could not write anything after 1870, and I could. And it has taken almost twenty years for my mind to frame words that will make some sense and yet convey my innermost feelings. I feel I can now complete the story and leave you with the following accounts of what happened to whom, when and (maybe) why.

Where to start? Chronologically, I think, and hope you can join the puzzle.

1868: William Cavanagh committed suicide prior to the discovery of substantial missing funds from the bank trust accounts he managed. For the reasons why, see Edward Gallimore's entry below.

1868: Anna Cavanagh, Irish-born, William's Irish-born mother, died of a stroke brought on by the shock of her son's suicide. Anna was not a happy person in her lifetime and turned to a lover during one of Septimus's long absences. She tried her best for her three sons but doted on her only daughter, Eliza (Lizzie).

1869: Septimus Cavanagh—an overbearing, pompous lawyer, with the arrogance that great success sometimes brings—died a bitter, broken, lonely and unforgiving man. Never got over his wrongly perceived abandonment by his second son Noah and never made his peace with him. Lost his young third son, James, to drowning at the age of five, and his first son, William, to suicide. Noah survived him by twelve months, and his only daughter Lizzie, my friend, survives to this day.

1870: Noah Cavanagh, my husband, died. A deathbed confession by Edward Gallimore admitted to Noah's murder by himself and others, but Edward's death
prevented him from being brought to justice. Noah's body has never been recovered, and that is one of the hardest things for me to bear. The "others" involved have never
been traced, but it was known that Edward had cohorts with criminal pasts.

1872: Edward Gallimore died. A flawed character, and the last of the people who would bear the Gallimore name. Although sickly at times, was thought to be the only male of the family to have escaped the deadly blood disease which had claimed stillborn twin sons and two other male siblings. Edward was the last of nine children born to Sophie and Sebastian Gallimore and was raised in comparative luxury, with no notion whatever of economy or abstaining from gambling with "never-fail" money-making schemes. He managed to fritter away a considerable inheritance, including the Gallimore estate, soon after his father died. He married Noah's sister, Lizzie, and they had three daughters. In order that his sister should not lose her home, Noah came to the rescue and purchased Gallimore from Edward, renovated and refurbished it, restocked it with cattle and settled Lizzie and her children in The Retreat at the bottom of the hill, giving her a buffer from the hard realities of life and penury.

Although she was not present when little James drowned, Lizzie always felt—correctly, it turned out—that William was somehow more involved than anyone had let on. She confided this to her husband during the early days of their marriage. Edward stored this information in the recesses of his twisted mind, embellished it a little and used it to "convince" his brother-in-law that a large loan would make them both wealthy men.

William must have felt duly threatened, because he secretly removed a great sum of money from several of his bank's trust funds and invested it in Edward's scheme to sell land up in the Hawkesbury area, land to which he had no legal title. None of this was helped by a severe drought in the area which left hundreds of miles of grassless earth.

When the land scheme invariably failed, William looked to Edward to repay the money "borrowed" from the bank, and, of course, there was none forthcoming. William could see ruin and disgrace staring him in the eye, and, before his embezzlement could be discovered, he died by his own hand.

Noah was devastated at the death of another brother and at a total loss to understand how two brothers of the same flesh and blood could be so different. When he heard rumours of his brother-in-law's involvement, he approached Edward for his account.

Edward was found in dark communion with his unsavoury friends, cooking up further nefarious schemes, one of which apparently involved trying to extract funds from Noah.

An argument followed, and Edward and his "friends" apparently bludgeoned my Noah to death and disposed of his body, possibly in the river, where it was carried out to sea.

Shortly thereafter, Edward, for whatever reason, succumbed to the heredity blood disease, which now has a name: leukaemia. It has been reported that Edward, who had nothing to lose on his deathbed, took great delight in confessing to the murder. He stated confidently that no body would ever be found and that, since William was dead and no records of any transactions existed, no monies could ever be traced to himself for that incident.

Edward and Lizzie's girls:

Charlotte, born 1863. Became very religious and married a parson, Bartholomew Higgins, a tall, awkward man whose bushy black eyebrows hung over the top of his thick glasses. An unfortunate look for a man of the cloth; on more than one occasion, Charlotte had to placate a small child frightened by his image.

Overwhelmed by what she said was the "moral disease of the population—intoxication," she devoted her life to following her husband wherever he went, preaching the gospel according to abstinence and the pain inflicted on those suffering from "the blue devils."

For two pounds three shillings, they bought an ancient old bullock and dray and walked, at about three and a half miles per hour, the thirty-five miles to Windsor. They settled in the Richmond-Windsor area north-west of Sydney, and she nursed her husband back to health during his near-fatal illness—influenza, the only deadly epidemic of the colony. Their lives were often upset by bushrangers driven to their depredations by starvation or possibly at the hands of a harsh master. They are so immersed in their work, and the distances between us are so great, that they very seldom come to Sydney. Lizzie contents herself with the news contained in the rare letters which come to her hand.

Theodora, born 1864. Married a schoolteacher, Hamish McEvoy. She and he founded a school in George Street, and *The Sydney Gazette* gave them glowing tributes when they eventually removed out west to establish a private school in what remained of the goldfields at Gulgong.

Theodora indulged us with wonderfully descriptive letters of her life there. We could smell, taste and feel the fear of fire, flood, drought, debt, loneliness and crop failure. We could see the slag heaps, the canvas tents, the corrugated iron sheds, the bark huts and hospital, the hotel of wattle and daub, the men in their raggedy dungarees and hot flannel shirts, their women in washed-out and patched gingham and calico skirts, and young boys chewing tobacco, spitting and pipe smoking.

We could imagine the awakening of the deep, silent darkness of the bush being dissolved by a rosy dawn, the cacophony of the settlers' clock, the laughing jackass, the smell of crackling, dry, dusty earth being turned to mud by a sudden downpour, a cow being driven home for the evening's milking, teams of eight bullocks yoked in pairs with their tongues hanging out, waterholes in summer all dried up and covered in thick snow and ice in winter. Immigrants and outlaws alike talking of home by day and dreaming of it by night. And the womenfolk who battled the elements, the tortured landscape and the grasshoppers, snakes, flies, parrots and hole-digging wombats to create gardens modelled impossibly on their English memories.

We learned about the surrounding goldfields in Sofala, Hill End— where they found the Holterman Nugget, the largest single mass of gold ever discovered (644 pounds)—Mudgee, Hargrave, Ophir, Windeyer and Pyramul. We learned the intricacies of panning for gold in that ancient home of the Wiradjuri people, surrounded by rugged mountain and gorge country, secret valleys, rushing rivers and gurgling creeks close by but not close enough to Gulgong to allow the washing of the dirt. We imagined the sudden influx of thousands of gold seekers, seeking both alluvial and reef gold. We marvelled at the building of hotels, butcheries, newspapers, banks and stamper batteries pounding ore twenty-four hours a day. There was even an opera house, the Prince of Wales!

Yet, in ten years, it was all over! The alluvial gold had mostly run out, and the reef gold was too expensive to extract. Businesses closed down, the population dwindled from thousands to hundreds in a matter of months and Gulgong battened down.

Theodora and Hamish remain there. She writes that too much of their lives has been spent there and they would feel disloyal, especially to some of their students, if they turned their backs on it all. Lizzie and I still enjoy Theodora's now-infrequent letters, and we feel with her the demise of the town.

Sarah, born 1867. What is there to say about little Sarah? As is the unfortunate custom, it often falls to the lot of the youngest daughter to stay at home and look after her aging mother.

In Sarah's case, I think it's very unfair. She did have a young man who called on her, and it is believed he proposed at one time—we'll never know for sure—but it came to nothing. We suspect that the care of her mother prevented it. Sarah is a very capable and loving daughter with a wry sense of humour, which is just what Lizzie needs. I think Lizzie is aware of Sarah's sacrifice, yet she leans on her heavily and would not be without her.

1889: Arika, my daughter, my very precious daughter, born 1869, married David Davies, the only son of a Welsh farmer, with a successful, large farm in the upper Hawkesbury River area. David is a congenial young man who exudes a calm dignity and authority. He makes me smile often. I have turned Gallimore over to Arika, and she and David live there. They seem blissfully happy, and David has put his considerable knowledge to enhancing the land and stockholding.

Gallimore has been restored to its former stature and I feel the name will live forever. The fact that no member of the Gallimore family will ever reside there again is of no interest to me at all, but I have a great love for the land and am glad that my daughter and her family will hold it in perpetuity.

1895: Lizzie Gallimore, my sister-in-law, still lives at The Retreat and is looked after by Sarah. There is only a year between us, she being the elder, and we are good friends. I keep a curricle here at Cathnoah and am glad that Noah taught me how to handle two harnessed horses at once.

I drive over from Cathnoah as often as I can, and she visits me occasionally. She is not a strong person and relies heavily on her daughter. We long ago tacitly decided not to dwell on the past, and we focus our thoughts on the present, enjoying Theodora's letters from Gulgong, the very rare visit from Charlotte and our speculations on which of our daughters, if any, will be the first to produce a first grandchild.

Noah, of course, resides in a permanent corner of my memory. It is now twenty-four years since his passing, and I am no stranger to dark days and thoughts. My world had great cracks in it, but I have been able to turn despair into acceptance, and memories and imagination now mingle hazily together to obliterate time.

Cathnoah provides me with the peace I crave, and I am content.

Catherine Cavanagh
Cathnoah, Sydney
23 June 1894

If you loved this book, please feel free to leave a review on any site, and thank you in advance for sharing your thoughts!

ABOUT THE AUTHOR

Dorothea (1930 – 2009) was born in rural Victoria, Australia in 1930 and moved to England aged 18. She returned to Australia in 1970, with her husband and two children, where she resided in Sydney until her death in 2009. Throughout her life, she worked as a Bookkeeper and Financial Controller and owned several gift and craft shops. She also pursued many creative hobbies, wrote poetry and was an accomplished artist and home chef.

Dorothea had a great sense of humour, and was renowned for having fun and mischief-making, often to the chagrin of her good-natured husband, Jim, to whom she was happily married for almost 55 years. Dorothea was also known for her wonderful poetry and story-telling, and would keep her children, and later her grandchildren, enthralled and often shrieking with laughter at the magical, and often nonsensical, tales she would relate. "Tell us a story, Grandma!" was a catchcry amongst all of her grandchildren, and she would happily oblige on the spot, making it up as she went along.

Dorothea was a friend to all and beloved by everyone who knew her. In her own words, "Humour has been a big and important part of my life and it will be till the last – and beyond. Don't cry – smile at lovely memories. No tears please, but if you can manage it, a smile or even a good belly laugh!"